The Gardener's Scrolls
Book of Scions

by Samuel R. Rodriguez, Jr.

The contents of this work, including, but not limited to, the accuracy of events, people, and places depicted; opinions expressed; permission to use previously published materials included; and any advice given or actions advocated are solely the responsibility of the author, who assumes all liability for said work and indemnifies the publisher against any claims stemming from publication of the work.

All Rights Reserved
Copyright © 2023 by Samuel R. Rodriguez, Jr.

No part of this book may be reproduced or transmitted, downloaded, distributed, reverse engineered, or stored in or introduced into any information storage and retrieval system, in any form or by any means, including photocopying and recording, whether electronic or mechanical, now known or hereinafter invented without permission in writing from the publisher.

Dorrance Publishing Co
585 Alpha Drive
Pittsburgh, PA 15238
Visit our website at *www.dorrancebookstore.com*

ISBN: 979-8-8892-5341-9
eISBN: 979-8-8892-5841-4

The Gardener's Scrolls
Book of Scions

This, my first novel ever, I dedicate to Martha, Michael, Joseph, Rebekah, and Angel. Thank you for believing in me, when all else failed, when others turned their backs, and bonds were forsaken. Thank you for remaining steadfast by my side. I especially thank you Michael and Joseph for your brilliant ideas and contributions to the story.

And to Nora, my editor, who also believed in me, and who helped to see my work to fruition, and for your amazing direction, your thoughts and scholarly insight in helping to shape my story. Your literary genius is stellar.

I also dedicate my book to the wonderful people at Dorrance Publishing. Oh, how you first stepped into my life and took me by the hand and walked me through the entire process. Thank you for believing in me, and for your patience with my hesitancy. I will forever be grateful.

My book is dedicated to my family, and my friends and acquaintances in my sojourn through life. Many conversations, realms, thoughts and ideas were crystalized and crafted into my world.

I am grateful to Life, the Universe, and the Ein Soph – the Great Without End who moved my quill and ink, the One who formed this passion for storytelling, from before the womb.

And finally in true mystical fashion, I dedicate this book to those who have presented antagonistic force in my life… couriers of drive and energy… for they always helped to propel me forward, without knowing it.

Sci·on

n.

1. A descendant or heir.
2. A detached shoot or twig containing buds from a woody plant, used in grafting.

To give the reader a better understanding of the cultures of Y'cromeca, this glossary has been divided into four sections – the people of the West, and the people of Upper and Middle Y'cromeca, the Isle of Feynhava and the Isle of Kaërybassad.

THE DESERT WORLD OF THE WEST WHERE THE BALLAI STILL STANDS, (FERÀN, RIHOVÀN AND CALASMORRA)

Aban – A friend of S'baladin and musician who served to play his lyre, and stringed instruments to help soothe the boys in their search for T'balidor

Anterros – A small trading village of shepherds and farmers in the region of Ferán, and birthplace of S'baladin.

Baltien – In the desert world of the West, a famous shepherd warrior from Anterros in Ferán. He rose to fame as a brilliant leader. Kalanit was his wife, and his children were T'balidor and S'baladin.

B'naiyth – In the language of Y'darit, it is a house comprised of patriarchal clans. S'baladin is descended from B'naiyth Eirun-Vala, from the clan of Alazar, in the land of Ferán.

The Br'thain – In Y'darit, Br'thain loosely translates to "Brothers", or "Brotherhood". It is commonly used in the plural sense in reference to the clan warriors in the desert world of the West. Chiefly, in the regions of Feran, Rihován and Calasmorra, it is understood that a clan warrior becomes a part of the Br'thain upon approval by the Fieradeem during his Maleor. It is noted in their desert culture, that a Br'thain lives by a strict code for the rest of his life serving first his family, his neighbors, and guarding the numinous role of the Br'thain.

Calasmorra – In the desert world of the West, it is the eastern region within the Ballai that still stands.

Didderäsh Mountains - In Rihován, near Messidia, the Didderäsh Mountains are a colossal maze of canyons, buttes and high desert valleys, containing caverns far below. It was Baltien who decided to provide tents and booths for the rescued children slaves to dwell in the Didderäsh Mountains.

Diero – He was S'baladin's close friend.

Dolscareb – In the desert world of the West, it is a unique attire worn in the regions of Rihován, Calasmorra and Ferán.

Duin Caeir - Located near the town of Messidia in Rihován, the ruins of Duin Caeir was the site of an ancient stone foundation built by the Faëynul. It was the Gardener who decided to use it as a platform to launch the Aerrukán beneath the ground through the Streams of Feynhava.

Eirun-Vala - An ancient sage who lived centuries ago in the region of Ferán. He drew a great following of students whom he mentored in the Streams of Feynhava, until his death. Afterwards, his devoted followers formed a B'naiyth after him.

Ferán - The southern region of the Ballai that still stands. It is the place of S'baladin's family, near the small village of Anterros.

Ferusat - A spike forged from the mines deep in the Isle of Feynhava. The Gardener gave the men of the West the knowledge to forge them in numbers in their missions of liberating the children slaves at the Fortress City. Hammered into the surface, a Ferusat channels the currents from deep in the ground, thus drawing up the Streams of Feynhava.

Fieradin – (Fieradeem - plural) In Y'darit, they are the elders over clans and houses. Fieradeem preside over a young man's entrance into manhood at his Shaiddzhim, electing whether or not he is validated into the world of the Br'thain.

The Gardener's Calendar - Long before the Thaed-Rú usurped dominion over the world of men, the Gardener kept track of time and marked the seasons according to his calendar. Later, with the people of the West, he would meet with them on certain Feast days. His calendar months flow in this order throughout the year beginning with the month called Zaiyot, then T'ziyur, Einruvan, Z'rev, Ein-riyon, Eiyyot, Yivev, Ghiil, Kayyiv, Entiyoh, K'nurith, and finally the last month of Baqquev.

Guaddeca – The customary robe and shawls worn by women in the West. In the desert world of the West, women hold a strong matriarchal place in society. As such, a Guaddeca denotes symbols of leadership or servitude, according to distinct colors, fabrics, and designs in each region. Some women carry the emblems of their clans, woven on their Guaddecas.

Javatiel – Friend of Vaez and Kelán, who joined in the quest to search for T'balidor.

Jubal – A young close friend of S'baladin who volunteered as cook for the lads searching for T'balidor.

Kal-Hezek (Root of Kal-Hezek) – The root from the Isle of Feynhava used by the Gardener to destroy the Fortress City. It was difficult for the Gardener to harvest this root, because everything that the Gardener grows brings life and healing. This root brought death and destruction.

Kelán – Friend of S'baladin who volunteered to help search for T'balidor.

Maleor - (Ascent of Light in Y'darit) In the West, this is the ceremonial coming of age for a young man or woman. It's also a festive occasion with food, song and gathering of attendees. In a Maleor, the celebrant proves his skills of fighting before a panel of Fieradeem.

Praeceptan – Clan leaders, trained by the Fierdeem to led the Br'thain. A group of Praeceptans can be mentored under one Fieradin in the code of the Br'thain as well as from the wisdom of the Streams of Feynhava.

Quinassa River – The largest river in the desert world of the West. Its headwaters start southwest of the town of Cerranth, in Calasmorra. It flows northwest through the Quinassa Canyon and empties into the Aoduin Sea.

Quispal – An elder Fieradin from the city of Tal-Coras in Calasmorra. He was present during the Gardener's meeting at Duin Caeir.

Rihován – The Northwestern region within the Ballai of the West.

S'baladin - Second son of Baltien and Kalanit. A young shepherd lad of Anterros in Ferán. He had an uncommon gift for poetry. Often his work was overlooked by the community, but his fiery words came into play with the revolution in the north.

Sabaca – S'baladin's friend from Urroz in Calamorra. Sabaca was the botanist and medical attendant for S'baladin's team in search of T'balidor.

Shiryon – A special breastplate worn by the Br'thain of the West. It was fashioned with twigs woven together from the Isle of Feynhava. The twigs held powerful energies.

Sibrion – Cousin of T'balidor and S'baladin, and eldest volunteer to lead in the search for him.

Streams of Feynhava - In the land of the West, this term carries two distinctions. Its primary understanding refers to the wisdom of the Gardener, though it was never codified, nor legislated. For this reason, it took on different interpretations from each of the Houses in the West. The second meaning of Streams of Feynhava refers to the underground currents of energy that the Br'thain travel through to rescue the children slaves in the north.

Tree of Y'crom – An epitaph used by the Gardener to describe the numinous lineage of Y'crom, the descendants of Alazar and Oliel.

T'balidor – The older brother of S'baladin, and eldest son of Baltien.

T'cayn Uloma – In the numinous tongue of Uraduin, it means to restore, or repair the broken and fallen world, one soul at a time, one day at a time, through acts of charity and by rescuing or liberating the oppressed.

Ulmeca-Dül – In the numinous tongue of Uraduin, it was the ancient description of the land of Y'cromeca before the arrival of men.

Va'Giyyel – In the tongue of Y'darit, Va'Giyyel is the land beyond the formidable Ballai that still stands. In a deep, mystical sense, it refers to a fallen world that is broken and shrouded in darkness.

Vaez – One of the older lads who agreed to join S'baladin in his quest to search for his brother in Hierundia.

Yashi – The docile, good-natured floppy-eared dog that belongs to Vaez.

Y'darit – The language spoken in Rihován, Calasmorra and Ferán. The Fieradeem teach that their language is descended from Uraduin, the ancient tongue of the Faëynul.

Yedara Mountains – Regional chain of mountains that run northeast and southwest in the territory of Ferán. The Yedara Mountains lie to the east of Anterros. It is also the favorite grazing spot for Baltien's flocks of sheep.

UPPER AND MIDDLE Y'CROMECA

Aejulan – a former citizen of Hierundia, he was rescued by the Aerrukán. Inadvertently, he was thrown into a dire situation against his will whereby he ended up with S'baladin's group searching for T'balidor.

Aidan Khalevad – He is the eldest son of Graeyba Khalevad.

Anil-Gevra – A race of people in Middle Y'cromeca, of unknown origin. Their mysterious language is not part of the Y'cromahein-Hierundiel family of languages. Notable writers emerged from their families who wrote about the romance of husbandry. Their techniques for planting and harvesting produced the best harvests everywhere they worked.

Ansuz (The Tribune) – Military Tribune over the Province of Hierundia, and close friend of Lord Sulla from Ir of the Fenrülk.

Aokenfana (Fields of Aokenfana) – A region of fields containing various crops, three days south of Dûenhallow. A fateful place where the Khalevad men were captured by the pursuing Rhunkai and Ulkyrien trackers.

Arban – In the Rhunkai armies, an Arban is the smallest unit of soldiers, usually consisting of 10 to 20 conscripted soldiers.

Arbantio M'zhalo – A farmer and miller from the region of Cerathmir, in Graëyhovan. He befriended the Gardener and agreed to help the good men of the West in rescuing the children slaves forced to labor on the Fortress City.

Baliencora Marshes – A vast expanse of swamps and marshlands in the Province of Hierundia.

The Ballai (Lit. "The Walls") – A plural form used to reference the earthen walls that surround the Eleven Provinces. Centuries ago, they were breached by the Thaed-Rü. Now, they are covered by growth and vegetation. The only one that still remains intact is the Ballai of the West that surrounds the regions of Feran, Rihován and Calasmorra. Deadly gases ascend from it, and at night it is characterized by a warm glow from its intense heat.

Bal Rú – (Conqueror of the Ballai) A title of the Thaed-Rú to rule over the Thaed-Rú Dominions.

Bisantior – The southernmost Province of the Thaed-Rú Dominions in the southern region of Middle Y'cromeca.

Breinhinod Kynara – In the language of Hierundiel, Breinhinod Kynara means the Early Kings who spread war, famine and terror over the Y'cromahein. The first king was Crimtha-Sûl, the second was Aed-Onach, the third was Sithienta, and the fourth was Druad-Alil.

C'nossa – Northernmost coastal port of the Province of Hierundia, in the district of Caethain. It was here that Ambassador Grioppa's retinue arrived by ship and were detained until they passed inspection.

Cahheramas – The last Province on the eastern coast of Y'cromeca.

The Caravan Leader – In the world of Upper and Middle Y'cromeca, a caravan leader acted as an independent contractor hired by merchants to safeguard their purchased goods, and dispense justice, if their representatives cheated in their business transactions along the trade routes. When the boys with S'baladin stumbled across the caravan leader, he was hired by the merchant families of Valassentio, Vol-Thaladuin, Kol'maquin, Dur Beddasain and Dar Hamuil.

Cethin Arda – In Hierundiel, it is the dark garden. In the past, there were three attempts to build the dark gardens, but each time was met with disastrous consequences. Bal Rú Íraban had plans to resurrect a fourth attempt, based on arcane manuscripts found in the city of Y'cromellah, in Teras Amin.

Cheüldric (the Master Scribe) – In the city of Y'cromellah, in Teras Amin, he was a famous chronicler centuries ago who documented the rise of the early kings to the forming of the Thaed-Rú Dominions.

Cian – The smallest Province of Upper Y'cromeca, with Hierundia and Cahheramas to the north, and Ir of the Fenrülk to the south.

Doernghâls – In Graëyhovan, these half bird, half crickets jump through the air, eating the cornstalks in fields. Farmers spring nets in the air to capture them.

D'thalien Khalevad – He was the younger son of Graeyba Khalevad

Dûenhallow – The ruins of an ancient fortress in Graëyhovan, famous for the brave men who died defending it from the newly formed Rhunkai tumens centuries ago.

Dul-Meggor – A labor compound near the Fortress City. It was run by the Rhunkai to force the Scions of Íraban into labor for the building of the Fortress City. In Hierundiel, it meant "builders of our world". Arkebalo was the elderly fellow who acted as though he ran the facility, when in fact, he was nothing more than an attendant who ran errands for the soldiers.

Eanair – The first month of the new year in the Thaed-Rú calendar.

Edict of the Scions of Íraban – Edict passed by Íraban, and administered by the Y'cromahein Guild, to oversee the use of children to labor in the building of the Fortress City, while experimented upon by the Necropulpa plant.

Fortress City – Located atop a high mountain in northern Hierundia, in the region of Caethain. It was the place where Bal Rú Íraban chose to build a city that surrounded the fourth Cethin Arda.

Ghost Kings – The hairy, wild men that inhabit the untamed hinterlands beyond the Eleven Provinces.

Graeyba Khalevad – A fellmonger by trade in the Province of Graëyhovan, he is the father of Aidan and D'thalien.

Graëyhovan – Central Province of Upper Y'cromeca.

Hanuthir – This city was one of the great centers of ancient Hierundia.

Hierundia – It was known as the northernmost Province and the place of origin of the Thaeyd-Rú. Hierundia became the first to fall to the Thaed-Rú when they breached the Ballai that surrounds it.

Hierundiel – It was the official language of the Thaed-Rú Dominions imposed upon all subjects of the Eleven Provinces. Although each Province speaks their own tongue from centuries of evolution within each of the Ballai, yet today, Hierundiel is the universal language of trade and commerce across the universal world of the Dominions.

Iemil – The estate of Lord Sulla in Ir of the Fenrülk. In an unknown tongue, probably that of the Anil-Gevra, it meant "Rock", or 'Stone".

Íraban Thaed-Rú – The last Bal Rú to rule over the Thaed-Rú Dominions. Son of Theragad Thaed-Rú, and grandson of Saerclusa the Great.

Ir of the Fenrülk – Province of Middle Y'cromeca.

Isayar – He was one of the young leaders of the four great divisions of the Anil-Gevra.

Ixzaril – The forests of Ixzaril is the geographical region wherein lies the Fortress City, surrounded by the glens of Vartenca, the southern ravines of Ganuyar, the western hill country of Vindakyr, and the marshes of Faeynoga. The forests of Ixzaril is the home of the ancient mountain clans of the Mon-Herra, the Fin-Faiza, the Ir-Aranon, the Breytha-Ul, the Ler-Bahnya, the Er-Orba Feron, the Bok-Faiza and the Tir-Volkai.

Ka-Lyn – The steward of the hidden refuge of Kol-Shebbala, as appointed by the Gardener. V'leshkah was her guardian.

Kelubragia – Village in the east coast Province of Cahheramas. It was the site of a wholesale execution of many families for attempting to hide their children from the Royal Edict of the Scions of Íraban.

Kiérbangaal – Capitol city of the Province of Hierundia, and seat of the Thaed-Rú Dominions.

Kol-Shebbala – A secret, hidden place of refuge in central Hierundia. It was fashioned by the Gardener himself for V'leshkah and Ka-Lyn, and later for those who escaped the Edict of the Scions of Íraban.

Laëthoban – This city stood as one of the great centers of ancient Hierundia. During the reign of Saerclusa the Great, he expanded its borders, and its highways to Hanuthir and Terasdagion.

Mechedül – A military compound in the Province of Rhühaven. Because of its extreme frost, it was used for training Rhunkai soldiers, turning them into. fierce warriors. The Thaed-Rú's bizarre gravitation to the frost became a philosophical technique for training Rhunkai to withstand fear in battle, and survival against the weather elements.

Merungild – A forest region in the Province of Graëyhovan. It is also the location of the Upper Vales of Miórgelân, the place where the Khalevad family came from.

Minghan –In the Rhunkai armies, a Minghan consisted of a company of one thousand conscripted soldiers.

Mishra-Olru – The shape shifting warlord who ruled a small region in northern Hierundia, long before the formation of the Thaed-Rú Dominions.

Molchaion – The westernmost Province of the Thaed-Rú Dominions.

Naddú – He was one of the young leaders of the four great divisions of the Anil-Gevra.

Necropulpa (plant) – Harvested in the Cethin Arda, this plant was used by the alchemists and engineers of the Thaed-Rú to heighten the strength of the Scions of Íraban as they labored in the building of the Fortress City.

Peiscavellan – A region of Hierundia, where Graeyba witnessed the Gardener defending himself from a band of Rhunkai malcontents.

Realmhold Thaed-Rú – The large fortress/ castle of the Thaed-Rú, set atop the mountains overlooking the capitol city of Kiérbangaal.

Rethin Bretor – In the capitol city of Kiérbangaal, The Rethin Bretor (the Royal District) consists of the gilded Hall of Towers, and other buildings of royal business.

Rhunkai – The soldiers of the Thaed-Rú Dominions.

Rhühaven – A Province on the northwestern coast of Upper Y'cromeca.

Saerclusa the Great – The grandfather of Íraban Thaed-Rú, who built the modern centers of Laëthoban, Hanuthir and Terasdagion.

Scepter of H'dhar – After the Breinhinod Kynara, (the early kings), H'dhar became the first ruler to consolidate the Thaed-Rú Dominions, hence the royal scepter of a Bal Rú is named after him.

Scions of Íraban – Íraban's description to denote the children slaves of his building program to create the Fortress City that houses the Cethin Arda.

The Seven Branches of Y'crom – The people of Y'cromeca (from the desert world of the West to the lands of Upper and Middle Y'cromeca) are all descended from the seven sons of Y'crom - Aeduthir, Aelgad, Dürthaliun, Visanthiel and Faëlgrey, Alazar and Oliel.

Sheddukem – The ancient giants who opposed the good-hearted Faëynul in their war for possession of the land of Ulmeca-Dül.

Shekülhorn – The standard currency in the Thaed-Rú Dominions.

Sovereign Tribunes – The Tribunes are the highest-ranking military officers commanding tumens. Each Province is presided over by a Tribune.

Ansuz is over the Province of Hierundia.

The Tribune Íthsaz is over the Province of Tal-Ciddion.

The Tribune Ríthas is over the Province of Rhühaven.

The Tribune Thurisaz is over the Province of Graëyhovan.

The Tribune Uruz is over the Province of Molchaion.

The Tribune Wunden is over the Province of Cahheramas.

The Tribune Hagalaz is over the Province of Cian.

The Tribune Urathsaz is over the Province of Ir of the Fenrülk.

The Tribune Dagaz is over the Province of Cerebantus.

The Tribune Kaunan is over the Province of Bisantior.

And the Tribune Gebor is over the Province of Teras-Amin.

Sulla (Master Sulla, Baron Sulla, or Lord Sulla) – the steward of Iemil, in the province of Ir of the Fenrülk.

Taenshuk – Tall-legged beasts used by the Rhunkai to patrol the wilderness.

Tal-Ciddion – Northwestern Province of Y'cromeca.

Teima – He stood as one of the young leaders of the four great divisions of the Anil-Gevra.

Teosifan – A member of the Thaed-Rú, and chief steward of the Y'cromahein Guild.

Teras-Amin – Southwestern most Province of the Thaed-Rú Dominions.

Terusdagion – One of the great centers of ancient Hierundia.

Terus Raynür – In Upper and Middle Y'cromeca, the vast wild expanse of the hinterlands beyond the Ballai that surrounds each of the Eleven Provinces.

Thaed-Rú Dominions – The Eleven Provinces of Rhühaven, Tal-Ciddion, Molchaion, Graëyhovan, Hierundia, Cahheramas, Cian, It of the Fenrülk, Teras-Amin, Bisantior, Cerebantus, ruled by the race of the Thaed-Rú.

Theragad Thaed-Rú – The father of Íraban Thaed-Rú.

Tumens – In the language of Hierundiel, the tumens were the largest organization of military forces.

Tzeytvara - One of the young leaders of the four great divisions of the Anil-Gevra.

Ulkyrien trackers – The dreaded trackers of the Rhunkai armies. They digested a certain plant from the Cethin Arda that heightened their senses, while disfiguring their appearances to almost beastly forms.

Va'Harot – A place in central Hierundia designated by the Gardener as a place of refuge should the Br'thain of the West become separated in their liberation of the children slaves. Va'Harot is an old ossuary of Faëynul bones far beneath the ground.

V'leshkah – Former midwife of the Thaed-Ru. When she delivered Ka-Lyn, she was ordered to put her to death. But V'leshkah grew tired of having carried out these atrocious acts for the Thaed-Ru, and finally escaped with the newborn infant. Pursued by Rhunkai, V'leshkah fled into the no man's land of Kol-Shebala.

Veyan Fehru – In Hierundiel, it means "The Ruler of the Veyasaen". It was the title given by the Gardener to Ka-Lyn at her coronation, for her subjugation over the Veyasaen.

Veyasaen – Large beastly fowl that terrorize the skies of Hierundia. Long ago they were harvested by the Cethin Arda.

Wind Ghouls – In the Province of Hierundia, they are hybrid canine creatures used by the Ulkyrien trackers to hunt down runaways.

Yaghun – In the Rhunkai armies, a Yaghun is a unit of 100 Rhunkai soldiers.

Y'crom – The First Patriot. He settled a primal colony in the desert world before the Age of the Ballai. Forging an alliance with the Gardener, he routed the Gardener's foe from Ulmeca-Dül, thus the Gardener changed the name of the land to Y'cromeca.

Y'cromeca – The land once known as Ulmeca-Dül. In the age of men, its name was changed in honor of Y'crom.

The Y'cromahein Guild – It was the royal group charged with the task of overseeing the building of the Cethin Arda. Its membership consisted of Thaed-Rú agents and Provincial Governors

The Y'cromahein – a poetic self-described name given to the sons of Y'crom. Later it evolved to refer to all citizens of Y'cromeca.

Y'cromellah – The capitol of the Province of Teras-Amin. It is the site of a large library of many authors and poets chronicling the history of Y'cromeca.

THE ISLE OF FEYNHAVA

Aerrukán – A predatory creature that inhabits the Isles of Feynhava. Long after the creature's death, the Aerrukán's skins continued to hold supernal powers, reflective of its predatory skills when it was alive. It was the Gardener who used its skins to protect the Br'thain of the West in their liberation of the children slaves at the Fortress City.

Faëynul – The Faëynul were the giants who settled Ulmeca-Dül before the arrival of the Age of Y'crom. Originally, they came from the Isle of Feynhava.

Feynhava – (The Isle of Feynhava) Place of the Garden of Ages, The Infinite Garden. Its fruits and properties are characterized by supernal agencies that defy description, or explanation.

The Gardener – Also known as the Steward of Feynhava for his care over an ancient garden of supernal, infinite power, on the Isles of Feynhava. It is known as the Garden of Ages, or the Infinite Garden.

Uraduin – The ancient tongue once spoken by the Faëynul, ages ago. Certain words carry great power that can shake the land, or cause other changes in nature. The modern language of Y'darit, spoken in the regions of Feran, Rihován and Calasmorra, is descended from Uraduin.

THE ISLE OF KAËYRBASSAD

Axzahiir – The false name and disguise of the Haruspec, posing as a sagacious old man.

Dreyshavuin – He was a composer of ancient Paradmah. He often wrote sonnets of rustic settings, and the poetry of nature.

Gershuvyk – Before the modern language of Paradmah, Gershuvyk was the primordial lingua franca spoken by the early tribes of Gershu who settled Paradmah.

Grioppa – (Ambassador Grioppa of the kingdom of Paradmah) Fatefully shipwrecked with his retinue on the Isle of Kaëyrbassad. The Haruspec used his concoction from the Mithengara plant to poison their minds to carry out his will.

Harmattan weed spies – After the breach of the Ballai that surrounded each of the Eleven Provinces, the Haruspec planted strange, eerie seeds in limited places throughout the Provinces. They served the purpose of capturing images of everyday life, from royalty to commoners. No one was aware of these weeds that informed the Haruspec hundreds of leagues across the ocean.

The Haruspec – The lord of the Isle of Kaëyrbassad, and sworn enemy of the Gardener.

Kaëyrbassad – The isle of the Haruspec.

Mithengara – A plant harvested on the Isle of Kaëyrbassad, used by the Haruspec as a special concoction to seduce others. Because he was very familiar with the sensual desires of man, primarily food, he engineered his into exquisite and delightful culinary preparations. The addictive powers cause the victim to fulfill the Haruspec's darkest wishes.

Namureyam – He was a famous composer of ancient sonnets and tunes in the country of Paradmah. His music reflected love, war, politics, history and patriotism for Paradmah.

The Kingdom of Paradmah – The country of Ambassador Grioppa and his retinue who were lost at sea, and became ship-wrecked on the Isle of Kaëyrbassad.

Serpent in the Garden – A deceptive pseudo term used by Axzahiir to describe his power of clairvoyance to see all things.

Table of Contents

Prologue xxv

Prelude xxxi
    Refuge at Kol-Shebbala
    The Provincial Capital of Kiérbangaal
    The Kelubragia Protest
    Upper Y'cromeca

The Khalevads 1
    Graëyhovan
    Dûenhallow
    Aokenfana
    Hierundia
    Ir of the Fenrülk
    Terus Raynür
    Peiscavellan Hierundia
    The Thorns of Dul-Meggor

A Storm from the West 55
    Anterròs of the West
    The Caethain Ascent
    Gloom Over Realmhold Thaed-Rú
    Threshold at Duin Caeir

The Gardener's Feast
  The Tales of Cerathmir and Duin Caeir
  The Harmattan Weed Spies

The Storm Breaks 111

  Envoys to Hierundia
  The Trap at Cerathmir
  Celebration in Anterròs
  A Stepping Stone
  A Cry in the West
  A Bold Venture
  An Escape
  Into the Va'Giyyel
  The Presage at Realmhold Thaed-Rú
  Mourning at Cerathmir
  The Caravan
  Sanctuary at Kol-Shebbala
  Capture at Va'Harot
  A Tribune in the West
  Northern Dreams and Visions

The Great War 247

  Gatherings
  A Summoning
  Raid Upon the Fortress City
  The Tip of the Sword
  Battle for Y'cromeca
  A New Seed is Planted

PROLOGUE

In the days of hallowed antiquity, in the primordial regions known as the First Fruits, there was the Gardener. Before the memory of time, beyond the Sea of Feynhava, on the Isles of Feynhava, he was the Chief Steward of the Garden of Ages. This garden prospered, giving life to seeds and fruits of supernal strength and wisdom. Even the minerals, mined from its depths, were composed of infinite, quantum energies. Only the Gardener knew the proper use and mixtures of these components. Thus, he appointed nine immortal sentinels, known as the Aelrük, to guard its borders. With his seeds, across the raging oceans, in a distant land known as Ulmeca-Dül, the Gardener wrought three ages.

In the First Age of Ulmeca-Dül came the race of giants known as the Faeynül. In their numinous tongue of Uraduin, their name meant "the First Fruits of Feynhava" for they were the first to arrive from the Isles of Feynhava. By their hands was the land of Ulmeca-Dül sculpted. Sower of seeds, from their work sprang valleys, mountains, rivers, gardens, boulders, and forests vast and infinite in design.

In the Second Age of Ulmeca-Dül, a race of man was borne of seeds brought from the Garden of Ages to dwell upon Ulmeca-Dül. This race of man became the Gardener's chief joy. From one of their earliest patriarchs, Y'crom, a father of seven sons, this people took on the distinction of Y'cromahein. The noble sons of Y'crom, Aeduthir, Aelgad, Dürthaliun, Visanthiel, Faëlgrey, Alazar and Oliel, became the Seven Branches of Y'crom.

Many generations after the Y'cromahein had settled in Ulmeca-Dül, far across the sea, there came upon the Isles of Feynhava the Sheddukem, the destroyers of all that was good. Black, smoldering fumes shrouded their appearance. Through stone masks, across razor-sharp teeth, their howls of anguish and torment filled the air. Their eyes glowed with pain from a Nameless Curse cast upon them in a dark place, far beyond the reach of daylight.

The Sheddukem charged the Gardener to rid them of their Nameless Curse with seeds from the numinous Garden. But the Gardener denied them this request, for he perceived the true desire of the Sheddukem: to use the supernal gifts of the Garden for evil. The Gardener's firm refusal drove band after band of enraged Sheddukem to open war against the mighty Aelrük for possession of Feynhava. The venerable Aelrük, nine in number, battled each new onslaught alongside Faeynül warriors across the breadth of the Isle of Feynhava in defense of the Garden of Ages.

As the last band of Sheddukem were routed into the sea, the alliance of Aelrük and Faeynül faltered. Though the Steward of Feynhava had forbade it, the Captain of the Aelrük gave unto the Sheddukem leader seeds from the Garden of Ages. His error, in ignorance of the Sheddukem's intent, was borne of compassion. His reward was swift and merciless. The foul Sheddukem beast drew out the captain's pity from his soul, leaving none within. So it was that the heart of the Captain of the Aelrük became darkened. Remorseless for his treachery, he cared not that the Sheddukem could now reap a harvest of untold destruction upon a thousand worlds.

When the Gardener learned of this great treachery and its consequences, a deep sadness fell over his heart. He knew that he must drive this traitor away from his Garden of Ages, into the sea. In his struggle with the captain, the Gardener put a mark upon him, contorting and disfiguring his face as a warning to all who might come upon him.

As the traitor withdrew into the sea by the ancient route of the Faeynül, he cried out, "I know of your special love for the Y'cromahein, how you consider them your chief joy above all creatures, great and small. For this reason, I will follow their course, and when I have found their small, frail forms, I will wipe their seed from the world. This oath of vengeance, I so swear."

The Gardener sorrowed at length over the loss of the Captain of the Aelrük and pondered the portent of his vow. As the Third Age waned, he retreated into the midst of the Garden of Ages to meditate and discern the signs of the future.

In the Fourth Age of Ulmeca-Dül, when the Faeynül had finished marking the boundaries of the land, the last band of Sheddukem wandered beneath dark oceans until they arrived at the icy cold northern lands of Ulmeca-Dül. They found a colossal underworld of vast caves far below the surface and made their abode therein for many generations. The evil of the Sheddukem fell upon the Y'cromahein. Capturing and sequestering men deep in their caves, they experimented upon them with the seeds of Feynhava. Hearing of the tortures perpetrated against man, a new war between the Sheddukem and Faeynül raged upon the surface of Ulmeca-Dül.

Finally, after years of conflict, the Gardener emerged from seclusion and travelled to Ulmeca-Dül. There he joined with the hero, Y'crom, known to this day as the First Patriot. Together with his armies, they struck back at the lower world of the Sheddukem. For many months, the Gardener and the ancient miners of Feynhava busied themselves in filling the cavernous tunnels far below Ulmeca-Dül with supernal ores of Feynhava.

Then it was that a colossal work transpired which was to shape the country of Ulmeca-Dül for eons to come. The Gardener, standing in deep meditation in the valley of Terus-Raynür, spoke in the sacred tongue of Uraduin to invoke life into the metal ores far below the ground.

The land shook with a mighty upheaval as a rumble peeled the sky. Fear and panic gripped all of creation. Molten fire moved through the depths of Ulmeca-Dül, consuming the lower world of the Sheddukem. Lava and molten ores mixed to violently rent the terrain, bursting forth as massive glowing walls. Their movement upwards waxed slow. Whole forests uprooted in their wake while rivers cooled their heat. For many weeks, the molten walls pushed through numerous vents in the terrain, across the land of Ulmeca-Dül, carrying with it the colossal bones of dead Sheddukem. The descendants of Y'crom termed this molten mix of ore and bone, the Ballai, meaning, "The Walls."

In the eerie silence following this event, the Faeynül gathered to the rents in the land and the lower entrances through which the remaining Sheddukem survivors would ascend. These were met with Faeynül swords, battleaxes, war mallets and maces. The vanquished Sheddukem laid as mountainous heaps throughout the land, rotting from flesh to bone, and thus was their race ended and the black name of Sheddukem passed into myth and lore.

In the years following the rise of the Ballai, armies of creatures and men attempted to scale these walls to plunder those within but fell to their doom amidst razor-sharp protrusions. They learned that none could pass beyond these barriers. In this way, the Gardener hid the offspring of men, Y'crom and his descendants, within the Ballai that surrounded each of the Eleven Provinces, so that the traitorous former Captain of the Aelrük still a wandering soul seeking revenge, could not touch them. And there, within the walls, the

Y'cromahein survived for hundreds of years. It was at this time that the Gardener changed the name of the land from Ulmeca-Dül to Y'cromeca, in honor of the First Patriot.

Yet, though the Sheddukem were slain, the scars they left on the land did not heal. All in the lower world of the Sheddukem was destroyed, save the life of one. The transmutation of a Sheddukem with a human host, survived. His beastly predecessors lent unto him an extraordinary height and an attraction to the cold which characterized his white, deathly pallor. He inherited superhuman powers which enabled him to wield profound influence in the world of men. He found his way up through the molten Ballai and used his influence to take wives and concubines which bred a special race of humans. In the dark tongue of the Sheddukem his name was Thaed-Rú, meaning "Mask of Rulership."

For eons to come, this race held sway over the world of men, growing great in number and gaining dominion over man. Implanted in their psyche is an ancient drive, another gift of their twisted ancestry, to resurrect the Cethin Arda, the Dark Garden of the Sheddukem. Throughout the centuries, the Thaed-Rú have used the ancient scrolls of the Sheddukem to nurture the perfect Cethin Arda and transcend into immortality. Through their dark powers, all but the Ballai of the West have been brought down. Though men may freely roam and trade, foul beasts, products of the dark garden, now terrorize the land. Turmoil and civil unrest lie heavy in the hearts and minds of the sons of Y'crom. To this need, the mysterious Gardener walks among mere mortals, vigilant for the day when the traitor to Feynhava returns to claim vengeance against the sons of Y'crom.

Prelude

Refuge at Kol-Shebbala

In the Province of Hierundia lies the obscure mountain country of Kol-Shebbala. The mountains are steep with valleys and gorges carving deep gashes. Through this forbidden landscape of snow-capped ranges wind endless mazes of twists and turns. People seldom venture into this region, for many have lost their direction and were never found.

    Deep in the heart of these mountains, as the third hour was drawing upon the last day of the week, a gray- haired man knelt in a field, pulling weeds. He wore a tiller's apron and his staff, with cryptic letters carved along its length, lay close at hand. The man was dirty from his tunic and apron to his arms and knees. Sweat sprouted along his brow and he wiped it away with a grimy arm. After a few moments more, he sought comfort from the afternoon heat beneath the shade of a sprawling fig tree. Eyes closed, he entered a deep state of meditation.

    I enter the Va'Giyyel, a world of darkness. I enter through the gate of knowledge of Hierundia, he spoke within. The light of the world fell away from him. For several moments, he occupied a negative space, at peace. Then, closed eyes squinted, and a deep frown curled the wrinkles across his forehead. A figure, tall and lithe, took shape before him. Spidery were his limbs, his visage skeletal. From darkened eye sockets, gleaming orbs spoke of a life in the shadow of evil. It was the face of Íraban Thaed-Rú. It was yet a youthful face, still handsome though scarred.

    The youth seemed to sense an intrusion on his subconscious. The train of his full black robe billowed as he pivoted slowly and took several steps forward, as if to draw closer to the gray-haired man. Perceiving the presence of another, in self-defense the young man's face shapeshifted into four wretched faces consecutively.

"I am the face of Crimtha-Sûl the Thaed-Rú," it said, in the language ancient.

A second face intoned, "I am Aed-Onach of the Thaed-Rú."

A third declared, "I come as Sithienta the Thaed-Rú."

And finally, a fourth visage uttered, "I am the first king of the Thaed-Rú order. I am Druad-Alil."

The gray-haired man well knew of these four Bal Rús. The Breinhinod Kynara, history students were taught, the early Thaed-Rú kings. In the days before the formation of the Thaed-Rú Dominions, they spread great terror, war and famine over the primordial world of the Y'cromahein. Each of these early kings, sustained by dark powers, each lived for hundreds of years. Under their influence, men became nefarious, practicing the art of deception, treachery and duplicity over each other. Neighbor cheated neighbor on their scales and businessmen dealt selfish agendas, with no regard for those that starved. Various enterprises turned to slavery for profit, with no regard for the sanctity of life.

"I am of them, yet they are not of me," the dark youth said proudly. "I shall surpass them all, I shall resurrect the Cethin Arda, and no one shall hinder my progress!"

The gray-haired man sighed wearily. It was to be expected of a Thaed-Rú to covet darkness and power. Yet his blood is mixed. He bears the blood of man also. And he is young.

Sensing hope, a sinister smile twisted the lips of young Íraban. *You think me promising? Good! My plans will soon unfold, and you will see their promise. You will see.* The youth raised his arms above him and turned his eyes skyward. Dark storms responded and his black cloak flapped wildly in gusts of howling winds. A thick fog enveloped him bit by bit until all that remained was his face. Once more, the faces of the Breinhinod Kynara imposed themselves upon his visage.

The grey-haired man shook his head in dismay and was instantly transported back to the field. A dark gloom hung about it now. The leaves of the fig trembled as gusts of wind shook its sturdy limbs. The man searched his surroundings for the little blonde girl. His eyes widened in concern as they fell upon her slight frame, bent to the ground. Her crystalline eyes peered at his through a cloying mist. He shook his head violently. The fog cleared, and once more the sun fell brightly upon the girl of four. Clad in simple brown tunic, she gathered a rustic bouquet of flowers in muddied hands. Her maternal figure guided her, watched her as the child chattered softly.

The man called gruffly to the little girl, "Ka-Lyn, come to me. I must teach you how to plant a garden. It is time you learned."

The lady standing beside her stiffened. Eyes wide, she urged her charge, "Go to the Gardener." She ushered the hesitant girl forward with a gentle hand, whispering, "You must listen to all he has to teach you. You will soon have need of it."

"I am going to plant an orchard here," said the sower as she knelt beside him. "But first, we must pull the weeds. If we do not, weeds will overrun the seedlings and choke them. One day, you will be like this seed. It is important that you grow roots deep in fertile soil, watered by the Streams, protected from the weeds. Many people will come from far away to eat from the fruits of such a place as Kol-Shebbala," he added.

The man squatted and hunched over his knee to seek her strange, peculiar blue eyes. A thin ring of lighter blue rimmed the deep azure of her iris. It was a curious oddity of which people often made note. She gazed intensely into his dark, brown eyes, then turned back to her flowers.

Her maternal guardian prompted kindly. "Ka-Lyn, did you hear the Gardener?"

The little girl looked up at the lady's long scar which ran the length of her right eye to her chin. Then she uttered indecipherable words, as children do, and shook her head.

Both the Gardener and her maternal figure chuckled forgivingly.

From the edge of the field, a man waved to the trio, then approached. He too was clad in a dark, rustic tunic. "More arrivals have come. It seems there are more each day," he said to them.

"Very well. Have your people attend to their needs. It is the last day of the week. I must prepare a meal, for twilight is upon us," said the Gardener.

The man nodded respectfully and turned to do his bidding.

The Gardener took up his tiller's staff and rose to his feet. To the maternal figure he said, "It is time we take the girl to see Íraban. She must understand the importance of all she is to learn."

The woman flinched but nodded.

The Gardener reached into his sower's bag and bent to show the girl a handful of dark purple leaves. "Where we are going, it is dangerous. Evil will surround us in Kiérbangaal. Yet, no one will detect us if we chew these leaves. The effects of this plant will shroud us," he reassured her.

He straightened and spoke again to the maternal figure, "Do not fret. She must see with her own eyes what a monster Íraban is. She must realize the darkness within her, and why she must confront it. In time, we will take her to visit the misery of other lands, else she will never understand why so many refugees seek sanctuary with us here."

"While all you have said is true, it will be difficult for me to return there. Dark forms, the misery of my past…they never cease to plague my mind," came her whispered response.

The Gardener frowned. The darkness in his meditations, and the impending darkness, long withheld, superseded her suffering. Soon it would plague the innocent and evil alike across all of Y'cromeca. Leaving this unspoken, he laid a gentle hand on the woman's shoulder and comforted her. "Just as grass which grows and spreads, healing too is a process. Come now, V'leshkah. Let us welcome in the day of rest. We will need our strength. After tomorrow's feast, we will gather our belongings for our journey."

The Provincial Capital of Kiérbangaal

"In the land of Y'cromeca, are the Thaed-Rú Dominions.
These are the vast domains sired from the loins
of that lonely figure who trekked across the frozen wastes,
the sole survivor from the lower world of the Sheddukem.
A seer long silent. A solitary monster.
Madness afflicted his mind. Agony wracked his body.
Conflict raged within his heart.
A deep, fathomless abyss carved into his soul.
He sought to fill it with power, wealth and glory.
But it was an endless chasm that could not be filled.
He sought vengeance for being born.
This is the heritage of every Thaed-Rú descendant,
The heritage of every Bal Rú."

Cheüldric, the Master Scribe
The House of the Y'cromahein Scroll
City of the Falls of Y'cromellah

In the land of Y'cromeca, in the northernmost province of Hierundia, wintry winds blew through the narrow streets of Kiérbangaal, the provincial capital. It was the twenty-third day of Eanair, but rather than celebrate the traditional new year of the Thaed-Rú calendar, this year brought about a rare occurrence. The coronation of a new Bal Rú. All classes of citizens were invited to witness this auspicious occasion.

Children in various drab tunics, scurried about the feet of those in the crowded streets that afternoon. All about them, the citizens of Y'cromeca gathered, some muttering, some shouting. Hoods, thick woolen scarves and fur caps covered every malcontented head that cursed the coronation.

"He is as evil as his ancestors!"

"He murdered his own father to seize the throne!"

"He may well murder us, too!"

Rhünkai soldiers worked swiftly to arrest and jail these protestors. Yet many in the crowds still shouted. Amid this angry clamor, little Ka-Lyn wound her way. Her two guardians firmly clutched her hands as they hurried through the crowd. A horrible, screeching howl caused her to pause and tug her guardians to a halt. Bright blue eyes turned fearfully skyward as monstrous black birds the size of a steed flew over the city. Though distant, their screeches vibrated through Ka-Lyn's body.

"The black birds from the banners!" she cried, pointing to a coronation poster on a stone wall. Upon it was an imprint of the Thaed-Rú coat of arms, two black birds, wings spread, flanking a black tree.

"Yes, the Veyasaen," said the Gardener from beneath an earth-toned hood that differed greatly from the materials and colors of the milling crowd.

"That tree is a symbol of the Cethin Arda, the dark garden." Never relaxing his grasp of his long, wooden staff, he moved to adjust the strap of a large shoulder pouch with his free hand. In it were various seeds and dried leaves. As the fowl above swooped, he grasped the girl's hand once more.

V'leshkah, clad in thick furs and a soft hood of her own, also gripped the girl firmly.

"What are Vey...a...saen?" asked Ka-Lyn, her tongue tumbling over the new word.

"An ancient breed of beastly fowl," her mother figure answered. "They terrorize the skies with their shrieks and wails. Worse yet, they prey upon men as victims, carrying them off with sharp talons. No man has ever slain a Vey-asaen. None are safe from those creatures. Not even the Rhünkai."

Early evening shadows crept through the streets. The Gardener scanned the crowd for pickpockets, muggers and other scoundrels as they snaked their way through the crowd once more. They turned onto a street lined on either side with tall, gothic spires.

"In half an hour, we should arrive at the Hall of Towers!" the Gardener shouted over the crowd.

The trio pushed through the masses to a steep, slope in the street where hundreds of spectators gazed expectantly upward. The sound of trumpets resonated triumphantly through the walled valleys of gothic buildings and towers. The people cheered wildly as a procession appeared upon the crest to ceremoniously descend the Avenue of the Bal Rús. A dazzling cavalcade flowed down the hill, surrounded by ecstatic shouts of praise. Dark armor, lances, halberds, shields gleamed and black and gray banners waved in the wind. Equestrian guards flanked the lengthy procession of foot soldiers.

Dozens of tall eerie figures followed the parade of soldiers. Clad in grim raiment, they flanked eight cloaked figures bearing a royal litter. Unruffled by the deathly white pallor of their skin, by their eye sockets as dark as pits, Ka-Lyn tugged eagerly at the Gardener's cloak and pointed to the ebony litter. It was emblazoned with the same Thaed-Rú coat of arms she had seen earlier. But the crowd was not as eager as the child. All about them, the cries of praise had ceased. Enslaved to their hegemony, the Y'cromahein held a deep-seated disdain for this strange and mysterious Thaed-Rú race.

The trio bobbed about those in front of them, following the litter, until they arrived at the Hall of Towers. There, they witnessed Íraban's descent from the royal litter. A tall youth, his long-flowing, jet-black hair contrasted sharply with the deathly pallor of a face veiled in part by an ornate gold mask. The armor protecting his body was a deep black with richly engraved scenes of battle and tales of ancient victories. His breastplate was emblazoned with the Thaed-Rú insignia and from his neck dangled long feathers of a Veyasaen long dead from his father's capture.

At the foot of the massive arched stairs which led into the Hall of Towers, a group of Thaed-Rú stepped forward to greet the prince. Clad in hooded cloaks, they reached out long, spidery arms to welcome him. Smiles wreathed their skeletal, canine features. yet they walked with a predatory stride. They offered him a ceremonial robe of heavy fur, and he flashed them a wide smile as he clasped it about his armor.

Beyond this gathering stood row upon row of the leading citizens of Hierundia. First among them were the Governors of the Eleven Provinces of Y'cromeca, then the Sovereign Tribunes of each province, then the members of the Y'cromahein Guild. Behind them were government officials, feudal lords, magistrates, merchants, bankers, and experts in the law. All heads bowed low before Íraban Thaed-Rú as he and his entourage passed through their ranks. Their boots rang out against stone steps, past elite guards, banners, and shields, and under the vast archways of the Hall of Towers which housed the Thaed-Rú throne.

Elite members of his court followed behind him. They paused to stand at the base of a series of steps leading up to a lofty stone platform. Upon it was a throne of shields and human skulls, deep red in color for it was completely covered in the blood of the Y'cromahein. The sculpted images of two Veyasaen eerily spread massive stone wings behind the throne.

Shields from the Eleven Provinces surrounded the courtiers as they murmured excitedly amongst themselves. The noble classes favored the rule of this young Thaed-Rú, as they had his predecessor. They profited highly from the Thaed-Rú, for it was they who taught the powerful to manipulate the lesser. Yet fear tainted their pleasure as the powers of the Thaed-Rú allowed them to enter the minds of all, discerning dissident from servant and coercing any who opposed them.

Meanwhile, common citizens poured noisily through a massive arched entrance. A vast, columned chamber stretched before them. Many among them shivered, some from the cold of the open-air atrium and some in fear of the screeching Veyasaen in the wintry sky above. Nonetheless, freezing common folk, exhaling cold vapors, filled three levels of platforms to witness this event.

Being the highest office in the Thaed-Rú Dominions, the coronation of a Bal Rú marked one of the few times when commoners were allowed to mix with royalty. Yet, iron-wrought trestles, a visible barrier dividing the classes, covered the commoners like caged prisoners. Amid these, Ka-Lyn and her guardians stood, peering far below. No one seemed to notice them, not even the Rhünkai who had searched everyone as they entered. "Your purple leaves cloak our identity here, the same as they did when we visited the cave, my lord," whispered V'leshkah to the Gardener.

Hearing these whispers, Ka-Lyn shivered in remembrance of their chilly visit to the cave of the first Thaed- Rú. Though the Gardener urged it was an important lesson, that she must see for herself where the first Thaed-Rú lived after he had survived the destruction of the Sheddukem world, little Ka-Lyn hated that cave. The ancient energies of that place had flooded her mind with a frightful image of the past, a dark figure hulking in the caverns, lord over the bones of slaughtered men. For this reason, she found this Thaed-Rú coronation a delightful contrast.

The Gardener, sensing her thoughts, urged her to dismiss the glory about her and discern the evil. "This young man being made Bal Rú today... he is powerful and elegant. But he is also as great a threat to Y'cromeca. In time, you will see all things with your mind's eye," he whispered in her ear.

The young Bal Rú, now paused dramatically before approaching the throne. His eyelids closed in ecstasy as he stood with outstretched arms and slowly tilted his head backwards. *Now I am Bal-Rú of all! This is my day of glory!*

Like many of the Thaed-Rú sovereigns, a great conflict raged within Íraban. Though his mother had wholly delighted in her child, the only inheritance she had left him was a thorough understanding of infidelity and the weakness of man. From infancy, Theragad had felt disdain for his only son. He had been acutely aware of the boy's weakness as a future monarch: his mother's blood was human.

Plagued by male dominance in their line, his race had relied on Y'cromahein women to further their line ever since the first such union in that frigid cave of the first Thaed-Rú. Handpicking certain Y'cromahein noblewomen of specific physical requirements and hereditary class, the Thaed-Rú had interbred for eons. It mattered little to them that the Y'cromahein had long equated such a mixture of blood to mating a human with a monster, the result being abominable offspring to rule their world. Nature however, seemed to agree as

Thaed-Rú power waned each time successive generations incorporated more human blood into their lineage.

Beyond his mixed blood, Theragad had further cause to despise his only son. Caught in a secret tryst with a handsome counselor of the court, the order for her execution was immediate. And Theragad forced their three-year old son to watch her beheading. It was Íraban's first memory and well he knew that, from that moment on, there was never to be any place in his heart for love. Thus it was that Íraban, through no fault of his own, was punished doubly by his father for his mother's betrayal and her blood. From the pressure of his father in his young life, emerged an arrogant, defiant prince.

Even today, before entering his coronation, the youth indulged his vanity. Two of his attendants stepped forward when he beckoned. One held a large mirror before him while the other arranged his attire and hair to his liking. Upon the faces of his fawning courtiers, several frowns of disapproval appeared, and a wave of titters ran throughout the crowd beyond. Though no one ever spoke of it, many secretly loathed the young crown prince for his narcissism and his brash ways. Yet, it was merely a product of his father's constant derision of every aspect of his character. Íraban had clung to the one thing his father could not disparage. A very handsome youth, at sixteen years of age, he made his first decree, that he must always be followed by two members of his personal staff. As they did now, their sole job was for one to hold a mirror while the other combed his hair and adjusted his clothing to his liking.

Theragad, who bore deep scars upon his face of his own father's violence, was outraged by such conceit. In turn, he passed the pitiful legacy of abuse on to his son. Soon after the vain decree of the crown prince, a drunken Theragad assailed his son verbally in hopes of goading him into a physical reaction. Although a frequent occurrence between the two, this time the frustrated youth bypassed fists for his dagger which he sank it deep into the flesh about his father's ribs. In a fit of rage, Theragad prevailed, wrestling the dagger from his son and turning it upon him, horribly scarring his son's handsome face to greater extremes than his own.

As he peered into the mirror, Íraban slipped a hand beneath his beautiful, golden mask upon his face, exploring the scar beneath it thoughtfully. He cringed at the memory of a young man coiled into a fetal position, like a new calf in a pool of blood, on the cold stone floor of his father's private chamber. He had cried in burning agony, yet Theragad had only jeered back at him with fiendish laughter saying, "Is your beauty and charm to govern when I am gone? Hungry for what is rightfully ours, my generals and Governors are poised to seize our dominion and divide it amongst themselves as a pack of wolves fighting over their game." He circled his son like the wolves of which he spoke, a grimace twisting his skeletal face. "You must understand pain if you are to rule. The ageless sun rises and sets on the miseries of all who live under our rule. How can you ever expect to rule them and understand them as subjects, lest you drink the bitter waters of pain and sorrow?"

Bending down to his son's pitiful form, Theragad had violently grabbed a tuft of Íraban's long hair, jerked the wounded face upwards, and smeared his hand in his son's blood. Holding his bloodied palm an inch before Íraban's eyes, he exclaimed, "Ours is a dominion built upon blood! The Thaed-Rú carry scars. We all do. It is part of who we are."

"A dominion built upon blood" indeed, Íraban thought triumphantly. He searched the reflection before him, half expecting to see his father's specter lurking behind him. Injured as he had been the night of his father's attack, and young as he was, it had taken time to understand his father's words, to learn the nature of his father's generals, their ambitions to preside over the Eleven Dominions in his stead. However horrible Theragad had been as a father, he had understood his dominion. His drunken taunts that night were founded in truth.

The Thaed-Rú lineage held great sway over the Y'cromahein. In ages past, many of the Bal Rú could discern the thoughts of their counselors. Others manipulated the wills of lesser lords and nobles through mental powers. From the Thaed-Rú, the age of the Y'cromahein learned the craft of violent rule, deceit, duplicity, and the betrayal of friends for personal gain. It was a craft that spread treachery across the whole of Y'cromeca, a craft which Íraban gradually discovered great strength. How right you were, father! the young Bal Rú crowed inwardly. A little of the day's joy returned to him as the new dawn approached. Oh, you taught me well, father. Through our hereditary powers of persuasion, I swayed your hungry generals, swayed them to aid in your assassination! And upon your blood I will build my own dominion!

The traitors eagerly believed his promises of co-sovereignty. They drank of his velvet vows to end the oppressive and tyrannical rule of the Thaed-Rú beasts, to free men to rule over their own dominions. Yet all their loyalty wrought them was the swift arm of Thaed-Rú justice. Beneath the sway of Íraban's influence, the courts of law were of his side and ordered them sized and executed for high treason. Unequivocally now, the stage was set for Íraban to become Bal Rú of the Thaed-Rú Dominions.

Pride widened the satisfied smile beneath his mask as the youth pivoted sharply on his heel. Grandly, he stalked past the members of his court to ascend the steps. His long fur cape trailing elegantly behind him, then swirled heavily about as he reached the throne and turned to look upon his people.

It is a shame, father, that you did not live to see what remarkable things I will accomplish! he thought sardonically. Then his eyes welled up with emotion on this most imperious of days. *Curse you for plaguing my thoughts today, old man! You will see! I will not disappoint you...as you imagined.*

With an imperceptible shake of his head, he banished such thoughts. Slowly, he surveyed the crowd before taking his seat upon the throne. Ka-Lyn's guardians lifted her up to see the seated figure. Her grimy fingers clutched the iron trestles as she peered through them, marveling at the scene before her. An intimidating row of dark-armored sentinels with lances, swords and halberds guarded the long, stone ramp that led to the handsome youth on the throne.

Her guardian pointed to the new sovereign. "Today he assumes rule over all of Y'cromeca." From beneath his hood, he explained, "There is much for you to learn from him. The Streams of Feynhava tell us that a wise man tends to his field. He protects it and pulls out weeds when necessary. Patiently he awaits the harvest. But a foolish man allows the weeds to choke out the plants. Let the actions of Íraban be lessons to you of what you must never do. Because of his dark ways, the rich and wealthy prosper under his rule while the commoners suffer and groan. Only death will come from such a man. You must never be like that young man on the throne — ever. Always be guided by the gentle voice of love and reason spoken over you from the days in your cradle," he whispered in her ear.

Her mother figure smiled, as she cherished the hooded man's teachings. Little Ka-Lyn listened dutifully, then cast her attention back through the trestles, to the ceremony. Yet it was the deathly skeletal features of the figure beside the one enthroned which haunted her. A little gasp of surprise escaped her lips as he stepped forward to speak. He was Teosifan, the Chief Steward of the Y'cromahein Guild. The tassels of his ceremonial black cap hung below his ears where tendrils of gray hair together with the leathery grimace upon his face characterized him as an elder.

In the velvety voice of a practiced politician, Teosifan called out, "On this eve, destiny calls upon the allegiances of the Governors of the Eleven Provinces to pledge their arms to the Thaed-Rú!" The cold vapors of his breath reached but a little way from his mouth, yet his deep voice echoed loudly across the vast, imperious hall.

The Sovereign Tribunes of the Eleven Provinces, all present, stepped forward in response. Each of them lorded over great tumens of soldiers in their respective lands. They answered now in the voice of their Governors, as dictated by the traditions of the Thaed-Rú. Their vow was meant for more than a declaration of fealty to their sovereign. It was a threatening reminder to the Governors of each Province that they did not rule alone, lest a need arise for the Tribunes' military power protected them. The Tribune Ansuz spoke for the Province of Hierundia. The Tribune Íthsaz was the voice for the Province of Tal-Ciddion. The Tribune Ríthas spoke for Rhühaven. The Tribune Thurisaz represented Graëyhovan. The Tribune Uruz spoke for the Province of Molchaion. The Province of Cahheramas was represented by the Tribune Wunden. The Province of Cian was spoken for by the Tribune Hagalaz. The Tribune Urathsaz gave his pledge for the Province of Ir of the Fenrülk. The Tribune Dagaz gave his word for the Province of Cerebantus. The voice of the Tribune Kaunan was given for Bisantior. And the Tribune Gebor sealed his pledge for the Province of Teras-Amin.

Teosifan prompted each of them, "Do you pledge your arms to serve the Thaed-Rú?"

"I do!" came each reply.

Infamous, the role of a Tribune was to press the rule of the Thaed-Rú over the commoners, often terrorizing the harmless and innocent with little regard to the light of justice and right standing. They cared little for the goodness of men, save only for their personal gain and advancement over the disgruntled masses. From the eleven Tribunes, and the Thaed-Rú whom they served, treachery, duplicity and deceit trickled out, then spread like a plague.

"From the hallowed days of the first Thaed-Rú, the power and promise of the Cethin Arda has always been our mark!" proclaimed Teosifan. "Therefore, if any province shall renege on this oath, this day or ever, should any aim to rebel against the Thaed-Rú, by plot or design, or desire to secede from the Thaed-Rú Dominions..." Teosifan paused for effect, "...then the fury of the

Thaed-Rú shall strike that province, its governor, his family and all his leaders with the wrath of the Cethin Arda!"

A dreadful silence engulfed the entire hall. Though the Tribunes nodded and bowed, this clouded the faces of many in attendance. The Cethin Arda, the dark garden. The flora and fauna which sprang forth from its darkness, promised no boon for man.

Ka-Lyn quaked as Teosifan's voice thundered threats into it, "Then shall your province be laid waste. Then will it become a haunt of ghostly specters and fowl beasts. Then will it become a graveyard for the rotting corpses of your men!"

Ka-Lyn's guardian patted her hand but frowned. Soon, these cursed words shall be realized upon your own heads.

After accepting the fealty of the Eleven Provinces, Teosifan knelt ceremoniously before the new liege. All present followed suit, bowing their heads before their new ruler, save for the hooded trio. Shrouded by the Gardener's powerful leaves, their failure to kneel went unnoticed.

Teosifan rose and took up the jeweled Scepter of H'dhar from an ornately carved stone altar beside the throne. Carved of hammered gold, the Scepter of H'dhar bore strange markings and symbols of the dark tongue of the Sheddukem which read: Uhtor Um Karreh "A Crown from Below." Handing it over with a flourish of pomp and circumstance, the elder said to the younger, "Behold the symbol of the Thaed-Rú, the Scepter of H'dhar. With it, assume rule over the House of Thaed-Rú, the Y'cromahein Guild, the Governors of the Eleven Provinces, the Sovereign Tribunes of the Rhünkai Armies and all who dwell within your Domains."

To the gathered masses in the hall, Teosifan introduced the new sovereign, "Y'cromeca receive your new sovereign. Behold your new Bal Rú, the Lord Íraban Thaed-Rú! A new day is dawning for the Y'cromahein. Bow lowly before the honor of your new liege." In a dignified wave, they bowed their heads, then rose solemnly to their feet. Mixed expressions of anticipation and angst governed their countenances.

Teosifan led the masses now in the centuries-old declaration of allegiance, "Command us through your will! Lead us into a stronger future!" the people impetuously recited after him. All declared, some fervently, some fearfully, save for the hooded trio. Ka'Lyn knew they owed this young Thaed- Rú no allegiance, yet she found him mesmerizing. Before this day, she had only heard of the Thaed-Rú. Their inhuman features were a curiosity, but it was the Bal Rú's eyes that drew her most. They were deep black with a bright yellow ring in the center, giving him a wolfish look. They flared triumphantly as he gripped the Scepter of H'dhar, rose from his throne and stepped to look out upon his subjects. Ka-Lyn tightened her hold around her guardian's arm as the Bal Rú spoke.

"Long ago, each of the Eleven Provinces of Y'cromeca was surrounded by thick, impenetrable walls of molten fire known as the Ballai. Trapped within these colossal walls, the Y'cromahein survived many ages until the first Thaed-Rú ushered in revolution" said the young Bal Rú. He extended his hand, palm upward to sweep it grandly over the people. "Here, in the Province of Hierundia, we harnessed the people's collective strength. Each successive reign of the Thaed-Rú, influenced each of the Eleven Provinces until these walls of molten fire fell from within. For this reason, we carry the title of Bal Rú, Conqueror of the Walls. We are the masters who breached the Ballai, so long ago. Their borders felled, the Eleven Provinces bowed to our might. In return, commerce and trade thrived across our Dominions," he strode forward with cold pride.

At the top of the stairs, Íraban raised his arms in a symbol of victory. "Now, in this Age of the Fallen Ballai, you are free to roam within and beyond each of the Provinces! Now you may live anywhere, you may buy and sell freely throughout Our Dominions! The walls that once held men inside, separating province from province, are forever gone!" he shouted.

The people applauded. Ka-Lyn's guardian shook his head under his hood. His words are spun in lies! What a mockery! To lead them to believe their lives are bettered through commerce! Yet, the truth remains...without the Ballai, the people are left ripe for plunder from an ancient foe. To his ward he whispered, "Ka-Lyn, the walls of which he speaks were not created to keep the people in! They protected from a great and powerful enemy, an enemy whose only allegiance is to an ancient oath of vengeance on this world."

Ka-Lyn's azure eyes held many questions, but Íraban's voice boomed on, drawing her in. At a nod from the Gardener, she turned attentively back to his address. "The Thaed-Rú have wrought order and balance in Y'cromeca. Today, we remember the benevolence of my grandfather, Bal Rú Saerclusa the Great, who built the modern centers of Laëthoban, Hánuthir and Terusdagion. He bridged these great centers of the North with highways beyond the fallen

Ballai. My own father, Bal Rú Theragad Thaed-Rú, saw to the restoration of our magnificent capital of Kiérbangaal. No city in the world rivals its splendor and beauty. These were their gifts to Y'cromeca!"

More applause ensued. The young Bal Rú raised the Scepter of H'dhar over his people and descended to move past them. In a hypnotic tone, Íraban continued, "I too have a gift for Y'cromeca! But I have seen the futility and vanity of my forefathers' gifts! Such fragile tokens as these do not heal a world of its strife. I am much concerned with the toil and tension undergirding the frustrations of my people." Pointing a frightful finger of judgement toward his audience, he uttered, "Many of you are not content to live under the rule of the Thaed-Rú Dominions." Softening his tone, he added, "I have spent much time and energy and, today, I vow to bridge our two worlds and end this thousand-year struggle, for all Y'cromeca."

The commoners exchanged nervous glances and quiet murmurs. Some in the court looked on knowingly, smiles playing at their lips, but many were as curious as the crowd behind them.

"Our ancestors three times strove to resurrect the Cethin Arda, each was futile. Too great to harness and comprehend, true knowledge of it has always been obscured in darkness, thus its name," continued Íraban as his masked eyes surveyed the people. "But now my alchemists have discovered that the Necropulpa plant, harvested in the Cethin Arda, can extend life. For everyone! For the young and the old. Seeds of this Necropulpa plant lend superhuman strength to those who labor under the sun. They heighten the prowess of soldiers in battle. And for those who thirst after knowledge and wisdom to improve their lives, the Cethin Arda promises infinite immortality by harnessing the thought process. Those who partake of these fruits shall become stewards of creations, inventions and bold enterprises."

To himself, Íraban chortled, For the benefit and advancement of the Thaed-Rú Dominions! To his subjects, he cautioned. "To ensure your security and to discourage seditious libel and rebellion, the Thaed-Rú masters will supervise the harvest and application of the Necropulpa. It is my wish today that my rule be marked by this journey of our minds, hearts and interests. Gradually our interests shall flow together, transcending into one collective thought."

Holding the Scepter of H'dhar with an extended arm for emphasis, he declared, "Under my rule, we shall wield powers beyond the clay of mere men.

We shall transcend into infinity. The Cethin Arda will unite the Thaed-Rú and the Y'cromahein as one omnipotent power! I bestow upon you now the greatest gift of all for everyone in Y'cromeca. The resurrection of the fourth Cethin Arda!"

Courtiers and merchants thundered shouts of praise, while the commoners squinted through the iron trestles, silently contemplating the implications of this proclamation. Ka-Lyn's guardian felt a deep well of sadness for the suffering soon to be unleashed upon the land.

Íraban strode to his throne. From his perch he laid out his plan before them all, his honeyed words placating the masses. "This garden will require a city, greater than this capital, and a powerful army to guard its borders. It will be a Fortress City, else those with selfish aims will attempt to strike and plunder the fruit of my great gift to Y'cromeca. To this city, I will appoint administrators for governance and commission housing for alchemists to learn and draw from its hidden wisdom and power. To ensure the survival and success of the Cethin Arda, its location will be my knowledge, but your mystery."

Beneath his ornate mask, Íraban's nostrils flared and his eyes widened. He raised a hand up over his subjects and concluded his speech with an edict. "And from each of our Eleven Provinces, thousands upon thousands of you shall join me in this City. I call upon the young men of Y'cromeca to build this new Fortress City, to resurrect my Cethin Arda. The sons of the Eleven Dominions will serve as builders and as Rhünkai soldiers. In return, the fruits of the Cethin Arda shall be extended to these scions, granting them heightened powers of skill, knowledge and immortality! Your sons will not perish in our service, but by their work our garden will prosper until all of Y'cromeca joins us in this immortality!"

A wave of mixed emotions ran through the crowd. Some shrank back or huddled in dread and fear, uncertain of the future of Y'cromeca. Others, enticed by the seductive words of this new Bal Rú, were more than willing to give their sons over, eager to see this new day for all Y'cromeca.

The Bal Rú rose and strode down the steps to be handed into his litter. Upon him rained great laud from the voices of his council and court for this new enterprise. A mass of commoners flowed, grumbling, into the streets, and the hooded trio followed. Yet many stayed behind, making inquiries about enlisting their sons.

Days would pour into weeks. News of the revival of the fourth Cethin Arda was to spread like malignant weeds through the whole of the Province of Hierundia. In taverns, marketplaces, inns and shops, this would dominate the talk of men who were to share ideas, suspicions and opinions over business transactions, cups of coffee, and goblets of ale. But, on the evening of Íraban's coronation, there was little speculation in the capital, so busily engaged were they in celebration.

The Thaed-Rú royalty, in colorful masks of all shapes and designs, mixed with the landed gentry and upper echelons of society. Their masks were neither ceremonial, nor optional. Long before his coronation, Íraban decreed that all celebrants be masked at royal occasions. This, he had hoped, would serve to normalize his own wearing of a mask. They drank, dined, danced, laughed and flattered one another as the rabble reveled in the streets.

Safely perched on the broad shoulders of the Gardener, Ka-Lyn sleepily observed the shadowy silhouettes of reeling drunkards and ruffians overpowering weaker vessels for their share of shekülhorns cast down to them from the wealthy in carriages and on horseback. As the night wore on, she fell into a deep sleep, nestled against the Gardener's shoulder. Her guardians remained in the shadows to grimly watch the prisoner wagons rumble forth. A final festivity of the coronation was an execution in the street of those who had protested Íraban's coronation; a token of Thaed-Rú justice.

The Kelubragia Protest

THE EDICT OF THE SCIONS OF ÍRABAN

THE VOICE OF OPPORTUNITY CALLS UPON THE YOUNG MEN OF COMMON CLASSES TO RISE UP AND BUILD A NEW FUTURE FOR TERRA Y'CROMECA.

HEREIN ARE THEY SUMMONED TO REVIVE THE PROMISE AND POWER OF THE CETHIN ARDA. ACCORDINGLY, ALL YOUNG MEN OF COMMON CLASSES SHALL COME UNDER THE ROYAL POSSESSION OF THE THAED-RÚ DOMINIONS BY THE AGE OF NINE.

IN ACCORDANCE WITH THE CENSUS, IN THE MONTH OF QUATANUIL, RHÜNKAI OFFICIALS SHALL RENDER THESE YOUNG MEN UNTO THE GLORIOUS WORK OF HIS MAJESTY, THE BAL RÚ ÍRABAN THAED-RÚ.

AS SUCH, THESE SAID YOUNG MEN SHALL BE KNOWN FORTHWITH AS "THE SCIONS OF ÍRABAN."

ANY FAMILY WHO RESISTS THIS EDICT BY WITHHOLDING THEIR CHILDREN FROM THE LOTTERY SHALL FACE IMPRISONMENT.

ANYONE WHO HELPS A FAMILY BY PLOT OR DESIGN SHALL FACE EXECUTION.

PROCLAIMED AND ISSUED THIS DAY, THE 13TH OF THE MONTH OF MEDDÍ

IN THE ISSUANCE OF HIS EDICT OF THE SCIONS, ÍRABAN DECLARED all children of the peasant classes to be property of the Thaed-Rú Dominions by the tender age of nine. Directly after his coronation, he ordered a new census to compare to that of his father's two years prior. By these records, he moved to make the child slaves a permanent fixture of the Thaed-Rú machine. Large sums were allocated to the Guild, which was composed of the Thaed-Rú court, various Governors, and lesser lords and nobles who held fiefdoms. In turn, they agreed to allow the Rhünkai soldiers in their territories to take possession of the children of commoners.

Across Y'cromeca, many took to hiding their offspring to avoid the Royal Edict, banding together in resistance to hide their children as best they could. But for all their good intentions, this course of action was ever in vain, for Rhünkai soldiers sought them out and imprisoned any who had aided in such deception. With each incursion, the Bal Rú grew angrier, his wrath more severe. As the jails filled across his dominions, whether parent or resistance, any who kept his scions faced torture and execution. Rapidly, despite the protests of many a village, his plan unfolded.

Autumn fell upon Y'cromeca, the cold in the wind matching the chill in the hearts of the Y'cromahein. In the high mountain country in the province of Cahheramas, the month of Quatanuil brought heavy rains from the eastern coast upon a cold and gloomy day. As they had done across the land, soldiers marched into the plaza of the village Kelubragia. The infamous call of the Horn of the March summoned parents and children to the town square where the summons messenger read from the Royal Edict of the Scions of Íraban. After a brief inspection of health and age, young lads were loaded into barred wagons destined for labor on the Fortress City in parts unknown. If a lad held potential in the Rhünkai army, he joined a separate caravan of recruits, which led to military training camps in the northwestern territories.

But today, the Horn of the March drew neither scions to the caravan nor protests from the villages. Soldiers kicked in doors only to peer into empty homes and shops. The brave villagers of Kelubragia in Cahheramas, despite the threat to their own lives, had abandoned their village entirely to sequester themselves and their younglings in the mountains. Guided by the screams of Veyasaen birds on high, the Rhünkai sought them out in the caves. There, amongst echoing choruses of grief and pain, the soldiers worked like soulless machines. Cold, regimented, they tore squirming children from their mother's grasps and slashed at fathers and elder brothers with swords. From the bloodied caves, those who survived were rounded up and led behind their youth, back to the village square.

As the children of Kelubragia were inspected one by one, weeping parents helplessly looked on. A Rhünkai minstrel sang the haunting Song of Íraban's Scions, accompanied by drummers.

> *"Heed the call of the fatherland.*
> *Strong arms to build a kingdom,*
> *The wisdom of our prince doth seek.*
> *To raise a land of sword and helm,*
> *Beyond the clay of mere men.*
> *Mothers weep not for your sons. Fathers do not resist.*
> *We are the Scions of Íraban forging a world for you and me.*
> *Our father is Lord Íraban. His justice tried and true.*
> *The fatherland of Y'cromeca is calling for me and you.*
> *A power to crush the world before us.*
> *And lay waste the enemies of House Thaed-Rú."*

"You lie," shouted a farmer, shaking his fist at the soldiers. That breath with which he spoke was his last as an arrow whizzed into his heart. As the caravans creaked away, bearing the children to their doom, each of the remaining villagers was butchered without mercy. In a nearby field, hundreds of dead bodies lay ripe for swarming flies and vultures, as a warning to those who disobeyed the Royal Edict of the Scions of Íraban.

Across the Provinces, many villages and townships suffered similar fates as Kelubragia. So it was that, one by one, the frozen wastelands of Tal-Ciddion and Rhühaven, in the Provinces of Molchaion, Cian and Graëyhovan, hamlets and villages gave themselves over to grim compliance. Weeping, they handed over their children to labor in the hidden Fortress City, a place of mystery whose location no man knew. The people of Upper and Middle Y'cromeca came to understand that many years of hardship lay ahead. And the soldiers of the Rhünkai fell into a dreary routine of trekking the land far and wide, ensuring each town, village and hamlet was harvested for Scions twice a year.

Upper Y'cromeca

Some weeks following the failed protest of Kelubragia in the eastern Province of Cahheramas, far away in the Province of Hierundia, a train of royal carriages wound through the dark, wet woods of Dhar-Thayn. Up from the muddy ruts of the forest road, they jerked and swayed. The carriages transitioned noisily to a wide, cobbled road leading to the great estate of the Tribune Ansuz of Hierundia.

Wearily Teosifan tucked his thinning hair behind his ears and prompted, "Lord Íraban?"

The Bal Rú, snored loudly in response. His masked face lolled to one side upon a wide cushion of red velvet. Though it was midday, their tedious travels from one estate to the other these many weeks had amplified his habit of drink. He was rarely sober.

"Shall I greet the Tribune for you?" Teosifan hissed, prodding his arm with long, skeletal fingers.

Reluctantly, Íraban roused. His own bony fingers pulled at his furs as he leaned to gaze through his window at the great iron gates under which they passed. The wooded view before him, promised no sign of the estate. He sank back against his seat and turned a blank stare upon Teosifan who was lecturing him sternly.

"The Feast of the Cethin Arda was your idea, remember? One hundred and eighty days of glory and splendor in Kiérbangaal, indeed!" he snorted, "Did you think to view each day's parades and games from your tower windows? To avoid the dining and dances and dramas?"

Íraban scowled. Though no longer a youth, he lacked maturity and he knew it. Planning the feasts had fed his narcissism, but ennui had overcome him. His appearances had quickly dwindled to a perpetual, and noticeable, absence. "I would rather take up residence in the Fortress City. It pleases me to watch its walls grow daily, to confer with my alchemists, and to witness the harvests of my garden."

"And your continual visits ensure progress there, of course," Teosifan conceded. "But in the meantime," he cautioned, "paupers and peasants and princes alike must see you, your administrators must host you, and you must draw out their support of your dark garden. Speak to the Tribune with care, sway him to your cause. Need I remind you, he holds the largest tumens in the land? We need his support as there is much resistance yet amongst his people."

Íraban's eyebrows narrowed beneath his mask. Teosifan coughed awkwardly and corrected himself, "...amongst your people."

The carriage jerked to a halt, sparing Teosifan a reproach. Bolting from the carriage, Íraban brushed rudely past the waiting Tribune Ansuz. The man bowed low at the waist in greeting, despite the rebuff, and called out loudly, "Your Majesty, welcome to my home."

Íraban spun, his dark furs swirling about his lanky frame. He threw the man a curt nod and scrutinized him as he rose from his bow. The Tribune Ansuz, unusually tall for an Y'cromahein man, stood eye-to-eye with the young Thaed-Rú king. In his hand he grasped a smaller version of the Bal- Rú's Scepter of H'dhar, representing the authority of his rank. Íraban noted the muscular frame of the overlord of Hierundia as the chill wind stirred his sumptuously woven, floor-length cloak. His broad chest was clad in military regalia denoting his many skills as a warrior. But it was the quality of the material of his cape which drew the Bal Rú's eye. Neither his military ornamentation, nor his stature impressed the young man.

Then, the Bal Rú's Thaed-Rú senses prickled. He shook off his wine induced stupor and focused on the man's face. Ansuz was many decades his elder, yet his finely chiseled visage lacked the deep signs of age that marked most counselors and officials in the dominions. This Tribune was in his prime. *He thinks himself my equal. He thinks himself a king,* sneered Íraban within.

For the past month, from his throne in Realmhold Thaed-Rú, Íraban had received streams of dignitaries bearing him gifts and offering repetitious praise. Among these men, the Tribune Ansuz had been notably absent. Íraban had only deigned to attend this week's feasts as they were assumed to be an attempt at reparation.

Smoothly, the Bal Rú spoke, "Tribune Ansuz, it pleases us to celebrate the Feast of the Cethin Arda in your home." Íraban's tongue, serpentine, licked hungrily at his lips as he worked to sway Ansuz. "I have much anticipated my stay here this week. Your prowess is of immense value to our cause."

The Tribune's dark eyes probed those of the Bal Rú before he replied. "My army is a treasure, indeed." To his servants he called, "Show the Bal Rú to his chambers, he is likely weary from his journey."

He bowed his head in deference, but as Íraban departed, he stared after him stormily. "Ready my horse!" he called. A member of his personal guard ran ahead to see to it, and he stalked after the man, his face clouded by thought.

In the great halls of feasts that night, wreathes adorned the archways, tall silk curtains lent rich color to each room, thick carpets softened the tread of courtiers, fine paintings dazzled the eye, bronze and marble sculptures inspired awe, and beautiful fountains gurgled merrily.

Íraban strode amongst this luxury as though it were his. In a way, it was. He was seated at the head of a massive table hewn of fine wood, with the Tribune Ansuz on his right. Before them lay a feast of oysters from Cerebantus, shrimp from the coasts of Teras-Amin, and hams, turkey, sides of beef, roast kid, and suckling pig from all over the vast kingdom.

An awkward silence hung between the two great rulers. Teosifan had long since given up on his ward and busied himself with the pursuit of women. Íraban busied his cupbearer. Far earlier in the evening than was customary for a host, the Tribune slipped away with ease. It was the only feast graced by the Bal-Rú's presence during his stay. And the Tribune Ansuz found this far more pleasing than offensive.

• • • • •

The following evening, the Tribune Ansuz attended a theatrical performance depicting the history of the Thaed-Rú dynasty. By the light of candelabras and flickering torches, performers crossed and re-crossed each other's shadows.

In the darkened theater, Ansuz slipped away from the balcony where several Thaed-Rú members of the royal court sat. He sank back against the wall of a dim corner below and waited, feigning interest in the drama before him.

"The Tribune Ansuz, it is an honor. Are you entertained by the history of the Thaed-Rú?" whispered a figure at his side.

Slowly, Ansuz turned his head and squinted in the dark but could see nothing of the man's face. The figure wore a strange cloak of earthen hues, the hood of which obscured his face. The Tribune's tone was also hushed as he asked, "You seek an audience with me?"

The man nodded. "Master Sulla's messenger reached you?"

"Yes, I came upon him yesterday during my evening ride," Ansuz said. "Sulla is an old friend, we have shared in many adventures, he and I." Cursing himself for sharing so openly with a stranger, he coughed, and inquired, "How fares his health today? I was saddened to hear he grows worse."

"He draws close to death, I fear," came the hooded figure's response.

Ansuz drew in a deep breath and scowled. "And who shall seize the estate of Iemil then?" A wave of trust in this figure came over him. It was beyond his comprehension, but, with faith in his senses, he clarified, "the true estate of Iemil."

"You mean the Anil-Gevra of Ir of the Fenrülk?" the figure returned quietly.

"Yes, Master Sulla is lord over their seat, is he not?" Ansuz said gruffly, thinking, *Who is this man that I should trust him so?*

Meanwhile, the hooded figure asked quietly, "What do you fear, Tribune? That the new Bal-Rú may seek to join them with his Rhünkai forces?"

The Tribune huffed at the impertinence of the messenger. "Fear?" he scoffed. "It is the young Bal Rú who fears the strength of Y'cromahein men, and of the Anil-Gevra. He fears any who might oppose him, should his powers of persuasion fail."

"It seems such opposition might satisfy you in turn, Tribune," the hooded man said craftily, prompting a response.

Ansuz chuckled, "It would indeed. Did you know, as a young soldier decades ago, I first served in policing the people?"

The man shook his head.

"Times were different," Ansuz shrugged. "But as I grew in rank and authority, I saw the Thaed-Rú shadow little by little tighten its grip over the land. One day, I realized what infernal monsters they were, and I ceased in unquestioningly following their orders. Now, I am no friend to those that cross me, as men well know. But, the Thaed- Rú order wreaks havoc on the ancient ways of our people. They conduct heinous acts of punishment against our own people for crimes they deem unlawful. And yet, they are beyond rebuke, even as they create reprehensible abominations from the Cethin Arda!" The Tribune struggled to keep his voice low as he fumed.

The messenger gazed upon the Tribune's stormy countenance and said gently, "It is heartening to hear of your disgust for these dark endeavors. To that end, I have been sent to speak to you by Master Sulla."

Ansuz nodded. "In conducting this new Edict, the Rhünkai target the young men of the Anil-Gevra. Sulla reports that many of them have fled, evading the Edict of this upstart. Íraban, whether through ignorance or arrogance, thinks them conquered and driven away. But they are a gathering force! It is not in the blood of the Anil-Gevra to be harnessed as slaves!"

"Nor is it in your blood," murmured the man.

Ansuz stepped forward slightly, peering beneath the hood in earnest now. The figure leaned forward, as if to aid his seeking. From forth the hood gleamed a pair of eyes as grey blue as a sea beneath the clouds. Inexplicably, a channel of trust emanated from that pair of discerning eyes.

Ansuz found this equally irritating and intriguing. He crossed his arms over his broad chest and leaned against the wall once more, casting his eyes upon the stage where players frivolously cavorted in celebration of the coronation of Bal Rú Saerclusa the Great.

Ansuz bit at his lip for a moment, then murmured, "Yes, the blood of the Anil-Gevra, in part, runs in my own veins. As you seem aware of that, you must certainly know that I will not yield the strength of my army to his command."

The figure commented only, "Yes, your blood is mixed indeed."

Ansuz blinked rapidly, eyes flickering, searching the man's countenance.

The messenger offered, "It is of the Anil-Gevra that Sulla wishes we speak."

"Oh?"

"He knows his time is short. Seeking a stable future for the people of his land, and of his heart, he offers you the armies of the Anil-Gevra under one condition."

Ansuz' eyes popped wide, and a wicked smile spread across his face. Eagerly he asked, "And the generals agreed to this?"

The man hushed him, and, remembering himself, Ansuz glanced around nervously. But the courtiers near them were deep in their drink, captivated by the play and ignorant of the conversation in the shadows.

"The generals?" urged Ansuz, eyes gleaming.

"All four generals of the divisions of Anil-Gevra are of an accord with his wishes."

Ansuz shook his head in wonder. Even by him, little was known of the Anil-Gevra. Though many a campaign had sent the Tribune southward, throughout the lands of Ir of the Fenrülk, the Anil-Gevra, descended from an ancient race of excellent tillers, had remained separate from the many wars of the Rhünkai. In times of peace, they were widely known for their passionate mastery of husbandry. In the darkest of times, and only against great evil, their menfolk had several times joined forces with the Y'cromahein to turn the tide of war for good. Yet a cloud of mystery hung about both their origins and intents.

"Why would such a force yield to my command?" he asked in wonder. "What is their condition?"

"They will bind themselves to you in allegiance, serving gladly at your will...if that will be to oppose Íraban and end the dominion of the Thaed-Rú over the Y'cromahein," came the answer.

A low whistle sounded as Ansuz sucked his breath in rapidly. The messenger looked about hesitantly, ensuring their continued privacy. But Ansuz succumbed to rampant thoughts. *Should we triumph, how well their might would serve to eradicate the Thaed-Rú! Such a war, when won, would place me on the Kiérbangaal throne!* Aloud, he merely scoffed, "Do they not know this alliance would jeopardize my position as Tribune, my lands, my estate, my family?"

"They know it to be the only hope of men," was the hooded man's reply.

Tribune Ansuz hissed, "As most men do, I too wish the Thaed-Rú reign to end. Their brutal enforcement of the Edict of Scions is a devastation to many a village and a detriment to the economy. But this is not the first such twisted reign in these lands. Like many comrades in arms, I buried my consciousness long ago. Like many, I know such tides will turn."

Ansuz hunched forward and lowered his voice to whisper. "The Thaed-Rú, they lose more of their innate powers with each successive generation bred. The blood of the Y'cromahein now dominates their veins. Though once a colossal ruling force, they are primed to fall. So, they have taken to using Scions for experimentation with their Necro-pulpa plant, a harvest of the Cethin Arda."

"Yes," interjected Sulla's messenger. "That is what I have heard from the nobles in Ir of the Fenrülk. It seems that in their cowardice, the Thaed-Rú experiment on the Scions of Íraban first, before trusting the plant's powers on themselves."

From under the hood, Ansuz spotted deep concern upon the man's face as he continued. "The Thaed-Rú draws near to higher levels of understanding. Should their concoctions succeed, they may well expand their own consciousness and transcend their bodies into immortality. What they seek is resurrection...but they are unworthy."

It was Ansuz' turn to prompt the messenger. "Unworthy?"

But the man merely shrugged and fell silent.

Though Ansuz found the offer of Anil-Gevra allegiance tantalizing, such an alliance was a risk. "You may tell Master Sulla this: Sedition brews throughout the Eleven Provinces. Protests and uprisings abound against the Thaed-Rú order and insurgents populate the countryside. But a great and terrible war may yet be avoided. The people know the Thaed-Rú blood is waning. Too long have they glorified their male heirs and murdered female babies." As he said this last, he watched the hooded man closely. Yet he saw no surprise in response to this exclusive knowledge.

Ansuz frowned but continued, "Íraban threatens to eradicate the Anil-Gevra. If the fruits of his dark garden empower him as he believes they will, despite my position, I fear for my sons. But I tell you truly, I will not risk my estate to save the people of Ir of the Fenrülk. Let the four great generals of the Anil-Gevra champion them! Only if the reach of this upstart threatens my lands, my people, or my family, will I consider such an alliance necessary."

Leaning close, the messenger whispered in Ansuz' ear. "Though a young man yet, Íraban channels the power of the Breinhinod Kynara. Wielding great power, he can conquer minds and rewrite history. He fears not the Anil-Gevra but hopes to wield their strength to make his garden prosper. His threats are grave, indeed."

"They are, indeed," Ansuz snorted. "But I also know the boy to be a drunk and aimless puppy."

At an impasse, a stubborn silence fell upon the two shadowy figures. Their attention drifted to the drama on stage. The play was ending and laughter and applause accompanied the narrative of how the Thaed-Rú dynasty had liberated and empowered the people of the Eleven Provinces.

"A liberated and empowered people have no need for violent resistance," remarked the messenger.

"Aye," said Ansuz shortly. After a moment he conceded, "Perhaps you are right. It seems a storm is coming," but, firm in his resolve, he repeated his terms. "Should this young Bal-Rú bring a great war upon my people, then, and only then, will I join with the Anil-Gevra against him."

Hearing nothing in reply, his eyes sought the hooded messenger in the darkness. His gaze was met only with inky emptiness and he huffed at the insolence of the man. He slipped out among his light-hearted guests, his mind heavy with concern for Hierundia's future.

The Khalevads

Graëyhovan

The winds of autumn swept across the northern province of Graëyhovan. Heavy rains, typical of the Thaed-Rú month of Meddí, pounded the deep forests. Lightning split the night sky and great trees trembled in the booming thunder.

Deep in the woods, Ulkyrien horsemen huddled under leather-hooded capes as twenty captured boys were herded past by Rhünkai soldiers. After five years of similar roundups, the soldiers had become immune to the fear and misery their odious task caused in innocent children. The poor souls, fated to become Scions, scrambled up slippery steps into the wagons of the child slaves.

Soldier and child alike shuddered as a flash of lightning lit the lead rider's scarred, ashen face. His marbled eyes in dark sockets, grotesque features, and pointed, canine teeth were far more fearsome than the storm.

"That is one of the ugliest Ulkyrien I have ever seen!" muttered one Rhünkai to another as he worked with three others to slam the gate of a wagon closed. His fellows grunted warnings and shook their heads, remaining silent.

A product of the Cethin Arda, where engineered, hybrid soldiery yielded substantial dividends, the history of the Ulkyrien was common knowledge in the Thaed-Rú Dominions. Yet, even amongst soldiers, such tales were not spoken of lightly. Historically, the Ulkyrien served as expert trackers for the Bal Rús. Once common men, their oath to serve the Thaed-Rú was rewarded with an order to ingest potions harvested from the Cethin Arda. This altered their genetic structure and heightened their senses, but transformed them into beastly creatures.

The twisted lips of the lead rider moved now. Baring yellowed teeth, he called out orders to the Ulkyrien above the storm. "I task you with finding three men." He sneered and spat through scarred lips, "A father and his sons."

Shouting into the rain he called out their names, "Graeyba Khalevad. Aidan Khalevad. D'thalien Khalevad. These three have managed to evade authorities thirty-nine times. They have killed at least fourteen of our men." Lightning lent ghastly shadows to the rage contorting his face.

"Their trail has led south for many months now. The eldest, Aidan, a youth of seventeen or eighteen is responsible for at least nine of those killings. His father is extremely dangerous as well. They are fellmongers by trade, trackers who know the country very well. Kill the father if you must but leave the boys unharmed. The Bal Rú wants his workers untouched."

With cries of, "We will find them," and "We have never missed our mark," the Ulkyrien departed.

On the morrow, through forests shrouded in thick mist, they rode. In and out of the fog, the eerie figures of five tall Taenshuks disappeared and re-emerged repeatedly. Like ghostly prehistoric giants, the elephantine creatures lumbered along, bearing Ulkyrien riders. Human skulls and shields laced their long necks.

Each of the five riders carried the staff of H'dhar, bearing the insignia of the Thaed-Rú Dominions and denoting their rank as captains. At the feet of the Taenshuks, a company of fifty Ulkyrien trackers trod through the mud, sniffing for any signs of child slaves.

High above, wild Veyasaen searched for runaway child slaves. Many were captured this way, the hybrid birds spotting them far below. Their keen eyes were bred to detect the slightest movements. The pleasure of the hunt alone drove them to seek the fugitives and return them live. Still, the Veyasaen required a daily feast of meat and the Rhünkai and Ulkyrien were all too glad to reward them in flesh.

Dark, oppressive, reigning the skies as the Thaed-Rú reigned on land, their ear-piercing screams worked in tandem with the Taenshuk guards. Yet they remained unfettered, beyond control. It was little wonder they had become the standard icon of the Thaed-Rú insignia. With fearsome screeches, the Veyasaen's black feathers spread out as the evil that spread across the land, its talons as sharp and merciless as Íraban's will.

· · · · ·

In a remote region of Graëyhovan, far from the reach of the Ulkyrien riders, autumn leaves of red and pale gray fell to the ground. A golden aura of late evening light hung warmly over the landscape as the sun set.

Graeyba Khalevad and his two sons Aidan and D'thalien ran through a tall wheat field, archery weapons held high above their heads. Sparrows broke into flight before them. Together, the three broke into a forest glen at the edge of the wheat field where the heady scent of the pines welcomed them. Behind them loomed the snow-capped Eifandir Mountains.

As the lads outpaced their father, Graeyba signaled for them to fan out into the darkness of the glen. They came upon their target suddenly. Large horns protruded from a massive skull bending heavily from an imposing body. Startled, it ceased grazing and began to run. But the two Khalevad boys closed upon it, forcing the beast to turn from the path. It froze in an abrupt halt before Graeyba, and, before it could wheel about, the man loosed an arrow deep into its throat. Two more arrows twanged from behind the creature as the lads released their shots. The mammoth elk galloped several hundred yards before slumping lifelessly to the ground. The men pursued it and as its body twitched, the elder son, Aidan, thrust his knife into its side. As the animal's warm blood splattered Aidan's face, D'thalien pulled a cloth from his sash and offered it to his older brother.

"These lands belong to M'zhalo, the miller. Let us load this up before the old man fires an arrow at us!" Graeyba heaved as he caught his breath. The boys moved to swiftly butcher the elk together.

When the faint sound of an eerie horn disturbed the silence of dusk, they all peered warily beyond the miller's crops toward the Eifandir Mountains. It was Graeyba who discerned a serpentine trail of caravan lights upon its shadowed slopes. They were accompanied by the usual howls of the wild and untamed Veyasaen birds.

"The Horn of the March! Let us depart before they are on to our trail!" Then frowning, he squinted up toward the mountains. "Are those—?" Before his sons could reply, he confirmed his own suspicions. "Yes! Rhünkai!"

The boys glanced nervously at each other but Graeyba reassured them, "They have found our secret passages in the Eifandir, but we should be safe as long as we stay in the low country."

"Our passages?" D'thalien asked anxiously. Hurriedly he wrapped the warm flesh of their kill in thin hides as his brother kicked at the ground and swatted angrily at low-lying limbs.

"The thought of them sleeping where we once slept, where she once slept..." Aidan trailed off. His anger and grief were too deep.

"Come on boys!" their father encouraged. It irked him also, but it would do no good to dwell on such thoughts. "I am famished! The woods will offer us shelter, come."

That night the Khalevad men sheltered in an obscure sticker patch deep in the forests. Surrounded by the sounds of crickets, far from maze of mountain trails, they feasted around a dimmed fire of low embers. Such good fortune seldom came their way. With Ulkyrien trackers pursuing them, they could hardly afford to leave a trail of campfires and the scent of a meal.

Satiated, Graeyba lit his pipe from their fire's glowing embers. The sweet smell of tobacco rose from its smoldering leaves. Leaning against a tree stump, he shifted his stare through an opening in the sticker patch. A puff of his smoke rose to mingle with what seemed like millions of white paint speckles dotting dark azure. For a moment, natural beauty erased the stress of hiding from the Rhünkai. His sons too, relaxed, the cool night air offering them a deep sense of connectedness to the earth.

D'thalien interrupted the quiet. "I wish we could live out here forever...in a world without the Rhünkai."

Aidan paused in jabbing his long knife into the air and replied thoughtfully, "I do not know how long we can avoid them, but I sense that something bad is going to happen with the Rhünkai."

D'thalien turned an uneasy look on his brother. Aidan often brooded this way, more so since their mother had died. Graeyba too turned from stargazing to stare, not at his son, but into the campfire's flames as he puffed rhythmically on his tobacco pipe. "Aidan...violence is not always the means to an end." Aidan sat and stared silently into the dying embers of the fire. "Aye papa...but violence is language of the Rhünkai."

"Yes, we use it to survive out here," Graeyba smiled in concession, then insisted, "But this is no game, no thrilling hunt." A gloom came over Graeyba. "We have managed to avoid them this long. But perhaps we should begin moving in the night, extend our lead on them. I have a mind to settle a new life for us... far from here, to the south, in the province of Bisantior." Aidan and D'thalien looked at each other. "Why Bisantior?" they asked in unison.

"T'is the land of my grandfather, your great-grandfather. T'is a land of stouthearted people. Even with the oppression of the Rhünkai, the people of Bisantior still appreciate the goodness of nature."

Taking another long puff from his pipe, Graeyba loosed a smile from the corner of his mouth and held up his fist. "They say strawberries from the fields of Bisantior are as big as a man's fist! 'Roll them in sugar and honey' they say, devouring them while juice runs down their chins."

His boys smiled at that. Graeyba blew several little clouds of smoke into the air thoughtfully. Then, he sat upright and said decisively, "Several days' journey from here, we will follow the trade routes of the merchant caravans who ply their trade into Middle Y'cromeca."

"But will we not be more noticeable in Bisantior?" asked D'thalien. "The merchants here, in Upper Y'cromeca, speak Hierundiel the same as we do. It is only the trading language in Middle Y'cromeca."

"When we follow the trade routes, we will do so at a distance, avoiding contact," answered his father.

Aidan balked. "I say we continue hiding! We will kill any who draw near. They will never take us! Papa, you have taught us so well to live and survive in the wilderness! Everything we need is out here!"

Exhaling smoke, Graeyba gestured to its fading shape. "Are we to constantly drift as does this smoke? I grow tired of running. We have killed too many of them already. I tell you, they will not give up until they have captured the two of you and imprisoned me...or executed me!"

"Well, I refuse to leave!" exclaimed Aidan. "Mother was born in the forest of Merungild. This is our home. I refuse to let the Rhünkai drive us from our own territory!"

"Aidan, we need not make her death our business any longer," D'thalien urged, grabbing his arm. "It will consume us if our hearts grow bitter. Father and his words are wise. Would you jeopardize his life in remembrance of hers?"

His brother huffed angrily but softened at the truth of his brother's logic.

"We must move away, far away from here. And never come back," D'thalien continued. "The forests of Merungild hold too much sadness. I have no need to tarry here."

Graeyba laid a hand on each of his son's shoulders and spoke a vow over them, "I do not know, my sons, what the future holds for any of us. But I promise you this: I will do everything in my power to protect you the best way I know how."

The boys grew silent at this. Graeyba gazed intently at each of them before speaking again. "There have never been such fine men as you. I admire you both, your strength and your words. No power in this world could ever take you away from my heart."

He smiled at them and ran reassuring fingers through each of the boy's bushy golden locks in turn. "You two sleep for a few hours while I stay on watch," he said fondly, "We must leave before the sun rises."

DÛENHALLOW

On the morrow, Graeyba woke with a start, and scanned the landscape for Rhünkai. Satisfied, he moved quietly to bury their fire. Then, while it was yet dark, he roused his sons. With matted hair and morning glory still in their eyes, they swallowed a quick breakfast of leftover meat from the previous day's game. Clasping their daggers about their waists, they slung their bows and quivers over their shoulders. Bo staffs doubled as walking sticks as their boots splashed through yesterday's puddled rain.

Soon, the swell of a hilltop rose before them in the predawn light. Atop it, the ruins of Dûenhallow rose eerily through the mist, its wisps like specters rising from the ground. The ghostly calls of elk and moose echoed from nearby glens. A frost enveloped the trio, leaving their noses cold and sniffling.

They drew their swords as they approached a cluster of old campfires. The area was littered with charred debris. Graeyba swept the shadows with a leery eye, scanning for bandits and outlaws.

From somewhere in the ruins, the melodic sound of a flute rose into the air.

Graeyba raised a cautionary hand.

"Maybe a traveler?" suggested Aidan.

"Perhaps."

"A shepherd?" D'thalien chimed in.

"Maybe. Keep your eyes open," said their father before waving them onward.

The sun cast its first rays of light softly over the valley. A pleasant scent of damp and ancient soil filled their nostrils. The volume of the flute increased as they approached the far end of the ruins. It was a slow and mournful song, a fitting accompaniment for the family's departure from their homeland.

Before them, the remains of an enormous stone balcony overlooked the mist-covered valley below. Yawning cracks, overgrown weeds and scattered debris lay beneath moss covered, crumbling arches.

At the far end of the balcony, a strange sojourner wrapped in thick covers, sat on the floor. Herbal tea brewed in a metal pot over a small fire before him. In his hands was a wooden flute. Its melody stopped abruptly as he spotted them. "Good morning!" he called. "Would you join me for some tea?"

Gripping the hilts of their swords tightly, Graeyba and the two young men surveyed the shadows with great caution.

"Do not fret. There are none here, but us," said the stranger.

The inviting aroma of the tealeaves engaged their senses, and a warm feeling of calm moved upon the Khalevad trio. Feeling no need for their swords, Graeyba and D'thalien slid them back inside their sheathes. Aidan, however, kept his in hand. Although the stranger radiated a sense of peace, he trusted not the surrounding area.

Graciously the stranger offered them tea once more.

Graeyba and D'thalien sat down around his fire and accepted cups of aromatic tea. "Aidan, come, sit, honor the hospitality of this man," Graeyba prompted his roaming son.

Aidan scowled and gestured to the ruins, "Someone needs to watch for Rhünkai, papa. Besides, you know I do not like tea."

Noticing a cloud come over the stranger's face, Graeyba frowned at his son's behavior. A rebuke was on his lips when the stranger said quietly, "He has his own path, let the boy be."

As Graeyba and D'thalien turned from Aidan to drink of their tea, a warm sensation flowed through their bodies.

"Where does this variety come from?" asked Graeyba. "Back home, I once grew my own leaves. Varietals of tea and tobacco to boot."

A warm smile lit up the stranger's countenance, banishing the sadness in his eyes. "Tell me, where are you men traveling?" asked the stranger.

The Khalevad men shifted nervously, noting his avoidance of their question.

"Do not fear, I am not in the service of the Rhünkai."

Aidan's head jerked their way at that word. He squinted at them appraisingly, then loped off to prowl a further perimeter.

"It is not that we fear your treachery," Graeyba reassured the man, "but other ears might lay nearby."

"I see." The stranger shrugged, then smiled. "Here, a gift for your journey." He offered Graeyba a pouch containing tealeaves. "They provide strong nourishment for your bodies, and for the soul."

Realizing his own question had gone unanswered, Graeyba pressed the sojourner, "Do you live nearby, or are you passing through?"

"I come from a distant land, beyond the Eastern Sea. I journey yearly to visit old friends in the West."

"What business have you with savages in the West?"

A bright smile lit up the stranger's face and he chuckled. "Savages they are not. Hearty and good natured are their kind," he said.

"No one I know has ever seen them. Perhaps that is why my people believe those beyond the impenetrable Ballai to be inferior savages," said Graeyba.

"How can you judge one whom you have never seen?" challenged the stranger.

The father and son sipped silently. Graeyba studied this peculiar man. He was dignified, his bearing regal. And why were they overcome with such powerful sensations from his tealeaves? Was he a magician? A sorcerer?

As they drank the last of their tea, the early rays of morn grew stronger, brightening their bleak surroundings.

"We must leave. A long trek lies ahead," Graeyba said. "Aidan!" he beckoned his eldest.

As the group around the campfire rose to their feet, the sojourner spoke. "I wish to speak good words over your journey, in the tongue from where I come." Smiling, he rested his hands on Aidan and D'thalien's heads. "If your journey be tumultuous, may you arrive safely at your destination. If you should lose your way, may you find your path again. If you are separated from one another, may you find each other. As a violent tempest rips apart branches from the tree, may you be grafted to an older tree with deeper roots."

As the melodic sound of his strange speech sent waves of power over them, a low rumbling rose from the ground. For a few moments, they clutched at each other in awe and fear as it trembled.

D'thalien grabbed his father's arm as it ceased. "What was that, papa?"

"It was the power of Uraduin, an ancient tongue," the stranger answered. "This land has been covered with evil words, dark deeds and unbelief. When the pure language of the Faeynül is spoken over an accursed land, it shakes the very ground."

The sun broke above the ruins. Its golden hue illuminated a part of Graeyba's mind he had long suppressed. Autumn leaves fell in soft sunlight and grain particles from the harvest drifted in the air over a pastoral scene. Numerous peasants, friends and family gathered by a running brook near tables of wineskins, suckling pig, fruits and vegetables. A lovely, youthful virgin veiled in rustic raiment of white stepped forth. Flowers adorned her golden tresses. Her hair and dress both rippled in the wind. His wedding day had been the happiest day of his life, beside the birth of his sons. But all was now tainted with the grief of her loss.

"I see a great burden in your eyes. It is heavy in your soul," said the stranger.

Graeyba stood motionless.

"The power of Uraduin has loosened that burden which lay hidden deep within your soul. It is good to remember those we have loved." The stranger turned to Aidan. "You are the firstborn, with the strength of many. But a great sadness shrouds your heart. Your anger is passionate, but you must learn to master it lest it consume you."

Aidan stood in stony silence at these words. The stranger turned to rest both hands on young D'thalien.

"Of great solace are your words. They are founts of wisdom in times of darkness, like healing balm on a painful wound. If you find yourself in danger and alone, do what you must to survive, my son. Submit, but let no one rob you of your dignity. Everything your father has taught you will serve you well in such times."

The stranger addressed the three men as a group, "A time approaches when all that is good will be sorely tested. Your hearts shall be proven, your strength summoned."

Moved, Graeyba put a strong hand on each of his sons' shoulders, "I pledge that I will fight to protect you both at all expenses. If we are ever separated, for whatever reason, I will find you, no matter how long it takes or how far you may go. I will not rest until I find you. Your purpose is to fight to stay alive and never lose heart in my words. If that day ever comes, I will find you."

Graeyba's words were met with a hearty smile from the stranger. To him he said, "Let your words serve as a reminder of the oath which I have made this day in the ruins of Dûenhallow." He held his sons in a tight embrace, then placed a kiss on their foreheads.

The Khalevad men thanked the stranger reverently. He waved cheerily and departed. As they watched him go, in all their minds was one thought, This is no common man. As they gathered their things, Aidan grunted and smacked a hand against his forehead. "We never asked his name!"

"I wanted to..." D'thalien said quietly. "...when the ground shook."

"Learn to speak up little brother!" Aidan said grumpily and made for the woods beyond the ruins.

D'thalien looked to his father for support, but Graeyba, deep into thought, followed Aidan silently. Heaving a sigh, D'thalien shrugged off his brother's criticism and joined them.

There is truth in the man's predictions, Graeyba thought. His mind attempted to comfort his uneasy heart. My sons are apt to any impending threat! Did I not spend every day of their childhood schooling them?

The Khalevad boys had worked alongside their father in the business of fellmongers, learning to set traps, to track. He had taught them both to hunt and to defend themselves with the bow and arrow, sword and bo staff. In the harsh world created by the Thaed-Rú, in an era of heavy hearts and downcast eyes, Graeyba had taught them it was still wholesome to laugh. But most of all, he had taught them to live from their heart with courage. He gazed upon his sons fondly as they left the ruins behind and entered the woods again. The Gardener's blessing echoed his own sentiments for the boys If your journey be tumultuous, may you arrive safely at your destination.

AOKENFANA

THREE DAY'S JOURNEY FROM DÛENHALLOW, THE KHALEVAD MEN passed through the Fields of Aokenfana. As Graeyba had planned, they pushed south toward the distant province of Bisantior in Middle Y'cromeca.

They moved together through an endless field of grain. Its stalks waved merrily in the breeze, unaware of the troubled times in which they grew. Graeyba longed for their ignorance. He rejected the politics of his time, abhorred its child slavery, despised the corruption of the wealthy. He simply refused to be harnessed to the Shekülhorn. Let them have their cities, it was the mystery and danger of the wild that drew him. In the mountains, pine forests, and fields, he was both lord and steward over the earth.

A flock of pesky Doernghâl feasted on the cornstalks of a neighboring field. Half bird, half crickets, these odd creatures preferred to jump and leap through the air than crawl.

"Heads up! Heave!" shouted one in the distance.

Large nets sprang up into the sky, cast by the peasants of Aokenfana. Doernghâl made for tender baked thighs and breast meats.

"Heads up! Heave!" More nets sprang over the cornstalks.

The Khalevad trio chuckled as the creatures evaded the peasants, hopping from stalk to stalk, while the men struggled with their nets. It was good to enjoy a bit of normalcy, to share a laugh. At Graeyba's behest, they had fallen into the habit of circumventing villages, towns and hamlets. These were hard times. Anyone eager for an easy profit, might turn them in to the authorities. Accordingly, Graeyba had taught his sons to be cautious of everyone.

As they trod through the grain, Graeyba's thoughts turned to the familiar fields of Merungild. A wry chuckle escaped his lips, dodging villages and towns was an old habit for his family. From the time Aidan reached the legal age of nine, Graeyba had honed their ability to evade the Rhünkai. Twice a year, his whole family accompanied him on a hunting trip, just as the Rhünkai were to pass through the borders of Merungild. Every year, he managed to evade losing his sons to the Edict of the Scions.

The scores of scattered souls in Merungild lauded him for his cleverness. In their eyes, Graeyba's defiance was heroic. Many of their sons and daughters were already in the service of the Rhünkai. Years ago, when the Bal Rú had ordered his census, Graeyba's father-in-law agreed to register Graeyba's cottage as his home while Graeyba's mother-in-law registered their home as hers solely.

But luck and wits could not hold his family together forever. A frown creased his face, and the fields around him faded to a golden blur. The seasons were wheeling by. Just two years prior to this trek, the cold autumn had heralded the deepest season of chilling frost their people had seen in years. Graeyba's wife grew sicker and sicker from the cold. To protect their sons from the soldiers marching through their borders, they sought refuge that season in the Upper Vales of Miórgelân until the Rhünkai danger was over. Navigating secret paths in the hideout in the Eifandir Mountains, they found shelter in the Caves of Tulenbaca.

A sad smile twisted at his lips as fond memories of that time together ran through his mind. Perhaps by way of the stranger's words at Dûenhallow, it was not the image of her fragile body, wracked by coughs, nor the sound of her frail voice whispering words of parting that he remembered most. The image imprinted most upon his mind was that of his spirited wife, the wind in her hair and the sun on her face as she merrily chased after their two sons.

"Heads up! Heave!"

Graeyba jerked at the cry, his reveries fading. His sons threw him a curious look. The peasants continued tossing their nets over the cornstalks, ensnaring the helpless Doernghâls. It struck Graeyba as a metaphor, the net the Thaed-Rú Order and the Doernghâls the child slaves.

His pace had slowed, yet Graeyba smiled indulgently at D'thalien whose outstretched hands drifted lazily over fuzzy kernels of grain. Aidan stalked ahead of them, glancing back now and again in frustration. A grain stalk protruded from his mouth and his brow was furrowed, his thoughts as distant as those of his father's. At eighteen years of age, Aidan was grossly affected by the untimely death of his mother. Graeyba recalled his son's woeful misery shortly after her death.

"If only she had stayed with grandpa or grandma rather than retreat to the Caves of Tulenbaca, she would still be here with us now" Aidan lamented.

"I would not risk it," Graeyba had protested. "Eventually, they would have discovered we were withholding you. They might have imprisoned her, tortured her! You know full well that hiding under Rhünkai law, hiding younglings, one's own or another, is punishable by the lash. The Rhünkai are foul beasts, even unto poor, defenseless women! She might have died of a far worse fate." He added, as if to himself, "Besides, she chose of her own accord to join us."

"I do not care what anyone says, mother could have been saved!" were the frustrated words of Aidan. In tandem with his own grief, these words often echoed in Graeyba's mind.

Today, as they traversed the Fields of Aokenfana, Graeyba could see the same look of frustration in his elder son's disposition. As was his habit, D'thalien sensed the mood of the men. Loping forward, he jabbed his bo staff playfully at the stalk of grain on which his brother gnawed.

Aidan spat out the stalk with a grunt and responded swiftly. Cocking his neck side to side, he fell into his usual stance, leaning forward slightly, his right arm angling the bo staff upward as one might do a lance. Lifeless as a statue, his only movement was the twitching of a grin. This stance served to build tension in the opponent. When or how Aidan would strike was unpredictable, yet D'thalien knew his brother all too well.

In a sudden flash, Aidan swung his staff. Just as swiftly, his little brother blocked it. A heavy thunk rang out across the fields. In a rare moment, the brothers laughed merrily.

Graeyba's affectionate smile at the pair was interrupted by the familiar shrill of large, ominous fowl. Before he could glance upwards in search of the Veyasaen, a net far larger than those of the peasants came over him. Another one sprang over his two sons and their bo staffs clattered to the ground.

The nets had yet to hit the ground when Graeyba, knife in hand, began to saw at the ropes. Ominous cloaked figures sprang from the tall rows of cornstalks. In a blurred flash, they surrounded the Khalevads. Hooves thumped against the earth as a hooded horseman came upon them from behind.

Adrenaline surged through his body as Graeyba sliced the netting. Aidan and D'thalien too worked swiftly with their knives now. The three of them wriggled free just as four or five figures descended upon him with lances and clubs, shouting, "Cease in the name of the Thaed-Rú Order!"

Aidan's blade surely made its mark as he sprang from his net and drove it through the heart of an Ulkyrien tracker, killing him instantly.

"That is for my mother!" yelled Aidan. Whipping around, he drove his knife into the thigh of another. He was wheeling about to find another foe when he heard his father yell, "Run!"

Aidan's eyebrows narrowed. Never in any prior conflict had his father issued that order. In confusion, Aidan scanned the field wildly for Graeyba but saw only gruesome, twisted faces and snarling, yellowed teeth.

"Seize them! Seize those boys!" they yelled.

As shouts from different directions overlapped, D'thalien clung close to Aidan's side. Following the sounds of battle, Aidan's eyes lit upon his father. Though surrounded, Graeyba urged, "Run!" once more, wielding his dagger in wide circles to keep the trackers at bay.

As the boys tore their gaze from him and fled, a wooden club came down heavily upon Graeyba. He reeled under a horrific blow to the back shoulders. Collapsing to his knees, he struggled to remain upright as the Ulkyrien circled him like a pack of wolves.

"I got him!" a man yelled in Graeyba's ear. The tracker spat in his face but Graeyba, stunned, did not flinch.

"Hold him down, boys!"

Pain seared through Graeyba's body, but a rush of hot anger roused him. From his boot he drew another blade. Rage propelled him forward. He rose just enough to thrust his blade into the upper chest of the closest assailant. A spray of Ulkyrien blood fell on Graeyba's right hand and sleeve in uneven stains. The man's face froze, and his soul instantly departed.

"Watch his knife!" came the call of a soldier.

The mounted tracker grew livid at his men's failure to suppress Graeyba's resistance. His voice thundered above them all, "I said 'Cease in the name of your sovereign!'"

On his feet again, Graeyba wrestled the club of another from its owner. Gripping it tightly with both hands, his powerful arms swung an arc, smashing the face of one and landing on the temple of another. Both slumped to the ground with terrible moans and heavy thuds.

The pastoral scene dissolved into chaos. Confused shouts came from the attackers. Another man swung his sword at Graeyba's waist, but Graeyba's quick reflexes evaded the blade.

"Get him, I say!"

"Bring him down!"

Doubling over on his haunches, Graeyba yanked with great fortitude on the net of an assailant as he made to fling it over him. The man's legs flew into the air, above his head and sent him crashing onto the ground. Falling headfirst, he lay there, stunned.

With a primal shout, a lancer lunged at Graeyba's arm. Its point bit deep through flesh, into muscle until it lodged in bone.

"Aaaahhhhhh!" His terrible scream of pain reached the edge of the cornfield, drawing the attention of both the peasants with their nets and his sons. Fearfully, the Doernghâl hunters gathered their nets and slipped away into the cornstalks. At the edge of the cornfield, D'thalien paused to cast a backward glance in search of their father.

Calls of, "Get those boys! Hurry! Get them!" echoed out. Three armed Rhünkai dashed toward him through the grain.

Aidan grabbed his brother, dragging him through the field, away from sounds of battle. "Run! They are gaining!" A sudden burst of energy from D'thalien drove him and Aidan into the corn. Their pursuers crashed into the stalks behind them, closing in,

Meanwhile, Graeyba had wrestled the lance away and driven a dagger deep into his heart. He made to rise, but the man he had sent reeling on his head had already leapt to his feet. Shaking off his pain, he let out a growl and brought his club straight down on Graeyba's skull. A lethal blow sent shock waves throughout Graeyba's body. He slumped forward to the ground on his side. The attacker then smashed his club directly into Graeyba's face. Relentlessly, he beat Graeyba as he lay there on his side, blood flowing into the field's furrows.

"That is enough! He is dead!" the officer called from his mount. "Leave him, go after the prize! The Bal Rú needs these guttersnipes to build his damned Fortress City," he fumed. "Get those boys!"

Aidan and D'thalien saw none of this. Running like the wind, they crashed through the cornfield. Their pursuers' shouts continued and tranquilizing darts zinged past their ears. It seemed as though their hearts would burst through their throats, yet still they ran.

Suddenly, a mounted Ulkyrien crashed through the stalks to their right. Flinging a net over them, he jumped from his horse to fall upon the captured boys with a growl. His heavy body knocked the air out of them both as they crashed to the ground.

Foot soldiers approached the scene, their crossbows in firing position.

"Tackled them, eh?" Another horseman emerged from the stalks.

Aidan reached for a blade to cut through the netting. Immediately, several crossbows were thrust pointblank at his throat and face.

"I would not do that boy! This net can very well be your shroud!"

An eerie laughter, like that of jackals, came from the men.

The Ulkyrien officer grabbed the net and yanked the boys to their feet with brutish force.

"You are the Khalevad boys from Merungild! We have been on your trail since Dûenhallow. Your father made sure of that!"

Fear blazed through their eyes and the brothers cast a glance at each other. D'thalien mouthed Father! but Aidan shook his head grimly and pursed his lips to indicate they should remain silent.

The hideous face of the Ulkyrien bared sharp teeth and cracked a wicked grin. "You know why we captured you here, boy? Your father led us here. He led us here so we could take you in to give you a better life! Like most boys, you will not appreciate this at first. But eventually you will. You could say we are one big happy family now!"

The laughter of jackals broke out at this. The officer's grin widened. He pulled his hood over his balding head, then gestured to the foot soldiers. Lifting the net from the boys, they placed iron shackles on their wrists and feet.

Aidan struggled to hold his tongue, then bellowed, "It is not true! Where is my father? What have you done to him? Where is he?"

D'thalien scanned the cornstalks desperately, hoping his dear father would leap out and rescue them. The scream of pain he heard earlier sounded like his father, but he held hope it was the cry of an enemy slain by Graeyba.

The Ulkyrien laughed. "Do not worry about your father, boy! He is long gone. He has abandoned you both for certain! I never saw a man flee so fast!" His ugly teeth showed again through the dark hood. Another jeer and taunt came from the men.

"That is not true! You lie!" Aidan lunged forward against his shackles, but the men held him back.

"He will come back for us! You will see!" D'thalien's voice cracked with fear and resentment for what this ominous figure said about his father.

"Your days of running and hiding are over! Wake up, boy. Learn your place! The breadth and width of the world is Rhünkai!" The Ulkyrien tracker lifted his cloak, revealing the Rhünkai emblem of the Veyasaen birds on his breastplate. "This is our symbol of our power over the Y'cromahein!" he uttered.

"Get them to the caravan!" ordered the officer.

Another wave of fear exploded within the boys. So great was their hopelessness it caused their legs to tremble as they walked. Rough hands shoved them up a ramp. It clanged behind them and an iron key grated against the lock of a barred cart.

Prisoners! The bitter taste of vomit rose in Aidan's throat. He spat it out angrily through the bars of their wagon. The Ulkyrien officer rose his whip high and cracked it over the horses and they lurched into a rollicking gallop.

A league's distance away, this small team of trackers and their captured prize, the Khalevad boys, slowed to join a larger caravan of child slaves. As they approached the long train of steel-caged wagons, a cluster of deplorable, miserable faces peered out through steel bars. Soldiers walked across the tops of wagons, jumping from one to the other. A tertiary wave of fear hit the boys.

The Ulkyrien leader reported Graeyba and Aidan's manslaughter of his men to the caravan company officers.

"Did you dispose of the bodies?" asked a company officer.

"Aye, sir! Five shekülhorns to the locals to bury their bodies - our trackers and the lawbreaker."

The boys' hearts sank. "The lawbreaker?" whispered D'thalien anxiously. "Do they mean father?"

Aidan merely shook his head and sighed. This was the third tale of their father told by the Ulkyrien. There was no knowing which was true.

The officers, meanwhile, had decided that Aidan was fit for service as a soldier. D'thalien's lot was the horrible fate of the child slaves, the Scions of Íraban. *They have finally won*, Aidan thought bitterly. *In totality, and in a single afternoon.* They had taken his precious father away, perhaps forever, and meant now to separate brother from brother. As soldiers pulled him away, he called out, "Remember what father said, D'thalien! 'Everything I have taught you was for such a time as this!' "

"I will be strong, Aidan! I promise!" D'thalien shouted as the men tugged his little brother away. His caravan slowly rumbled forward. Fearing he would never see his brother again, D'thalien's eyes locked upon Aidan until he could see him no more. Even in the company of hundreds of young lads, D'thalien had never felt so alone, so uncertain of his future. But his father's memory, he knew, was etched deep in his heart, his words of wisdom too. He would draw strength from Graeyba's love and courage to fuel him through the turbulence ahead.

HIERUNDIA

IN CAGES OF IRON, HUNDREDS OF YOUNG BOYS CRAMMED miserably against each other. The caravans stopped only when the drivers needed to relieve themselves. The child slaves were not allowed this privilege. They relieved themselves outside the bars of the cages or sat in the shame of their own stink. Some cast their eyes downward, lost in their thoughts or fears. Some peered beyond the bars at passing fields. Some threw furtive glances at the mounted soldiers.

Neither the Khalevad boys nor the Rhünkai noticed the strange weeds in the fields around them. They were oddly shaped, almost amphibian in nature, like spiky lizards. As the wind blew over them, they bent in the wind much like any normal plant. After the boys were trundled off to their fates however, these weeds became animated and slithered back into the ground. No one, not even the peasants in the fields, noted their existence or disappearance.

A very thin, wiry man with a wretched disposition guarded D'thalien's wagon. The man fed small pieces of bread to the boys through the iron frames. Oftentimes, he coaxed the stronger ones to bully the weaker ones for their share. He also gave small portions of water to the boys from wooden scoops drawn from metal containers. At times, many boys were passed over. Some became sick from dehydration or exposure to the weather elements.

The nights became extremely cold during the autumn months. Soldiers afforded the children a certain number of blankets. But their guard only issued a few blankets, which the children tried to share, uncomfortably.

D'thalien passed his time in silence, staring at the harsh country of the North through wrought iron bars. He was in awe of towering mountains, snow-capped crests and dark clouds. But their dark characteristics echoed those of the ones who ruled this great expanse. Bleak weather swept down the mountains and filled his lungs with a deathly cold.

The very air seemed full of death and darkness. Day after day, he searched for the sun, but was met with only mist and fog. He watched as shrunken leaves fell from the trees they passed. The dark, hybrid fowl of the Cethin Arda flew overhead, searching out fugitives. There was little hope of rescue. He knew his father was likely dead and the faces of the peasants in the fields were either miserable or callous as they passed. The will of man had long since shattered in these forsaken lands.

Finally, the caravan entered the unforgiving wastelands of the province of Hierundia. They passed within its crumbling Ballai. Over the following weeks, the weather turned. Autumn was short and winter long in the North. Each night a miserable cold crystallized the earth with fresh frost. The chill mist turned to sleet, then snow. The elements whipped endlessly across the children's poor faces and bodies. They huddled together in small clusters to produce any ounce of body heat that they could.

Although the Rhünkai issued them thick-sleeved, hooded garments, many were barefooted while the soldiers wore heavy boots and cloaks of fur and warm, fleecy masks. Tucking their feet beneath them and burying their heads in their arms like little birds, the boys shivered, cried and coughed incessantly in their wagons.

One grey morning, D'thalien gasped in horror as he awakened to the cold, grey face of a young boy, his lifeless body falling heavily upon his own as the caravan ground to a stop. "Guards!" D'thalien called urgently. "Help!"

Several guards peered between the bars. Seeing the boy's corpse, they grunted, unlocked the wagon, heaved the body out, and locked the gate once more. Stripping the body of its clothes, they tossed the pitiful form irreverently to the roadside and turned away, unphased. Tears sprang up in D'thalien's eyes and a horrible feeling of despair came upon him.

As the caravan progressed, several times the boys pointed out little piles of children's corpses along the road in varying states of decay. Thinking they too might suffer a similar fate, the frozen corpses traumatized the boys into a grim silence.

• • • • •

Days blurred to weeks as the Dark Road of the caravan wound through endless fog and endless cold. One morning, already huddled against the elements, the child slaves suddenly shrank further still. Large grotesque figures, glowing darkly in the fog, loomed above them. D'thalien peered upwards in fear, then sighed in relief. Mounted into the walls of the pass, torches illuminated a series of the primordial guardians of the Sheddukem underworld carved into the wall. Rising out of the fog, they gave the appearance of giants emerging to attack them.

A lad beside D'thalien commented, "I heard the soldiers speak of these. These markers mean we are now in the heart of Rhünkai country."

To D'thalien, this news brought relief. In his mind, it promised respite from the harsh cold of this horrid journey. He, like so many of the boys, hated this country with every fiber of his being. He and the boy struck up a quiet conversation, sharing what little they knew of the Rhünkai, of their plans.

After one final, intolerable week of cold, a large, dim glow on the horizon drew the attention of the boys. Descending the crest of the last of the mountains, distant light spread warmly across the sky in a wide arc. An hour later, they came through the mountain pass below and beheld a large valley where thousands of flickering lights stretched across the floor.

"T'is it, D'thalien," remarked his new friend, "This is the place where they will keep us to work."

Eager for freedom from their wagons, many of the boys rejoiced at the sight of their destination. As if in warning, the fog thickened into a dark, icy rain.

D'thalien hugged his shoulders and asked through clattering teeth, "What do they call this place?"

"I think I heard the soldiers call it Du-Meg-gu, maybe Du-Men-na. I cannot recall." the boy answered.

The caravan creaked along the road until it approached a massive stone wall. Its towering black spires stabbed into the sky. Upon it, strange markings and symbols were faintly visible. In the language of Hierundiel, they read Dul-Meggor: The Builders of Our World.

A shrill cry from above caused the boys to cast their eyes upwards. Dozens upon dozens of the Veyasaen perched upon the stone wall. D'thalien caught his breath as a flock of them spread wide, dark wings and ascended into the night. Others returned from the day's search. Never had he seen so many of the creatures.

A rough laugh sounded from a caravan guard. He jabbed upward and leered, "Thinking of running away? Best to think twice about that!"

Soldiers within labored against large, oak gates. At least fifty feet in height, they swung inward sluggishly.

"Escape," scoffed D'thalien to the boy who seemed to know so much. "How are we to escape over that?"

They exchanged grim expressions. When their turn came to pass beyond the gates, they peered through their bars. Soldiers were everywhere. Some led groups of young boys while others carried equipment over their shoulders.

D'thalien marveled at how late into the night the Rhünkai worked. More startling still was the beastly countenance of shadowy silhouettes of the child slaves. It might have been their uniformly bald heads, but their appearance was startling. All about the compound, the child slaves stopped momentarily to stare at D'thalien's caravan. Eerie grins and menacing eyes flashed in the darkness from a few. The visages of the rest were blank, lifeless.

From the darkness of the street a haunting song was heard:

> *The Ulkyrien ride across the land.*
> *They gather the harvest of gloom.*
> *We shall reap broken hearts of sorrow.*
> *The end of all good things is here.*
> *Sing of the memory of our mothers,*
> *for they are no more!*

Eerie laughter rose from the child slaves in the compound as the voice faded. Chills ran down D'thalien's spine. He tried to discern from whence the song had come, but the children had already slipped into the darkness. An evil foreboding came over D'thalien. Suddenly he wanted to be anywhere but here. Surely it would be better to remain in the cold frost than inhabit a place where loss of freedom and family seemed a joke to the slaves themselves.

They rolled through the compound several hundred yards more before stopping at a large adobe building. After months of infernal creaking, the caravan finally fell silent for good. Mounted escorts shouted orders to each other, barely audible in the heavy, ice-cold rain. The gates of the wagons clanked loudly against the ground and the caravan emptied.

A light appeared in the door of the large adobe building. In its glow, D'thalien saw the short and gangly figure of an old man. Clad in a leather apron, he carried a lit torch in one hand and a stick in the other. D'thalien's eyes narrowed. A torch was necessary in the dark, but the stick did not bode well for the quality of their welcome. The man's bow-legged steps were surprisingly fast and he clipped sharply along the length of the caravan.

"Here we are at last! Look what the rain and thunder yield! More workers for the harvest of the Rhünkai!" Loftily, he introduced himself, "I am the Steward of Dul-Meggor!" Then he growled an order to boys and guards alike, "Come in out of the rain, you fools! Make haste!"

There was more threat than welcome in his words. As they moved inside, bile rose in D'thalien's throat. The place had a foul stench. Soaking wet, the boys filed into a massive chamber where armed soldiers waited. Row after row of them submitted to the shaving of their heads. D'thalien hated the scrape of the blade against his skin. His crop of soft blonde curls fell to the ground to be trod upon by the filthy, frostbitten feet of his fellows. He cringed when they were forced to strip down naked like animals. He abhorred the shouts of pain from each of the boys as the hot fire brands bit into their right shoulder blade with the emblem of the Thaed-Rú Dominions like cattle. Soldiers cursed as boys squirmed. But slaves they were, and each received the brand.

Next, the Steward ordered the boys into another expansive chamber. Dozens upon dozens of wooden tables stretched before them. Soldiers stood beside them, waiting to collect what remained of the children's personal articles. Those who lagged were rapped soundly with their sticks and admonished, "Make haste! Make haste!"

Officers grouped together, jesting and mocking the boys as they walked into the chamber.

"Silence! Shut your stupid mouths, you damn worms!" shouted one of the officers.

A hushed silence came over the masses. Instead of words, the soldier's eyes grew vicious. They taunted the boys silently with their swords. Still, D'thalien was grateful as their hateful cacophony faded.

"Now listen to me, all of you!" the officer's voice rang out again. The boys bobbed this way and that, straining to catch a glimpse of the speaker.

"According to the Royal Edict of the Scions of Íraban, you are now property of the Thaed-Rú Dominions. As such, any personal articles or merchandise that you have on your person you are hereby ordered to surrender on these tables!"

Murmurs and groans filled the room.

"What?"

"But this is my father's belt!"

"My grandmother gave me this locket!"

Officers walked about the tables, smacking protesters with his stick. "Stop your bickering at once. Do as you are told!"

The groans continued, but the boys deposited their valuables onto the tables under watchful eyes. D'thalien painfully yielded a soiled sackcloth containing the crumbled remains of four sunflower petals. He had gathered them weeks before being captured, for sunflowers were his mother's favorite. As he peered within the folds for one last glance, a soldier's wooden stick came crashing down on the table before him. "Leave your damn articles on the damn table! Now!" yelled the soldier. Frightened, D'thalien released the cloth at once. From that sacred day in Dûenhallow, the stranger's words came to D'thalien in a quick flash...do what you must to survive, my son. Submit, but let no one rob you of your dignity. A warm feeling filled his heart in that cold chamber surrounded by callous souls. An uncharacteristic fierceness surged within. Take the petals, but you will never take the memory of my mother, or my father, or my brother, or their love.

After the boys were issued working garments and a hot soup with bread, the Steward ordered them all into another chamber with more soldiers and scores of medical attendants. Several strange apparatus with needles and beakers lay interspersed throughout the chamber. D'thalien struggled to identify the heavy odor hanging in the air. He listened half-heartedly as an officer called out the next round of orders.

"Hear me, every one of you! You are now in the service of the Thaed-Rú Dominions! According to the Royal Edict of the Scions of Íraban, you are called upon to serve as builders of the Bal Rú's new world. To ensure maximum efficiency and productivity, you must hereby receive medication. It will enable you to work more efficiently for his honor!"

A wave of fear rippled over the boys. They cast nervous glances at the equipment. Some of the younger ones huddled together in little groups. As the soldiers ordered the boys into file, the medical attendants began injecting them with needles from the strange apparatus. As promised, a sense of euphoria rushed into their veins leaving many feeling invincible. Others felt a sort of peace. Still more were resigned to feelings of passivity.

In their varied states, before they were allowed to retire to the night, officers led the boys into a final chamber. The stench of rotten wood hung heavily in the air of this dark, damp chamber. A long row of crescent-shaped candleholders hung from the middle of the ceiling. Archaic statues of past Bal Rús stood against high, cracked walls. Withered, dead weeds nestled in crevices and ascended to a wooden vaulted ceiling where shadowy, heraldic banners hung beyond their reach.

At the far end of the room, a lone dark figure, half-shrouded in the shadows, occupied a black throne. There were no seats before him, so the boys sat on the cold stone floor. Even in their euphoria, they moved stealthily, hesitantly. The sound of rain and thunder added to this lone figure's strange aura. Boys continued filing in quietly, awed by the figure's presence. An odd tranquility overcame the room. Still, soldiers lined the hall, scanning the child slaves with swords at the ready.

An officer in full armor moved to stand beside the lone, dark figure. "I am the Marshal of Dul-Meggor. According to the Royal Edict of the Scions of Íraban, you are all here to build the new world! In a show of benevolence, the Bal Rú himself has come here to personally address you and your mission."

A low wave of murmurs went through the crowd and several soldiers moved their hands to their hilts. Most of the boys were stunned that the Bal Rú was among them, but many felt a surge of fear taint their excitement.

The Marshal demanded of them, "I order you to give your immediate respect and undivided attention to the Bal Rú Íraban Thaed-Rú! Fall before his greatness in obeisance!"

The multitude of boys and young men, D'thalien among them, fell to their faces. The young Bal Rú chose that moment to rise from the shadowed throne.

His tall and narrow build slowly glided toward the first row of boys. Reveling in his power over them, he called out, "Rise to your knees. Rise and heed my words."

Through his ornate mask, all that was visible of his face was a ghastly smile and sharp, crystalline eyes. "You have made a long, perilous journey here. You faced hardship, cold and hunger. And you saw death. Some of your cohorts did not make it here, but you did. This terrible journey serves as a threshold into a new world, a new life. Your old life is behind you. You are now scions...my scions."

The Bal Rú's stare and the euphoria of the medicines held the lads in a mesmerizing grip.

"A new wind is in the air. In it is the spirit of young men like yourselves. Slaves are you no more. Henceforth, you shall be known to the world as the Royal Scions of Íraban."

D'thalien frowned as, all around him, faces beamed upward gratefully. He was quick to ease the frown from his face, however, as the tall figure turned sternly on one of the young boys. Impetuously, he grabbed his cheeks in his palms.

"Do you know what a scion is?"

The young lad gave a frightened nod. The intimidating figure released his face and gazed out on the crowd.

"A scion is a branch that has been grafted to a tree or a plant. Within time, it grows into the tree or plant and becomes part of it."

Walking through the rows of boys, the Bal Rú spread his arms open in a wide embrace. "Today, you become my scions. Together, we will build a new world. Through arduous toil, you too will become part of the Thaed-Rú tree. I graft you into my family."

The eyes of hundreds seemed attached to his dark cloak, for as he moved, they followed, riveted. "Many of you come from poverty, from families with nothing to offer you but harsh words and hard labor. And for what in return? What legacy will they leave to you? A noble father is what you need to take you out of your miserable lives. You think I do not understand your plight, your misery? You think I do not know what it means to suffer? Verily, I tell you, you are not alone in your suffering. My own father abused me!"

Visible only to those nearest him, tears glistened beneath the mask in the dim candlelight. As if none could imagine any abuse on such a personage, he expounded, "Oh yes, he did. Beyond the emotional torture, the mental anguish, there was corporeal abuse, too. I was punished by him for having pity on those who were his slaves."

Capitalizing on his tears, he wept openly as he continued walking through his scions. "One day, he took a dagger to my face because of my compassion for those whom he treated as chattel. He punished me for my compassion toward his slaves. That very day, I decided I would never harm another as he had. To this purpose, I decreed the Royal Edict of the Scions of Íraban. I offer you a life of purpose and the true love of a father. But," he lifted a skeletal finger in the air, "as any father, my paternal love also has set conditions which must be met." Pointing from one boy to the next he said sternly, "Like any child, you will be given certain chores to perform in order to help your new family."

He passed D'thalien as he spoke. The boy's heart blazed, and he cast his eyes downward, for he knew that no love could ever replace the love of his father. Especially not the love of the very man responsible for Graeyba's demise. And what of the frozen corpses that marked the path to Dul-Meggor? Had they not died at the Bal Rú's behest?

A vile grin leered within the ornate mask. "Fear not, my Scions. Thrice daily, you shall be fed well. Nightly, a warm bed and bath shall entreat your weary souls. The medicines, which you just received, shall be administered to you from time to time to sustain you as you build the glories of my illustrious Dominions."

Cruelty chilled the warmth in the Bal Rú's voice. "However, should any of you fall behind in your performances or tire your masters with rebellious ways, then, as in any family, there will be consequences for your disobedience. On that day, you will have turned your back on all that I have done for you and I despise rejection. If you so decide to seek your old, pitiful life, you will suffer consequences for spurning my fatherly love."

Though the boys around him nodded their consent in a stupor, D'thalien's stomach lurched as the dark figure stalked from the room. *What if I fail in the smallest detail? What will become of me?* He needed his father more desperately than ever before.

The Bal Rú's words of fatherly love and the inheritance of the scions profoundly disturbed him. Surely, some of these boys had fathers who had lost hope, who were apathetic toward the Edict of the Scions, or whose abuse was worse than the threats of Dul-Meggor. But Graeyba was an uncommon and noble man. If his father yet lived, D'thalien was certain he was searching for him within and without the fallen Ballai of the Eleven Provinces. In an ironic contrast to the Bal Rú's offering tonight, conditions had never limited his father's love, nor was it ever darkened by threats. Yet as a scion, he was now legally a child of this looming Bal Rú.

These complexities troubled him deeply as he was ushered to comfortable bunks in a large barrack with the other boys. Their hum of chatter gave way quickly to the sighs and snores of sleep. But D'thalien, dreading his first shift, slept little.

In the great hall, the withered, dead weeds - which had barely been visible through the cracks in the walls - became animated and slithered out of sight. Not even the Bal Rú himself, with the intuitive powers of a Thaed-Rú, sensed their supernal presence.

Ir of the Fenrülk

The evening skies were dark and shadowy over the fallen Ballai of Ir of the Fenrülk. In heavy battle armor, his sword and archery bow in a cross form on his back, Aidan's dismount was an uncharacteristically clumsily one. He left his horse to graze and strode about in a field of wheat. The morning had stretched across one delay after the other.

"The enemy approaches!" had woken him early, but they had yet to appear.

An hour ago, the call of "Ready your weapons!" had come, and still no battle was to be had. He frowned at the emblem of the Veyasaen seared into leathern cuffs upon his wrists. Though useful, but as sentries the creatures were unreliable. "Better a foot runner than those beastly fowl!" he growled and plucked at stems of grain.

Upon his shield and armor, was the insignia of an unearthly beast representing their shape-shifting warlord with the inscription in Hierundiel "705TH MISHRA-OLRU TOMEN." It was with great personal satisfaction that Aidan served in the Archers' Arbans of the 705th. He bore it proudly and had eagerly accepted their storied history as his own. Formed under the Thaed-Rú warlord Mishra-Olru, in the 705th year of the Thaed-Rú dynasty, their prowess in battle came from their warlord's ability to shape shift into a beast. This ability was a unique gift from potent seeds of the second Cethin Arda.

One of the stalks of wheat, by habit, made their way to his mouth. In such a field as this, I was attacked! With a grimace, he spat out the wheat as it triggered a faint image of the past. His little brother jabbed angrily at him with a bo staff and a blur of tall cornstalks flashed through his mind. A rush of fear remembered came over him and he flinched as the scream of his father "Aaaahhhhhh!" rang out, almost audibly in his ear. So real it seemed, he cast an uneasy glance around to see if perhaps the other men in his arban had heard it too. He sighed, remembering the teachings of the Rhünkai masters. Such recollections are merely lies of the heart. The hazy form of that same young brother climbing the steps of a steel-clad wagon, to join dozens and dozens of filthy boys and young men often twinged his heart. Yet now, as always, he remembered. My family was unfit for service in the Rhünkai order! Whereas I am well on my way to becoming a captain!

Like D'thalien, Aidan too had endured the wretched elements of the northern country. But his caravan took him further, beyond Hierundia where he had fallen deeply under the sway of the Necropulpa plant.

Within the fallen Ballai of Rhühaven, Aidan's caravan had deposited its shivering passengers in the military compound of Mechedül. Mechedül, Aidan thought with a frown. Then, ineffably, his thoughts shifted back to the words of the powerful young Bal Rú. Just as he had spoken to the Scions at Dul-Meggor, Íraban initiated his military scions personally. His Thaed-Rú powers, and the gifts of his dark garden, swayed each lithe youth from any willfulness of their own.

"You are but poor images of your fathers. They bequeath so little to your posterity! I offer you adventure! I will give you glory!" the Bal Rú had declared. "Those of you who once opposed us are pardoned this day. I waive all manner of indictments and convictions against you. Instead, I graft you into my family as scions of my most benevolent order. Forsaking all bonds, we enter a new life. This day you are my Scions, and I am your father. I give you the world of the Y'cromahein for you to rule!'

These words extinguished the light of Aidan's family, supplanting his past with a new identity and a new purpose. Though the memory of his family was but a faint vapor in his mind, a deep hurt yet lay within. It often served as kindling for his battle rage. All he could do was bury the pain of his memories and manifest aggression on weaker souls. Indescribably, he hated this. Yet, the more he pressed into his training, the more the code of camaraderie and exhilaration of warfare gave him a new sense of identity and purpose.

It was not the Rhünkai he lay in wait for today, but innocent villagers fighting against the Thaed-Rú edict. Under the instruction of Rhünkai masters, he honed his great prowess with the sword, crossbow and lance. During many a battle simulation, he forgot they had all been innocent youths but weeks, then months, before. In violent rages, he exacted vicious kills in battle and maimed countless men-in-training. The masters condoned his wild constitution, his fellows applauded him.

He sighed now, left the field and swung heavily into his saddle to return for their midday meal. But before he could partake of it, an officer bore down upon him at a gallop, pulled his poor mount to a rough stop and called out, "Aidan, the captain calls for you! A band of armed men approach from the east."

"Finally!" Aidan responded with real joy and galloped toward those shaping into battle formation.

"Aidan, the Strength of Many!" cried the captain of the Royal Rhünkai Archers as Aidan's horse galloped past. Cheers ran through the seventy-five crossbowmen at the captain's laud. Aidan raised his right fist into the air.

One soldier called out, "Come now Aidan! How many hundreds more than us will you take down today?"

"Indeed Aidan, you make our tasks easy!" bellowed another, drawing out laughter from the soldiers.

"He's slain how many now? Two hundred?"

A soldier loading his crossbow laughed to another soldier, "Aye, in battle. But it is more than three hundred...if you include those who fell in training!"

As he galloped on, one soldier sang a little ditty popular in his village. "There is an arrow much faster, yet younger than most. A bow or a blade in the hands of Aidan, the great wrath of Mishra-Olru holds."

Despite his youthful tenure as a novice soldier, Aidan's prowess brought him rapidly to the attention of the generals. Never had such a young man been asked to serve in the Archers' Company.

The laud he received for his skill not only fueled him for battle, but also swelled his heart with pride. He had hearkened to the words of the Bal Rú and eagerly sought glory amongst the Royal Rhünkai Archers. The agony of his beloved mother's untimely death still clung to his heart. Often, he hoped that, were she alive, she would be proud of his many daring conquests. Yet his humble roots, his common father and brother, were a shame to him, a shame best buried.

He wheeled his horse into formation at the shill warning calls of the Veyasaen above. Their shadows fell darkly, fearfully upon the field before them. Finally!

The captain of the Royal Rhünkai Archers trotted past his soldiers. "Look alive! Man your weapons. Look to the trees, but wait on my command."

Aidan and his comrades tore their eyes from the dark fowl. His arban held their crossbows in check, at the ready to aim, to fire. Throughout the Province of Ir of the Fenrülk, petty insurrections and protests against the Royal Edict of the Scions of Íraban had brought about a merciless policy of death on sight to such as these. Always, these skirmishes went the same. A tattered band of men and lads, untrained, armed with rustic weapons and simple farming tools attempted to take on their elite force. Aidan shook his head, perturbed. Why do they fight when they must surely know it is in vain?

Within the space of half an hour, a band of a few dozen insurgents gathered hesitantly at the tree line across the far end of the open pasture. In place of helms, they wore knotted peasant caps, where the Rhünkai wore armor and leather, they wore only threadbare homespun.

Seventy-five Royal Rhünkai Archers laid low beneath a hedge of wild bush before Aidan's mounted arban. On the far side of the open pasture, twenty-five more archers, and dozens of Rhünkai soldiers armed with razor-sharp battle-axes, swords and lances lay along a thick grove of trees, ready to surround the insurgents once they charged.

Aidan's heart pounded with anticipation, but his forefinger remained steady on his crossbow trigger. Though the day was as chill as all had been of late, perspiration moistened his head underneath his helmet.

Warily, the first of the peasants emerged into open pasture, tightly grasping pitchforks, shovels, and scythes. They glanced nervously about the field and upwards at the sky, but neither Rhünkai nor Veyasaen attacked. Untrained as they were, when those few brave souls remained unharmed, the rest followed suit. They trudged into the open pasture, seeking a battle they little knew was already upon them.

At the captain's command, the Rhünkai Archers rose from behind the hedge and loosed a volley of arrows across the open pasture. Many peasant insurgents fell. Aidan's steady stream of arrows brought down dozens more. Those few who escaped the onslaught, retreated to the tree line only to be met with the rear archers' volley and butchered by the flank of soldiers who sprang forth from the grove. Blood drenched the soil and the Veyasaen flocked to feed upon the corpses.

With the battle nearly over before it had begun, Aidan led an arban of twenty soldiers into the forest after survivors. In the melee, Aidan spotted a peasant and a young lad disappearing at a distance into a thick grove. Dismounting, he broke from the men to pursue them into the woods.

The shouts of confusion or other peasants faded as he chased them further. Despite his heavy armor, Aidan rapidly gained on them. Fluidly, he notched an arrow as he ran, then, jolted to a stop to aim. Seconds later, its sharp stone tip burrowed deep between the shoulders of his target, who toppled to his knees with a grunt. The lad wheeled about to help the wounded man.

"Papa!" he shouted. He tried desperately to yank the man to his feet, but his father merely groaned and grasped desperately at the arrow. His efforts were futile however as it was beyond his reach.

"Come, Papa! Please! Let us go, Papa!"

Aidan stepped forward and the boy and he locked eyes for what seemed an eternity. Hazel doe-eyes softened the boy's dirty face. His look of fear seemed all too familiar to the young archer. They both stood paralyzed.

For a moment, Aidan saw D'thalien's panicked countenance in the young lad. His father's urgent cry of, "Run!" rose to his own lips as a horrible, nauseous pain gripped him. His heart beat widely, wretchedly, rendering him powerless to react at all.

Bewildered, Aidan's bow arm trembled, and his arrow slipped from his grasp. The boy's brow furrowed in confusion. His father groaned, but the boy turned from him to step forward hesitantly, as if to plea for help. Though the boy was no threat to him, an unreasonable anger at his insolence overcame Aidan. In one smooth move, he whipped another arrow from his quiver. It burrowed in the man's heart, ended his suffering. Hardly had the boy's eyes widened at the sight of this before they two went blank, devoid of life, as a second arrow found his own heart.

Aidan sneered down at the body of the young boy, laying atop that of his father. Before turning to follow the distant sounds of the Royal Rhünkai Archers, he threw savage kicks at both their bodies. "Peasants," he snorted. "They never amount to anything."

Terus Raynür

Beyond the Provinces of the fallen Ballai, the Aberfelus River meandered through moonlit gorges in the valleys of Terus Raynür. Across craggy cliffs high above the waters, lay a thick old oak tree, felled long ago to serve as a bridge. A man limped slowly across the massive oak and passed into the thick darkness of the forest just as a monstrous howl pierced the night. Strange beastly yelps echoing out in response from the darkness of the forest. Heavily populated with shrubbery, bushes and thick groves of pine, even the full moon did not penetrate its darkness. Thus, the dense vegetation concealed the tall, dark figures watching the man.

His garb was of animal fur and he wore crude, leather footwear. A wild mass of wavy hair flowed beneath a soiled bandage which wound around his head and over his right eye. Scars crossed what was visible of his face to disappear within an unkempt beard. Exhaling cold vapors in the moonlight, his good eye scanned the thick brush. The stillness of the cold, winter air heightened the man's senses. His grip on his bo staff tightened in response to another chorus of eerie yelps. He sensed something observing him, studying his every move. His heart thrummed with anticipation.

Slowly, he crouched to the ground. On one knee, he bent to smell the low-lying scent of an animal's musky odor. It hung over the tall grass from which a faint rustling indicated movement toward him. Several hooves clopped softly, moving through the darkness. The familiar gave way to the peculiar as a series of yelping vibrations pursued the prey. He frowned, the sound was both familiar and strange.

Suddenly several deer dashed through the trees directly in front of the man. The moonlight fell upon their panicked eyes as they wheeled to avoid him. Behind them, branches cracked and snapped, breaking under the thud of heavy, gigantic footsteps careening after them.

A gigantic, hairy creature emerged out of the dark foliage in mad pursuit of the deer. Briefly, their eyes locked. The man stood motionless. Opposite the creature, another massive figure crashed through the dark foliage. Both had smashed through large branches as though they were twigs.

A little way in front of him, yelps turned into howls that pierced the night air. A chill ran down the man's spine as he felt the presence of a third creature standing quietly at his rear. Every hair on his arms stood on end. Slowly turning around, and peering upward, the man came face to face with the giant figure.

In the darkness, he could see the whites of the creature's big eyes, and a hideous scar that ran from its forehead to its chin. They struggled to convey something he could not decipher. From the distance came the bleat of a deer's anguish, then the crushing of bones, then silence. There were more than just these three.

The man squinted his eyes against the same eventuality. He cringed backward. After several moments, summoning his courage, he peeked and gasped. He was alone. Warily, hesitantly, he walked a radius of several yards, gripping his bo staff, not knowing what the creatures would do next.

The man's curiosity drew him to press further into the darkness until faint sounds came to him. The indistinct chatter of a sentient language interspersed with clicks, chirps and whistles led him to a gathering of wild, hairy creatures dividing their game. Despite the dimness of the woods, he could just make out their massive forms bending over the deer carcass.

Hours later, he found himself following two of them several yards behind, while the third creature followed many more yards behind him. A terrible headache plagued him. They came suddenly into a clearing and the moonlight silhouetted their gigantic, hairy forms. One helped another slump the dead carcass over his shoulder and the third turned to gaze at him.

He sucked his breath in deeply. On a similar moonlit night, it had been this creature, the one with the soulful stare and scarred face that had found him near death. In a fogged memory, he remembered how the creature had slumped him over its shoulder and carried him to safety. In a state of miserable pain, he had felt too weak and powerless to respond. Had it been weeks since then? Or months? He furrowed his brow and thought, *Just how severe is this head injury of mine?*

Clearly now, the man recalled a flood of memories, the creature setting him down beneath a tree, smearing sticky sap all over the man's eyes, a crude blindfold, then carrying him for several hours crashing through brush, splashing through rivers and ascending a steep mountainside to its windy peak, only to descend the other side. The creature had finally deposited the almost lifeless man in a deep ravine where he must have passed out from exhaustive pain.

The man had awakened to a creature smearing away the sap from his eyes. The morning breeze had ruffled their long strands of hair which covered the whole of their bodies. Too weak to feel fear, he had wished for death, to end his horrible pain and suffering. But the creatures had offered him an array of berries and wild figs and occasionally raw meat. They kept their distance, man and creatures both, observing each other for many days. They chattered amongst themselves with those strange whistles and calls. Eventually, he was carried to a river where he mustered enough strength to bathe. His reflection bore deep gashes on his face, the source of continual pain. The creatures had watched with great curiosity as he tore strips from his clothing to bind his wounds. They emitted a series of excited clicks when he stooped to strip away the rotting bark from the largest flotsam he could find. He smiled as sturdy oak emerged beneath the softened bark, then laughed aloud as the creatures imitated his use of the cane, some with imaginary canes, some hunching over the leg bones of their prey. When he, with the help of his staff, could finally walk on his own, they had chosen to allow him to accompany them in their nocturnal hunts. *Weeks for sure, months perhaps.* The man thought as the memories of his recovery came in waves.

Under tonight's full moon, he scrutinized these dark and hairy creatures. They stood eight to ten feet tall. *The Ghost Kings!* he nearly exclaimed aloud. *Then I must be in the forests of Terus Raynür!* Few brave souls ventured out from beyond the fallen Ballai of the Provinces and fewer still had ever seen these creatures. Part human, part simian in their features, their intelligence, shared language, and ability to detect the slightest movement in the deepest dark from hundreds of yards away had always seemed a myth before.

One of the creatures grabbed the man and slumped him over its shoulder. He grinned wryly as they loped smoothly through the woods. He was accustomed to their frustration with his human pace. They came upon a tree running with sap, and he grimaced.

"I wish you would not do that every time we go to the cave!" he protested. "I will never tell anyone where your cave is!"

The creature, annoyed by the man's complaints, answered only with a growl, swiped at his eyes with the sap, then slung him over his shoulder once more. The faint sounds of a roaring waterfall grew louder and louder until finally its waters crashed down upon them as the creature carried him through it. Once behind the waterfall, the sounds of water faded as they passed the mouth of a small cave.

The creature clamored through it and descended a steep wall. The man heard its feet thump against wood debris and the crunching of discarded bones. Here and there, a clang underfoot rang out from what must be manmade armor or weaponry among the corpses of dead soldiers among the prey. The indistinct chatter of a great gathering of creatures echoed across the walls and ceiling. The echoes of their odd sounds bounced off distant walls of the massive chamber. The now familiar stench of earth mixed with something ancient assailed the man's nostrils and he sighed. His hunting excursion in the forests and the mountains had been a welcome change after his secluded recovery.

Beastly hands removed the man's sap. His eyes adjusted in the semi-darkness. He watched gigantic forms and shapes ripping apart the limbs of the dead carcass. Beyond his view, he heard as the deer's flesh and muscles tearing beneath the powerful strength of their hands. The creatures casually stole glances at the man as they went about their business. In the cave, their unearthly, guttural language of chirps, clicks, high-pitched barks and strange phonetic sounds echoed in the air around him.

After many months together, their tolerance of each other's presence remained cautious. After all, these creatures had retreated in total oblivion for centuries. Very few humans had ever seen their kind. Though a few lone woodsmen and hunters had likely caught a glimpse, their existence prevailed, for the most part, in folklore. Still, the people of Graëyhovan understood the forests of Terus Raynür to be a wild haunt of these mysterious creatures, hundreds of leagues from civilization where very few souls ventured.

Though grateful they had spared his life, with the strength of his body returning, he longed to be out of the cave, roaming the forest freely. More than that, he longed to return to his world. Each night as he lay on his pallet of moss, the world beyond seemed to call to him with increasing urgency. A heavy spirit of melancholy deepened daily as the memories returned one by one from the muddled corners of his injured head. Finally, there came a night where the pieces of his former life fell together so completely, so vividly that it prevented him from sleeping.

On the morrow, the man awoke to the rise of guttural sounds, chirps and barks as the creatures stirred. On high and motionless, the scar-faced creature perched on a massive rock, observing him. Standing himself up with his staff, the man looked directly at the creature, and spoke firmly, "I must leave."

The creature turned from him and scaled the rock, to depart the cave, leaving him behind. The man sat, disheartened, awaiting his return and the delivery of his daily fare. Hours later, the ghost king returned, not with berries and figs, but with more sap in its hand for his eyes. From behind a cluster of boulders, the creature withdrew a crossbow, a quiver full of arrows, and a leather belt from which a sword hung heavily. He offered them with a grunt. The man's heart leapt as he realized the creature intended to release him. He submitted eagerly to the sap, one last time.

An hour later, the creature halted his loping pace abruptly and set him down in a little clearing. The beast removed the sap from his eyes and the man blinked against the sunlight. He cast his hand over his eyes as they adjusted, then rose. Turning to the hairy giant, he spoke his farewell. "I must leave now. I need to find my sons."

The creature seemed to understand what the man was saying. Its eyes conveyed the permanence of a mystical connection, forged over the last six months. Then, he urged the man into the forest with a rough gesture of his hand, as if to say, "Find them!"

The man took several steps toward the beast and spoke humbly, "You have brought me back to life," he murmured. "I will never forget that." He lifted a hand high above his head to touch the creature's muscular chest, but the creature bent to meet him, and the man's fingers fell upon his scarred face. The creature's fleshy fingers gently probed the man's own scars, and their eyes locked in a primordial bond.

Wheeling abruptly lest he lose his resolve, the man departed. The sword thumped against his thigh and the bow bounced upon his back in a familiar rhythm to which he added the thudding of his oaken staff. Hundreds of yards were between them before the entire forest of Terus Raynür was suddenly shaken with a beastly howl of anguish. It echoed off the mountainous walls. The birds and beast of the glens and upper vales fell silent in fear of its power.

The man understood such anguish. Tears streamed down his sap-stained, scarred face. Before continuing onward, he cast a backward glance and cried out, "I know, my friend. I know."

Peiscavellan Hierundia

For months, Graeyba limped slowly westward, throughout the Province of Molchaion, then turned north to the Province of Tal-Ciddion in search of his sons. Disheartened by the fruitlessness of his efforts, he turned east from the frigid wastelands of endless snow. He skirted Graëyhovan to the north, for how could he return, without a wife, without his children? He was equally hesitant to enter the Province of Hierundia as its environs were the heart of the Thaed-Rú Dominions. Nevertheless, enter it he did.

He had long since swapped his tattered bandages for fresh clean cloth. Posing as a beggar along the highways, he struck up whatever conversations he could with wayfarers and soldiers alike. He interspersed pleas for help with questions about the labor camps or training camps of the child slaves. Curses, grunts, and the occasional curious frown showed they knew nothing. He peered into wagon after wagon of captured boys as they passed, but never did he see his sons.

Graeyba endured the frigid nights of the North huddled inside caves, deserted farmhouses, abandoned granaries. One night, he sheltered inside an ancient mine, another he passed huddled within the steaming warmth of the carcass of an elk he had slain.

A miserable depression came upon Graeyba. As he moved doggedly through the harsh reality of endless, unforgiving landscapes, dark voices plagued him. "Aidan and D'thalien are dead." "You will never see them, again." "End your search now." "You will never find them."

One snowy evening brought him to the edge of a steep ravine. Graeyba approached it, staring into a black abyss. A great conflict raged within him.

His will clashed against his despair until, from deep within his memory, an echo of his own voice came to him. *If we are ever separated, for whatever reason, I will find you, no matter how long it takes or how far you may go. I will not rest until I find you.*

Driven by the memory of his vow, yet only with great effort, he pushed himself away from the edge of the ravine and fell awkwardly onto the snow. A stabbing pain shot through his body as icy sludge met injured eye. It merged with the cold loneliness in his heart. The sorrowful reality of his near attempt to take his own life within burdened him with shame. Convulsively, his body gave way to tears.

Sometime later he hauled his body up and into motion. Trudging despondently through the snowy forests of Peiscavellan Hierundia, he came upon a river crossing. A lone, hooded figure trod across the bridge, leaning heavily on a wooden staff. Graeyba made to join him, then shrank into the trees at the sound of horse's hooves. A detachment of equestrian soldiers galloped out of the forest and forded the river.

Graeyba counted twenty men. Several of the horses circled the hooded figure, and their riders began to heckle him.

"What business have you in these parts alone?"

"Do you not know that lone travelers are often robbed and murdered?"

"Aye! Brigands and bandits hide in these forests!"

The men were young, brash, emboldened by power to make sport of the weak. Anger sent Graeyba's hand to his sword. He was prepared to redress the effrontery should it turn violent.

"I journey to visit friends far away. I am just passing through," the lone figure calmly answered. "I thank you for your concern for my safety, gentlemen."

The soldiers cackled. One of the soldiers dismounted and tugged at a leather bag slung over the traveler's shoulder.

"What have you here? Let us share!" a young soldier taunted.

"These are a harvest gift, seeds for my friends."

"Well, then you must know that there are taxes for transporting any seeds or properties of harvest across the provinces." Saying this, the soldier confiscated the leather bag and peered inside it.

The man did not resist.

"What is in there?" asked another soldier.

"Just as he said... these puny old seeds!" Saying this, the soldier grabbed a handful of gray seeds from the bag. With a leer, he poured them into the snow and crushed them into a drift with his heel. The others cackled again.

A white-hot anger seethed in Graeyba. Quietly, he drew his sword and began to edge toward the scene.

Another soldier dismounted to study the man's staff. "What are these strange markings?" He reached out a curious finger to trace the engravings.

"This is the language of Uraduin," the lone figure patiently answered, pulling it slowly back from his reach.

Graeyba squinted. Uraduin, now where have I heard that word?

One soldier asked the rest, "Where is Uraduin spoken?" but they shrugged and shook their heads.

It was the stranger who answered. "It is the language of the One True Infinite Garden."

The soldiers froze.

Then a soldier billowed, "What are you doing with seeds from the Cethin Arda? Theft of this kind is the greatest of treacheries!"

"Seize him!" cried another.

The soldier who had been curious about the staff, grabbed at it with both hands, while another soldier dropped the leather bag and seized the figure by the arms.

Graeyba, dashed forward, but before he could intervene, an astounding feat of incredible power unfolded. The lone figure assailed them all. One by one, twenty soldiers met their fate as his staff swung about raining deadly blows upon them with lightning speed. The men screamed in pain as their skulls cracked under his force. A fine mist of blood sprayed the air, staining the snow. In mere moments, each of them lay dead.

Steaming heat rose from their cracked skulls as the lone figure stood silently over this carnage. Their blood poured down the riverbanks and seeped through the wooden bridge to meet the swirling river.

The lone figure sensed his presence and addressed him. "What is your name, friend?"

He moved forward hesitantly. "Graeyba...Graeyba Khalevad, from the Province of Graëyhovan."

The man peered closely at Graeyba's bandaged face. "You look very familiar," he said with a friendly smile.

Graeyba's eyebrows raised in surprise as he too recognized the man. "You...you are the one who gave my sons and I the tealeaves last year! That language on your staff, Uraduin, you spoke it over us and the world about us trembled!"

The lone figure nodded casually, then asked. "What business are you about? Do you not know how dangerous it is out here, alone like this?"

Both broke in hearty laughter. Graeyba surveyed the bloody mess and chuckled, "Indeed."

Then his smile tightened into a polite grin, "I am in search of my sons. They have been taken away from me, much as you foretold at Dûenhallow." Gesturing toward the dead soldiers he explained, "They are the reason my family has been torn apart."

"I reckon that explains your bandaged eye and those new scars you bear," the lone figure said. He looked intrigued but did not ask for details. "I can certainly tell you where they are, your sons. I just passed through there, myself."

Graeyba closed his eyes briefly in relief, then exhaled a deep sigh. When he opened his eyes, they were wet with unshed tears of joy. The man smiled kindly at him when Graeyba stuttered out, "They...they are alive?"

"Alive and well," he said. "Several weeks journey toward the Forests of Ixzaril will lead you there."

"I have searched for months! The journey of a few weeks means little to me. I thank you for your news." As Graeyba turned to go, the man cried out.

"Stop!" With a kindly laugh he said, "I have yet to tell you the place! And a word of caution, you will know when you arrive, the very ground under your feet will rumble for leagues in every direction. The Rhünkai masters, they are continually experimenting in nefarious ways. But they can never seem to get things right." He paused, his expression dark. A great weariness overcame his demeanor. "They lack the proper knowledge of the Garden of Ages," he added.

Graeyba knew more of the Rhünkai brutes than their masters. Perplexed, he knew not what to say.

"Stay a little while with me, away from this carnage," the man offered. "Let us break bread this evening."

They left the bloody bridge to seek shelter in the forest. Before long, a fire crackled warmly, and they ate.

That night, Graeyba shared his entire story with the kind stranger, an intent listener. His sons' plight at the hands of the Rhünkai deeply concerned the kind stranger. The power of the man's blessing in the ruins of Dûenhallow, and his display of skill in battle, caused Graeyba to trust this man more than he had trusted anyone in years. It was a great release for Graeyba to share his burdens.

When his tale was done, the man said kindly, "Do not give up. You will be reunited with your sons."

His word seemed law. It strengthened Graeyba, and a renewed sense of purpose surged within him. "Will you join me on my quest?" he asked.

The stranger declined, "I regret I have a previous engagement to fulfill."

Seeing Graeyba's disappointment, he clicked his tongue soothingly. "We will meet again. Soon, and in better circumstances."

Graeyba was heartened by this promise.

As they parted, the kind stranger heartily embraced Graeyba and bade him farewell. Graeyba felt an enormous peace and calm emanate from him. He pondered the remarkable nature of the man as he went on his way. Suddenly Graeyba turned, and called out, "Wait!" But the man was gone. "Again?" he laughed aloud. In all his excitement over finding his sons, Graeyba had once more neglected to ask the kindly stranger for his name.

The Thorns of Dul-Meggor

Several weeks later, cloaked by night, Graeyba arrived at the gates of Dul-Meggor. He was disguised in the uniform and armor of one of the slain Rhünkai on the bridge and rode upon one of their horses. He had filched the finest of their weapons. A sharp dagger had tamed his wild beard and hair. A black eye patch formed from one of their cloaks now covered his injured eye.

He fell in now behind a rear guard, pleased to go unnoticed. But once inside the compound, the gloomy sight of countless child slaves in tattered clothes, hunched submissively as they scurried by erased his grin. What troubled his heart the most was seeing children working into the night. Torches and lanterns throughout the compound cast deep shadows on deathly-pale faces. A wave of panic came over him. *Is this the fate of my sons also? What oppression has tortured these poor souls so?*

His mount fidgeted as a great creaking of wheels and clattering of hooves approached. An officer appeared at the head of three caravans. In the tongue of Hierundiel, he ordered, "Arban Five, Arban Six and Arban Seven! Move out!"

The wagon masters cracked their whips at the team of horses. As the caravans exited the compound walls, the kind stranger's words rang true. For leagues in every direction, the very ground rumbled. The soldiers struggled to calm their animals. Graeyba felt no fear but smiled instead. As he calmed his horse, he reveled in the blossoming of a new hope. *You will be reunited with your sons*, the man had said. If the ground had rumbled, then, surely, that too would come to pass.

Feeling he had seen an omen, Graeyba was drawn to the caravans and followed them at a distance. It wound its way from Dul-Meggor through the snowy pines, into the wilderness. Graeyba's vision, honed on his lonely trek, discerned beyond it, through the forest, an enormous cluster of lit torches, too numerous to count. It was in that direction the caravan moved.

Cautiously reining in his horse, Graeyba gradually fell out of sight from the caravans. No one seemed to have noticed his arrival and none now noticed his departure. He urged his horse up a steep trail. A short while later, he dismounted high above a deep gorge. Far below, the sound of creaking wheels ceased. Patiently, he scanned the forest, along the ravine's edge. A precipitous mountain jutted up from the chasm's far end. At its base, he caught the curious sight of tiny, little torches scaling the wall of the peak. Squinting, he followed their slow ascent. Occasionally, trees or brush obscured them, but gradually, they rose far up into the snowy summit of the towering mountain.

A large Veyasaen glided lazily into his sightline. Graeyba flattened his back to the ground and followed its flight. Only when it was a mere speck on the horizon, did Graeyba flop to his belly to return his gaze to the darkness of the ravine floor. Distant echoes of harsh commands, the moans of children, and the crack of whips rent the crisp night air. In particular, the miserable sound of leather meeting skin and bone echoed loudly from the mountain walls.

Graeyba winced in sympathy. Had his sons suffered such whips of late? Spurned by this thought, he edged closer. But the furious cold whipped across his body, chilling his very bones. How the children could sustain themselves in such frigid weather in threadbare clothes was beyond Graeyba's comprehension. Frustrated by the limitations of his body and with a troubled mind, he slipped into an uneasy rest in the slight shelter afforded by some shrubbery.

The next morning, recalling advice from the Peiscavellan stranger, he dug deep into the snow, then covered himself in mud from head to toe to hide his scent from the Veyasaen. He shivered uncontrollably as he smeared it on his skin. So disagreeable was the sensation that he found himself longing it was the Ghost King's sap smeared warmly over his eyes instead. Shaking his head wryly, he gritted his teeth against the chill and began his ascent.

The threat of the Veyasaen patrolling above soon caused him to forget the chill. Their screeches and howls, shocking in volume and doubled by echoes, reverberated against his skull. He longed to clap his hands over his ears. Several times he very nearly lost his grip as instinct battled instinct.

It was nearly nightfall when the mountain rumbled once more. Graeyba lurched forward, boots slipping on ice, scudding through snow. Desperately he grasped at the mountain, his fingers seized a cluster of shrubs. The rumbling ceased, but fear still pulsed through his veins as he scrambled to his feet. In relief, he sought carefully for a foothold and came upon a little shelf of snowy rock. Breathing hard he sat upon it and massaged his frosty hands until their strength returned, then resumed his climb.

After several days, with Veyasaen above and rumblings below, the treacherous mountain suddenly flattened into a broad summit. The dark stone walls of what must surely be the Fortress City stood some fifty yards away. A foreboding landscape of giant thorns and thistles covered the ground. They, in turn, were wreathed in thick shrouds of fog. At the height of his chest, the undergrowth, thick with age, stretched over the walls of the Fortress City. Like giant thorny serpents, the vines crawled over the walls.

The walls of the Fortress City were close, but the army of thorns and thistles divided them. Not a single spot of ground seemed free of the vines' barbs. A frightfully unnatural sight, it was as if the mountain itself desired to bar all who dared set foot upon it. Treacherous as it was, the barbs could not dissuade a father from searching for his sons.

Graeyba fell to his belly and crawled. Despite his Rhünkai armor, the spikes still snagged above his boots and pricked at his arms and head as he squirmed along beneath them.

The ground below him rattled slightly, then crescendoed to a rumble so great the whole mountain seemed to groan. Graeyba cried out in pain as trembling thorns above violently pierced the back of his right leg. Nonetheless, he pressed onward toward the outer walls of the Fortress City.

Minutes later, a great pain spread around the pricks where highly potent poison made rapid progress. A green tinge spread around the edge of his sores, then oozed an unnatural pus. With ragged breaths, Graeyba dragged his body into a briar patch with enough space for him to flop to his back. The blood in his veins cooled, his body stilled, and all about him the vines began to sway, drifting in and out of focus.

Desperately, he pushed aside delirium to search his mind for a solution. The only thought that came to him was the stranger's tea seeds, gifted him in Peiscavellan. Weak fingers sought them in his bag.

He clutched at a handful and strove to muster the strength to push them into the frosty ground. Before him appeared the visage of his deceased wife, her long tresses floating as golden liquid in a haze of dusk. For the second time, he faced his death. "I am sorry, my love, I have lost our boys," he moaned as he slipped into unconsciousness.

The following morning, he lay there still. Pale, inert, he stirred only a little as another rumble violently rattled the mountain. Half conscious, he awoke to the unmistakable smell of tea. Beside him, in the frozen briar patch, a sturdy tea plant grew. As if in a dream, he willed his arm out slowly, slowly to reach for and break off its leaves. One by one, he chewed each of them, then waited.

Moments later, a warm sensation flowed throughout his body. He found that he could breathe more deeply and gulped at the icy air. Gradually, his strength returned. He gathered burgeoning tea leaves to rub on his wounds. An hour later, Graeyba searched his flesh in awe, unable to find a single sign of his wounds. Such powerful herbs transcended all alchemy known to him.

Throughout the day, the stem of the tea plant thickened, fresh leaves budded, then burst forth. He ate from the plant once more and was nourished. Remembering the stranger's promise that they would meet again, he imagined ways in which he might express his gratitude. Yet it seemed he could ever truly repay such a debt. He was still resting as the sun began to sink, but the thump of boots and clank of swords drew his eyes to the massive gates.

By nightfall, Graeyba felt strong enough to continue his search for his sons. Peering out of the briar patch a second time, he grinned to see the fog thickening about him. Torches glowed dimly through it near the gates. Beneath the fog, he began to crawl again.

As he approached the fortress walls, soldiers bore torches on high as they ushered child slaves into the Fortress City. He had noticed that only guards patrolled the misty summit during the day. Remembering the children of Dul-Meggor, he mused, perplexed. So, the soldiers work the children only at night.

He managed to edge closer to scan for the source of the trail of human traffic. The children shuffled along a narrow stone walkway built against the wall. Thorny vines covered it, reaching high up the walls. This walkway ended at the fifty-foot-high entrance of a massive adobe wall, parts of which were still under construction.

Another rumbling rocked the mountain. Instinctively, Graeyba's hands flew upward fingers searching through the barbs to push the vines away. Once the rumbling subsided, he crawled toward the edge of the walkway.

As the last of the soldiers passed, he emerged from beneath the vines to balance carefully atop their solid limbs. Surveying the scenery with great caution, he climbed gingerly along them. Whether through dark science or naturally over time, the vines had been made to arch over the path before snaking up the walls. Here and there along the walkway, gaps appeared where branches wound together. Eventually, one of them yawned wide enough for Graeyba to crawl through.

Inside the walkway, he stood erect once more and winced in pain. He stretched cramped muscles and creaking joints and dusted caked mud from his uniform. After two days lying prone, it was good to move freely once more.

"Please, sir," he heard a child cry out behind him.

He turned, eager to help, but froze as a soldier herded two young boys away from the entrance toward him. The boys, in chains, begged the soldier tearfully for pardon.

The soldier, soulless, ignored their pleas.

Dark as it was, the boys' sooty faces were indiscernible. Graeyba studied their eyes as they passed for any flicker that might show they were his sons.

The soldier marched past Graeyba, oblivious to his interest in the slaves. Graeyba watched them disappear into the fog. He longed to come to their aid, but he continued grimly up the walkway instead. Scores of guards patrolled a series of scaffolds where child slaves worked by torchlight to construct the walls. Merging with a group of these, he passed undetected through the gates and into the Fortress City.

On the summit of the snow-capped mountain, an evil garden all about him, Graeyba walked through the unfinished streets of Íraban's Fortress City. Domiciles, buildings, towers and large edifices in various states of construction lined streets populated with debris and scaffolds. Harsh taskmasters cracked their whips over deathly pale children, yelling, "Pick up your feet, you sluggards! We will fall behind schedule with such sloth! Do you wish to personally incur the wrath of the Bal Rú? Now hurry!"

Fear and sadness gripped Graeyba's heart equally as he witnessed hundreds upon hundreds of the Scions of Íraban hammering, chiseling, sawing, lifting, rolling, heaving, pouring, wobbling under burdens in their labor. And all occurred under the bloodied whips of taskmasters. Agony scared their filthy faces. His impulse was to run through the semi-finished streets of buildings and debris, calling frantically for his sons, slaughtering every Rhünkai who came between them. Every fiber in his being struggled to hold him back from this instinct, for it would mean the end for him and for his sons. Thus, it was that Graeyba slipped away and descended the mountain to decide on a thorough plan of action before continuing his search.

A Storm from the West

Anterròs of the West

"Unto the West we shall all return; the land where time began.

The place where the Sacred Work of the Faeynül was laid out.

In all the land of Y'cromeca, only there does the Ballai still stand, because of the faithfulness of the Br'thain unto the wisdom of the Gardener."

S'baladin, son of Baltien,
of the house of Eirun-Vala,
from the clan of Alazar,
in the land of Ferán.

In the summer month of Yi'vev, the evening sun cast golden hues in waves of heat across the valleys of Ferán. But high amongst the rocky crags of the Yedara Mountains, cool breezes accompanied a gangly, suntanned shepherd boy as he climbed. On a solitary ledge near the mountain's peak, he sought a moment of repose from his watch.

Breathing heavily, he pulled the loose folds of his earthen brown Dolscareb more tightly about his arms and legs, shivering as he sat. He squinted large, brown watery eyes against the elements and coughed as his lungs adjusted to the thinness of the air. Though his body plagued him, his spirits were high. He chuckled to himself as he watched several shepherd boys below attempt to ride the largest of their sheep.

Lazily, the boy turned his almond-shaped face to the desert far below, enjoying the expansive vista afforded him by his perch. He imagined various animals and crops within the geometric patterns of carefully irrigated fields below. On the edge of the southwestern horizon, the Ballai cut a rough diagonal from the northeast. The shepherds of Ferán often competed in attempts to make out any high reliefs of the Sheddukem faces etched on the Ballai. Yet, they never could distinguish the grotesque features from so far away. The winds blew his hair into his face as he pulled his long, black hair out of his eyes. A race of giants with dark intent, trapped forever in their rocky prisons, now the subject of child's play reflected S'baladin grimly.

Off to his right, five leagues northeast, his township of Anterròs lay nestled in the cool shade of a canyon's steep wall. He leaned his back wearily against a massive wall of jagged granite and meditated on the middle distance. After some time, his eyes squinted suddenly. He leaned forward excitedly, his eyes fixed upon a rising cloud of dust. A vast movement of horsemen approached Anterròs from the southwest.

Below him, the young shepherds too had spotted them. They leapt upon large boulders to point excitedly with shouts of, "Look! Look!" and "The Br'thain are headed to Anterròs!"

S'baladin closed his eyes with a smile and imagined he was riding amongst them, a great warrior. The wind swept softly over his dark brunette locks, caressing the sun-browned skin of his face. After a little while, a bout of coughs roused him, and he clutched at his ribs until it passed. Then, stretching his arms out wide, he released a deep, soulful sigh. *The desert, it gives people wonderful ideas!* he thought. *Great wisdom is borne of a dry and barren landscape.*

In this arid country of sagebrush and mountains, shepherds often slung a leather hide sack over their shoulder. Like his fellows, the young lad always carried goat cheese and round, flat, unleavened bread, but he also toted another sack, the contents of which only close friends and family were aware. The items within were of greater value to him than food.

Now, as the winds of inspiration blew through his soul, he reached into his special sack for a small bottle of ink and a wooden pen which he laid on the rocky ledge. Next, he pulled out a thick roll of weathered parchment.

He wiped at his runny nose with his sleeve as he rifled through its pages. Finally, he found a certain sheet that held his last writings, and a look of glee came over his ruddy face. He glanced down toward his sheep below, satisfied that they were safe, he dipped his pen and began to write.

It was the language of Y'darit which filled the page. He fancied its features of hooks, triple dots under certain characters and swirling majestic curves. Every time he wrote, he felt a delightful connection to the venerable history of this ancient script.

A garden was planted in the west which grew wild berries and sweet figs with plenty of orchards and vineyards of every kind. All manner of creatures rested underneath the shades of its trees. From everywhere, fowl came to perch on its branches. But in the north, wild beasts planted a dark garden of thorns and thistles that poisoned the minds of men. These wild beasts spread their wrath across fields and forests, over mountains and valleys, leaving desolation in their path. They attacked the numinous garden in the west, devouring its orchards and vineyards...

S'baladin imagined the gigantic workers, the Faeynül, of ancient times. Where the Sheddukem had birthed chaos, the Faeynül had spread only peace. He imagined one approaching, his head reaching the summit of the Yedara Mountains, his colossal countenance pleasant, friendly.

...The people will one day combine their strength again, becoming as one of the Faeynül. In their restored power, this new Faeynül will burst forth from deserts and glens to green fields and valleys. The colossal one will rise forth to drink from the Streams of Feynhava.

On impulse, he added: All these things must happen, when all will think hope dead, beginning with a small seed. He savored that last line until a voice called, "S'baladin! Where are you?"

Sparrows broke into flight from a nearby bush as T'balidor his older brother, and Sibrion, their eldest cousin, appeared on horseback from behind a massive boulder with a third lad. Though a cousin in name, in both his swarthy appearance and his closeness to T'balidor, he might well have been his brother. As they picked their way up the steep slope, they shouted once more, "S'baladin?"

In the heavy rustic drawl of the West, T'balidor gibed, "There he goes again! The dreamer! What are you writing about this time, brother? Dirt? The pungent odor of sheep?"

A roar of laughter erupted from the lads as S'baladin rolled his eyes in annoyance.

"Come, scholar! It is nearly dinner time."

The third lad dismounted. Ready for his evening watch, he was heavily armed with a bow, a short desert saber and a battle club. Over his shoulder hung a shepherd's flute and leather hide sack.

S'baladin nodded to him, then mounted the boy's horse to join T'balidor and Sibrion. In their descent toward the town of Anterròs, their younger cousins and friends similarly relieved others who pastured flocks along the slopes of the Yedara Mountains and joined them. They chattered about the Br'thain warriors, about the battles they too would someday wage.

S'baladin ignored them, his physical ailments prevented him from voicing such dreams. His silence did not go unnoticed. Abán, a lad near S'baladin's age nudged his horse over and spoke casually of their day, the flocks, the weather, and his eagerness to dine amongst the Br'thain. His chatter lightened the gangly youth's mood considerably.

On the valley floor, though the gentle light of dusk softened the appearance of tall cacti and the scraggles of sagebrush, nothing could soften their pricks. Expertly, the boys maneuvered their mounts. As their mountain path merged with the road to Anterròs, they came upon two young girls dressed in the robes and shawl known as the Guaddeca, riding on a mule toward town. The boys' eyes were drawn to their fair-skinned beauty and hazel, almond-shaped eyes.

"Good evening young ladies," bid T'balidor. "My name is T'balidor from Anterròs. Are you headed there also?"

They giggled and one shyly replied, "Good evening, sir, and no. We make for Vadenquas to visit our aunt."

Running his hand through his windswept dark locks, T'balidor raised an eyebrow. With a toothy grin he said, "Ah! Vadenquas!" He clutched his garment at his heart. "I once knew a girl from Vadenquas who broke my little heart!"

The two girls erupted in laughter.

Encouraged, T'balidor spoke to them again. "They sing ballads now of the string of broken hearts that she leaves bleeding! Have you heard of such a girl?"

When they shook their heads, Abán, grinned, drew his lyre from off his shoulder where it hung upon a leather strap and prodded T'balidor, "Go on then, sing it!"

The older lad needed no urging, he bellowed out to Abán's accompaniment:

> There was a lovely girl from Vadenquas.
>
> Her beauty dark her smile, glorious.
>
> In the Feast of Duenibas,
>
> when men gathered in wine.
>
> All hearts lay broken. Including mine.

They were rewarded with a peal of laughter from the girls.
"If you come across this girl, tell her that T'balidor still longs for her!" he said in mock bitterness.
"Very well. We shall tell her."
"If we find her," the girls tittered.
"Have a wonderful evening, young ladies," grinned Sibrion.
"Thank you," they responded in smiling chorus.
Such were the pleasantries exchanged by youth.
They moved beyond the girls to pass a series of watering holes where palm trees lent their shade to a caravan watering their beasts of burden. Beyond this was a large oasis where women filled leather sacks and crude ceramic jars of colorful designs. Children splashed happily in little pools nearby, their nakedness partly obscured by the evening shadows and the surrounding brush.
As they passed through Anterròs on their way home, merchants and vendors called out to the boys.
"T'balidor! How fares Baltien, your father?"
"See you at sundown!"
Finally, they reached the humble domain of the family of Baltien. Though he was a man of esteem across the West, his home was simple. With its patches of unrepaired straw and clay walls, thatched roof and brushy overgrowth, the old stone house resembled the fallen ruins of a fortress. Centuries ago, his wife's ancestors had ruled over Ferán, but her great-great grandfather was the last of these princes. With the fortune long spent and the title irrelevant, all that remained was the weathered estate.
Its grounds were extensive however, and these were unusually busy with activity tonight. Dark shadows stretched down the steep canyon walls and filled

the valley where they met the glow of several crackling fire pits. Children dodged each other's wooden swords, laughing as dogs frolicked with them. Women dressed in Guaddecas carried baskets of unleavened bread from the house, their robes swishing pleasantly as they passed. Another group of women, the shawls of their Guaddecas cast aside, prepared stews and meats over blazing pit fires. Meanwhile, other women rolled animal furs into tight bundles and set them aside for the Br'thain's upcoming mission. Several men, all clad in flowing Dolscarebs, loaded mules and horses with these furs, along with bundles of provisions and weapons. Their faces, darkened by the sun, spoke of the harshness of desert life.

The clang of swords turned S'baladin's head. He peered into the darkness along the edge of the crumbled wall to the arena and frowned. There, men and youth shuffled back and forth upon the sand, practicing nocturnal fighting skills. Never would S'baladin's own body allow such training, even in the light of day. He knew well from his many failed attempts that his skills lay elsewhere.

Beside the arena, in a far corner of their property, several blacksmiths toiled in his father's smithy to sharpen dozens of swords and replace the crystal tips of Ferusats. S'baladin's frown tipped upward at the pleasant sound of ancient Uraduin spoken over their work. Their ceremonial use of words and phrases evoked a supernal covering of protection over the use of these weapons. It was their language more than their work that wrought S'baladin's joy.

"Little brother, time for dinner!" T'balidor called.

His stomach growled in response and, along with T'balidor and Sibrion, he headed for the indoor kitchen. Just then, the beautiful, olive-skinned lady of the house, Kalanit, stepped outside, her body swayed to a graceful halt and uttered a stream of orders to the women in the yard. They moved hurriedly in response to her bidding. By rights, she should have been a princess. Though she bore no title save lady, she bore her body with the same regal bearing as her grandmothers before her.

Noticing the boys, Kalanit's softly rounded face lit up with a beaming smile. As her almond-shaped eyes noted S'baladin's slow pace toward her, they filled with concern. "How was your cough today?" she called out as she brushed back dark, gray locks against the cool wind, "Did you take your syrup?"

"Yes, mama, I took it. My cough was not as bad."

"Good!" she replied. "There is a hearty stew in the kitchen for you boys. And your papa wants to see you before he leaves. He has some news for you, unless your brother already spoiled it with his big mouth!"

"T'balidor told me nothing."

"No?" Kalanit looked skeptically at her eldest.

T'balidor shook his head and threw his hands up in mock surrender.

"Good. Your papa will give you the news."

"Yes, mama." Distracted by a familiar smell emanating from their home, he asked, "Did you make your delicious bread?"

"Yes, there is plenty for you and the boys. Hurry along." She waved them in and moved to oversee the other women.

They entered through the great room where, amongst a clutter of old maps, weapons, rolls of animal furs, and rustic wear of interwoven twigs, two dozen men stood in small groups around a long table, speaking earnestly. As always, whether the lowliest warrior, or their leaders such as these, the presence of any of the Br'thain - the brethren of clan warriors of the West - stirred in S'baladin a profound sense of awe and respect. These powerful and valiant men, their prowess in battle, and their storied history was the stuff of local legend. Tonight, the fervor of an impending battle filled the air with a palpable charge. The men greeted his brother and cousin with a respectful glance. But the gangly boy who coughed excessively was, for the most part, ignored.

In one corner, the boy saw the Ferusats leaning against the adobe walls. The Br'thain travelled with these special staffs, and their presence gave the boy a thrill.

The gangly youth covered a cough, which caused Baltien to looked up from the map he was poring over. "Bad cough today, S'baladin?" he asked. The men paused respectfully.

"I am fine, papa," S'baladin answered.

"The women have a veritable feast prepared. Have you eaten yet?"

"No, not yet. Mama said I should speak with you," he answered respectfully.

Tilting his head in the direction of the kitchen, Baltien said, "You boys go on now, eat. S'baladin, we will speak later." Then he turned his attention back to the conference. "Sir, we were discussing how many men to send through the first wave of attackers," a man reminded him.

S'baladin struggled to hide more coughs as he followed T'balidor and Sibrion into an open courtyard. They crossed it, passed through an archway of hanging red peppers, and entered the large adobe kitchen where poultry cutlets sizzled on a large skillet in a nest of garlic and onions. From a domed adobe oven just outside, the yeasty smell of unleavened bread mingled with the savory fragrance of the kitchen. Women chattered animatedly in Y'darit as they chopped cilantro, celery, spinach, and tomatoes.

The boys hurried to dip their hands thrice in a basin of water and dry them. They helped themselves to a steaming stack of unleavened bread onto which they ladled roasted vegetables and shredded poultry from a large pot atop a wood-burning stove.

They exited the kitchen to the yard and were greeted by several younger cousins and friends. "Come, we are going to try our new bow and arrow on a pack of coyotes outside! We heard their howls not far from here!" they exclaimed in excitement. Chuckling, T'balidor and Sibrion declined and made for the arena, but S'baladin followed them into the sagebrush. Grease ran down his fingers, dripping onto the sand as he savored every morsel of his mother's cooking.

In the deepening dark, the boy's missiles missed the coyotes. He left them to their howls and returned to the great room to lean against a wall and listen to their strategizing. After some time, the last of the men filed out of the room. Baltien embraced his son and kissed him on his forehead. "Where did you pasture our sheep today?"

S'baladin raised a finger upward. "Near the summit," he answered.

"Ah! Your favorite spot. That is good! There is excellent pasturing up there," his father smiled.

"When do you leave?" he asked his father.

"Midnight." Baltien frowned and began to fold the maps.

The boy's eyes fell upon an unfamiliar land and he cocked his head to the side.

Seeing his interest, his father offered, "This is the area of Va'Harot, a place of refuge designated by the Gardener. If any of our men should find himself separated in the fray, they are to flee to Va'Harot and hide deep underground until it is safe for our men to return and rescue him."

He waited patiently for his father to finish with the maps and speak.

Laying them aside Baltien sighed and turned to his youngest son. "It is time for Maleor, son."

"I am to try again?" S'baladin asked quietly.

The Maleor was a ceremony in which a young person earned validation with the community. To become a young woman, a girl proved themselves by their knowledge of the Streams of Feynhava, while young men demonstrated fighting skills.

His father sighed heavily. "For so long, this illness has plagued your body. The Fieradeem have agreed to allow T'balidor to be your sparring partner during your Maleor. The boys from Anterròs would not be so understanding of your ailment in the sparring arena."

S'baladin rolled his eyes in frustration. "You mean, he will let me win? Papa! You know I do not wish to prove myself before the Fieradeem."

"But the Maleor requires a show of strength!" Baltien retorted.

"Thrice have I honored my Maleor since I was twelve. Is not knowledge a strength? I would like to share my knowledge of the history of Y'cromeca to the Fieradeem that they will judge my worthiness by that, not by my physical strength, of which they well know I have none."

Baltien shrugged. While his son's plea rang true, he feared such an unprecedented request would never be accepted by his peers.

Seeing his son's despair, he softened his tone. "S'baladin, the men of the West are shepherds and rangers, farmers and metalsmiths. Everyone knows of your interest in writing. And it is a good thing. But a young man must prove his Maleor by demonstrating the skills of the Br'thain."

"Each time I have tried, the Fieradeem reject me for my weakness! And now you think a staged fight, an invalid's triumph over one of our best fighters, will satisfy tradition?" the lad's anger dissolved into coughs. He clapped one hand over his mouth, clutched at his ribs and sank into a chair.

"S'baladin, you are making yourself ill!"

But S'baladin, spurred on by his father's impending departure, could no longer hold his tongue. "I know that I am an embarrassment to you!" he fumed. "A disappointment to the great Baltien, leader of the Br'thain."

"Son!" The boys coughing fit cut short his father's rebuke. Forgiving his son's petulance, he said kindly, "While your ailment has been frustrating for you, for all of us, you are blameless. Your body is beyond your control, but you are strong of mind and heart. We Fieradeem do understand."

Baltien hesitated, and his eyes grew stormy. He rose and paced, attempting to calm himself. When he spoke again, his words tumbled out in a stream of rebuke. "There are other reasons why the Fieradeem did not accept you into the Br'thain. The leaders of Ferán have watched your company every time we gather for the Gardener's Feasts. Your friends from Rihován and Calasmorra have also been passed over many times in their Maleors. I have spoken often with the Fieradeem of your friends' wild and undisciplined constitutions. They are reckless, S'baladin, with such little regard for the Gardener's ways! Mind the old Ferán saying, 'Tell me whom you join with, and I will tell you who you are.'"

The gangly youth was quick to defend his friends. "You speak of Diero and Jubal? They are wild. I do not deny that. How could they not be? Diero was orphaned as an infant and suffers the abuse of a drunken master while Jubal knows poverty better than he will ever know his father! Where you and mama have schooled me in kindness, their hearts are genuinely good, noble even, despite their hard exteriors and poor decisions. I am proud to be their friend, Papa!"

Baltien shrugged. The two sat for a moment, and the tension between them slowly diffused.

Finally, S'baladin cleared his throat and asked quietly, "Could you ask the Gardener? When he comes during his next feast? Perhaps he might have something to say in this matter," urged S'baladin.

Baltien's eyebrows raised at this suggestion and its wisdom. "Very well, when the Gardener appears for his next feast, I shall consult with him."

S'baladin nodded his thanks and bid his father farewell and luck in battle. Kalanit moved softly forward from the shadows just beyond the door as he departed for his bedchamber.

"Are the men ready and packed for the morn?" she asked quietly. Her husband nodded absently, his eyes upon his son's departing figure.

"I will miss you, and T'balidor."

He laughed then, turning to her with twinkling eyes, "You will be sleeping, my love!"

"I certainly will not!" came her quick response.

Softening, he took her into an embrace and whispered, "Our first two missions went perfectly, not a single injury! I have every reason to believe this will go the same."

She pulled back, her gaze skeptical, then changed the subject, "How was your talk with S'baladin?"

"I am less confident there," he admitted.

"Indeed, he has much of your stubbornness," Kalanit laughed.

Her husband chuckled, then grew thoughtful. "Despite his frailty, he has a strength I do not."

"His failings burden him with grief. At times, it overwhelms him. He tells me this often."

Baltien nodded and a heaviness came upon. "I want him to be a part of the Br'thain, but he can never do what we do in the Va'Giyyel. I sometimes wish even T'balidor had never joined us. I have seen things there that rob a man's soul of the purity of life. T'balidor too is burdened."

"I see a darkness in his eyes sometimes. The boy in him is gone," Kalanit agreed. Her eyes misting, she whispered, "I wish neither of our children suffered as they do."

They sat, hand in hand, silently awaiting Baltien's departure, the room shadowed by gloom and tears.

The Caethain Ascent

IN THE NORTHERNMOST DISTRICT OF HIERUNDIA, STRANGE CLOUDS mushroomed along the southwest horizon of Caethain. It was the month of Zeccul of the Thaed-Rú calendar, and moonlit snow fell upon the Scions of the Fortress City. The boys were at the end of their spell of labor. Across the building sites from many pipes rang strange melodious tones for several minutes. The young slaves paused to listen. Their breathing slowed, the aggression of their working state was pacified. Their moods grew melancholy, it was time to rest and repair their bodies.

As D'thalien Khalevad's group of weary laborers made their way down the slope of the mountain, an ominous sight drew their eyes upward. "Look at that!" cried a boy near him.

Their tones grew hushed and low as they murmured nervously.

"Odd how quickly that storm is moving."

"Those clouds seem…different."

"Does that lightning seem more blue than white to you?"

The Bal Rú's alchemists and scientists still toiled in the nefarious experiments of the Cethin Arda, which shook the land from time to time. As it often did, a low rumbling of the ground rolled now beneath the child slaves. It grew to a loud and heavy vibration, rattling everything for leagues away.

Within the barracks, D'thalien was restless. He paced the room, peeping through chinks in the wall at the storm, but his peers did not. These were the effects of the Cethin Arda's Necropulpa plant, which they were still forced to ingest. The slaves were always listless at labor's end. Although all forms of recreation and entertainment were available and readily used by the Rhünkai, the boys had no desire for entertainment, creativity, or competition. Those who did not immediately seek rest in their bunks stood in groups, with little or no communication at all. Some stared into space, heaving quietly, as a tired dog would. They joined in one collective effort during their nocturnal work, yet individually, they were soulless components.

Only once had D'thalien tried to approach a boy in conversation. He merely asked his name, but the boy's heaving breath intensified. Slowly he turned to address D'thalien, but despite an answer lurking in his eyes, only a low, guttural growl came through a grimace of bared teeth. Fearing a physical attack, D'thalien resolved to speak to no one. But sometimes, like today, he studied their curious faces. Their deathly pallor fascinated him. It gave them an eerie glow in the darkness, accented by their balding heads.

Weeks ago, breaking away the ice from a trough to seek refreshment, D'thalien had gawked at his own visage, completely unaltered by the Necropulpa plant. The faces of the others had paled, their eye sockets darkened. D'thalien, fearing detection or punishment, took to lowering his face, averting his eyes.

The physical stamina of the slaves was heightened too, and sleep fell heavily upon them during the day. D'thalien's training with his father and his brother, and their time on the run from the Rhünkai equipped him well to fall in with these habits, though the Necropulpa plant afforded him no added strength.

The lightning storm crested the mountain. Its flares bit through the trees and gleamed upon the bars of a caravan preparing for departure. A palpable wave of tension assailed the caravan's patrols. White knuckles gripped at lances and crossbows. Eyes twitched nervously, scanning the snowy ground. The men lifted their heads to scan the tops of frosted trees and tall, icy brush. Highly trained as they were, nothing prepared them for the terrible sense of foreboding wrought by this unnatural storm.

The barrack's guards gathered at the doorway and murmured nervously amongst themselves. One covered his mouth to conceal his concerns from the children, not because they were children but because they were captive.

Less than a league away, from the base of the towering mountain, ranks of children approached. They passed within mere feet of where a man crouched hidden amongst the undergrowth, in Rhünkai disguise. From behind the trees, Graeyba observed the activities as he had done every night for weeks, desperate for a glimpse of his sons. He rubbed at his injured eye, adjusting his patch. The extreme Caethain frost had stalled the healing process. He glanced uneasily at the storm gathering above and considered seeking shelter.

As the storm thickened, the darkness roused the child slaves. Noticing the clouds, they slowed and spoke amongst themselves, pointing upward.

"Fall into place, you vermin! Be Quiet! Move forward!" soldiers sharply ordered them into formation.

Placidly, hundreds of boys complied. But for the effect of the Necropulpa plant, their marching would have been a grim shuffle. It had been another night of breaking their backs, of scraping the flesh off one's knuckles against perpetual stonework, of perspiration burning their cuts, of aching sores and bruises. It was the requirement of the Bal Rú, their newly proclaimed father. There was no absolution in sight.

Despite this, the ranks of boys and young men trod along in neat formation, stomping thick furrows through the open field of snow as they marched toward the depot. Countless soldiers, heavily armed, cautiously shuffled backward as small electrical currents hummed in the snow around their feet.

The ringing of a hammer upon iron rent the morning air. Accompanying it was the deep thudding of a stake bearing into the ground. The soldiers paused at the unfamiliar sounds and several drew their weapons. The humming slowly rose to envelope the depot in a roar. Soldiers and slaves alike stood as frozen as the snow. At the blaring of a horn, panic entered everyone's veins. It seized their throats like sharp poison. Amongst a thousand men, there was a sudden, fearful silence.

Into this silence crackled a fierce bolt of lightning. An intense heat emanated from where it struck the ground with a thunderous boom. The steaming, snowy ground gave way to a depression in the earth. It stretched to a radius of about five feet. Curious, the soldier nearest the strike edged forward, then drew back rapidly, fighting clumsily against the slush of melting snow.

Great horror wreathed his face as an explosive mound of dirt and snow rose from the depression. A set of horns atop a beastly head with bony protrusions and long quills sprang upward. Though he moved to shield his face with his arms, millions of tiny dirt clods, snow, and twigs bit into his flesh. A flash of rippling azure light filled the air and rose about the creature to form a dome around the strike.

A rapid series of similar terrestrial explosions flared between trees and across the snowy fields by the thousands. With momentous speed, terrifying horned beasts sprang forth, each thick body ascending from an individual explosion. Dark, brownish fur and bony protrusions and quills lent natural armor to their backs. As the currents of these explosions faded, the frightened slaves and soldiers gazed upon the vastness of the army. Then, they clutched at their ears in unison as a chorus of otherworldly howls of rage assailed them.

So frozen were the Rhünkai in their fear, they were struck down with razor-sharp talons before they realized the creatures had moved. In bi-pedal locomotion, the beasts moved rapidly through the ranks of men. Soldiers were sent hurling into the air from the blows of powerful, furry arms. The creatures released deadly volleys of quills from their backs into the faces, chests and backs of hundreds more.

Blood splattered the snow, melting the snow and pooling into rivers of pink. Panicked screams filled the air. Children cowered, screaming in terror as older slaves and soldiers ran for their lives. Accustomed as Graeyba was to scanning the slaves for his sons, the sweep of his searching eye grew panicked. He fell to his belly, crawling through the icy slush of snow, edging closer to the depot.

The Rhünkai armor seemed no match for the creatures whose great hairy arms bludgeoned them to death. Professional soldiers, many of them trained since birth, and all well-seasoned in battle, they fell like peasants. Violence had been their tool to breed hate and discontent in the weak, to sow the seeds of fear of their very uniform throughout the populace. But now, their screams of terror far surpassed the wails of the countless victims they had mercilessly violated. As he neared the battle scene, despite his fears for the safety of the children, Graeyba's lips twitched upwards in a sick grin. Though the creatures were truly terrifying, he felt a deep satisfaction in the terror of the troops whose habit it was to misuse children so.

A squawking sound preceded the crunch of bone, the thud of bodies. It was the muffling of a young bugler squad's nervous call. Their trembling lips had clamped bravely about their trumpets, but a bloody strike from one horned beast truncated it, and their lives, abruptly. Everywhere, from just a single-handed swoop, clusters of five to ten soldiers collapsed lifelessly in a swift and powerful assault.

The air was full of beastly howls, screams of agony, and blood. Yet, somehow, Graeyba found the strength to gather himself, chest heaving against his cloak, and continue his crawl toward the bloody carnage.

Though time stretched interminably, it had only been a minute or so of mass confusion. Yet, another series of terrestrial explosions and blinding flashes of light suddenly rippled on all sides. As the first group of creatures continued striking down soldiers, a new group ascended from the ground. The shrill screams of frightened children rose above screams of agony as this new army, their missions differing from the first, grabbed at them. Dozens of these creatures were massive enough to swoop up a pair of wriggling children.

Each of the beasts in this second wave of creatures, children firmly tucked under their arms, rapidly produced an odd-looking stick, a staff or club of some sort. These they drove in a sudden strike into the ground. Instantly, multiple explosions of dirt and snow, followed by a blast of light erupted with the impact. Hundreds of explosions swallowed up the creatures and children.

As they disappeared, a forlorn Graeyba rose from his prone position to his knees to gape in dismay. Utterly forlorn, his quest a failure, he awaited the swift death promised by the horned beasts. About fifty yards away, one of the children not yet captured ran toward him, yelling indiscernible words. Graeyba stumbled instinctively upward to aid the child as best he could. As the boy neared, Graeyba made out the words, "Papa! Papa! It is you?"

Graeyba's eyes grew large. "D'thalien!" he shouted at the top of his lungs. He slushed through the mire of blood and snow and mud between them. But a furry arm came between them, yanking D'thalien high into the air to pin him against his massive frame.

"No!" yelled Graeyba. He lunged forward, seizing its muscular hind leg as the creature drove his staff into the ground. Instantly the three of them disappeared in a blinding flash of light.

The first wave of beasts continued to butcher what remained of the troops. When the last of the soldiers fell, just as the second wave had done, they drove their staffs into the ground and disappeared. The lightning and clouds receded as the rippled electrical currents faded. Into the dark silence left behind rose the groans of a handful of survivors. Each of them carved their outlines into the snow, squirming in maddening agony from quills embedded in their flesh.

From the dense forest floor, a dozen figures, hitherto camouflaged into the environment, crawled forth to survey the bloody massacre. One of them removed a long metal spike from the soil. At its center gleamed a blue crystalline blade.

Approaching shouts of more soldiers rang out among the trees. Apparently, the brave buglers' brief call had been enough to rouse support. The figures stole away with the metal spike, merging invisibly into the pines. On the edge of the forest, a cluster of weeds in the snow suddenly became animated. It too crept away unseen.

Gloom Over Realmhold Thaed-Rú

The howl of a frosted wind greeted six royal carriages as they rolled through the tall, oaken gates of Dul-Meggor. A large, mounted force, the Thaed-Rú Dominion's elite guard, accompanied them in snow-covered furs. Deserted, but for a small contingency of soldiers on patrol, the depot was strangely quiet.

Íraban, Teosifan and several Guild members emerged from their carriages. Thinking of them as his children, Íraban believed he must personally and regularly inspect the living conditions of the Scions. These visits served his advisors well to ensure the Thaed-Rú machine was well oiled and working smoothly.

They were welcomed into the housing barracks by Doctor Tirzheul and his medical staff. At the precise moment the doors closed behind them, they belched open again with a gust of icy wind as an officer burst through them. "Doctor Tirzheul," he cried out, then froze at the sight of Íraban. Kneeling he said, "We have terrible news from the Fortress City! Last night there was another attack on our soldiers and your Scions. This time, there were but eight survivors, all gravely injured."

"Take me to them!" ordered Íraban. His entourage hurried after him as he whirled out of the barracks and across the windswept compound. Screams of pain and misery met their ears as they passed into a medical building of stone and thick rusted metal walls. A flurry of attendants and soldiers paused momentarily to bow before the Bal Rú, then continued with their attempts to save the survivors. From deep gashes across their faces, their necks, and their backs, blood had saturated the tables, pooled on the stone floor, splattered the attendants' aprons. From glazed eyes, tears streamed down the faces of the wounded.

Íraban approached. Expressionless behind his mask, he frowned at their delirium.

A soldier cried out "Sound the alarm!" and pointed past the foot of his bed, past the attendants while another peered in the opposite directions, whispering anxiously, "I see their horns behind the bushes!"

Several attendants worked to remove dented armor from another raving soldier, gasping shallowly as though he were drowning. They glanced at each other in despair as his breastplate sprang free to reveal a sunken chest and collapsed lung. Beyond him, another attendant busily applied pincers to quill after quill, removing them from a soldier's back, chest and face.

Íraban's gaze fell upon a pool of blood beneath the soldier nearest him. He sighed deeply and moved on to the next one. Upon the farthest table, he found a soldier with wounds less grave who appeared less frantic than the others. Taking up the soldier's face in his palms, Íraban studied the agony in his fearful eyes. In silent concentration, he used his innate powers of mental persuasion to pacify the man.

"Soldier, tell me! What did you see out there?"

The man momentarily adjusted his attention on the mesmerizing eyes behind the ornate mask, but his concentration broke, and his head lolled back and forth as he moaned, "The creatures! They disappeared. Do any yet remain?"

Íraban tightened his grip, intensified his gaze. "Listen to me! You are safe now. There are no more creatures. They are withdrawn. Now tell me, what happened at the Fortress City?"

The soldier's chest heaved with deep gulps of breath between sentences. "We...were about to descend...the mountain with the children. We heard the sound of...hammer on metal...A sudden, blinding flash of light...i-i-it came up...from the ground!" The soldier paused. Whether his delirium was dissipating under the Bal Rú's mental powers or he merely needed to catch his breath was difficult to distinguish.

"Tell me soldier! What happened next?" asked Íraban.

"Lightning bolts! Flashes!"

No one understoodnd the import of his words.

"But the creatures?" pressed Íraban.

"They came...in flashes of light..."

"From the ground?"

The soldier stared into the depths of dark ceiling above, labored for breath, then nodded.

"How many more flashes came up from the ground? Ten? Twenty?" pressed Íraban.

"Too many."

"Hundreds?"

The soldier nodded again. "An army."

"What happened next?" Íraban pressed.

The soldier's eyes darted back and forth, accessing more information. His face contorted in fear and he stuttered, "T-The-Then...they came up out of the ground...the lot of them!" Here, the soldier began to hyperventilate. "They...came...out...of...th...ground..." Tears began to stream from his eyes, and he sobbed.

Íraban leaned closer, the man's face still in his hands. Through his tears, the soldier responded to his ruler's dark influence. "They tore us apart, ripped at our flesh, hurled us in the air..." The soldier shook violently, crying again. He stammered, his words dissolving into tears.

Íraban grabbed the soldier's shoulders. "Who were they?" he demanded.

"No!" the soldier grunted. "N-No! No! Not people. Terrible creatures...wild beasts with horns!"

Íraban frowned and stepped back from the man to pace about his bed. "Are you certain they were not simply men wearing horns?" he prodded.

The soldier studied the ceiling again as if sifting through the images of battle, searching for reality. Stubbornly, he repeated. "Wild beasts...with horns...T-They were larger than a man! Fur all over! And horns...protruding from their skulls...their shoulders...their backs!"

Teosifan's leathery face framed by gray hair brooded over the tormented soldier. Teosifan and the others glanced fearfully at their Bal Rú.

An urgency charged Íraban's voice as he asked, "Did they carry weapons?"

"Claws and fangs...claws and fangs." The soldier's wild panic returned and again he hyperventilated as he spoke. "They ripped the soldiers apart! The agony...we were helpless...and the slaves..." the soldier trailed off.

Íraban's thin frame stiffened. "Exactly what did they do with the children? Did they kill any of them?"

With effort, the man composed himself, caught his breath, and shook his head. "No! Not even one! They seized them... and...and...took them back into the ground." The soldier frowned, struggling to understand his strange experience. Then he muttered, "I remember no more." A deep shuddering sigh escaped his lips as he passed into the shadows. An attendant gently closed his eyes, frozen forever in a glaze of hopelessness.

Íraban released him roughly with a grunt. Behind him, the doctor, Teosifan and the others stood in stunned silence. With heads bent in deference, medical attendants removed his lifeless body.

The officer who had summoned Íraban and his royal entourage stepped forward. "Bal Rú, our people are still determining our casualties, but we estimate—."

"You estimate?" Íraban interjected. "You heard the man! He said there were only a few hundred of these beasts. How many of ours did they kill?"

The officer hesitantly offered, "My Bal Rú, thousands of our soldiers are dead."

Íraban's eyes narrowed. Tension filled the air.

"And what of my Scions?"

The officer's eyes grew large with fright as he inhaled nervously. "My Bal Rú, we estimate the number of missing Scions in the thousands as well."

Although his eyes flared hatred, Íraban's hand flew absently, fearfully to grip the hilt of his sword. He whirled upon Teosifan. "How long have these phantoms been sequestering my Scions?"

"Over many years," answered Teosifan.

Red-hot anger boiled inside Íraban. "Many years?"

Teosifan's long and skeletal face paled. "But only in three attacks, spread out," he rushed to explain.

"I see. And, per attack, what are the casualty totals?"

"Accounts vary, but they increased each time. At first it was a hundred or so of the scions with approximately three hundred soldiers slain. The next attack doubled those numbers. The third time, the casualties were thrice the first," answered Teosifan.

"And now this fourth attack..." muttered Íraban. "Everyone out, except Teosifan," said Íraban. The attendants hesitated, glancing at their groaning wards.

"But the soldiers," Doctor Tirzheul urged quietly.

Íraban glared at him and screamed in anger, "They are useless! I said leave!"

Fearfully, the doctor and his staff fled the room.

Edging closer to the Bal Rú, Teosifan pointed out, "We never had witnesses till now. Now we know our enemy!"

"Do we?" Íraban balked. "Even with this soldier's account, no one really knows what they are!"

Teosifan pursed his lips and fell silent.

Íraban crossed thin arms across his chest and queried. "How are we to conquer creatures from another world who appear, vex us, plunder my Scions, and disappear?"

Both men turned troubled eyes upon the groaning wounded. Sighing deeply, Íraban relented, "Go, fetch the doctor. Perhaps there's more to learn from these men yet."

Toward evening, the remaining seven survivors, quills removed, and gashes ministered to, began to show signs of improvement. The young Bal Rú returned to interview them. They bore the same witness as their fellow: their enemy was not of human form. Each man told of quills and horns of furry arms snatching children, thumping mysterious clubs of terrifying figures disappearing under domes of rippling light. But why they stole the Scions was a great mystery to all.

A waning moon shone weakly on six royal carriages groaning their retreat to Kiérbangaal that night. Within them the inspection committee murmured amongst themselves, wondering at the implications of the attack. "Do they use the children for ritual sacrifice?" "Do they devour them as food?" "Perhaps they too will use them as slaves."

In his private carriage, Íraban's thoughts swam in utter frustration. He wondered if the unusual creatures were products of his own dark garden. Perhaps the Cethin Arda had opened a portal for their entry to this world.

In the capital, the young Bal Rú withdrew, restless and depleted of energy, to his private chambers. He drew his curtains tightly and flung himself upon his bed. Not only did attacks from these phantom beasts threaten his ambitious building project, but the loss of lives also meant the loss of an immense sum of revenue. Any more of these attacks and the economy of Y'cromeca would suffer. What vexed him most was the mysterious nature of these creatures. In a mood as icy as the bleak cold winds which whipped Realmhold Thaed-Rú, Íraban sulked for days, descending from moodiness to utter drunkenness.

We Thaed-Rú are slowly falling away. This world, which we have gathered, is slipping from our hold the haunting words of his father came to him in his stupor. The only strength and direction for the young Bal Rú – the balm that young men require for indecision and frustration – came in the form of dark and bitter memories from beyond the grave. His heart led him from the truths of his father's teachings to the pain of his venom. *A Thaed-Rú is always alert and mindful of his surroundings! But you are playful, curious, vain! Change or you will lose your place in history. Change lest you be remembered as the last of the Bal Rús, a careless ruler!*

"I will not lose my place in history!" Íraban fumed and drank still more. Hatred ran like poison through his feverish veins. Alone, drunk, the days and the nights became a blur. His only solace, a twisted one at that, was the memory of his father's assassination.

"I showed you, did I not? I will prove to you that I have changed, that I can hold this world together!" He shook a tight first heavenward. But how was he to defeat an unknown enemy with unknown aims? "My scientists and engineers are on the brink of this discovery while these wretched creatures continue to interrupt my plans!" he raved.

But in the meantime, he well knew the attacks would escalate. As he sank further into despair, his shaking hand was barely able to pour more wine from his crystal carafes. In the darkness, it ran over his chalice. A rich ruby stain spread on the table as the blood of his soldiers had spread in the snow.

So it was that Íraban, after many days of seclusion, did only what he knew to do with the mask of a Bal Rú. As winter passed into a chill spring, it was the people who felt the burden of the phantoms' raid. The wholesale purchase of child slaves grew to an unprecedented level, ripping families apart. Cities fell to ruin and the people became restless. Across the hinterlands of the Eleven Provinces, Y'cromeca plunged deeper into protests and revolts.

The Rhünkai Archers, their greatest champion still found in Aidan Khalevad, fell into a cycle of constant action. Swift destruction came to all who opposed the Royal Edict of the Scions of Íraban. But the Bal Rú Íraban cared little for how his subjects reacted. After all, Theragad had constantly reminded him as a young lad, "The Thaed-Rú carry scars. We all do. It is part of who we are."

Threshold at Duin Caeir

Near Messidia, where once the council halls of the Faeynül giants towered thousands of years ago, lay the great stone ruins of Duin Caeir of Rihovàn. All that remained of Duin Caeir now, was a wide field of massive stone blocks, tightly packed, the length of one league in all directions. A single jagged crevice the width of several inches ran across the center of this stone field from east to west.

Ferán, Rihován and Calasmorra, these three regions comprise the land of the West where the Ballai still stands. And from these regions, as morning dawned, mothers, wives, and sisters gathered around the perimeter of the ruins of Duin Caeir. A hum of anticipation moved throughout the crowd as they awaited the return of their faithful and valiant, those who fought for the weak and the oppressed. The women and elderly sat upon rows of stone steps that once served as the seats of the colossal ones. Behind them, children ran about, their mothers and sisters calling stern warnings to them, "Keep to the grass!" "Stay off the stone field!"

They need not have worried as hundreds of clan warriors kept the expansive stone floor clear of any wanderers whether child or curious adult. All complied respectfully as even the children were well aware the stone field would become a hotbed of dangerous activity.

The clang of iron rang as a gentleman in a light gray Dolscareb hammered a strange metal pin, a light blue crystal embedded in its mid-section, into the stone floor. Murmurs of "The gatekeeper!" rippled through the crowd and they fell silent.

Like Baltien, the gatekeeper was a Fieradin, a leader well-schooled in the Gardener's wisdom. His Preceptan, a Fieradin in training, approached. Pushing back his deep brown Dolscareb, he knelt nearby and watched as the gatekeeper placed his ear upon a large iron cylinder the length of one cubit embedded into the stone floor. The man was skilled in reading how many people were coming through the Streams at one time, based upon the sound coming through the large, iron cylinder. If the sound generated a heavy and low hum, this indicated a thousand souls or more were travelling through the Streams. If the sound produced a high pitch ring, he determined that under twenty people were about to appear through the stone foundation. If one or two people came through, there would be no sound, for very little energy was used to carry them through.

The gatekeeper's eyes widened as a distant rumbling emanated from the stone floor. "I hear it! There are thousands of them" he cried in Y'darit to the clan warriors. Rapidly they moved to form a tight formation around the edges of the stone field.

The distant rumbling became a tangible humming vibration felt by all who stood or sat upon the stone field. His ear still pressed to the cylinder, the gatekeeper called, "Here they come!" He and his Preceptan rose and made for the edge of the field with calls of "Stand ready!"

Seventy clan warriors blew their ram's horns in response. The crowd began to cheer and shout. As the echoes of their mighty chorus faded, hundreds upon hundreds of bursts of azure lightning set the stone field aglow. The warriors shoved the horns into their belts and gripped the hilts of their swords.

The same army that had devastated the forces of the Fortress City arrived in the order in which they had left. Out of each burst of light, a creature ascended from the stone floor with children in their arms. A wild wave of shouts swept the crowd.

Released by their captors, most of the children ran in fear, but some stood as if paralyzed. The tight hedge of clan warriors prevented the runners from going any further than the edge of the massive stone field. The children turned in panic, fearful eyes scanning the crowd. But everywhere, friendly faces of men, women, and children greeted them with smiles and joyful applause. Clan warriors and creatures alike were quick to reassure each of them. They knelt to greet them in Hierundiel saying, "Son! Do not fret!" and "Children, you are safe now!"

As the children looked upon their captors in horror, the creatures removed their beastly heads to reveal sun- tanned faces of men within their blood-stained furry disguises. Hearty smiles and twinkling eyes turned kindly down upon astounded children and they offered reassuring words. The poor souls were incredulous. One moment they had cowered amongst calamity and chaos, the next they had entered a strange field of stone where wild beasts turned into kindly men, all surrounded by the fervor of a wild, ecstatic crowd.

As each little dome of light faded, the crowd descended onto the stone field in a rush. Eager eyes searched for sons, brothers, cousins. Among these, Kalanit struggled through the crowd, scanning for familiar faces. She stumbled over a lone boy. In the sea of legs around him, he babbled tearfully, "Where am I? What is this place?"

Kalanit, remembering her sons as small boys, was moved by his fear. She paused to take each of his cheeks into her palms. "Hush now, hush. You are safe. You have been through a terrible ordeal. But you have been rescued! You will begin a new life here, in the Ballai of the West!"

He quieted a bit, his wails dissolving into sniffles. Kalanit smiled encouragingly at him and turned back to her search. Just then, the shouts of a clan warrior rang an alarm in Y'darit. "A Rhünkai!"

Instinctively, Kalanit clutched the boy to her, then whirled to face the hiss of swords drawn from leather sheaths. The crowd shrank away from the soldier. He was on his knees, clutching a lad.

"Release the boy!" called nearby clan warriors as they ran toward him.

"Wait!" came a shout. Baltien stepped forward from the crowd, at his side was T'balidor. The boy tugged to free himself, his experiences with the Rhünkai was enough to send him dashing away into the crowd. Relief flooding away her tension, Kalanit smiled brightly and released the boy who dashed away into the crowd. With Baltien nearby, a single Rhünkai was nothing to fear.

"Weapons down!" urged Baltien. Respectfully, the men complied.

"D'thalien! Oh, my D'thalien!" the Rhünkai sobbed.

Tears streamed down the lad's face also. "Papa! I knew you would return! I just knew it! Many times, my mind had doubts, but my heart never failed to believe!" The boy frowned and asked, "But papa, why are you dressed like a Rhünkai?"

"It was just a disguise son, just a means by which to find you," his father explained.

Baltien smiled at that. Still clad in his own disguise, he stepped closer and tapped the stranger on the shoulder with his staff.

The man glanced tearfully upward. Removing his mask, Baltien asked in Hierundiel, "How did you enter the Streams?"

But it was T'balidor who answered, "Papa, Just as I entered the Streams with the boy, this man leaped forward and clung to my leg."

Baltien and the others stared down at him incredulously. "And this boy is your son?" he asked.

"Ay!" choked the man through his tears. Yet still he remained, kneeling, gazing in wonder at the face of his son. He caressed his child's shaved head tenderly and wiped at the boy's joyful tears, murmuring words of comfort. After a moment more, he explained. "Both my sons were taken from me during a Rhünkai ambush. Left for dead, I was found by…by wild creatures that nursed me back to life. I have searched for many months for my sons."

By now a large crowd was pushing forward, each of them peering at the stranger. Never had any man from beyond the Ballai of the West entered their lands through the streams. Only young men and boys were brought into their world through the Streams, and only as they were chosen by a Br'thain.

Father and son stood and scanned their surroundings. "Where are we? What is the name of this place?" the man asked.

"This is the Ballai of the West. These ancient stones on which we stand are the ruins of Duin Caeir in the land of Rihovàn," answered T'balidor.

"Ay, and I am Baltien, a Fieradin from Anterròs in the southern land of Ferán." With a hearty grin he asked, "What is your name, friend?"

"Graeyba Khalevad. And this is my son, D'thalien."

"I am eternally grateful for this rescue! What you and your men do is valiant…it…it is beyond description."

Baltien and Graeyba embraced in a potent salutation.

All around them, emotion charged the air as people continued attending the newly arrived children. Scores of clan warriors divided the boys into smaller groups and began an inventory of the rescued. Baltien received this report and made for a high ledge above the stone floor where all could see them. Moments later, Baltien gathered his family, along with Graeyba, D'thalien and several of his captains about him.

"Numinous is the Gardener! Infinite are the Streams of Feynhava!" Baltien shouted in the ancient tongue of Uraduin. He raised his staff victoriously to a chorus of enthusiastic cheers. Next, Baltien spoke in Hierundiel to the rescued children. "We began this undertaking years ago, our first operation saving a dozen children. But, with each new mission, our success swells and, today, you are our greatest number! Today, there are thousands of souls with us!"

Graeyba was surprised how fluent Hierundiel was in this distant land. He also marveled at the darkness of the skin of the crowd, as all he had ever seen was the fair skin of the north and the pale skin of the Thaed- Rú.

The crowd sprang to life. Children were hugged, tossed into the air, and pulled around in gleeful dancing. Finally understanding that they were truly free of the harsh edict, the children laughed and giggled. Kalanit seized T'balidor in a fierce hug, he smiled and lifted her off the ground in a whirl. Both chuckled as she yelped, "Set me down!"

"Where is S'baladin?" T'balidor peered around her, eager to greet his brother.

Kalanit shook her head, her smile vanishing. "He was too ill today to greet you here. Wisely, he rests at home, saving his energy for the feast."

T'balidor lost much of his joy at this. He pressed his lips together in a thin line of worry.

The crowd about them hushed as well as Baltien held up a hand. "I have more good news to share!" he declared. "Never has a man crossed through the Streams by his own will. They are powerful, dangerous, and can alter a man's mind and body if his heart be not true. But today, as fate would have it, a father, reunited with his son the moment we slipped into the Streams, has made the journey safely! Graeyba Khalevad he is, and his son D'thalien."

Baltien extended his hand to summon the smiling father and son. The shouts, cheers and praises ensued again. T'balidor and the captains clapped them on their backs as they passed.

Baltien concluded his speech. "Now we will take you children to your homes. You will be cared for in the colonies of the Didderäsh Mountains."

On the edge of the stone ruins, the number of rescued children far outnumbered the waiting wagons. But they trotted merrily alongside the wagons, peering about them and giggling as the warm desert sands shifted beneath their wriggling toes. Those who boarded the wagons were delighted at the sight of long wooden flatbeds softened by sweet smelling straw and hay. Giggling they lay comfortably on their backs, closing their eyes to the bright, warm sun, a novelty to them. Graeyba's heart warmed at the sight, no more would these children be carted about in barren wagons barely fit to cage a beast.

Many clan warriors, their wives and daughters chaperoned these wagons with pitchers of water and tin cups. Chattering amicably with the children, they offered the lads peculiar fruits from the Garden of Ages. As they consumed its juicy flesh, the hollow deformities on their faces filled and began to heal.

Young D'thalien watched in wonder and relief. Eagerly, he pointed to them. "Look at their faces, father! The fruits are healing them!" Graeyba shook his head in disbelief at their transformation. "But...how...?" he stuttered.

Hearty laughter rang out beside him and Baltien reigned in his horse to match the steps of theirs. "They are the fruits of the Garden of Ages, a gift from the Gardener," he said simply.

The Khalevads turned to him, puzzled.

Baltien only laughed and said shortly, "You will soon learn. One cannot be long in the West without learning of our Gardener." Cheerfully, he added, "You may even meet him. Our greatest feast day fast approaches."

Before they could ask more explanation, they crested a large hill, and their senses were assaulted by the delightful aroma of citrus fruits hung romantically in the air. All about them, children gasped as they beheld a vast valley floor of crops and orchards.

As the caravan traversed the road to Didderäsh, workers in fields and orchards stopped their toil to gape at the massive caravan passing through. Some were natives, but most were young men from Y'cromeca, rescued by the clan warriors a year or two ago and helping now to feed the burgeoning population of rescued children. A great many of them crowded by the edge of the dirt road waving and shouting greetings in Hierundiel.

From his shared mount with D'thalien, Graeyba asked of Baltien, "How much further will we travel, friend?"

"Within the hour." Baltien pointed toward the western rising of the sun, "See that range of high mountains? Those are the Didderäsh. There are many large caves deep inside where we have fashioned numerous camps for the children."

"How many live there?" asked Graeyba.

A smile flashed across Baltien's face. "Many more than you would expect, my friend. And every few weeks, we discover more caves further below. The children enjoy living there, and so will you."

Relief flooded Graeyba's countenance, the Khalevads had once, indeed lived happily in a cave, hiding from the Rhünkai. Warmly, he patted his son's thigh with fatherly affection, a rush of gratefulness welling within for this unexpected reunion with his D'thalien. Yet a heavy gloom shared the same room in his heart for Aidan.

Beside him, Baltien frowned, "Does something trouble you, friend?"

"Aye," said Graeyba. It is a joy to see my youngest son once more, yet my eldest remains in the north."

"Ah," said Baltien. "I have two sons also." He frowned and added, "And I worry for one as well."

"Worry?" Graeyba asked.

"My eldest, T'balidor serves in our cause with the Br'thain, but my youngest has battled illness all his life."

"It sorrows me to hear that. I too, have been burdened by the illness of a loved one." Proudly, Graeyba added, "Like T'balidor, my eldest, Aidan, is greatly skilled in martial arts as well." Then muttered darkly, "Skills the Rhünkai are likely using to their benefit."

"You speak of your sons, but what of your wife?" Baltien asked curiously, his eyes following Kalanit as she offered water to the lads.

"It was of she I just spoke," Graeyba explained. "I lost her to consumption a few winters ago. Sometimes I blame the Rhünkai for her death, driving us into the cold as they did," he added, eyes smoldering.

"I am sorry to hear of this loss," Baltien offered.

The men fell silent as images of wracking coughs plaguing the bodies of their loved ones consumed their minds.

Before them, a dry riverbed cut a ravine a quarter of a league wide at the base of steep canyon walls. Humming swarms of flies and gnats sought the moisture in their eyes and the flesh of their food as they passed through it. Soon after, they arrived at the base of a sloping hill that took them three leagues up the side of the Didderäsh, through a maze of monstrous boulders, to a yawning mouth. Beyond, a precipitous path wound down into the darkness of the caves.

Mystified, the boys murmured amongst each other, then laughed as their voices echoed off the high cavernous ceiling. A long row of torches marked their descent to a spacious cavern floor where children moved about on a soft carpet of palm leaves. The liberated slaves inhaled deeply of the cavern's fresh cool air, sniffing curiously at the scent of something ancient mixed with dirt. The smell triggered Graeyba's memories of the wild, hairy creatures in Terus Raynür and he chuckled. Twice saved by creatures, I am! he thought.

The column of people and wagons noisily passed through the gathering room. Further down, the trail of torches revealed a series of larger chambers. After nearly an hour, they entered a cavern that was gigantic beyond description. Slack-jawed, the newcomers gaped at its immensity.

"Look, papa!" D'thalien pointed out pillars of smoke wisping upward to wind their escape through crags and cracks.

So happy was he to hear "Look, papa!" once more, that Graeyba barely noticed his stomach rumbling responsively to the delightful aromas emanating from the base of these pillars. Around pit fires, grills and domed ovens, men and women chopped meats and vegetables, deboned chicken, skinned game, shook savory spices into thick sauces and mixed and formed massive amounts of unleavened bread.

Nearby, rows upon rows of low-lying wooden tables stretched beneath a canopy of nets overlaid with rustic ornaments of dried flowers, leaves, and peppers. From stone pillars these canopies depended, supporting hundreds of candles whose glow fell invitingly on vibrantly colored, woven mats. Countless more palm branches carpeted the cavern floor.

"Is all of this just for us?" marveled D'thalien.

"Surely not," said Graeyba. "More likely preparations for some sort of feast."

The clang of swords and shouts rang out and both pivoted sharply, then sighed in relief. Hundreds of yards away, near a tall outcropping of boulders dozens of young men practiced at sword fighting and hand-to-hand combat, their instructors looking on with care. D'thalien found their shadows, cast ten times their size against the cavern wall, mesmerizing. Graeyba, however, was more impressed with the extent of this cave system. The magnitude of this single chamber was beyond anything his family had seen in the Caves of Tulenbaca of the Eifandir Mountains.

A little way from the training arena, blacksmiths skillfully attended young boys in the forging of metals for weapons and tools. Where the caravan stopped, wainwrights inspected them while heartily instructing young boys in making repairs. Beyond them, amidst waxes and chemicals, chandlers busily taught children to make candles. In a secluded area of the cavern, teachers quietly lectured more studious children peering at torchlit scrolls. Others taught children to weave, sew, tan leather, and cobble shoes, sandals, and the unique desert boots of the Dolscareb.

As the boys from the caravan milled into the cave, people everywhere paused in their work. They gazed in astonishment and exclaimed at the number of newcomers pouring into the cavern.

"We have never seen this many liberated!"

"Look! There are still more pouring in!"

Beaming, Baltien gestured widely at the cavern. "Welcome to your new home! In the cool shelter of these caves, we teach the children to fight, read, clothe themselves."

In wonder, Graeyba commented, "Our little village had no such education to offer my sons!" With misty eyes, he added, "I taught them all they knew."

"And taught them well, I am sure," Baltien comforted him kindly. "Of what did you teach them?"

"The use of various weapons in defense and in the hunt, the tracking of animals, and the use of the hands to build and repair."

Baltien nodded approvingly, then prompted, "Various weapons?"

"My eldest took to it best, but D'thalien too is competent with the bo staff and excels in the use of blades and bows."

"If it please you, we would gladly offer him a position in training to join the ranks of our brotherhood, the Br'thain."

Graeyba smiled his thanks and nodded, unaware of the greatness of the honor just offered his son.

"And you, Graeyba Khalevad," Baltien said, "if they learned by your hand, you too must be quite skilled in weaponry."

Graeyba smiled proudly, "Aye," he said, then hurried to defend himself, "though only self-taught. I never served amongst the Rhünkai."

"By the scars on your face, I take it you have seen battle?"

Graeyba's fingers gingerly explored his scars. "In defense of my people, my lands, and my family, I have taken Rhünkai lives."

"To you then," said Baltien, "I offer a position amongst our Preceptans. Amongst them you will learn of the wisdom of the Gardener and, should the Fieradeem find you apt to it, they will train you for a position of leadership in the Br'thain."

At this, Graeyba bent briefly down to one knee in deference and acceptance. Baltien seized him jovially by the arm and pulled him upright with a laugh.

Graeyba's face remained grim. "We will be grateful to have a purpose here, unrooted as we are from home," he said. Seeing the smile slide from Baltien's countenance, he hurried to explain. "I mean not to be ungrateful! But my son and I long to search together for his brother Aidan, yet it is not safe for us to return. And the loss of my wife is augmented by the distance stretching between our old home, and this," he gestured widely at the cavern, "our new one."

Baltien nodded his understanding. "I cannot imagine your pain. But work, I think, will be a welcome distraction. For now, please, join my family in our eleventh-hour meal."

So it was that Graeyba and D'thalien sat together at a low table with the leaders of the West. Halfway through the meal a gangly boy, Baltien's younger son, S'baladin, quietly joined the table to sit beside his brother. Together, all ate of the sumptuous meal with voracious delight while thoroughly enjoying the sounds of regional music as warm as the desert and as soothing as the hospitality.

The Gardener's Feast

As thousands of rescued children slept on palm-woven mats, a meeting took place. Eighty-six women and men filed in to a large, natural chamber off the main cavern. Dozens of tables and chairs formed neat rows at its center. When the wife of Baltien joined them, drawing a thick curtain of multi-colored cloth behind her, their chatter hushed.

Kalanit acknowledged several of them with nods, as she seated herself at the head of the longest table. She called for the inventory accounts of their food and textile supplies. Together they worked out orders to procure supplies from the vendors and caravan merchants from Andovias. Her brow furrowed as they wrote out orders for larger quantities of bartered produce than ever before. "We must seek larger wholesale to sustain our burgeoning population," she urged.

From the maze of corridors beyond their chambers, came wild cries of childish delight. "The Gardener is here! He has arrived!"

Forgetting the troubling economics before them, the stewards of Didder-äsh smiled, rose to draw back their curtain and poured into a vast concourse of people towards the great cavern hall. A tingling sense of euphoria rushed through them all. Everywhere, a cacophony of voices, shouts and cheering overpowered echoed against the caves. "He is here! He is finally here!"

Kalanit hurried to the straw pallet where S'baladin rested. Together they pushed through the crowd until they spotted him. Beside Baltien was a man clad in strange garments of old from another world. They joined the people in applause as Baltien aided him in donning a ceremonial robe of deep blue.

The ancient Steward of Feynhava, a myth to those of Upper and Middle Y'cromeca, was known simply as the Gardener to the people of the West.

Shouts of "Long live the Gardener!" echoed in the cavern as dozens of the Fieradeem gathered around. Behind them crowded eager Preceptans, clan leaders, in training with the Fieradeem, who hoped to one day rise to leadership positions amongst the Br'thain. And all about this tight circle of men, children spun and danced and clapped in glee.

Upon a high and rocky ledge forty men lifted ram's horns to their lips to blast a call throughout the caverns. A clamor of shouts and applause rose. As they subsided, Baltien's lone and powerful voice broke forth.

"Behold, the Feast of In-gathering has begun! The Gardener returns again, at his appointed time, to meet in the land of the West! Across the dark and accursed land of the fallen Ballai, he has journeyed! All who have been faithful to his ways, rejoice, for he desires again to meet with you! With ram's horns we proclaim the goodness of the Gardener! And may it be heard throughout every corner of the West! May the Streams of Feynhava always water his garden in the desert."

The ram's horns echoed once more, but the people's shouts of praise surpassed them. A galloping riff of stringed instruments hushed them as they built to a crescendo. The sound cascaded into an ancient melody played upon cymbals, horns and tambourines. It moved the people, causing them to remember that they were part of a larger story and to reflect on the infinite power of the Gardener. Waves of excitement coursed through them and everywhere, the people began to dance. Men linked arms and stomped rhythmically in circles about the women as they swayed and spun, their Guaddecas swirling gracefully about them. Throughout the night, wine and food flowed plentifully as friends and families from all three regions were arriving at every hour.

As the people feasted, the Gardener moved amongst the most esteemed men in the West, offering laud, "I am enormously proud of you all. Baltien has led you to the rescue of a vast number of innocents!"

"Our success bears the mark of your wisdom," said Baltien respectfully.

The Gardener put his arm around Baltien with a smile and led him toward the chamber of refreshing. The Fieradeem, Preceptans, and the greatest of the clan warriors followed, talking and laughing amongst themselves. Momentarily, the Gardener pulled Baltien in closer. "I must tell you my friend. I have known many good people for hundreds of years. Among them all, second only to Y'crom, I consider you my dearest friend in the West."

Baltien bowed his head deferentially, speechless at this compliment.

"Accept my praise, accept my thanks. Years ago, you managed to settle feuds between the Houses – a feat that no other Fieradin could do. And now, this campaign to liberate the child slaves carries your personal signature, my friend. Across Ferán, Rihován and Calasmorra leaders now seek your counsel, they depend on your leadership, as do I. More than that, they value your friendship." And with a smile, the Gardener added, "As do I."

In great humility, Baltien kindly thanked the Gardener, misty eyed.

They entered the spacious chamber of refreshing where they were seated about a long, wooden table, the Gardener in the great seat as its head as the rituals of the feast began.

A supplicant appeared with an ornate basin of water, which one of the Preceptans took and brought before the seated host. Baltien knelt before the Gardener and took up a colorfully designed cloth. He wet it ceremoniously and washed the desert sands from the feet of their venerable guest. Following this ritual, men and women filed respectfully in and out of the chamber, to kiss the Gardener's hand, his cheek and his tassels.

As the people streamed about them, they were presented with a sumptuous meal of spiced foul, lightly cooked in olive oil with roasted onions and tomatoes, platters of wild salmon from Messidian brooks over a bed of wild rice and nested among in leafy vegetables and roasted potatoes and a spicy, regional soup with crusts of hot buttered bread.

Baltien and the clan leaders of the Br'thain offered stories of their rescue missions to the Gardener as they supped. In turn, the Gardener shared more wisdom from the Streams of Feynhava. Following the stream of adults, children flocked to greet the venerable host. Having heard legends of his great deeds, some of the little ones shyly fingered his ceremonial tassels, some held his strong gaze, others giggled as he let them stroke his beard.

S'baladin approached hesitantly with another young lad, Sabaca. He dared not bring Diero or Jubal before the Gardener, they were viewed as delinquents by all. Sabaca too was not without his shortcomings. But, a budding botanist, he had begged for this introduction to the Gardener.

"S'baladin, son of Baltien," the Gardener greeted him with a smile. "And who is this?"

"I am Sabaca," the boy said, eyes popping wide in awe.

The Gardener's smile widened into a grin. "And what is this you carry, Sabaca?"

The boy's passion for his hobby flared. From a leather pouch he eagerly displayed rare seeds, dried leaves, and pressed blossoms collected from mountain cliffs and desert floor alike. His curiosity piqued, the Gardener leaned forward to engage in conversation with the lad.

A young Preceptan, noticing the Gardener's unfinished plate of food grew agitated by this interruption. Peering out at the line of children awaiting their turn, he stepped forward and ordered the volunteers to stay the children and allow the Gardener some rest.

But the Gardener spoke for the children. "That will not be necessary," he said. "Never withhold the children to come unto me. They are the reason we fight. One day, they will fight as you do." He turned to gaze upon Sabaca, "Even you my child, will one day play a part in the course of history." To the Preceptan he said sternly, "As long as the Ballai remains standing in the West, we must treasure our youth."

The young Preceptan blushed furiously and bowed his head. The rest of the Fieradeem and their Preceptans smiled politely, some bowing their heads in reverence.

S'baladin was deeply satisfied by the Gardener's attention to his friend. My father and the Fieradeem may question my friendships, he thought, but he understands. He sees the good in them.

As the Gardener and his fellows joined the rest of the celebration, wild plants sprouted everywhere he trod. Astonished adults marveled at the rocky flora while children gathered them in bunches. Sabaca plucked several to press and treasure.

Everywhere in his wake, as they had always done, the elderly gathered little groups of these children to them for stories of noble deeds, of frightful creatures subdued, dark enemies vanquished. From the painful toil and turbulent choices of times long gone, the children gleaned a wealth of wisdom. In truth, both young and old were spellbound by these fanciful tales.

Countless threads of stories of the Gardener's feasts, accounts and tales that intertwine and converge over time, could be told. But nowhere in the universe were there enough scrolls to house them all. The wisdom of the Streams of Feynhava flowed forth from his bosom with great love for the valiant people of the West, the ones who had clung to his ways since time immemorial. Bolstered by that love, his loyal followers were honored at these feasts to pass the rich heritage of his wisdom on from generation to generation.

Amongst the ancient stories long shared, this year's feast included many a new tale. Stories of children freed from enslavement and stories of how it came to be that the men of the West, together with a small band of strong armed, good hearted men of Graëyhovan wrested thousands of Íraban's scions from his grasp.

The Tales of Cerathmir and Duin Caeir

Hemmed to the north by the Eifandir Mountains, a miller of grain dwelt in the region of Cerathmir within the fallen Ballai of Graëyhovan. Married to a good and respectable lady, with seven sons and three daughters, M'zhalo was a noble and caring man, generous with his good fortune. It was he and his men who drove the spike into the forests near the base of the Fortress City, opening the Streams of Feynhava for the Br'thain of the West. Arbantio M'zhalo's mill had passed from father to son for many generations. Respected as men with strong backs and sturdy hands, the M'zhalo name was well known in his small farming community. His neighbors little knew, however, of his role in the rescue of children from the wretched slave camps in Hierundia. This is the story of how he came to bear that responsibility.

Like many of the farmers and millers in the shadows of the Eifandir Mountains, Arbantio M'zhalo lost his two youngest sons to the lottery of the child slaves. While many other souls gave up hope and manifested their grief in various forms, M'zhalo chose to act.

Long before the Edict of the Scions, the Gardener had habitually passed through Cerathmir on his annual journey to the West. More or less, the locals of Cerathmir ignored his curious ways. So busy were they with their toil, they turned coldly from his warm, friendly chatter. As was the habit of their land, they denied him, a stranger, lodging of any kind, even amongst the hay in their stables. The only citizens of Cerathmir to offer hospitality to the Gardener was M'zhalo and his family. For seven years, when the Gardener travelled to the West, he stayed as a guest at the M'zhalo homestead.

Several months before the brave men of the West began their operations, the Gardener had arrived as M'zhalo's sons and laborers finished their toil for the day. As they chatted and cajoled outside M'zhalo's domicile, the eldest squinted toward the Oaks of Uradhuil. Emerging from the forest in the twilight mists, was a hooded figure, bearing an oaken staff.

He pointed and exclaimed, "The Gardener is approaching!"

"Very well, indeed!" exclaimed his father, coming to his door. "Take the donkey to him," "M'zhalo said, "that he may ride into our midst! I am sure he is famished, and weary from travel!"

M'zhalo welcomed the Gardener into his home, gesturing for them to sit on straw mats. The lady of the house and her daughters offered them tea, then busied themselves preparing a large cauldron of beef stew.

"Tell me, M'zhalo, of what clan are your forefathers?" asked the Gardener.

The miller's large blue eyes brightened, deepening decades of wrinkles upon his face. "The oral traditions of my family say that we are from the clan of Faëlgrey," the miller said proudly. He rose to light up a pipe of scented tobacco from the kitchen fires, then returned to the mat.

Drinking from his tea, the Gardener nodded his appreciation. "One of the seven sons of Y'crom, along with Aeduthir, Aelgad, Dürthaliun, Visanthiel, Alazar and Oliel. They became the Seven Branches of Y'cromeca, today. Yours is a distinguished line indeed."

M'zhalo leaned forward with a chuckle. "Tell me again of the sons of Alazar and Oliel in the Ballai that still stands. I never tire of hearing how wrong my people are to think them savages!"

The Gardener grinned. "Far from savage, the people of the West live simply, yet their hearts are free. They live for the song of the sparrow in the early morning dew. They seek wisdom in the trickling sound of a quiet brook. For them, the whole of the universe is contained in one breath of laughter." The gentle smile upon his lips dissolved into a troubled frown as he continued. "The men of the West are a valiant people who fight wholly on the side of life. Their lives differ greatly from those in these northern lands."

M'zhalo's face, reverent at first was darkened by a scowl. "It is the Thaed-Rú masters who deny us a similarly peaceful existence."

"Aye," the Gardener concurred. "As you mention, the people of the West descend from the seven clans of Y'crom, just as you," he said. "This brings me to a grave question." His brows lowered a shade of concern over his countenance. "Has there been any news of your sons? Since they were pressed into service by the Thaed-Rú?"

At this, the miller's eyes revealed an abyss of sadness within. He exhaled a deep sigh and the glow of the fireplace cast deep shadows about his frown. "No, and my poor lady..." he paused and turned to watch her at her work. "Her nights are restless as she struggles yet to cope with our loss. We M'zhalo men are strong-willed with strong arms. Yet we can do nothing but hope that strength keeps our sons alive. The thought that they work to prosper the Thaed-Rú burns our souls. We hope that the light of their precious lives has not been extinguished...discarded..." the miller's voice trailed away.

The Gardener was touched with sympathy at the sight of his trembling lips. Leaning forward, the Gardener reached a hand out to his arm. "It has been many years since the issuance of the Edict of the Scions," he said. "Long years have passed since your boys were pressed into service. Despite the pain of your grief, you remain hospitable, generous, with a great wellspring of compassion for those less fortunate."

M'zhalo bowed his head in acceptance of these well-earned accolades.

"Yet because of the Edict," the Gardener continued, "I also see in you a great sword of indignation, long repressed, set against the Thaed-Rú. It is time."

The miller looked up from his misery with an inquisitive look, his eyes boring straight into those of his numinous guest. "Time?"

The Gardener nodded. "It is time to draw that power into great deeds, for the sake of your two sons, and for the sons of all those whose lives have been blighted by the Thaed-Rú." He finished his tea, set the cup upon the mat and explained. "The sum of all Y'cromeca has come to this. Of all places, Cerathmir, who slumbers in the shadows of the Eifandir, is called to make hallowed the pages of history, to summon all that is glorious of the past, to bind to the noble cause of liberation."

"What do you propose my lord, the formation of an army? Rebels to brew sedition within the borders of Graëyhovan?" asked the miller, his eyes gleaming.

"No, my friend. No. Such would only be the vanity of futile dreams," the Gardener replied gently. The two sat quietly for a moment and then the Gardener stirred. Raising a finger in the air he said solemnly, "But unto you I have come, for the wisdom of the Streams of Feynhava has afforded us the opportunity to steal them away these children. Within the free lands of the Ballai of the West, these children too may once again be free."

M'zhalo's eyes flared wide, and in his heart, hope kindled for his missing sons. "But the Ballai are impenetrable, and the Thaed-Rú threat insurmountable. By what means could we rescue them from the Thaed-Rú's miserable plot?"

A slow smile turned the Gardener's lips upward, "We will do it right before the very eyes of their task masters. In the space of several minutes, we shall transplant them by the hundreds to the West. There, they shall be grafted to the Tree of Y'crom. Then they shall truly be scions in more than name."

• • • • •

Upon the Fieradeem of Ferán, Rihován and Calasmorra lay the burden of duty to serve as judges in all manner of arms, civic and private matters. Of the seven hundred and seventy Fieradeem throughout the West, only one hundred and fifty-seven men responded to the Gardener's call to gather solemnly at the stone ruins of Duin Caeir. But on this solemn day, the one hundred and fifty-seven patriarchs and their entourages were gathered. Tall staffs and multicolored Dolscarebs distinguished the Elder Fieradeem who stood in a circle at the center of the gathering.

As the ground began to hum and rumble, this circle widened, and all stepped backward in anticipation. All in the gathering shielded their eyes as an explosion of azure rose from the ground. When the light faded, they blinked in surprise at the sight of foreign men, oddly clad in the warm furs and cloaks of the north.

In an unprecedented act, the Gardener had ferried four guests with him into the Ballai of the West. This was done through the infinite power of the Garden of Ages, for it is otherwise impossible to pass through the walls of the Ballai that still stand. Known as the Streams of Feynhava, subterranean currents of energy passed deep beneath the ground like rivers of water, through the walls of the Ballai and far below the surface of Y'cromeca.

Recovering slowly from the shock of travel, the Gardener's four guests gazed about in wonder at the vast, stark beauty of the West. Meanwhile, the Fieradeem and patriarchs conversed intently.

"I have summoned you, the Fieradeem and Preceptans, to these ancient ruins for a historic meeting. Night is upon us and a time of harvest is fast approaching." With these opening words, the Gardener cast a hush upon the gathering. "I bring with me," he said, gesturing to the men one by one, "A miller of Cerathmir, Arbantio M'zhalo, his two eldest sons, and the Tribune Ansuz of Hierundia."

Where the men were puzzled at the presence of a simple miller and his sons, they were aghast at the introduction of one of the eleven Sovereign Tribunes of the Thaed-Rú provinces. Distrust coursed through the veins of many.

"Why bring him here?

"Why allow him Knowledge of the Streams?

"Does it not endanger us?"

Lowering his countenance to the ground, the very breath of the Gardener stilled. This sudden moment drew the men's attention, silencing all. The rustling of his robe and its tassels in the breeze accentuated his stillness. Suddenly, the Gardener began to tremble, gripping his staff with both hands. The ground began to rumble and quake, transfixing each man where he stood.

The Gardener lifted his countenance to the evening sky. Ancient words of Uraduin arced from his lips across the evening sky. Their power shook those in attendance to their core. Although only a few understood a handful of his words, all stood in awe as the evening sky lit instantaneously at his voice. About them all the heavens flared for several seconds, the clouds shape and color as visible as day, then darkness returned. Faces paled at the wonder of such power.

A groan erupted beneath them and the stone floor split open. From east to west, a rent yawned several inches wide across the length of the stone floor. As the quaking subsided, the gathering scrutinized the figure of the Gardener. His eyes searched the group and they beheld his anger. "A rage of a thousand sorrows rents my heart, as a sword! The infamy of the Thaed-Rú knows no bounds, reaching even unto the shores of Feynhava! I have called you, my people unto me, yet even the small portion of faithful in attendance here today lack faith in what matters most."

A sense of deep, dark foreboding overwhelmed the men as the Gardener strode past. "A great tyranny and injustice plague the distant lands of Y'cromeca. The dark one on the Thaed-Rú throne, wields child slavery on a massive scale to build and revive the fourth Cethin Arda. Already civil unrest and upheaval plague their lands. Already, they are powerless against the Thaed-Rú, but their greatest trials are still to come."

Low, indecipherable murmurs rose. The gentler souls among them expressed grief at such mistreatment. Some of these men were grandfathers who prized and loved their own grandchildren dearly. It was into a deep well of sadness that they plunged upon hearing of such cruelty to the families in the north.

"Fieradeem, barons of the desert, this threat seems distant, but, left unchecked, darkness shall soon fall upon the West. I call upon the intervention of the Br'thain to rid the north country of this infamy. I call upon the help of Arbantio M'zhalo, his sons, and his workers to be our allies in the North. And I call upon the Tribune Ansuz to ally his vast tumens, still beyond Íraban's control, to rid us of Thaed-Rú rule and all its darkness."

All present heartily gave their agreement, save the Tribune Ansuz. The Gardener nodded his acceptance of their pledges. Then, collectively, all turned to the Tribune Ansuz. Their eyes were full of questions and the hearts of many brimmed with suspicions.

Though the man was sweating under his thick, brown furs, his demeanor was cool as he stepped forward. His voice rang out, "I come, at the behest of this man," he gestured to the Gardener, "to consider forming an alliance with you. The toil of the Thaed-Rú to intensify their dark power, is tiresome at best. Their work is ceaseless, these many centuries past. Thus, I see no reason to lend the lives of my thousands of men to their discretion. Now, as punishment for my refusal to submit my tumens to Íraban's command, my own sons, my two youngest, have been made child slaves by this upstart."

Quietly, the Gardener said, "Yet you will not concede to an alliance with us."

It was a statement, not a question. An oddity that did not pass the Tribune's notice. His eyes narrowed as he thought Who is this man that knows my mind so well? Once, in the guise of a messenger, he offered me the might of the Anil-Gevra army! Now, to this seeming leader in this foreign land, he offered not but requested.

"Already, my youngest sons are taken from me," the Tribune said. "Should I join in your venture, I fear for my eldest, and for my daughters. For these reasons, I must decline and bide my time." Silently, he thought, And for my own life, my title, and my estate.

Many hissed, "Coward," under their breath at this, yet the Gardener merely nodded. One elder murmured to another, "If he already knew the man's response, why ferry him through the Streams? Does he not know how rare that is?"

He turned and ordered the Fieradeem to take a census of every man twenty years and older, according to their families and clans. From this, they would select clan warriors from every clan militia to mount an insurgence. While the men toiled to this end, the Gardener ushered the Tribune Ansuz back through the Streams to his bleak and frigid homeland.

Soon after, the Gardener returned. Calling forth a hoary Fieradin from the city of Tal-Coras, he said, "Quispal, I hear you have an interest in the study of exotic creatures."

The elder, surprised at this designation, hesitated then nodded.

"What know you of the Aerrukán?"

"As I understand it, the Aerrukán is a nocturnal hunter, borne of the Garden of Ages. At night it lies on its back under a mess of branches, twigs and leaves, for hours at a time. When prey wanders nearby, foraging for food, the Aerrukán emits a substance into the air. Its prey senses this and becomes temporarily paralyzed. Finally, it moves cautiously across the undergrowth, then springs up to seize its prey, talons driving deep into its vital organs."

Another elder appeared from behind a group of men to add his knowledge. "The Aerrukán has also been known to discharge a volley of poisonous quills from its back. Its quills can kill its prey from twenty yards away!"

A murmur of agreement rose from several others at this.

With a smile, the Gardener said, "The Aerrukán is a unique creature, worthy for our cause."

For several days, they planned the requisite logistics, housing, and education required to create in the Ballai of the West a refuge for the child slaves. Magnanimous as their intentions were, the Fieradeem argued hotly over which territory would host such a settlement. Finally, Baltien's proposal of the Didderäsh Mountains won out. His branch of the Br'thain were the strongest and greatest in number, but also the network of large caverns far below offered unique and affordable protection and shelter to the thousands they hoped to save. He drove his argument home by pointing out its proximity to the ruins of Duin Caeir. The location settled upon, their meetings shifted to transporting the children and their food, clothing and housing and the education of the children in knowledge both practical and mystical.

After seven days, the series of meetings concluded. A treasurer among them had transcribed the events and facilitated planning with lists and timelines. Before the men departed, the Gardener asked this treasurer to write a letter stating their accord. All signed, including the Gardener, so that there would be no wavering. Among the patriarchs and elders, even the lowliest amongst them - Arbantio M'zhalo, the good miller from Cerathmir in Graëyhovan and his two sons - were asked to attach their signatures.

The Harmattan Weed Spies

Following the Caethain raid, as the M'zhalo men retreated with the spike, a small cluster of weeds near the carnage had become animated and slithered into the ground. Though the men were certain they had retreated unseen, they were oblivious to a hidden evil that followed them beneath the ground. The animated weeds thickened with supernal strength, pursuing the sounds of their footsteps as the men ran through the forest. Night after night they were followed, the weeds as unseen as they believed themselves to be.

Weeks later, when the M'zhalo men reached Arbantio's homestead, the animated weeds sprung to the surface, posing as dead overgrowth. In ignorance of the spies within their midst, Arbantio greeted them with a paternal embrace. In his customary greeting to their return from such journeys, he offered them seeds from a leather pouch. They were supplied by the Gardener himself to offer the supernal power from the Garden of Ages. Arbantio and the three men chewed on them, savoring their nourishment, as he welcomed them into his home. "I rejoice at your safe return. I want you refreshed, bathed and well fed, so that tonight, you can share the details of how well your bartering went."

With Íraban's edict now in full effect, the Gardener's orders were to keep the true nature of these excursions hidden. Many would eagerly share the details of their secret operation for rich profits from the Thaed-Rú. Spreading over a small storage shed behind the mill, that night, the dark weeds labored after information. As each of the men crossed the shed's threshold, they touched a metal article nailed to the right side of the entrance. A gift from the

Gardener to Arbantio, upon it was the carved design of a waving river to remind them of the Gardener's love for those who drink from the Streams of Feynhava. Though the animated weeds tried to eavesdrop on their conversation, the gift rendered their speech incomprehensible. Thinner vines slithered stealthily from the main cluster up the edge of the shed's window. But the men inside, protected by the power of the Gardener's sacred gift, appeared in hazy, vaporous forms.

Speaking in Uraduin, as taught by the Gardener, they reported eagerly to Arbantio.

"Our greatest rescue yet!"

"The number of Rhünkai slaughtered was vast."

"Aye! The snow ran red as soldiers fought blindly in the darkness, gripped by chaos and fear. But all went well on our side."

A smile wreathed the miller's face, as he puffed on his fragrantly scented tobacco pipe. "Excellent! And how many boys were rescued?"

He searched their eyes for a glimmer of hope regarding his own two sons. The three men hesitated, knowing the tenderness of his heart which longed for his sons to return to his bosom. Gently, one of them relayed his regrets. "A great many boys were saved...but there were no signs of your sons."

Arbantio removed his pipe from his mouth, slowly dropping his gaze to the candles on the table. "I still hold hope that...perhaps...they were rescued this time, taken into the Ballai of the West."

While Arbantio slipped into a melancholy, the miller lifted his gaze to the men with a lightened countenance and said, "Well these are good tidings! Another group of young boys set free!"

All four men smiled and agreed. They conversed into the night, conveying more details of their campaign over Graëyhovan wine. Unbeknownst to them, even as they spoke, hundreds upon hundreds of weeds sprouted out of the ground.

They snaked across the breadth and width of Y'cromeca to spy and eavesdrop on a thousand conversations, from paupers in the fields to manors of feudal lords. The greatest secrets in Realmhold Thaed-Rú were laid bare before this dark verdure. The supernal sprouts recorded every weakness, every strength, and no one was aware. No one ever suspected something as innocuous as a weed could threaten their land and their people.

Wherever conversations ended, business concluded, or friends parted, the weed spies shrank away and withered, their particles carried away by the wind.

The dust of the shriveled weeds drifted in the air to meet with stronger currents above which carried them far away, across the ocean in a shadowy mass.

They came upon a very curious island, in an unchartered region. It was a strange land, its shores obscured by a perpetual mist. Shipwrecks in various states of decay along the stretching shoreline stood silent witness to the isle's mastery of countless ages.

The dark cloud of weed particles floated over this world through hazy half-light until it came upon a sprawling mass of bizarre buildings upon a mountain peak. Small clusters broke away from the cloud to descend into several oval portals atop these structures. Swirling down mist-filled tunnels, the clusters made for a cavernous chamber far below.

Winged creatures flapped chaotically across the chamber. Small heaps of dark, hideous insects moved over each other along the skeletal ridges along the ceiling of the chamber. Their humming, clicks and chirps filled the chamber. Above these tortured screams of agony rose to reverberate across the chamber. In cages suspended high above the chamber floor, bloodied humans and other hybrid creations wailed. Freakish cocoons large enough to host humans, were also suspended. Homunculus creatures crawled up and down the cavern's bony ridges, attending these caged souls. Some prodded them with tools while others injected them with various concoctions.

Far below, the clusters continued their descent until they reached a monstrous pile of bones. It stretched for several yards inside a cage whose frame had been set on fire. Flames leapt from the pile, biting ferociously at the darkness of the chamber. As the clusters of weed particles sank into the flames, instead of disintegrating, they were energized. They whirled rapidly, forming a dark vortex above the fire.

Several yards away, the powerful mass of an unfathomably large figure was perched high atop another heap of skeletons. His dark eye sockets glared into the caged fire. Each painful breath he heaved spoke to an exhaustion of living. Heinous features of stitched flesh carved his face served as visible markers of battles waged long ago. The grim set of his jaw, the gnarled fingers gripping his staff and his labored breathing indicated a life of constant physical agony. As the dark cyclone form, he stirred to cast his ghastly eyes upon it.

Several wretched figures in black armor and robes stood at the base of his skeletal perch. The language with which they spoke, a sinister arcane tongue, cursed the very air itself with vapors reeking from their cracked, stitched lips.

The hulking figure grunted to his minions who uttered words of control to manipulate the cluster of weeds, to dispense its information to the large figure.

As the vortex shifted to a slower spin, the mysterious figure spoke in a loud voice. "My harvest is come! My Harmattan weed spies have arrived here, in Kaëyrbassad. Heralds from across the seas! Tell me, what dark power looms over the sons of Y'crom? Relay your secrets, from countless words collected shape with me their destiny!"

Instantly, innumerable voices emanated from the whirling mass of weed particles. Some were in Hierundiel while others were the various provincial dialects of Upper and Middle Y'cromeca. The figure sank back upon his heap of bones, absorbing all they told.

For many weeks, the Haruspec, as he was called, and his cronies heard hundreds upon hundreds of conversations from prince to pauper, from the lowly fields of peasants to the stately manors of noblemen. Though their forms were varied, they shared a common thread. The plague of their land was the enslavement of children for the building of the Fortress City, for the harvest of the fourth Cethin Arda.

They heard the grief of peasants, laments of mothers, and boasts of nobleman. And the Bal Rú Íraban himself spoke of his plans to use the power of the fourth Cethin Arda, once revived to build a master race. Through the many reports of young boys in caravans of caged wagons, the Haruspec perceived something far more important. He leaned forward with great interest as myriads of peoples spoke of traversing through the open Ballai of Upper and Middle Y'cromeca.

The Ballai, after countless ages, they are breached? he thought in wonder. A fiendish delight flared in his ghastly eyes as report after report confirmed this suspicion. His withered face of stitched flesh and tendons receded back to reveal a hideous, cracked grin. It stretched so wide that it encompassed not only his decayed teeth and jaws, but the bloodshot sides of his eyeballs also. *Ages ago, the raising of those cursed walls prevented my plunder of the world of men! Fools were they to think themselves safe within them! The seeds I sowed in ages past, from the first are ripening. It is time to fulfill my oath of vengeance!*

"At last!" he growled aloud.

Energized by this news, he descended his perch. "Summon my generals," he ordered his minions, shoving back those who attempted to help him. "I will need them to superintend the details, to initiate my possession of Y'cromeca!' he growled. "Send them to my chambers."

The rooms of the Haruspec, populated by lengthy tables and shelves strewn with flasks and jars, scrolls and tomes, were extensive. For many years, he had been growing and developing an eerie plant to use in his takeover of Y'cromeca. With a grunt, he seated himself before an oily parchment and scratched away, carving out a plan.

'The Mithengara plant was sown in gloom. It was grown in the shadows of Kaëyrbassad, on the hill sides of Geala-Dor. It loathes sunlight. I spoke incendiary words over it as I stroked its prickly petals. Now bring about the most delightful taste for those who digest your petals. Baked sweetly in bread, minced in meat, or mixed in drinks. Allure them with your sensual pleasures, with feasting, with wine. Let the bonds of laughter, debauchery, revelry galvanize the effects of the Mithengara, deep inside their minds, overcoming their wills."

His pen grated against the ancient fibers of his page. The sound reverberated against the walls of the cavern. It was as if, just in the act of writing, his words were amplified in power and reach.

"Plant within them a dark seed," he wrote. "May it bloom as a desire to serve me. Let your poison flow through their veins. Find your way into their minds. With the force of my will, dominate them to seek nothing but my will. When they fulfill my order as I see fit, tighten your grip on their lungs. Cause their brains to diminish, to lose faculty. Cause their body to fail without protest. Leave only the sight of their eyes that they, lying paralyzed, may behold my gaze into theirs, with no strength to resist. At that moment, they shall realize the futility of their lives in serving me – in serving darkness, even as the shadows of life descend upon them."

With the Mithengara, the Haruspec wielded his alchemy to make delightful foods of every kind. The many captives in his caves found his concoctions delightful and addicting. Sensations from another world spread throughout their body, yet they remained completely unaware.

From their indulgences of these salacious appetites, blossomed an unnatural desire to serve the Haruspec. Eagerly, the Haruspec tested the lengths of this desire. His twisted whims commanded them to murder their fellow comrades, sink boats and burn villages. When each task was executed, he had but to speak into the Mithengara plant and they too were destroyed.

Thus it was that the Haruspec sat upon the precipice of a new era. The burgeoning new Cethin Arda and the breach of the Ballai called to him, goading him to enter the land and take mastery of every living thing. After centuries, his plan for revenge was nearly complete. He lacked only the perfect servant, one who would pave his entry into the world of men. The Mithengara will aid my conquest well, he cackled within. With it I shall shape the perfect emissary of my evil.

• • • • •

For years, he had plied a select number of his prisoners with Mithengara tainted food and drink. Among these, one was apt unto the Haruspec's needs. For the Ambassador Grioppa of the kingdom of Paradmah and a small contingency of his fellow countrymen, the Haruspec had designed a special lair. There, they engaged in endless revelry. Alternately feasting and dancing, men and women fancifully adorned in dark-colored animal costumes with beaks, horned masks and feathered capes, glided and twirled about a vast prison cell.

From beyond the bars at the end of the chamber, the Haruspec's scarred lips smiled as he watched his handiwork. "This is one of my favorite tunes by Namureyam!" exclaimed Ambassador Grioppa, while the others concurred in grunts, so busy were they in voraciously masticating juicy meats and gulping goblets of wine. It was evident that the power of the Mithengara had consumed them, twisted their reality.

"Once a Gershuvyk, always a sly fox! For we deal in trickery!" said Grioppa. He spoke nostalgically in the language of that name, Gershuvyk, rather than their mother tongue of Paradmah. "With sly tongues, our forefathers stole the rich lands of Paradmah centuries ago! With trickery did they bloodlessly conquer the snow-covered mountains and the rich, green valleys of our home!" All present raised fine goblets in a toast.

The Haruspec sneered and muttered. "Of all the prisoners who have dashed their ships upon the rocky crags of Kaëyrbassad, these insipid fools have indeed garnered the post of entering Y'cromeca as my bait to lure in the lion. "This task will justify his years of feasting."

He motioned for his servant to unlock the cell door and walked amongst his victims, unnoticed. "Every one of you! Wipe your faces! Stand in my presence, you fools!" he called.

Immediately the music ceased, the dancers froze, and everyone around the table stood, wiping food-filled faces. Swine-like, they stood amidst the mess of crumbs, grease at the corners of their mouths, wine dribbling down their chins. Yet years of digesting his food had made them pale and gaunt.

Grioppa bowed low as the Haruspec hobbled his way around the table toward the ambassador. "My Lord! I congratulate you for this auspicious feast that you lavish us with! How can I ever repay you for your hospitality?"

Standing tall over the gaunt and withering frame of the ambassador, the Haruspec breathed laboriously as he spoke. "Indeed, I have fed you long enough Grioppa, you and your people. Your services as an ambassador are much needed in a distant land," spoke the Haruspec in their own tongue of Gershuvyk.

"I have longed for this day, for a way to show my gratitude, to use my skills in your service," replied Grioppa.

"Excellent indeed, ambassador!" heaved the Haruspec. "In the business of diplomacy...we are poised to embark on the opportunity of a lifetime, to seize the sum of a vast realm." He paused struggling to catch his breath. "You...all of you...you will shape the fortunes of history at my side."

"We serve at your pleasure," Grioppa said smoothly.

"You will be envoys," the Haruspec wheezed. Inhaling laboriously, he added, "You will represent my counsel to the Thaed-Rú Dominions."

The ambassador's chest swelled. In euphoria, he looked at his fellows around the table and was greeted with lustful grins oozing pleasure.

"I wish to fulfill my obligation. Master of my will, if I should please your eminence, would you grant me a principality of my own? If I were to rule a small portion of a humble estate, I could show you my loyalty, a tribute to your magnificence."

The Haruspec played along to advance his own personal aim. Placing his massive hand on the ambassador's shoulder, the towering figured peered into his soul.

"Y'cromeca is vast. I require you and your diplomatic retinue to enter in, to open the gates to the roots of their Eleven Dominions, forging my own entrance therein. Execute this task with convincing authority, and I shall grant you much more than a principality, ambassador. You shall have a place to rule at my side."

Grioppa spluttered in amazement and sank in a low bow.

Ignoring him, the Haruspec turned his attention to the gaunt, withering fellows around the table. "All of you shall help to rule this new dominion under Ambassador Grioppa."

The air was charged with ecstasy.

Grioppa rose. "There is an old saying in our faraway land of Paradmah, 'the skin of a Gershuvyk is the fur of a sly fox!' The art of deception runs in our blood. We shall convince them with great authority for you!"

But he was made to wait. His desire for wealth ate away at his heart as the Haruspec staged his possession of the distant land of Y'cromeca. There was the grooming and training of fantastical creatures bred from his dark garden on the Isle of Kaëyrbassad, the arranging of an impressive show of political and military power and glory arranged, and the schooling of Grioppa's retinue to attend to in perfection. In a final touch, the Haruspec forged ancient legal documents and letters of introduction with meticulous detail to sway the sharp minds of the Thaed-Rú, bending them to his will now as they had bent the men of Y'cromeca for centuries.

The Storm Breaks

Envoys to Hierundia

The Ambassador from the kingdom of Paradmah, shifted creaking joints against the misery of the cold Hierundian rain. At one time, as a legitimate ambassador, he had delighted in the thrill of regularly arbitrating between kingdoms. That was long before his fortunate shipwreck on the shores of Kaëyrbassad. Now he found no pleasure in travel and felt only pressure from the work at hand. The incredible destiny offered him by the Haruspec should he succeed hung heavy in its promise.

Already, his progress had been made frustratingly slow. As he and his entourage disembarked in the icy port of C'nossa, Rhünkai soldiers detained them, searched their equipment and seized their credentials. It had taken an entire week before permission arrived granting entrance into Realmhold Thaed-Rú. Grioppa spent the week fraught with anxiety. Not only was a governing seat in the Haruspec's kingdom at stake, the rulers of the Thaed-Rú Dominions might well kill him if they did not accept his forged documents. And should his mission fail, the Haruspec would destroy him. At all costs, he must succeed.

Now, as the sharp and icy peaks of the coastal district of Caethain fell behind him, the ambassador shifted nervously in his carriage, pulling thick layers of protective garments more tightly against the chill. He wondered how any soul could endure such a bleak world. It was a relief when the crystal world of glinting ice was swallowed by the vast darkness of the highland woods surrounding Kiérbangaal.

"Once a Gershuvyk, always a sly fox!" he repeated firmly to himself as his carriage creaked through a winding pass and into the capital. It was late in the evening when the caravan finally arrived at the gilded Hall of Towers, in the Rethin Bretor, the Royal District. Their only welcome at the ancient gates was a guard of eighty or so sentinels. Under the cold watch of a heavily armed guard, the Bal Rú's minions escorted the retinue to a dimly lit council hall. This breach in ceremonial protocol unnerved Grioppa and his staff.

The stone columns of the open-air atrium flared white in flashes of lightning as the rain resumed. A colossal mural depicting the Cethin Arda stretched across a smooth expanse of stone behind the throne. High above the courtyard, the Bal Rú Íraban reclined against his throne. His golden mask shone dully in the shadows as he turned to offer scraps of meat to a small Veyasean bird upon his arm.

A cupbearer stood beside him, proffering a royal goblet of Graëyhovan wine. An arc of thirty-two shadowy dignitaries sat around Bal Rú, seventeen chairs on each side of him. This was the Thaed-Rú court. Impervious to such the wintry weather, the Thaed-Rú sat staidly while Grioppa and his retinue stood, drenched and shivering.

Íraban cast a glance at Grioppa, then nervously drank of his wine. Delaying the mysterious Kaëyrbassad retinue for a week had left him no more knowledgeable of their aims than when he had received their unexpected request for an audience.

A guard approached and glared at them. "You are to stand here until the meeting begins. And wait for Teosifan, the Chief Steward of the Y'cromahein Guild to address you! When he introduces the Bal Rú, you and your staff will bow low before our great Bal Rú. Is that understood?"

Ambassador Grioppa's nervousness suddenly came together in a lump in his throat, but he nodded courteously. His shrewd eyes scanned the colossal chamber, searching for a weakness in this inhospitable court. Countless armed guards populated its walls and from the balcony above them stood row upon row of archers, their bows trained directly on them. A smile twisted at his lips. This young ruler is edgy, he thought. He gestured to the actors among his entourage to begin setting up their props.

The guard barked out, "I said, do not move beyond this point."

Grioppa smiled widened. Edgy indeed! He shrugged casually and threw his hands up in mock surrender.

Moments later, a tall, greying figure approached. In his hands were a copy of the ambassador's letters. His eyes never straying from the ambassador, he cleared his throat and began what was to be a brooding conference. "Behold the great Bal Rú of the Thaed-Rú Dominions, the Lord Íraban Thaed-Rú."

When Grioppa's entire diplomatic retinue, even the standard bearer of the Kaëyrbassad flag, bowed low before Íraban, Teosifan grinned in satisfaction.

"Ambassador Grioppa, of the Realm of Kaëyrbassad," he said, "welcome to Kiérbangaal."

To Íraban, he proffered the ambassador's letters and said, "My lord, these letters from Ambassador Grioppa outline his purpose as diplomatic in nature. His illustrious leader, the Lord Azxahiir, claims descent from an ancient dynasty of stewards known as The Serpent in the Garden. Furthermore, he claims knowledge of an arcane art of divination. These letters detail his ability to manipulate events, bring balance to nature, and divine the secrets of all. This clairvoyance, he claims, has revealed to him the Dominions' most guarded secrets, including the source of the ills which plague our land."

Íraban leaned forward slightly, out of the shadows. Through his mask, piercing eyes as sharp and icy as the shores of Caethain glared down upon Grioppa. "Your Kaëyrbassad master, a stranger to us, knows much of our world! The Thaed-Rú Dominions, an ancient dynasty, stretches across the vastness of Eleven Provinces, from coast to coast. As such, we do not treat with petty nations, or strongholds bereft of legitimate sovereignty. And yet..." he dangled the phrase, toying with Grioppa, "we are curious how you came upon this knowledge. Share with us your mission. Have you tidings of some profit, some benefit in which we both may share, ambassador of Kaëyrbassad?"

Íraban took a voracious gulp of wine. The cupbearer retrieved the empty goblet and made to fill it. Teosifan threw them both a warning look and gestured for the boy to leave it empty. The cupbearer hunched forward, averting his eyes while Íraban scowled.

Unperturbed, Teosifan turned from them to Grioppa. "Ambassador, give voice to this congress!"

Grioppa smiled inwardly and launched into the bluster of diplomacy. In flawless Hierundiel he said, "My master, the Lord Azxahiir, offers many gifts to you in your time of need. Gazing into his ancient craft, he can see the past and present of Y'cromeca. He sees your society teetering on the brink of collapse. Now, I could detail your various conquests and your struggles, but that would be a tedious task indeed. You have read of them already in his scroll.

But your highness, it would please me if you would allow my actors to entertain your court with a little play of his making."

I loathe this foreigner! I should feed his flesh to the Veyasaen! Íraban fumed. But the words 'In your time of need' circled through his mind as well. Perhaps borne of drunkenness, perhaps of hope, he consented. "Make clear your mission," he said gruffly.

Grioppa bowed and signaled to his retinue. Immediately, dozens of actors clad in dark masks and black garments responded. Black vines and roots protruded from their costumes. Onto the wet, stone floor, they cast hundreds of peculiar pod-like seeds. These fell in a circle, encompassing the throne room. The troupe master of Grioppa's retinue clapped his hands high in the air. From them, a black powder exploded into the air with a puff.

Suddenly, the pod-like seeds opened to reveal hundreds upon hundreds of brownish weed-like stems. They burst forth, stretching high into the cold rain. They joined each other, thus forming an impervious wall. The Thaed-Rú court, accustomed to fantastical entertainment chuckled and applauded. The soldiers however, squinted suspicious eyes over trained weapons. Some turned bows and spears upon the peculiar props.

"Tonight, we reach back into hallowed antiquity to an age when colossal forces ascended from the ground. Behold the great Ballai that once surrounded the Eleven Provinces of Upper and Middle Y'cromeca. For millennia they prevented the expansion of the Eleven Provinces, inhibited free trade among your people."

As Grioppa spoke, actors clad in various garbs from noblemen to peasants clamored desperately along the walls. "Throughout the centuries," he continued, "these mysterious walls kept the populace from advancement of any kind. Eventually the people rebelled against this limitation on their lives."

Majestic robes billowed about the actors' shining black armor as they mimicked the strife of war. When they touched their regal scepters to an area of the wall, an explosion of fragmented debris erupted from the wall in a crackling cloud of sparks. The peasants and noblemen both pretended amazement, bowing before the Thaed-Rú actors in mock worship.

Grioppa gauged the Thaed-Rú court. Their beastly eyes were dilated with a cold, dark pride as they exchanged approving looks. Íraban sneered a hideous grin at the reenactment of the Thaed-Rú breach of the Ballai.

A nebulous clump of black vines and roots, propelled by a line of black clad actors, floated ominously across the stone floor to the center of the throne room. The clamor of the court rose in fervor and pride, but Grioppa spoke to them in stern rebuke. "Three futile attempts at resurrecting the Cethin Arda lie in your past. Now, the eyes of destiny are fixed upon the fourth attempt as you struggle to harness ancient power in a modern age."

At this cue, actors beneath the massive figure of the dark garden began to writhe and shift. Some appeared in hideous, disfigured forms and some as white furred creatures. Several of them flapped dark wings of the Veyasaen and attacked the peasants and noblemen. The violence was realistic enough to drop a hush upon the court as they watched the actors leap high through the cold rain to crash down with screeches upon their victims.

"There remains one thorn in your flesh which stirs great unrest in the populace, disrupts your economy, increases revenue and expenditures, and thereby halts the progress of your Cethin Arda. Otherworldly beasts, by violent force and plunder, are seizing property which does not belong to them. Herein, lies the source of a great ill which has affected your lands."

Eight, or nine, horned beasts gave the illusion of ascension from the ground in a blinding flash of sparks and debris. Five soldiers advanced toward the creatures, only to be struck down violently. False blood sprayed into the air from the victims' bodies and the actors fell, lifeless, upon the ground. With this, the play ended.

Ambassador Grioppa watched as the court, which loved violent entertainment, cringed at these visceral attacks. A confidence bloomed within him. The spines of Íraban, Teosifan and the thirty-two dignitaries all stiffened. Their faces formed defensive blanks. Many among the court, murmured in puzzlement as only a handful were privy to knowledge of the beastly ambushes.

Grioppa strode to stand before the throne and turned upon the Thaed-Rú court. "My master, the Lord Azxahiir, knows of your attempt to resurrect the fourth Cethin Arda. He knows your bloodline wanes and that you hope to cross the Necropulpa plant with seeds of Thaed-Rú and the Y'cromahein, to breed a new race of longevity and power."

"Ravenous beasts, products of your garden beyond your control, haunt the environs of your Fortress City. This threat will only grow. Above this very capital flock growing numbers of the Veyasaen who prey upon your citizens. But my master, in possession of ancient knowledge, can subdue them. He alone knows the proper mixture of seeds to help bridge the gap for your quest to breed the bloodline you desire. All-powerful from the beginning of the primordial world, he stood witness to the first seeds of the Y'cromahein. He offers you his power, power to control the beasts who plunder your Scions, Scions who dutifully belong in your lordship's service."

Íraban's eyes dilated. So, the omniscient master of Kaëyrbassad sympathized with his cause! This is what his soul searched for. Yet, skilled in the machinations of diplomacy, he protested,

"But no one knows what these beasts are! Neither do they know their origins, nor their reason for abducting my Scions! Tell me, what does your master knows of these beasts?"

Bowing his head, Grioppa answered promised, "Your Excellency, my master desires to bring these nebulous beasts to justice, with a swift and sudden stroke." Fixating a shrewd gaze on Íraban, he declared, "He chooses to share the details with you in privacy."

A force of vengeance ripened in Íraban. The beasts from another world that abducted his Scions had indeed become a thorn in his side. His knuckles tightened their grip around the armrest of his throne. Surely, the breadth and accuracy of knowledge possessed by this foreign lord indicated truth to all that this man claimed. Still, he remained leery of foreign aid.

Out of the shadows, he breathed, "Your master promises a solution? An offer like that must come at a great price. Tell me, ambassador, what does the steward of the Serpent in the Garden ask in return? Wealth? My kingdom? My head?"

With head still bent, Grioppa said, "Your excellency, wealth and riches mean little in the economy of Kaëyrbassad. And your defeat is not the impetus needed to fulfill his vision."

Through a haze of drunkenness, a thought struck Íraban. ""What is his vision?" he asked, brows narrowed suspiciously. "To know so much of my Dominions, he must have agents dispatched strategically inside every corner of Y'cromeca! What more does he plan for my domain?"

Dramatically, the ambassador raised his face up gradually, peering incrementally upward, beyond the throne, through the rain. Everyone followed suit as the distant sound of gigantic wings beat thunderously above. The council hall began to shake.

"Archers, at the ready!" cried the captains from the balcony and a hundred crossbows rose toward the dark void above the atrium.

Suddenly, a massive Veyasaen burst from the clouds to descend upon the council hall. The court shrank back in fear, their eyes locked upon it as they grappled for hiding places. Then, they froze, murmuring in awe as they discerned a mount upon the fowl.

Veyasaen and rider hovered above Ambassador Grioppa and his retinue. Lightning and thunder rattled the council hall, momentarily outlining the mysterious form above. Shrieks and screams heralded the arrival of a flock of smaller Veyasaen above the council hall. They flew chaotically, diving and swooping through the open-air atrium. Their calls rose to form a cacophony so deafening that even the most regal of courtiers cowered in fear, clapping their hands to their ears.

Then there arose a great clamor of armor and weaponry as soldiers rushed to shield Íraban. Courtiers foolishly sought safety behind high-backed chairs. Many ran to the nearest exits, even as guards cordoned them off, fortifying the ancient gates against a breach. The monstrous fowl landed ponderously. Its razor-sharp talons grated the stone floor as it came to rest between the diplomatic retinue and the Thaed-Rú court.

The mysterious figure spoke in a sinister, arcane tongue, unknown to any in the court. This intensified everyone's fear. More archers on high, accompanied by lancers, swordsmen, and soldiers bearing battle axes below, poured into the council hall. A vast array of them thickened the defensive shield around the Bal Rú and spread to encompass his Thaed-Rú court.

Meanwhile, Grioppa and his retinue moved slowly, positioning themselves behind the Veyasaen as the gigantic bird slowly lowered its body to the stone floor, seemingly in response to the arcane tongue. The Veyasaen laid its thick neck heavily on the ground, but its head craned upward. It gazed about with eyes so piercing that many a hand trembled upon its weapon. When it remained still, all eyes moved to its rider. Clad in a flowing black robe, the giant figure dismounted laboriously from the fowl's lowered neck. He drew a wooden cane from within his cloak and hobbled forward. Though hunched with age, the hulking figure yet stood several feet taller than the Thaed-Rú and towered over the Y'cromahein.

The stranger spoke again in its arcane speech. As if the Thaed-Rú coat of arms had come to life, the giant fowl rose to stand on high behind him. It stretched massive wings about the figure, turning over chairs and courtiers alike with their span. Íraban interpreted this as a gesture of attack and nodded to Teosifan. "Open fire," Teosifan called to the captains. Immediately, a volley of missiles whistled toward the stranger.

The Veyasaen monster curved its colossal wings around the stranger. They emitted a powerful whoosh of wind which threw many a missile off course, but the remaining projectiles, even explosive gunpowder, were deflected by the creature's wings. Ambassador Grioppa's retinue remained protected from the volley as well.

Captains ordered the primary arbans to reload and called for a volley from the second string. The flock of Veyasaen swooped down to seize them and bore them upwards into the clouds. As their screams of terror faded, fearing his own demise at any further incursion, Íraban called out loudly into the fray, "Cease! Cease!"

Teosifan and the captains exchanged looks of frustration, but the cries of fowl and men alike quelled their urge to fight. "Cease," Teosifan grunted and all along the lines of men, captains called, "Cease!" and "Down with your weapons!"

In the aftermath of the skirmish, the eerie silence was punctuated only by the icy rain and rolls of thunder. Who was this stranger that the greatest of the wild and untamed Veyasaen should bear his weight, let alone obey and protect him?

From behind the throne, Íraban's wine bearer peered out fearfully. Though neither supplied the smallest modicum of protection, he gripped a goblet and bottle defensively. The little Veyasaen perched upon Íraban's shoulder squawked in surprise as the Bal Rú' sprang from his throne and descended toward the stranger. Beneath his mask, Íraban very nearly blushed at the absurdity of his pet in comparison to the giant fowl before him.

Ambassador Grioppa stepped forward. The thudding of his boots rang out loudly in the hushed atrium. With an air of exaggerated dignity, he and his standard bearer walked in a wide arc past the Veyasaen monster, who still sheltered the stranger in its wings.

Grioppa broke the silence as he neared Íraban. "Your Excellency, I present to you my master, the Lord Azxahiir, ruler of the land of Kaëyrbassad and chief steward of the Serpent in the Garden."

As if on cue, the Veyasaen monster spread its wings to reveal the Haruspec. He hobbled his way to the foot of the stone steps. Grioppa and his standard bearer followed behind. Íraban and Teosifan both weaved back and forth, anxiously peering around the shield of soldiers.

The Haruspec dismissed the court dignitaries, attendants and soldiers in a glance as though they were but weak and foolish children. He cast a loud shout to the skies in his arcane speech and it reverberated across the council hall. The flock of smaller Veyasaen wheeled away, disappearing amongst the dark clouds above.

No one, not even the Thaed-Rú, had ever seen wild Veyasaen respond to a command. Grabbing the goblet and bottle from his cowering wine bearer, Íraban poured a drink to overflowing and gulped it down. He sent both cup and bottle clattering to the stone floor and strode forward. The Haruspec glanced casually down, skirted the glass, and ascended the remaining steps between them. Teosifan, hand upon his dagger's hilt, followed close behind the Bal Rú while the Ambassador Grioppa and the standard bearer of Kaëyrbassad tailed the Haruspec. Together, they met upon the steps to the Thaed-Rú throne.

From a step below, the Lord Azxahiir looked down upon Íraban's ornate mask, gazing piercingly into the Bal-Rú's eyes. Even from a lower position, even huddled with age as he was, the giant figure towered over the Bal-Rú. Yet, his expression remained sagacious, of seeming concern, and Íraban's nerves eased. In a glare of lightning, the young ruler noticed that the Haruspec also bore a scar across his face. Instantly, Íraban felt the pull of morbid curiosity. In perfect, flawless Hierundiel, the Haruspec began to speak.

"Lord Íraban, I come not as a conqueror, but as an advisor to your court. I trust my ambassador and retinue accurately represented my vision. If you would but allow it, I wish to help stem the tide of revolution and harassment that plagues your lands. What I offer is a solution that transcends far beyond the clay of mere mortals."

Íraban's demeanor shifted. Yet, he offered no grand welcome. "Your display of power truly is immeasurable." Íraban looked beyond Azxahiir toward the giant Veyasaen monster, subdued yet menacing still. "My soul searches for such transcendence."

The Haruspec also cast his gaze about. His eyes traveled from Íraban to Teosifan to the soldiers whose weapons were still trained on him. Slowly, he looked upwards upon the numerous troops along the balcony.

Íraban's gazed returned from the Veyasaen in time to note a violent fire in the Haruspec's gaze. He prickled in fear and bellowed, "Cast your weapons down! Immediately!"

The clangor of weapons clattering against the stone around them surpassed the thunder above. Azxahiir issued a vile grin. For show, the Bal Rú shouted, "If you so much as point a finger in his presence, I shall have your head, and that of your captain, and those of your very family too!"

The Haruspec muttered a quiet word and the colossal Veyasaen surged upward into the darkness. The force of its thrusts caused the courtiers to clutch at their robes as they swirled violently about. Íraban returned to his throne and whispered to Teosifan who called for servants to usher Grioppa's retinue to sprawling chambers, where they would be treated with the highest hospitality and decorum of Thaed-Rú protocol. To the Haruspec, Íraban issued an invitation to his own private chambers where they spent the better part of the night conversing privately.

Íraban began their talk with eager questions regarding the beasts who plundered his Scions, the Haruspec readily replied "Yes, the Serpent in the Garden has shown me visions of these perpetrators. However, their identities come to me only in shielded voices spoken in an arcane tongue, not in visions. To fully establish their identity, I must ask something of your magnificence."

"Anything," said Íraban earnestly.

"Given that I am but a humble guest in your country, provide me a protective escort of your most lethal soldiers, those unwavering in their loyalty to you, that I may pursue the one I most suspect. Clad these troops as commoners to avoid implicating the Rhünkai."

"I will see to it personally."

"Out of deference to you, I wish to conduct an investigation of this source in obscurity. I would not wish to incite further unrest. Once I determine the veracity of my suspicions, I shall bring before Your Excellency my discovery."

Íraban leaned forward in his seat. "I apply to you, as one ruler to another. Your arrival to my Dominions comes at a time of great need. Not only do those infernal beasts wreak havoc on my plans, the greatest amongst my armed tribunes bucks my authority. Your ambassador did not mention him before your arrival…"

"You speak of Ansuz," the Haruspec interjected. When Íraban nodded grimly, the Haruspec laughed. Had not his words already begun to sway the Bal-Rú, it would have been a chilling sound. As things stood, an eager smile spread beneath the ornate mask.

"He will bend to our will, worry no more."

The affection which flickered in the young Bal-Rú's expression was nearly filial. He leaned in closer, and his tone intensified. "Ambassador Grioppa spoke of your understanding of the suffering my Dominions have endured. Tell me, how is it that you know what weighs on my mind? Is it through the Serpent in the Garden?"

His countenance wise and sagacious, the Haruspec replied, "My son, I read it in your eyes. I am well acquainted myself with such struggles."

The young Bal Rú of the Thaed-Rú world was accustomed to dominating his court, his city, and his kingdom with both his innate strength and political prowess. But in these words, for the first time in his life, he felt a power far greater than his own. It seemed to hover over him. He felt keenly the validation offered by this powerful personage. It was the validation he had failed to earn from his father. In place of his drunkenness, long since faded, a raw vulnerability throbbed.

"What clairvoyance do you have regarding the private matters that govern the deepest, darkest regions in my life?" he asked.

A smile played upon the Haruspec's lips and his voice grew fond, familiar. "Young Íraban, there is much for you to discover concerning my roots. I was once a tree, tall and proud. My strong branches offered shade and protection to a very old king. But when I offered shade to countless others, this king became enraged with me and chopped my tree down to the very roots."

The Haruspec's eyes gazed hypnotically, and the young man shifted to the very edge of his seat. Leaning so far forward he was very nearly squatting, he asked, "Why enraged? What was this shade that you offered?"

"The seeds of knowledge, the forming of unlimited power, the consciousness to transcend. It was the inevitable course of humanity that presented itself. But this king was jealous to share his shade with others. He simply would not have it," answered the Haruspec.

The man stretched a crooked old finger out and traced a line down the cheek of Íraban's mask. "Tell me, young Íraban, what causes you to wear this?"

"By my father's doing! In a drunken rage, when I was sixteen. Claiming I was the weakest link in the chain of our dynasty, he took a knife to me," answered Íraban.

"I know the treachery of that tale! It is all too familiar," the Haruspec gazed into Íraban's weak and searching eyes. "The king I once provided shade and protection for, he drove me away from his realm. He pursued me far across the ocean, and when he found me, he too, assaulted me mercilessly."

"Is that the source of your scar?"

"Yes." The Haruspec traced the ridge of skin upon his own cheek. "This is precisely why I know your struggles and sufferings far too well. I am very well acquainted with the brute force of a fiendish authority figure. I have seen the jealous rage that rules such a person, the atrocious ways they act out on a son, a pupil, or a servant. Jealousy flares in the face of a greater glory. What master desires to be weaker or less knowledgeable than his pupil?" He paused to peer intently at the young Bal Rú before adding, "Which father wants his son to outshine his merits?"

The Haruspec leaned heavily on his cane and rose to hobble about the room, but his eyes never left the Bal Rú. "In spite of Theragad's wretched flaws and failures as a father, you rule one of the greatest and most magnificent cities in the world. You bear the immense weight on your shoulders of holding together a world that is crumbling and falling apart, a world built on the labors and merits of your ancestors."

The young Bal Rú's cold heart gravitated toward this sympathy. His eyes were held in the powerful gaze of the Haruspec as the man moved back and forth. He moved now to hover over the seated Bal Rú. He grunted in pain as he stooped down to remove Íraban's mask.

Tracing his scar he spoke, "Destiny has crossed our worlds together, young Íraban. It is our time to restore balance to nature. It is time to give transcendence to the Thaed-Rú Dominions. Let us prove your father's jealous accusations wrong and rewrite a new paper for all Y'cromeca."

Íraban's heart thrilled as promises of all he had ever hoped to be were laid before him. It was no wonder that the Gardener deemed so long ago never to cross seeds without the proper mixture of benevolence and wisdom. The humanity inherited from his mother's side gave him weaknesses that conflicted with the Thaed-Rú monster inside. He bore deep scars, emotional and physical, from his father's twisted teachings and abuse. Many of his father's fears were coming true. The older he grew, the more his Thaed-Rú powers waned. But now, this perceptive giant brought a new hope. He offered freely the relief and respect for which young Íraban yearned. His acceptance of it now was as unconditional as he had once hoped his father's love might be.

The Trap at Cerathmir

The torrential rains that fell over the Province of Graëyhovan usually lasted for the space of an hour or so. The laborers in the fields welcomed such respite. Today, with the barn doors wide open, several of the workers of M'zhalo enjoyed a card game while others sought a nap in the hay. Their heads jerked upward suddenly today as they sensed a presence. Six strange men clad as commoners, heavily armed, spanned the width of the barn doors. They were eerily silent and still as statues. The M'zhalo workers froze in a temporary stupor. Had these strangers materialized from thin air? How was it they had approached unheard?

Cries of anger and fear came from the homestead where another group of strangers violently seized Arbantio M'zhalo and his family. Forcing them to their knees, powerful grips held each one firmly in place by the hair of some, the shoulders of others. His wife and daughter screamed curses at the strangers and struggled against the mud.

"Leave my mother alone, you vile bastard!" Arbantio's oldest son raged at the captors. His brothers joined his cries with threats against the men.

Their threats were empty. Even Arbantio M'zhalo could not wrestle off the weight of his captor. He cast a desperate glance across the open courtyard at the side view of the barn. His hope failed him as screams of agony rose from the barn above the onslaught of pouring rain.

"Please leave my family alone! My children have done nothing to you!" pleaded his wife.

Once more Arbantio's eldest issued curses and threats. This time, a wooden club struck him in the face. Rendered semi-unconscious, he writhed in the muck as blood fused with the rain upon his face to form a pool of umber beneath him. His mother's wail filled the air.

An enraged Arbantio struggled vainly against his captor. Movement at the barn door drew his gaze away from his family. Six strangers strode from the barn. They shoved and dragged a dozen of his workers who crawled and hobbled along, clutching at their injuries. Their blood-stained garments, ripped and torn, grew sodden as the men booted them into the pouring rain like dogs.

Arbantio's heart sank to see their wretched forms. Good and faithful workers they were. Poor souls! Strong as he was, Arbantio's lips began to quiver as a surreal reality dawned on him. He knelt in a line with his entire family and all his workers. Brutish men towered over him. The tallest carried the signature features of a Thaed-Rú, while others were Y'cromahein. Before wild thoughts of *Who sent these men? How much do they know?* found answers, still more brute strangers, clad as commoners but fully armed, approached the courtyard from the fields. These men marched into the homestead and began tearing apart the miller's humble abode. Arbantio's outraged howl was truncated sharply as his captor's grip wrenched at his hair. Overturning furniture, they searched through every room.

The M'zhalo family and his men fell into a grim and anxious quiet. Fear and panic gripped the miller's heart. *Who would betray my trust? Surely not my men! Perhaps a spy in the fields...*

He flinched at the screeches and howls of Veyasaen in the distance. The cries crescendoed as the dark, monstrous forms appeared above the tops of the trees. The storm which should have broken by now, thickened. The birds careened in circles, illuminated by flashes of lightning, heralded by the booms of thunder.

Suddenly, the trees bent backward beneath powerful currents of air. The largest Veyasaen the miller had ever seen descended from the clouds. Arbantio blinked, then gasped, "Inconceivable!" Upon its back, sat a rider.

Rider and fowl landed just beyond the courtyard. Arbantio and his family watched the giant figure descend and hobble toward them upon a wooden cane. His black cloak swept through puddles and mud, dragging cumbersomely behind him. He paused several feet in front of them to cast an evil glare across the line of captives. Involuntarily, they shivered.

He spoke several phrases in a sinister tongue and thunder shook the ground beneath their knees. The Veyasaen flock screeched and howled ferociously. The colossal Veyasaen, still several yards away, lowered its neck and released a bone-chilling shrill.

"Is it going to eat us?" asked M'zhalo's youngest son. M'zhalo found himself, for once, unable to offer comfort to his trembling children as a gripping wave of fear seized him.

In Hierundiel, the giant asked the captains surrounding him which was the man in question. A deep hatred roiled within the Haruspec as he approached Arbantio. *They are all as little children, spoiled and repulsive. Even these Rhunkai brutes are not beyond the Gardener's love for Y'crom. The seed of Y'crom is ripe for possession and takeover of the land!* Aloud, the giant called to a captain who, in turn, ordered a soldier to bring the giant's leather pouch.

The giant point to a worker. "Bring him closer," he ordered. Reaching into his leather pouch, the giant brought out a handful of tiny seeds mixed in a dark green powder. He beckoned to another soldier and ordered, "Hold him." Forcefully the two brutes pushed M'zhalo's man into the mud. With a grunt of pain, the giant stooped down over this pitiful form.

The giant lifted the powdered seeds up to the rain. The mix turned muddy, then sprouted dozens of tiny, thorny vines which prickled with thistles.

In his arcane tongue, the giant shouted, "I bring the curse of thorns and thistles to spread, to cover the land, to choke out the flower of life from all who oppose me! I crush the seed of Y'crom and any who stand against me!"

No one understood his words, but his portent became clear when the giant smeared his concoction onto the worker's face as his captors held him in place. Instantly, the thorns and thistles sprouted vines which multiplied across his unfortunate face. The poor worker closed his eyes in pain. He shook his head violently against the vines to no avail. Tiny tendrils spread into his nostrils, into his ears. He pressed his lips together in anguish but they pried his mouth open and entered there as well. The worker writhed in pain as portions of his face turned ashen, then gave way to a pallor of green. Arbantio and his people watched in horror as the man's struggle gave way to a blood-curdling howl.

The giant whipped ferociously to face the kneeling miller. Speaking now in the provincial dialect of Graëyhovan, the giant breathed laboriously words over Arbantio, stooping down to stare into his face. "Tell me, M'zhalo, who are the beasts that cross into this world without permission, or tribute? Who are those vermin that abduct the Scions?"

"I beg you, release that man! Take me instead!" cried M'zhalo.

But the giant clenched his teeth. "I do not treat with vermin like you! Tell me what I want to know, or your wife will suffer the same fate!"

Arbantio peered through the heavy sheets of rain at his shivering wife and children. Thunder and lightning shook the ground with a relentless and unnatural intensity. In shame, Arbantio hung his head as a miserable weakness overcame his will.

"Very well! I will tell you!" he said quietly. "They are not the creatures you suppose them to be." The miller fought for breath in heaving gasps, so close was he to panic. "They are...the hallowed Br'thain...they live beyond the Ballai of the West. Now release my wife and children!"

Some of the M'zhalo people gasped, some lowered their heads in shame and some offered looks of sympathy. Together they lamented that the greatest secret in Upper and Middle Y'cromeca was now revealed.

The giant seized Arbantio by the shirt. Lifting him straight up with little effort, he met his gaze with hate-filled eyes. "Tell me, M'zhalo," he snarled, "why do these vermin commit this plunder of the Scions?"

Arbantio hesitated. He looked to his worker, still writhing in unfathomable pain. He knew he could never bear to see his family suffer thusly. The weight of a single man's torture already weighed heavily enough upon him. "It...it is the design of the Steward of Feynhava. It is he who decreed the Scions of Íraban be ferried away from the Thaed-Rú Dominions," confessed Arbantio.

The giant clenched his teeth. "Why? Tell me!"

"They were forcibly taken from their families, enslaved to build the Cethin Arda. The Gardener is also aware of unlawful experimentation on them...to increase their strength and stamina for labor in service to the Bal Rú."

"The Gardener!" seethed the giant. "It has been his infernal work all along!"

The Rhünkai men threw puzzled glances among their ranks. The Gardener was but an obscure, superstitious tale. To them, it was far more disconcerting to consider the men of the West, supposedly ignorant shepherds and farmers, had found a way to traverse the Ballai. Impenetrable, the mountainous walls ascended so high into the sky that no man had ever scaled them.

For centuries, the land of the West had been the stuff of fables in Upper and Middle Y'cromeca. Thus, even the most educated citizens knew nothing of the true history of the land, only fanciful stories of rustic peasants in the barren desert descended from Oliel and Alazar and destined to isolation by the Ballai of the West.

"I would believe the creatures appeared from another world before I will believe simple-minded Br'thain have knowledge of such power and might!" scoffed one soldier and his fellows grunted in agreement.

An officer suggested to the giant, "Surely, the miller fabricates this tale to protect the real perpetrators!"

But the ominous giant ignored them. His narrowed eyes remained trained upon Arbantio. He held up a hand and they fell silent.

"The Faeynül," he muttered to himself. Loudly, he addressed the prisoner, "Through my Harmattan sources, I have seen you convene with your trusted men, M'zhalo. I have seen them travel a long distance to help those desert vermin with their abduction of the Scions. You speak in a riddled tongue to thwart espionage. Now that I understand the Gardener has been behind all of this, I know it is the ancient tongue of the Faeynül."

Arbantio wept as he looked up at the giant and nodded.

"But why could my Harmattan spies, well versed in Uraduin, not decipher it?" asked the Haruspec.

When Arbantio hesitated to disclose their tactics, the Haruspec made to withdraw more powder from his pouch and turned toward the man's wife.

"Wait!" Arbantio called.

The Haruspec turned back again.

Despising his weakness, hoping for forgiveness for his betrayal, he whispered, "Seeds, the Gardener gave us seeds."

The Haruspec gestured for him to continue.

"We swallow them before we speak. They garble our speech to any who overhear our words." The poor miller hung his head as he spoke. He felt as though someone had just dropped him down a bottomless well of indescribable misery. His words compromised the valiant warriors of Oliel and Alazar. His words might jeopardize thousands of innocent lives, but once begun, he knew he would now lay all his knowledge bare in hopes of protecting his household.

"The Nebarraweth plant," the giant murmured with a nod.

Arbantio looked up in shocked surprise. He wondered how such an evil man could have knowledge of the wholesome powers of the Gardener.

"That accounts also for your undeciphered voices in the shed. But my Harmattan sources could not see your people there. What trickery is used there?"

Soldiers yanked Arbantio toward the shed. The giant and his henchmen followed. Arbantio pointed to a metal article mounted on the right side of the entrance. Its carved design of three waving lines represented a running river.

The Haruspec leaned closer to observe it. "What is the purpose of this talisman?" he barked.

"The Gardener instructed us to touch it every time we entered the shed to discuss the business of the Br'thain. It shields us from spies," answered the poor miller.

The giant traced the lines upon the talisman. "The Streams of Feynhava, I presume?" Through clenched teeth he growled, "Your Gardener seems very clever."

The miller shrank back as the giant's arm reached out toward him. But his bony fingers shot past the miller to wrench the numinous article from its nailed place on the threshold and whirled about in a huff.

Several brutes dragged Arbantio back to the courtyard, following on the Haruspec's heels. They slammed him violently to the muddied ground beside his family with several swift kicks to his torso.

Fingering the Talisman, the Haruspec asked, "When will these Br'thain vermin strike next?"

When the miller hesitated, the brutes shoved his wife down beside him and made as if to kick her too. "On the Gardener's next feast," Arbantio babbled, "during the fall of leaves…the first full moon in the Gardener's calendar."

"Where? How?"

Tears ran down his cheeks as he betrayed his friend. "The Gardener instructed us to be at the Fortress City on the third hour of the morn after the first full moon. They will drive a special spike into the ground to draw the underground currents of the Streams of Feynhava to the surface."

"How is it they return?"

The miller drew a shaky breath. The forced confession of the Br'thain's most guarded and valuable secret was too much. It was painful, exhausting.

"Each warrior…they carry a Ferusat spike in their animal skins. When a warrior grabs hold of a child…they drive the Ferusat into the ground and are ushered back into the streams."

"So, without these Ferusat spikes, no one can travel the Streams of Feynhava?" the Haruspec said shrewdly. "Is a host needed to channel a return opening?"

The miller peered up through sheets of rain at the Haruspec. His look of shame confirmed the Haruspec's anticipations. "A brilliant strategist the Gardener is! Very well. We shall foil the next attempt of these abductors of children, at the Fortress City."

As if in response to his words, several massive, crackling fingers of lightning streaked the sky. The giant booms of answering thunder and the screeches of the Veyasaen, still circling somewhere in the clouds above, rattled the nerves of the M'zhalo and Rhünkai alike.

But the miller's shame gave way to hatred. He gazed directly in the Haruspec's evil eyes. "It is the Rhünkai who abduct children. The Br'thain are their saviors!"

The Haruspec's eyes flickered rage at the man's defiance. With the supernal faculty of one hand, he bent the Gardener's token article, crumpling it into a clump of metal.

The miller's body quivered with a rush of adrenaline, and he raised his voice against the thickening storm, "You may strike at the Gardener's heel, but you shall not prevail! He will remove the curse of thorns and thistles so…"

The Haruspec hurled the token into the miller's face with such force it made those words his last. So passed Arbantio M'zhalo, of the clan of Faëlgrey, descendent of the Seven Sons of Y'cromeca.

"Say your farewells!" the giant figure sneered at the M'zhalo's and their workers. As they sobbed and clutched at one another he shouted to the Rhünkai, "Sing a song of their deaths! Their futile attempts to thwart the progress of the Cethin Arda are done! And this is but the first turn of the wheel."

He raised a hand to the sky and lightning streaked toward him in response. Ominously, he declared, "A violent maelstrom is coming! The great storm I bring shall utterly destroy the Tree of Y'crom planted in the West!"

Celebration in Anterròs

Across the valleys of Ferán and into the Yedara Mountains, harvests ripened and foliage darkened. Within the city of Anterròs, a tent city burst forth all about Baltien's estate housing hundreds of Br'thain. In the heat of the afternoon, they erected a massive tent to serve as reception for the scores of guests arriving from all over the West. There, old friends embraced in a tearful reunion while young and old alike exchanged pleasantries. The time of the Gardener's Feast was fast approaching.

For days, the matriarchs of the wealthy clan propers from across Ferán had aided S'baladin's mother in preparing flatbread, savory stews and soups, and tasty delicacies. As was Kalanit, they were princesses and ladies in all but name and ruled their communities with wisdom and love. Yet all week, they had worn their hair in simple buns and donned humble aprons in servitude to Kalanit, to whom they were entirely devoted.

From within his home, S'baladin watched the tent city grow and the guests arrive, all the while following the sun's descent with nervous eyes. He had rested all day in preparation for his Maleor. As the sun met the horizon, the inviting sound of stringed instruments and drums rose all around his home. His feast was beginning.

Steeling himself, S'baladin strode out into the cool spring evening arrayed in a special black Dolscareb. The ceremonial tassels of the Br'thain swung from each of the four corners of his robe. All he passed paused to offer smiles and well wishes. Used to going unnoticed, he blushed at the attention but nodded politely.

The young lad joined his family on a special mat situated under a canopy. It was large enough for the celebrant's family as well as the elders of the Fieradeem. His parents smiled at him briefly in welcome but were occupied in receiving the many noble souls offering gifts and blessings as tribute to their son.

"Where is T'balidor?" he whispered to his mother.

"Off to spar with your cousin Sibrion and their friends Javatiel, Kelán, and Vaez I think," she said. With a pat, she urged him, "Sit, eat, save your strength," then turned back to attend to their guests.

S'baladin, his stomach in knots, nibbled absently at a crust of unleavened bread. Thoughts of his impending performance consumed him until the distant shouts of "The Gardener is here! He is here for S'baladin's Maleor!" interrupted them.

Approaching the property was a caravan of wagons and horses transporting the Gardener himself. People rose and made their way to greet him with warm embraces, touch his tassels, or kiss his hand. In his great love for the people of the West, the Gardener reciprocated their rich and warm pleasantries, yet his eyes searched the crowd anxiously.

"Where is Baltien? Where is my old friend and his son?" he asked. Baltien and Kalanit appeared through the crowds.

As S'baladin followed, his brother T'balidor dashed up at his side breathlessly. "The Gardener didn't attend my feast!" he said. "A great privilege, little brother!"

"Baltien, my good friend! It is so good to see you again! And S'baladin!" he turned to greet the gangly boy with a beaming smile. "The celebrant of today's Maleor! You do your father's house a great honor. This is a special day that will be long remembered in the West, my son."

S'baladin smiled at both the words of his numinous guest and T'balidor's compliment. Nervous fingers toyed with one of the ceremonial tassels on his Dolscareb. Why was everyone acting as if this same event had not played out twice before? Two feasts, two failures.

Baltien spoke, "The pleasure is ours, my lord. My house is so honored that you could join us for S'baladin's Maleor."

Another wagon rumbled to a stop and, from it, descended a familiar man and his son. Baltien extended them a hearty smile which the man reciprocated.

"Graeyba!" called Baltien. "We are so glad you could join us!"

"It is an honor to join you in this special occasion!"

"How goes your training?" asked Baltien.

"I am learning much of the ways of the West and bettered by the wisdom of the Gardener," said Graeyba. "And D'thalien here, accustomed only to combat with his brother and I, is learning much from the discipline and order of the Br'thain."

So caught up in their greeting from Baltien were they, the Khalevads had not noticed the Gardener. As their eyes fell upon him, both men gasped and bowed respectfully. He smiled upon them kindly.

Baltien directed the Khalevads to the refreshment tent, then ushered the Gardener toward the guests. S'baladin followed at a distance, seeking the warmth of a nearby fire pit as Baltien sat to speak at length with the Gardener and two Fieradeem. S'baladin watched their lively expressions in the glow of a nearby fire pit. He knew his father was asking the Gardener one last time for his approval of S'baladin's unusual demonstration for his Maleor. The Gardener's wide smile conveyed his clear support and S'baladin felt his nerves settle, only to be jolted by the ram's horns chorus announcing the commencement of his ceremony.

Baltien rose and spoke in a loud voice for all to hear. "Friends and family, people of the West, on behalf of my family, I wish to thank you all for celebrating my son's Maleor! You have traveled long distances and many of you have honored my son with gifts. May the Garden of Ages grow strong roots in your lives."

Glad shouts and cheers rang out from the crowd. The Gardener moved to stand beside Baltien. "I am honored to join in S'baladin's Maleor as a guest of Baltien's house," he said. "On this hallowed occasion, a boy becomes a man," he turned to S'baladin. "His Maleor tonight will be as special as the special mark he bears. It carries the breadth and depth of the Garden of Ages. In time, his influence will ring across the West. It will bring the fury of the Faeynül to the vile lords of the Thaed-Rú."

The people fell silent in deep awe. Then murmurs swept across the mass of guests.

"He speaks of our sickly S'baladin?"

"Greatness? In Baltien's youngest son?"

Baltien's family exchanged nervous glances. S'baladin himself was taken aback. The Gardner merely smiled and gestured for the ceremony of the West to begin. The guests grew silent once more, out of respect, as Kalanit lit two candles. She too thanked the Gardener for meeting them at this feast.

Then, the Gardener laid hands on S'baladin and spoke in the ancient tongue of Uraduin. His undulating voice rang out in a song of wisdom from the Streams of Feynhava.

On this hallowed eve, I confer on you my words of life.

S'baladin, son of Baltien, of the house of Eirun-Vala,

from the clan of Alazar, of the land of Ferán,

leave behind your former ways of a child, and rise as a young man.

May the ancient wisdom of the Streams of Feynhava flow within your heart, always.

The Gardener turned to the Fieradeem. Still speaking in Uraduin, he commanded them. "Barons of the West, stewards of the Seat of Y'crom, on this Maleor, judge the words of the son of Baltien. Decide for yourselves if they hold substance enough for this boy to be welcomed as a man into the world of the Br'thain."

Few of S'baladin's guests had known of this unorthodox approach to his Maleor. They spoke quietly amongst themselves in confusion.

"He is not to fight?"

"I thought he was to spar with T'balidor."

The crowd fell silent as the four elders stepped forward and spoke their agreement and beckoned for S'baladin to join them. Under the full moon above, a large cloud formed over the desert mountains north of this gathering. Eerily, it floated in the direction of the gathering at Baltien's property, hovering above everyone. The people gazed wordlessly upward. Lightning and thunder rolled forth. Amongst the flashes could be seen glimpses of a garden paradise atop the cloud. Graeyba and D'thalien were amazed at this great sight, but the people of the West were used to great signs and wonders such as this and welcomed such blessings from the Gardener.

S'baladin smiled gratefully at the Gardener as he handed the young man a tea of crushed leaves. When ingested, it would amplify his voice above the sounds of the Gardener's signs and wonders. Turning to his guests, he unfurled an ancient Y'darit scroll and began his recitation in a loud voice that moved across the large gathering.

"'I am the Gardener before the memory of time. Chief Steward of the Garden of Ages beyond the Sea of Feynhava. Out of the shrouds of mystery, order begat our world. From the hallowed sod of Feynhava, the abode of the sons of the ancient powers, the foundation of the Garden of Ages, flowed an

Ancient Fount from eternal springs. For men, I crowned this land Ulmeca-Dül in the ancient tongue of Uraduin.'"

The ground shook as images of colossal figures trod heavily across the clouds. They appeared to descend the surrounding mountains toward the spectators who gasped appreciatively. Children squealed and clapped their hands at the sight of giants towering hundreds of feet above the feast. None were more excited than D'thalien who tugged at Graeyba's sleeve, saying, "Look Papa, the Faeynül! Just as we have read!" Baltien smiled at this enthusiasm and beckoned for Graeyba and D'thalien to sit with him so he could translate.

S'baladin too was excited by the wonders of the Gardener's powers, but he steadied himself, returned his gaze to the scrolls, and continued reading. His words flowed forth, telling the tale of how these giants had shaped their land and their people. He told of the coming of the mysterious Sheddukem, thought to have ascended from the coldest regions in the depths of the sea to steal the seed of the Garden of Ages.

As he told of their ill intentions, the guests of S'baladin witnessed strange beasts appear from the clouds to clash with the defenders of Feynhava. S'baladin took several deep breaths in this pause. Many of these turned ragged with coughs. Composing himself, he relayed to his guests the clash between the Sheddukem against the Aëlruk guardians and the Faeynül and their victorious routing of the dark ones into the sea. Momentarily, S'baladin himself paused to gaze at the Gardener's props high above as they acted out his words. It thrilled him to see these images reinforce his story. A gentle cough from the Gardener behind him reminded him to continue.

S'baladin's guests moaned and murmured audibly as he read the frightful tale of how the Sheddukem preyed on the pity of the Captain of the Aelrük, sapping all compassion from his soul and leaving his heart as corrupt as theirs. To most of them, this tale was a new one and they looked upward with great interest as a dark, hulking figure appeared behind the mountains. "'Before this dark figure was vanquished, he vowed one day to return, to eradicate the seed of Y'crom,'" S'baladin gravely relayed.

At this, the guests murmured worriedly. Many times, had they heard of how the Gardener routed the dark figure out to sea. Never had they heard of this vengeful threat. The people murmured in fearful awe as rippling clouds of white formed waves which swallowed up the ominous figure.

All the while, Baltien had continued his interpretation of Y'darit to Hierundiel for Graeyba and D'thalien. As they realized the cause of the stirring of the crowd, the father's brow furrowed, and the son's hair prickled. The two had faced evil enough.

S'baladin shuffled awkwardly. When the guests understood that he was not yet finished, they quieted. As he continued with his story, more flashes of lightning and thunder gave way to cloudy images of cavernous cities far below the ground where Sheddukem giants forged a dark garden with these seeds. The people sighed, well versed in the righteous war of the Faeynül against the Sheddukem and their dark garden, of the joining with them of the First Patriot Y'crom and his seven sons, and the great defeat of the Sheddukem. Riveted, they watched the battle scene unfold above them in the sky.

S'baladin's loud voice rang out in sacred Uraduin, speaking the words used by the Gardener so long ago to raise the Ballai:

> *"I speak the words of ancient life*
> *over metals harvested by the Faeynül.*
> *I command them, buried deep within the ground,*
> *to rise to shape the destiny of Y'cromeca.*
> *Rise high into the skies as Ballai.*
> *Cover and protect the sons of Y'crom.*
> *The faces of these infernal beasts*
> *wreath in stone, frozen in time.*
> *Never again shall beast or man rise over these walls*
> *to prey upon or slay those who dwell within*
> *And for ages to come,*
> *all those traverse the land will ask*
> *'What great feat doom this race,*
> *and triumphed over these colossal creatures?'"*

Many of the guests, students of the Gardener's wisdom, mouthed these words with him. But a great shaking of the ground beneath their mats ended their reverie. A massive stormfront above them swelled to cloudy heights of fifty to seventy feet to form puffy Ballai in every direction across the sky. The bright light of the moon cast a white glow upon the Ballai, but the images of dead Sheddukem glowed red as if illuminated by molten fire. Not subsiding until just before sunrise, this master prop of the Gardener remained all evening as a festive backdrop for the Maleor.

Cheers and shouts of praise erupted from the guests. The Gardener surveyed the crowds with a stoic, yet hearty smile. His bosom was filled with a deep well of love for the people. S'baladin too was overwhelmed, not with emotion but by his ailments. His body trembled and ever so slightly, began to sway. He cast a lingering gaze over his family and friends. His mother's brow furrowed as she saw sweat beading his brow, but his father beamed encouragement at him, nodding for him to continue.

Weakened by his performance, and hesitant for the last part of his tale, S'baladin frowned as he pressed forth with his narrative. "'Five centuries of the Sheddukem threat ran its course until each of the pods in the corrupt garden were burned or destroyed by molten fire. All save one. The final experiment of the Sheddukem had crossed one of their own with a son of the Y'cromahein.'" To his people, he relayed the origins of the Thaed-Rú' and their supernal powers, descendants of a single transmutation of the Sheddukem experiments with an Y'cromahein. The Gardener's props grew vague. Only a dark cloud, full of lightning and booming thunder hovered over a vision of a corrupt garden, thorny and wild.

The son of Baltien unfurled his last scroll tightly, raised it in the air, and addressed his guests. "This scroll has yet to be written upon. It remains blank. This will be our story, yet to be fulfilled. It is a wonderful story of beauty and adventure, but it is also frightful, its conclusion unknown."

A surge of strength flowed through him and he stood a little taller, a little steadier, as he spoke to his people. "The Thaed-Rú threat lies heavy in the north. Into these troubled times, the dark one, filled with vengeance and hate, lacking in mercy will return. I have seen visions of this. We now enter into a new chapter, crossing a threshold. Each of us has a role to fulfill. By the Gardener's wisdom has our country prospered, our Br'thain grown strong. I have always admired the strength and bravery of the Br'thain. I have always wanted to become one of you. But my affliction has led me to this most unorthodox Maleor. Tonight, I have shared the history of Y'cromeca, and I share with you what I have seen of the future." Surveying his guests, he concluded humbly. "I rejoice that you have travelled so far to celebrate my Maleor."

An awkward silence followed. Though the minds of his family and guests were still troubled by his vision, their hearts were touched by S'baladin's honesty. S'baladin's literary skills had hitherto been unknown by all save his family and a few in his community. Never had he spoken to anyone of his visions.

Baltien broke the hush. He leapt from his mat and strode proudly to his youngest son. He clapped him heartily on the back and lead the guests in a great clapping of hands for his performance. Into S'baladin's ear he whispered, "I am proud of you, son. You showed great strength and courage, reading as you did. You spoke from the Streams of Feynhava, the oral traditions of our forefathers. From this day forward, other young men will follow your example. They too will read from the oral traditions of our history."

The Fieradeem conferred briefly, then announced their unanimous decision to confer upon S'baladin the honor of joining the Br'thain, placing a special mark upon him, just as the Gardener had said.

An elder spoke over him. "You are a man now, son of Baltien! We welcome you in the Br'thain as the first ever Chief Scribe. From the beginning of our people, our history was always passed down through oral tradition. But now you will hold a sacred place in our ranks to tell the history of our people."

At this news, S'baladin's father cried out joyfully as Kalanit scooped her son into an ecstatic embrace. Guests showered a flurry of congratulations and gifts upon S'baladin and his family. Many expressed their appreciation for his words.

Many clan warriors congratulated S'baladin, men whom he respected and admired from his infancy. S'baladin, elated, felt as though he was floating among the puffy Ballai yet hanging in the clouds, a lingering decoration for his feast. Truly, the Gardener's spectacle was the greatest reward, blessing his Maleor with an immense validation. Second to the Feasts of the Gardener, no other celebration in the West had carried such glory and scope.

In the days following his Maleor, the people of the West returned to their work, and the Br'thain prepared for another mission to rescue child slaves from the north, but over them all hung the shadow of S'baladin's tale. Placing great faith in visions, a gloom hung over all who had heard of S'baladin's dark, compassionless figure. Indeed, their faith was well found. A great change loomed on the horizon as gathering remnants of the dark one's vengeance threatened to spill its evil across all of Y'cromeca, even into the West.

A Stepping Stone

The early morning darkness, tall pine trees and thick forest brush veiled a hidden threat. A hyena laugh rang out sharply from the rocky border along the forest's edge. It fell silent with a little whine as the sound of a hammer upon a spike signaled the presence of men.

Strange, ominous clouds formed high above and a low humming sound began. Across an open field electrical currents rippled against rocks and stones. These sounds rose gradually until hundreds of azure rings of light illuminated the field. Explosions of clods, twigs and debris announced the ascension of the clan warriors in Aerrukán skins. T'balidor and Baltien were amongst them.

T'balidor swept the field anxiously. An empty clearing stood where thousands of Rhünkai and child slaves should be. The hyena resumed his laughing, and an otherworldly shriek pierced the early morning darkness to join it in a howling chorus. Baltien frowned and gestured for the men to form tight ranks.

In a sudden fury, the forest came alive with horned wolf-like quadrupeds. They jumped out of the darkness to pounce and attack, devouring clan warriors. Some stood on two legs, much like a human, the height of ten or twelve feet tall. Shock gripped T'balidor at his core. Speechless, the cry of "Ambush!" froze upon his lips.

An order in a fiendish tongue shrieked across the darkness. Instantly a volley of wooden missiles erupted from the forests onto the open field. In the darkness, two hundred or more strange weapons, eight spears loaded into each, fired a lethal volley. Mounted on wheels, nearly twenty feet tall, and with ten to twelve men operating each weapon, these superseded Rhünkai ingenuity.

The men of the West sprang for shelter behind boulders and trees. These afforded little safety however as missiles whistled through the air from every direction in the valley.

One such missile struck the Ferusat of T'balidor at knee height. The entire staff exploded into tiny stinging shards. T'balidor panicked. It was as if his will had been snapped along with the staff. He swung his head about wildly, searching for his father. It proved difficult also to avoid the missiles while surveying the chaos for his father. In his state of distress, wolf and Aerrukán skins blended in a whirl. He soon abandoned all hope of locating his father as hundreds of clan warriors fell swiftly about him, impaled by the hurtling spears. These were the lucky ones. Others were torn apart by the fangs of the bloodthirsty beasts.

Wildly, T'balidor swung his head about. His gaze fell upon an arban of Rhünkai archers, an unearthly beast engraved upon their armor. From their ranks, a young captain, his face framed by blonde curls oddly familiar to T'balidor, leapt upon a boulder and shouted, "Archers of the 705th, aim, fire!"

The young Br'thain fell to the ground. As the volley of arrows flew arched overhead, he met the terrified eyes of a fellow warrior. The young man raised his Ferusat and fled into the safety of the Streams.

The archers bellowed their triumph as many Br'thain fell and many more fled. T'balidor heard one cry out to his captain, "They are on the run now, Aidan!"

"Aye, stop them!" their captain ordered roughly and ordered them to ready a second volley.

A primal fear surged through T'balidor as he scrambled awkwardly on his knees. Pushing his muscular frame between several tall boulders, he hid, ashamed of the Ferusat wielding Br'thain deserting the field in azure light, ashamed of himself for huddling like a child as the shouts of his countrymen filled the valley with a maddening noise. Yet, this was no ordinary battle.

The second wave of Br'thain emerged into chaos and confusion. Disoriented, many met a tragic fate in their confusion. Some managed to retreat through the Streams. A handful took with them the injured and the dead.

As several of the beasts leapt over T'balidor's boulders, he lay, unflinching, beneath his furry coat. It concealed him well in the shadows of the boulders. Steadying his breathing, he willed away his panic. All along the edge of the forest, Rhünkai reinforcements emerged, weapons drawn. They mean to kill us all, T'balidor thought grimly. As the last of the clan warriors disappeared from the field, the Rhünkai moved among the injured, their swords and axes mercilessly ending lives. Knowing Baltien would never have deserted such a fray, T'balidor clapped a hand over his mouth to quell a scream of Father!

When the field had quieted, but for the sound of the massive beasts devouring the flesh of men, a trembling T'balidor crawled out of his Aerrukán skin and away from the boulders. He feigned dead, collapsing to the ground, each time Rhünkai neared him. In misery, he crept past the corpses, searching for his father and his friends. After nearly half an hour of painstaking progress through the carnage, he once more sought concealment behind boulders, this time along the canyon walls to observe the carnage below. A wave of deep trauma at such defeat came over him and his vision misted. But his eyes sharpened at the sight of a giant figure moving slowly through the carnage.

The Haruspec's hideous, stitched face revealed a vile grin as he surveyed the carnage of T'balidor's dead countrymen. It caused T'balidor to looked warily about him. The creatures had been so numerous. Were there more of this new dark figure too? For a moment he was certain that a horde of evil entities were about to descend upon him. You are a warrior of the Br'thain of the West! he scolded himself. He shook his head as if to ward off his irrational thoughts. Steadying himself, he allowed a hatred of this forsaken land to replace his fears. "The very air is evil," he breathed quietly. This declaration brought a bit of calm upon him.

T'balidor's eyes narrowed as he followed the large figure. It hobbled through the carnage. Every step pained him. Yet, his voice was strong as he commanded a crony to collect an abandoned Ferusat from the ground. Holding it in his monstrous hand, the large figure observed its design. It stooped down to strip the Aerrukán skin from the body of a clan warrior. T'balidor breathed a sigh of relief. It was not Baltien.

Several beastly aides approached the giant with more Ferusats recovered from the dead. "Master, bid us to make our way to their land," they suggested. "Let us plunder their world as they have done ours, but to a greater extent."

"No," he spat. They shrank from him as he whirled upon them. More to himself than to them he said, "That is impossible, for now. M'zhalo said they have an agent at their base, a steward in charge of removing his Ferusat once their vermin return."

He bent with a grunt and fingered the dirt in one of the pits left behind by a warrior's Ferusat. "To follow them now," he said, "would only leave us trapped forever in the Streams. We have struck fear enough in their hearts for today."

A sense of foreboding came over T'balidor as he remembered his brother's Maleor, the vision of the pitiless, compassionless Aelrük. Was this figure one and the same? In the face of such evil, his instincts took over. A voice within him urged, the Va'Harot!

He tried to recall the Gardener's instructions to the Br'thain to find a hidden place of refuge in Hierundia, should they ever become separated in an attack. It came to him in hazy forms, his mind a fog of grief, his heart still thrumming with fear. "...a place of craggy foothills...I have called it Va'Harot. The features of this country...many rocks and boulders resembling skulls...fifty leagues distance from the Fortress City, northeast ... as the crow flies."

T'balidor made his way through the forest until he was clear from Rhünkai presence. Anger toward the Gardener ruled his thoughts. *You and your war have destroyed our army, taken my father from me, perhaps forever!* Hot tears slipped down his cheeks as he scrabbled down the mountainside. He threw a glance upward, gauged the sun's position, and redirected his steps toward the foothills of Va'Harot in the northeast.

For many days, he survived on the sparse vegetation along the shallow river that once roared through an endless canyon. Finally, his weary feet brought him to a collection of rocks and boulders resembling the skulls of creatures and men. The river, which had become a trickle, disappeared altogether to give way to the desolate landscape of Va'Harot. A frightful gloom hung over the place, as T'balidor glanced nervously about.

You said to meet here, Gardener! Yet where are my people?

For the first time since he began his dogged trek, waves of panic returned. Consciously avoiding the massive skulls above him, he kicked through the dust and pebbles below. *I have found only hopelessness here, not my father, not my friends!*

He found himself at the end of the canyon and gazed upward. The largest of the skull rocks rose some fifty feet in the shape of a gigantic monster. "This is it! The entrance of Va'Harot!"

The howl of wolves cut short his triumph. A pack appeared, eyes glittering. They chased him, snarling, higher up the rocks. Sharp teeth snapped at the flesh of his ankles. He stumbled in the darkness then yelped as his foot drove forward into nothingness. One of Va'Harot's deep crevices silently received the son of Baltien. As he fell, scrabbling for a handhold, he had but one thought: I am as cursed as this land!

• • • • •

For weeks, the young Bal Rú awaited the return of Lord Azxahiir. Still keeping to his chambers as he had for months, his days were consumed with nervous pacing, his nights with wild dreams of triumph and equally vivid nightmares.

From the skies above his tower came a great, shrieking cry. A wide grin spread across his face as he raced to the window and beheld the Haruspec upon his Veyasaen, descending into the courtyard below. Calling for his attendants, he cast away his rumpled clothing and to be dressed in finer garb. "Bring him to me!" he commanded eagerly.

Although they greeted each other formally, Íraban could barely contain his excitement. They sat in a pair of large armchairs, the Haruspec dwarfing his, to speak in private conference.

"It is as I had suspected," the giant heaved, short of breath from his trek to Íraban's rooms. "The Serpent in the Garden led me to the miller M'zhalo's homestead in Graëyhovan. His information led me to uncover those pathetic desert rats who have been sequestering your Scions, transporting them to the deserts of the West."

"And?!" pressed Íraban.

The Haruspec cackled. "With detailed knowledge of their plot, we laid a trap." Relaying all he had learned of the Br'thain's methods and their ambush, he concluded triumphantly, "We slaughtered them by the hundreds and plundered the equipment with which they travel so freely, Ferusats they call them."

"Let us enter their world and strike back!" the young Bal Rú responded. He grinned wickedly and straightened in eagerness. He rose a fist to pound it upon the arm of his chair, but the Haruspec arrested it mid-air, swallowing it up with his own, massive hand.

"Should they open the Streams again, we can certainly cross their Ballai, enter into their desert, and wipe out their entire life!" he said. Then tempered it with, "Yet we will not."

"We will not?" the Bal Rú echoed stupidly.

"We will not. They will know we now possess their Ferusats. If I were in their position, I would most certainly not allow our entrance."

The Bal Rú scowled and muttered, "Ah, of course."

"Lord Íraban," the Haruspec offered, "your Fortress City is wisely guarded by a strong Rhünkai presence. This is much to our advantage. I have seen the future through the Serpent in the Garden. Those vermin will return. There you have the upper hand, there, it shall be finished."

Íraban sighed his acceptance of this plan, then returned to his old complaint. "Why do they seek to take what does not belong to them? The Scions are rightfully mine. I own them."

The Haruspec leaned forward to gaze hypnotically into Íraban's stare. He quelled the young ruler's petulance with a promise. "There will be another day of reckoning. I have seen it. It is coming to these lands."

"What has the Serpent shown you? What do you know?" Íraban pressed.

From his Harmattan weed spies, the Haruspec recalled how numerous conversations had centered around the people's ignorant beliefs regarding the Gardener. Conveniently, their stories characterized him as a mythical and benevolent man who traversed their land to bear of tidings from another world. Careful to conceal his hatred for the Gardener, the Haruspec spun the myths of his immortal nemesis to his advantage.

"The Serpent has shown me the superstitious lore of your people surrounding a hermit wanderer - a purveyor of fanciful dreams, spreading homespun wisdom. He trespasses your Dominions every year as he journeys into the West. Time has exaggerated his importance."

"Yes, yes," the young man said dismissively. "Let the people tell their stories, what of it?"

"It appears it is he who leads those rustic scavengers of the West to sequester your Scions from their duty."

The young Bal Rú gaped and fell limply into his seat. He grabbed a flask of wine and poured himself a drink. What impotence, the Haruspec sighed internally. He forced a smile upon his lips as he ponderously hauled his massive girth upward to loom over Íraban's spidery, seated form.

"This wandering hermit, he is the sole impetus behind the infernal works against you. The Serpent in the Garden has shown me it is he who designed and engineered the raids that plague your progress. Allow me to remove him. Then these vermin can no longer capture your Scions."

Íraban was quiet a moment. When he spoke, it was with surprising shrewdness. "Could it be that this little hermit's power runs deeper than we know? Are my legions equipped to handle this task? Are you equipped to terminate him for me?"

It took everything within the Haruspec to refrain from breaking the Bal Rú in half like a twig. To the Haruspec, the lord of the Thaed-Rú Dominions was like a worm. *You are but a stepping-stone,* he seethed, *through you shall I possess this land and all the people in it.* But, mustering all the decency he could, he spoke calmly, "Did not I reveal the identity of those phantom raiders?"

Íraban merely blinked.

"Did not my minions, creatures, and my weaponry successfully thwart those vermin from the plunder of your Scions?"

"For this, I am beholden, Lord Azxahiir," said Íraban, unconvinced.

"Many an enemy lays slain. And not a single Scion was taken nor a single Rhünkai injured," the Haruspec continued. He widened his eyes hypnotically. "The great scope of my power comes from the Serpent in the Garden. Your alchemists struggle to unravel these mysteries in the Cethin Arda, but I can help you."

The Haruspec's lips twisted in satisfaction and he laid out his plan. "The Serpent in the Garden, henceforth, will stem the tide of war, Lord Íraban. Your vast army will shake the world, the fourth Cethin Arda will be revived and together we will defeat the vermin of the West. But so long as their fabled hermit lives, neither the engine of armed forces nor dark science can begin to touch a single hair of their heads."

His arcane ways gradually worked to ignite a fire of retribution in the Bal Rú's eyes. "Then we shall be rid of him," he agreed.

The Haruspec hobbled about his chambers, as if deep in thought. "You must understand," the Haruspec explained, "this hermit heralds from another world, a world far more transcendent than your own. It is this transcendence that he brings to the West. To this purpose, your Dominions must lean on the ageless wisdom, power and might of the Serpent in the Garden to strike this fabled hermit, and his vermin dead, once and for all."

Over the course of his stay in Realmhold Thaed-Rú, the Haruspec spent a great deal of time opening his mind to young Íraban, sharing with him ancient knowledge from the Serpent in the Garden. Young Íraban spoke highly of Lord Azxahiir to his counselors and the court began to buzz with talk of his power.

Winds of a new age blew afresh upon those who ruled over the Dominions. The Rhünkai captains and generals stood in awe as the Haruspec instructed their engineers in the building of weaponry far superior to their own. Lord Azxahiir lent his power to Íraban's Cethin Arda, where he taught the alchemists to incorporate his seeds of dark knowledge into their harvest. Thus did the highest echelons of the Thaed-Rú hierarchy gather in support of Íraban as he proposed to offer Lord Azxahiir the highest position in the Dominions, Lord High Counselor, second only to the Bal Rú.

Within weeks, the court of Realmhold Thaed-Rú drafted a charter to grant Lord Azxahiir the position. In return, they pressed him for his constitutional wisdom and guidance to benefit the Thaed-Rú Dominions with the Cethin Arda.

On a moonless, pitch black night, wind whistling eerily through the cracks of the Hall of Towers, the thirty- two members of the Thaed-Rú court played host to the Haruspec, his entourage, and various dignitaries from the Bal Rú's Dominions. All were treated with the highest decorum and protocol.

In the third hour of the great banquet, the vast chamber was cleared of all but Íraban's court and the Haruspec' entourage. The charter was formally presented to the Haruspec and he accepted the title of Lord High Counselor of the Dominions.

It was with a fiendish delight that Íraban's court set him upon a high throne over the whole of the land, second only to the Bal Rú Íraban. They saw in their minds a primeval and sagacious figure that would lead their world into an age of transcendence. They saw the Thaed-Rú lineage eclipse Y'cromeca and transcend into immortality in the path of Lord Azxahiir.

As the Haruspec ascended his magnificent throne, all within the chamber stood transfixed. The court of thirty-two witnessed hundreds of tiny black insects float away from the confines of the dark robes of the Haruspec. They stared in awe and wonder as the gnats grew larger until they resembled a flock of crows. Many of the dark fowl swarmed around their master, while some floated aimlessly around the chamber as still others dissipated into clumps of black feathers which fell upon the stone floor.

A rumble shook the chamber. Íraban would soon learn that this rumble emanated beyond the hall in a wide radius to include the entirety of Realmhold

Thaed-Rú. It thrilled him now to watch as black thorns and thistles eerily sprouted from between the stones on the floor and on the walls to surround the Haruspec's massive throne. *An omen! He will make my garden flourish!* the young ruler foolishly thought. But a drunken euphoria ran through each of the men in the chamber. The entire court were instantly imbued with a palpable sense of otherworldly power. They tasted a glimmer of immortality in the shadow of the Haruspec.

The Haruspec spoke in a voice that thundered through the chamber. "Sense the foreboding that is gathering. Breathe it in. I behold a city whose scope and power stretches across the Eleven Provinces. I see a vast dominion of creatures, a great army and people harvested from a dark garden beyond domestication. It is a world awakened to fleeting beauty, pain and suffering. The beasts of the field moan and wail in anguished anticipation. The sower in the fields awaits a day of gloom and fire that will consume the harvest. The soldier sharpens his sword for a day that is fast approaching. Anger, blood, hatred and fury will be unleashed throughout the Dominions. It will scatter every man, woman and child into the four winds of the land. A day of reckoning is coming to Y'cromeca!"

And the foolish court, feasting upon Mithengara-tainted fare as they had these many weeks, nodded merrily to this, raising their goblets in a toast to the Haruspec's dark threats.

A Cry in the West

Following the Gardener's Feast, far away in the West, the sun rose on the ruins of Duin Caeir. A large crowd of families, friends and loved ones awaited the return of the Br'thain, laden with rescued child slaves. The steward of the Ferusat, kneeling on the stone surface with his ear to the ground heard the low drumming sound and called out, "I hear them moving through the Streams! People move yourselves back!"

The people complied, shouting in anticipation as a humming grew, its vibrations culminating in rippling electrical currents. Azure rings of light burst forth, illuminating the field as clan warriors ascended. The enthusiastic cheers of the crowds rapidly dissolved to alarm as they became aware of the state of the Br'thain before them, the absence of liberated slaves. Limping warriors yanked off the beastly heads of their disguises and cried out loudly, "Draw your weapons!" to the guards.

Immediately, swords, shields and lances were fixed into position. Those who had returned exclaimed, "Ambush!" and "Many have been slain!"

Clan warriors in various states of injury trod heavily off the stone field, making way for the second wave. The people let out murmurs and moans of shock and confusion at the sight of their beloved Br'thain bearing dozens of the deceased upon their shoulders.

A hush fell upon them all as domes of azure lights appeared once more. The second wave of surviving warriors bore with them many injured and fallen brothers in arms. As the lights faded, the steward in charge of the Ferusat stiffened for a moment at the command of an officer. Then, in a dramatic, two-stroke move, he swept his spike upward and smashed it down upon the stone surface, thereby closing up the Streams of Feynhava.

The field grew silent but for the moans of the injured. The people, galvanized by these cries, moved rapidly to aid the injured and retrieve the dead. Wails of grief began as some identified the dead body of a father, a son, a groom soon to be married, cousins, uncles. It was a calamity of great distress never experienced in the Ballai of the West.

In the confusion, Kalanit, along with several attendant relatives, searched nervously through the crowds for Baltien and T'balidor. A horrible knot gripped her stomach. "T'balidor...Baltien!" she shouted, as she surveyed the chaos.

Behind her, S'baladin shouted, "Papa...T'balidor!"

As a sheep that knows their shepherd's voice, Kalanit's family recognized the voice of the Gardener's loud wail of grief. Indeed, it rent the crowds. The venerable matriarch hurried her family along until they came upon the Gardener. He had fallen to his knees. In his arms was a lifeless body clad in bloodstained Aerrukán skins. Their hearts sank the instant they recognized the face of Baltien. The Gardener tore the fur skins apart with supernal strength, to expose a severe gash on Baltien's chest. Kalanit's family hovered near. Onlookers drew near and murmured from one to the other that the great leader of the West was dead.

Kalanit fell upon her deceased husband, crying in a loud voice, "Baltien! Oh, my Baltien!"

S'baladin stood frozen, looking helplessly down upon this tableau. In a moment of quiet strength, the sickly child placed a steady hand upon his mother's shoulder. All about them, the gathering of souls tore at their robes, cast dust upon their heads and lamented their slain patriarch.

"My dearest friend is done!" lamented the Gardener.

A clan warrior in bloodied Aerrukán skins approached the Gardener. "A terrible ambush, it was. We arrived in the wilderness, far from the Fortress City! More than just the Rhünkai, there were monstrous beasts among the trees who devoured our brothers! We retreated rapidly amidst much chaos. I barely escaped. Most were killed upon sight."

Those within earshot muttered curses amongst each other or wailed in grief. The warrior glanced about him grimly, then continued his report. "As I drove my Ferusat into the ground, on my left I saw a missile strike the Ferusat of one of our warriors. It shattered into pieces. Immediately, a volley of missiles struck between us, or I would have him with me. As I slipped into the streams, I saw him crawling on his belly for a rocky outcrop. Perhaps some of us survived, perhaps they will meet at Va'Harot as you instructed."

The Gardener's eyes flared with hope at this. Gently, he shifted Baltien's heavy head to his wife's lap, and rose. It was then that a look of horror came upon Kalanit. She grasped pitifully at the Gardener's robes as he made to leave. "Where is my T'balidor?" she cried.

"I have not seen him here," the Gardener frowned. "Perhaps he is among those who escaped to Va'Harot."

Lips trembling, Kalanit expressed a burdensome fear, "My lord, what if he is in their hands?"

The warrior said, "My Lady, none were taken prisoner that I saw."

Finding this more grim than reassuring, she collapsed forward against Baltien's chest, sobbing.

The Gardener turned to the warrior again. "Tell the remaining division captains to draw up a list of the survivors and the slain. We must find all who are unaccounted for!"

The clan warrior nodded and turned to set about this task at once.

To Kalanit, the Gardener gently urged, "Do not worry too gravely on account of T'balidor. I know that all seems lost, but your son is a skilled warrior. If he survived that massacre, he will be found."

She turned woeful eyes upward, wiping fiercely at her tears.

"Years ago," the Gardener explained, "I designated a place of refuge should our warriors ever become stranded. Any who survived will know where to go while we plan a rescue party to retrieve him."

He expected hope to bloom at this, but Kalanit's eyes remained hopeless. If Baltien lay slain, what hope was there for her son?

As the day waned, the stone ruins became a hospital. Doctors arrived from nearby Messidia to attend row upon row of the wounded. With the setting of the sun came the list of the unaccounted, which ran in the hundreds upon hundreds. T'balidor was among those named.

At dusk, the Gardener met with many of the Fieradeem to discuss the details of the ambush. In all the confusion, fear and loss of heart, the Gardener offered the Br'thain just one directive: develop a safe approach for rescuing survivors from Va'Harot.

That night, inexplicably, the Gardener disappeared. He simply passed through the Streams without a word to anyone. With no knowledge of his intentions or destination, the next day's sun fell upon a mass of confusion and anger. After such a terrible day of death, the Gardener's departure was salt upon their wounds. A crowd gathered before the Fieradeem, shouting complaints and voicing fears.

"It was his idea to rescue those children of the north!"

"Aye, and now he leaves us so discourteously!"

"To bury our dead alone? With no words of honor?"

"What are we to do?"

But the great men of the West were at a loss of how to proceed. No one could recall a more frightful and disheartening time. As their enemy now possessed the Ferusats of the dead, their passage to the north closed. With the bulk of their warriors slain or injured, their courage was lost. Thus, leaders and villagers alike abandoned vengeance and sank into mourning.

• • • • •

In the aftermath of the greatest disaster ever to strike the Br'thain, families travelled far across the land to Calasmorra, Rihován and Ferán to bury their fallen in their hometowns. Grief-stricken clan warriors carried Baltien's body on a wagon from Duin Caeir to Anterròs. As they travelled, the caravan behind them swelled with mourners giving precedence to the funeral of Baltien over blood of their own. They laid him to rest with his forefathers in the land of Ferán, near Anterròs.

On the evening of Baltien's funeral, the sun set on a gathering of hundreds upon hundreds of souls. Large numbers of clan warriors from every corner of the West, held their flags, waving in the evening breeze. Families, friends and strangers from across the West came to pay their respects to a great leader and patriarch. Tales of how this noble soul had touched so many lives moved many to tears and laughter alike.

Graeyba and D'thalien were among the mourners. They spoke fondly of Baltien's heartfelt welcome upon their arrival in the West. "At the start, my sudden separation from all that I knew, and my inability to search for my eldest son left me utterly defeated..." Graeyba paused, eyes misting, he turned to gaze at his son before continuing, "Despite my reunion with D'thalien, despite the beauty of the West and the hospitality of its people, I felt as though I had died."

A gasp erupted amongst those gathered, several frowned at the foreigner's inappropriate choice of words. But he raised a hand to silence them and continued, "But Baltien, occupied as he was with the missions of the Br'thain to thwart the evil abuse of children in the north, took time to carve out a purpose for my son and I here. As a Preceptan amongst your people, I have been grateful to learn your ways. As I learned of the Gardener's wisdom, I also learned of Baltien's kindness and saw how beloved he was by his people and his family. It is no surprise to me now that so many of you have gathered to respect him. I mean not to intrude upon your customs, I mean only to convey that, in my lands too, he would have been a great personage, and his passing would have been equally honored."

The crowd settled, and Kalanit nodded to him gratefully for his words. Yet he rubbed at his forehead in frustration, feeling he had expressed himself inadequately. Within him worked a complex grief beyond his grasp. The loss of Aidan, the loss of his homeland, and so similar were these funeral rites to those of Graeyba's wife that it moved him to tears.

Into the fog about his senses, D'thalien expressed similar thoughts. "Papa, do you think Aidan is dead?"

Graeyba's eyes narrowed. He frowned but firmly shook his head against such thoughts. "I would know it if he was. I am certain he yet lives."

D'thalien pressed his lips firmly together in a frown of doubt. Only out of respect for the mourners all about did he hold his tongue.

The last to bid Baltien farewell was Kalanit. Choking back tears, her words were brief. "Every one of you here I love with all my heart. You are all dear to me. But today, I find no joy in your company as it marks the loss of my dearest friend. The West has lost its greatest son. The Br'thain has lost its bravest warrior," said Baltien's widow.

As the ceremony ended, dozens of the Br'thain tore their robes from the collar down. As their wails erupted, the land shook with a thunderous quake.

A Bold Venture

It was now K'nurith, the eleventh month of the Gardener's calendar, the beginning of the winter season. Cool winds blew gently across a desert landscape of dried cacti, wildflowers, trees, shrubs and grasses that surrounded the ruins of Duin Caeir. There, the Fieradeem and Preceptans of every clan of the West were gathered. Their standards fluttered gloriously in the evening sun.

Quispal, the Elder of Tal-Coras from Calasmorra, began the meeting. The man was never without his tobacco pipe. Never had he attended a meeting without sending little puffs of aromatic smoke above the heads of all. But today, he stood without it. "This has been a very dark time for the sons of the West. Be it son, father, kinsman, or a dear friend, each of us bears a loss from the ambush. As many of you know, the Gardener's mysterious disappearance perplexes us still. Perhaps he has a just reason, but it is his choice for it to remain hidden," he said.

"I disagree, Quispal!" uttered a Fieradin of Maluenda. "There are many here who take offense with the Gardener leaving without explanation. Many in my region accuse him of deserting his own cause. The Gardener is gifted with visions, yet he had no knowledge of the ambush? He must surely have left in shame," added the Fieradin. Such an accusation would have been shocking weeks ago, but today, many heads nodded in agreement.

A young Preceptan raised his staff to speak and Quispal conceded. "Suppose he has left to seek the aid of outlying kingdoms beyond the western sea?"

His fellow, seated at his side, scoffed and was recognized. "And supposing he has sheltered himself in some unknown sanctuary? Protecting himself from the dark one spoken of by S'baladin?"

Quispal struck his staff loudly against the stone field to quiet the eruption of conversations. "We are divided by the Gardener's willful disappearance; of this it is certain. But this is the measure of his ways. I too am puzzled, yet I trust that in the end, all things will be revealed."

"So, what is to become of young T'balidor?" asked another of the Fieradeem.

"For the time being, it is not safe to venture into the Va'Giyyel. With Ferusats in their possession, they could capture our rescuers and force their way into the Streams. Let us trust the wisdom of the Gardener. Together, our collective hope will guide young T'balidor to hide safely within Va'Harot," said Quispal.

• • • • •

Months passed and the Gardener failed to appear. Yet, still the faithful gathered again at the ruins of Duin Caeir for his feast, clinging to mere threads of hope. For that hope, people came from far and wide to set up their tents near the stone ruins. They joined hundreds upon hundreds of loyalists who had camped there ever since the Gardener's departure, faithfully awaiting his return.

On the outskirts of the festivities one evening, from a butte a hundred feet above the stone fields, a peaceful melody drifted from the lyre of a shepherd boy. He sat at the center of a small ring of boys surrounding a campfire.

Overcome by the music, tears welled up in S'baladin's sickly features. He wiped at them and explained apologetically, "I fear my body sickens further with the anger and grief which consumes me."

"Abán, still your fingers," Sabaca murmured quietly. He toyed with a clump of vegetation in the awkward silence which followed. Unable to uproot the leafy stalks from the crack through which they had stubbornly sprouted, he peered upward and asked, "S'baladin, are you upset with the Gardener? Do you blame him for what happened to your family?"

S'baladin stared at the stone floor of the sprawling butte. "My family," he muttered. He sighed deeply, a sigh which erupted into a series of coughs. Then, a stream of grief poured forth. "I always admired T'balidor's strength, his skill with weapons, but I little considered my father's skills. Now, my home is full of the stories and accolades of visitors paying their respects. My father's diplomacy, leadership, generosity and benevolence to all was every bit as admirable as T'balidor's prowess with a blade! Yet now..." tears gathered in his eyes, "now he is gone, and he will never hear from me of this new and deep respect I have for his legacy."

The boys murmured condolences to S'baladin, but he was beyond comfort. Hotly he turned to Sabaca, "You ask if I blame the Gardener? I believed the Gardener's plan was foolproof, perfect. Never did I think a single one of the Br'thain would be slain in those raids!" Heaving breathlessly, he gazed into the fire a moment. Quietly, he said, "I do not know what to believe anymore. The Gardener's ways, the Br'thain, all of it has failed."

Diero, always quick to side with S'baladin mused, "Aye! If we were executing his will in rescuing children, should we not be covered by his infinite power from the Garden of Ages?"

"My papa and brother did so much for this cause and look what happened to them!" S'baladin scowled. "And the Gardener offers no wisdom, no consolation. We are on our own now, my mother and I." Though his body was weak, there was a strength in his eyes as he declared, "I must go after my brother. If he survived, I must find him and bring him back. If the Br'thain can enter the vast Va'Giyyel, the hinterlands beyond the Ballai, to rescue children, why can I not do the same to rescue my brother?"

"Well, for one damn thing," bellowed quick-witted Diero, "in their last meeting, Sibrion sought permission from the Fieradeem to take a group of the best warriors to find your brother. And you know damn well what happened to that cousin of yours, S'baladin!"

The gangly boy appeared too lost in thought to reply. The fourth among them, busily consuming lamb's meat wrapped in flat bread, finally spoke in a chortle. "They sequestered him! Day in, day out, he may speak with no one. And all the Ferusats were confiscated because of his crazy ideas!"

"That was months ago, Jubal!" Diero huffed. "And still no one can leave the Ballai! And a good thing too! They say the ones who ambushed us plundered many a Ferusat. Do you want them slipping past us in the Streams, to ambush innocents in the West?"

"This is the reason we cannot search for T'balidor, much as we want to," interjected Sabaca.

Abán, who had resumed strumming his lyre, began to think aloud. "I wonder...what if we were to take...just one?"

The boys all turned to him and urged him on in chorus when he paused, "One what?"

Abán strummed a chord to punctuate each word. "Just...one...Ferusat..."

"Your senses are scattered!" quipped Diero. "It would still mean opening up the Streams. Are you suggesting we disobey the Fieradeem?" he pressed.

The musician shrugged, strummed his lyre, and sang a ditty. "On wings of hope we fly afar, with a Ferusat in our beak, to bring our brother back."

The lads' chuckled yet remained skeptical.

Around a last large bite, Jubal snorted, "You have lost the plot, Abán." He wiped breadcrumbs from his pudgy fingertips, folded his hands behind his head, and laid down to gaze upward at the stars.

"Oh, now you all have found a conscience?" the musician jibed. Jubal groaned and turned away but Abán persisted. "You think I encourage your delinquency, but I ask you, does the Gardener's disappearance negate his wisdom?" Again, the boy sang a little snatch of a tune, this time giving melody to a lesson they all knew well. "When we are willing to seek help, the universe responds in kind."

S'baladin's grief-stricken gaze cleared at this and he cocked his head to one side in consideration.

Diero's laugh echoed out against the stone. "You are mad as a bag of ferrets, Abán! You are using the words of the Fieradeem against them, to justify illegal actions – just to help a single person!" A wicked grin broke out as he cried, "I love it!"

He leapt to his feet and waggled a finger in the air, "Listen to me, you raggabrashes! If we are caught, do not – and I mean DO NOT divulge our plan to anyone. Is that clear?"

The boys gaped up at him.

"Leave everything to me," he said, "I know how to talk my way out of anything."

The lads exchanged mixed looks of concern and excitement.

"We'd need a spike too, not just a Ferusat," Jubal mused. Then grunted, "Diero, what brilliant idea fills that head of yours?"

Reaching into his pouch which hung underneath his arm, Diero unfolded a piece of cloth that revealed several blades. "Finally, my apprenticeship to that old drunk is paying off! See these? Javatiel, Vaez and Kelán placed orders for me to make these for them. I'm to deliver them to their posts."

"My brother's friends," murmured S'baladin, a glimmer of hope in his dark eyes.

Jubal sighed heavily and hefted his body upward to peer at the gleaming weapons. "What does that matter?" he grumbled.

Diero stood eyeball to eyeball with the portly youngster. "They guard the storehouses where the Ferusats are kept, jackass! While S'baladin and I are busy with those blaggards, you, Sabaca and Abán will sneak into the storehouse from behind. All we need is one Ferusat and one spike to open the Streams."

• • • • •

The following day, Diero and S'baladin warily approached a large cluster of smooth, massive boulders. Their figures appeared as two tiny ants against the rocky backdrop.

"There is the entrance to the storehouse," Diero pointed to a low-lying hole in the boulders. "Where they keep the Ferusats?" responded S'baladin.

The two youths hesitated as they spotted three guards at the mouth of the cave.

"I know them," whispered S'baladin. "Javatiel, Vaez and Kelán. They are friends of T'balidor!"

"Here comes the blacksmith's apprentice with our blades," said Javatiel to the others as they approached.

Still, Vaez ordered, "You, there! Do not come any closer, by word of the Fieradeem!" The three men moved toward Diero and S'baladin who halted. Diero smiled and withdrew their blades.

Engaged in inspecting the weapons, the guards remained unaware that three other youngsters had previously crawled on top of the cave. Jubal, Sabaca and Abán now scrabbled down and entered the cave.

S'baladin feigned nonchalance as Diero rambled incessantly, "Yes gentlemen, so after I hammer the ore down well, I dip them in the Quinassa River. You know what they say about the water – it has mineral properties that can galvanize any metal stronger than most others out there. You will not find anything more durable than my blades, gentlemen. I give you my word."

Inside the cave, Abán, Sabaca and Jubal stumbled onto Yashi, Vaez's floppy-eared sheep dog snoozing by the campfire. "What good is Vaez' sheep dog here? Everyone knows he never barks!" scoffed Jubal.

"I heard Vaez used to tie him up, but the silent mutt always escaped and followed his trail," said Sabaca.

"Silent and faithful," Abán murmured, "a dog such as that is the stuff of songs."

"Come," urged Sabaca and the boys followed him past Yashi, toward the rear of the cave.

Jubal gestured to a rusted steel cage frame with a locked door, "The Ferusats and metal spikes lie beyond that door," said Jubal, "and here I have Diero's lock picker." He moved to examine the lock, then yelped as Yashi's wet nose pushed at him, sniffing about his pouch.

"Yashi! Get away. I am busy here," Jubal urged quietly. He pushed at the dog with a leg while still struggling with the door lock.

"I think he is hungry. You wouldn't have any food in there, Jubal?" teased Abán.

With a low whimpering bark, Yashi rested his paws on the portly lad's arms. Jubal chuckled at Yashi's wide-eyed begging and relented. "Of course Jubal has food! Sssh now!" he whispered. He reached into his pouch and gave Yashi some bits of lamb meat. "Here! Now leave me alone." Satisfied, Yashi gulped down the snack and retreated.

As he continued to struggle with the door lock, it suddenly snapped in half. "Ugh! Damn this pick lock!" Jubal cursed quietly, "Diero said it could open anything!"

Abán reached into his pouch and pulled out his flute. From there, he removed a small pin. "Here, let me give it a try." It sprang open in an instant. Jubal gaped, dumbfounded.

The young musician wriggled his fingers at him with a grin. "These are good for more than a tune!"

Quickly but cautiously, the three lads reached for a Ferusat and a metal spike. Stealthily, they moved toward the mouth of the cave. But Yashi arrested their progress. Playfully, he jumped at Jubal's pouch a second time. In response to the boy's rejection, he emitted a pleading yelp, as if to pledge a new allegiance if he could but have a bit more.

"This dog will be our ruin!" muttered Jubal. He reached into his pouch a second time and tossed the lamb's meat behind him, far behind him. In nervous haste, the boys had forgotten to close the jimmied door. Now Yashi's prize fell within the pile of Ferusats. The three boys watched in horror as he leapt to fetch it. As an avalanche of metal spikes clattered noisily to the floor, the boys cast their eyes about nervously for a place to hide but found none against the gently sloping walls of the cave. Without, Diero and S'baladin exchanged nervous glances as the guards whipped their heads about and clutched at their weapons.

Diero, feigning deafness to the noise, bid them a nervous farewell. "Well gentlemen, I guess this concludes our trade. Thank you for your business. May we meet again."

Javatiel ordered Kelán and Vaez to the cave and Diero and S'baladin made ready to leave. In one smooth move, Javatiel detained them, grasping each of them so firmly by the shoulder that they winced. Moments later, Kelán peered out from the cave and beckoned Javatiel to join him with the boys.

Vaez, chest heaving and seethed through gritted teeth, "We just caught these three damn whelps!" He spluttered in disbelief, "They were trying to steal a Ferusat...and a metal spike!" To the boys he bellowed, "The Fieradeem will hang you boys for this crime!"

"I have seen you five together at the Feasts," commented Javatiel. "What are you thinking, you bunch of saddle-gooses? You think you can steal from under our noses? And at such a grave time as this?" Javatiel's voice rose with every word as he processed the deep offense of their actions.

"The Fieradeem are going to hang you upside down! Then they will smash your wedding jewels in front of all the girls!" Vaez threatened.

Sabaca and S'baladin winced in fear but their fellows glared back at their captors in defiance.

"Speak up as to your intentions!" pressed Kelán.

Remembering Diero's instructions, the juveniles cast their eyes downward and held their tongues.

But Diero burst out, singing like a canary, "Please do not tell the Fieradeem! We just wanted to borrow a Ferusat and the metal spike. We wish to open the Streams so that we can go into the Va'Giyyel by our ourselves, to search for T'balidor, to bring him back! Honest. That is what we plan to do. And that is why we stole the spike and Ferusat. Here, take them back, just do not tell the Fieradeem! Please?"

His friends stood speechless as he babbled. The guards gaped openly at the boys. Then Javatiel's laughter rang out, echoing from wall to wall. Vaez and Kelán exchanged looks as puzzled as those of the five friends.

"You are a real gasbag, you know that? You have less common sense than a sleeping two-year old rocking in his mama's arms!" Javatiel flung at the apprentice blacksmith. Yanking the metal spike from Jubal's hand, Javatiel shook it in the boy's face. "Do you even know which of these to use first, and how? Do it wrong and the Streams remained closed. You bunch of jackasses will pop up just feet away!" Javatiel, Vaez and Kelán erupted in laughter, while the boys exchanged looks of embarrassment.

"Maybe we should send them into the Va-Giyyel and let the Rhünkai spank them for their own good!" jeered Kelán.

"Yes, that might teach these boys a lesson!" Vaez chimed in. More earnestly, he asked, "What happens next, Javatiel? Should we turn these jokers over to the Fieradeem?"

Javatiel's grin flattened. "We will do no such thing."

Guards and delinquents alike expressed astonishment, but Javatiel held up a hand to silence them. To his two comrades, he said firmly, "Strange as this sounds, I sympathize with their cause."

"Javatiel, you lost the plot," frowned Vaez. "Maybe I have. Maybe all this is wrong, or worse, foolish. Perhaps we should just turn them over to the Fieradeem. However," he paused, cast a shrewd gaze at the boys, then continued, "I cannot help but agree with them. Somebody needs to rescue T'balidor! Sibrion tried, did he not?"

Vaez nodded and Kelán stuck out his lower lip in thought.

"Tried and failed, and through proper channels too," Javatiel pushed. "And what did they do to him? They sequestered him with a Fieradin and drove fear into the hearts of all." Javatiel snorted and crossed thick arms over his mighty chest. "Never have the Br'thain given up their Ferusats to official confiscation!"

Vaez nodded again and offered, "For years, we Br'thain have risked much in the Va'Giyyel to rescue foreign children, at our own peril. How is it that the ambush of the Rhünkai erases that bravery, that honor?"

"Sibrion's arrest, I must admit, drove me to fear too…" Javatiel confessed, "…at first. Then, when we were stationed to guard this storehouse, I thought again, 'Why are we guarding these Ferusats in here? We should be using them to search for our brother!'"

Vaez and Kelán stared at the Ferusats, pondering Javatiel's words. Diero, grinning, jabbed at his friends and motioned excitedly. They were all smiles in response, all but S'baladin who remained respectfully attentive to Javatiel.

"As young as you lads are, and as dim-witted as your plan sounds, you five lads have brought back my courage." Javatiel's eyes flared with fresh fire. "I would be ashamed to call myself Br'thain should I not join in your endeavor."

All five of the boys gasped, then whooped excitedly. Javatiel smiled kindly at them, but his expression darkened as he turned to his comrades. "I ask you honor a single request. Delay your report to the Fieradeem until after we have passed through the Streams. I will gladly face the consequences upon my return, whether I find T'balidor or not."

"No. I cannot do that," said Vaez.

Javatiel heaved a heavy sigh, and the joy of the little band faded.

"Indeed, I cannot either," agreed Kelán, "for I wish to join you."

"That makes two of us," agreed Vaez.

Seeing smiles all about him, Javatiel glared and challenged them gravely. "This will be no picnic! Decide now if you wish to withdraw yourself from our enterprise. And no blame will attach itself to you."

The eight youths exchanged a nervous glance, but none spoke.

"Then we are all in. This pact is sealed," spoke Javatiel. "But first, we will free Sibrion that he might join us also. T'balidor is like a brother to him."

Vaez issued one instruction. "Before we move to free him, let us procure winter gear and food surplus from this cave. There is a secret place I know where we can store them, along with a Ferusat and one or two metal spike conductors to open the Streams. Then we will free Sibrion from his isolation."

And with that, the fellows moved in haste and excitement.

An Escape

A DAY'S JOURNEY FROM THE STOREHOUSE OF FERUSATS, SIBRION stirred from a deep meditation and rose. A cool evening breeze blew gently across an endless landscape of dried desert brush and cacti, but it was not the breeze which stirred him. Sensing no threat, the young Br'thain warrior stretched his limbs before following a strange rustling sound. He moved past bowers heavy with blooms, past the gentle lapping of the water against the banks of a small pond where small fish swam lazily about, further and further away from the house of a certain Fieradin tasked with sequestering him from all manner of visitors.

"Sibrion! Over here!" Javatiel hissed to his friend.

The youth smiled as he spied familiar faces amongst a band of eight youths. Glancing around for guards, he hissed, "What are you doing here?"

"We came to break you out!" Kelán and Vaez chorused.

"Break me out?" he laughed. "I am under no heavy guard and have no jailer. Still, best keep hidden as my host would not joy in seeing you as I do. Is that you, S'baladin?" he asked peering wonderingly into the bushes at the sickly boy making such a journey.

"Aye, the eight of us formed a pact to search for Sy's brother," Javatiel said proudly, patting S'baladin's shoulder.

Diero interjected excitedly, "We even have a Ferusat and a metal spike to cross the Streams!"

Sibrion gaped incredulously at them as Javatiel jabbed at Diero and added, "But we need you to lead us."

The captive youth squinted at them. "You have traveled far for such a jest!"

Sabaca stepped forward, brandishing the Ferusat and metal spike. Sibrion sobered instantly.

"Your hearts are in the right place," he said, "But, in my seclusion here these many months, I have come to understand it is indeed foolhardy to enter the Va'Giyyel beyond the Ballai." He rebutted their protestations, urging, "Yes! Even to search for T'balidor! It is a foolish quest."

Several of the boys crossed their arms over their chests in irritation. S'baladin stepped forward, "Cousin, your leadership would aid us greatly in our search."

"Have you forgotten that the Rhünkai now have Ferusats?" Sibrion shook his head despondently. "None of you are safe on this mission, but you also risk them entering the Streams to annihilate our people."

"Sibrion, my name is Diero," piped the apprentice blacksmith's voice.

"Yes, I know of you from S'baladin."

"You may have also heard of Abán here too?"

Sibrion nodded and Diero continued, "His father and my father have never been in our lives. For years, his mother has barely made ends meet, and he has often stooped to theft. And I suffer the master blacksmith, my guardian, a drunk whose fists fly in the night." He shrugged and said nonchalantly, "I often run away."

Seeing Sibrion's attention drifting, he hurried to arrive at his point. "You may think us bad seeds, delinquents bucking the decisions of the Fieradeem,. but we are fiercely loyal to S'baladin. It was your courage that inspired Javatiel to join us, and his courage, in turn, inspired the others. And over all our loyalties, a powerful truth from Abán reminds us of the wisdom of the Fieradeem. 'When we are willing to seek help, the universe will respond in kind.'"

Sibrion sighed heavily and held up a hand for silence. He let it fall to rest lightly on S'baladin's shoulder. "Sy, aside from the threat to our people, the journey is full of danger. Imagine the great depth of pain your dear mother would have to endure having lost her husband and her sons."

S'baladin slumped at the thought but met Sibrion's gaze steadily. "While that is possible," he said, "suppose we succeed? Am I to simply watch a flock of sheep each day? When my brother might still be alive? We have no wish to force you into this, indeed we did not expect reluctance on your part! I dare say that you and T'balidor were much closer than we have ever been."

Tears welled up in both Sibrion and S'baladin's eyes, but the lad was not yet finished. "Sibrion," he said, "you have six brothers and sisters at home, but my only brother is trapped somewhere in the Va'Giyyel." His lips trembled and he breathed heavily, bracing himself to continue.

"Very well, Sy," Sibrion interrupted. He threw up his hands in mock surrender. "You conquered me! You and your mouthy friend there," he laughed, pointing at Diero.

As the boys chortled, albeit more from relief than at his teasing, he looked anxiously back at the peaceful safety of the Fieradin's lush desert garden. Sibrion sighed, closed his eyes, and tilted his head up to receive the sun's warm rays. These eight young men were far from the great warriors he had requested the Fieradeem grant to him. Grimy, lacking in discipline or order, one rather weak and one rather large, it was a ragtag group which stood before him. There was no time to properly prepare for such a hazardous mission, no time to train these volunteers. Their only qualification was a hardening of their resolve by the bitter forge of life.

Together, the boys conspired to sneak Sibrion past his guards. It was not a challenging task. They were few in number and given to drink in the evening. As they left behind the Fieradin's estate, Sibrion's doubts eased, and his Br'thain training took hold. He issued a string of directives as they hurried along. "It will soon get rough, boys. Once the Fieradeem discover my absence, local clans will be on full watch. Trust me. I know how they operate. From Kir-Geyzot to Messidia, all the men will be out looking for us. For what we are about to embark upon, it may be considered treason. Night travel is safest. Let us leave the main road and go into the wilderness. I know of an outcropping of stones which will serve as our portal to enter the Va'Giyyel."

The evening sun was swallowed up by darkness as the young fellows hurried through the desert wilderness in semi-darkness. Just a couple of hours into their trek, they spied the small glowing orbs of torches far behind them.

"A search party?" asked Diero.

"Yes," Sibrion responded shortly.

"They are far behind us, worry not," Javatiel reassured the younger boys.

"Spread out! When you find Sibrion, sound your ram's horn and seize him," were the orders a faraway Br'thain captain issued to his clan warriors.

But Sibrion's company had already come to the secret place where Javatiel, Vaez and Kelán had previously hidden thick, wooly coats and a pile of shiryon, the rustic raiment of woven twigs worn by the Br'thain in days past when they had travelled with the Gardener into the Va'Giyyel.

"Courtesy of the storehouse," said Kelán, waving a hand grandly at a supply of food stores, candle wax, and fuel in metal cannisters. No one chuckled at his gesture. Peering about in fear of search parties, they hurried to equip themselves and pack their bags.

Then, the fellows perspired and heaved their way across the nocturnal landscape until they finally arrived at the stone outcroppings. For several minutes, the fellows climbed up rough stone stairs. Unbeknownst to them, a shadowy figure stealthily followed their footsteps at a distance.

The fellows crested a jagged surface and looked about. Crumbling ruins, peppered by dried brush, surrounded a small stone field. The walls of stone about them were riddled with natural holes large enough for a man to crawl through. Tired and famished, they built a sheltered campfire deep within a crumbling wall.

As they ate, Sibrion gave further instructions. Standing up from his seated posture, Sibrion took the Ferusat from Javatiel's care. He held it up for all to see. Slowly, he paced around the campfire. "We will travel as one through the Streams by holding on to one another once I drive this Ferusat into the ground. But, without the aid of a metal spike on the other end, we run the risk of popping up in different places. We could end up hundreds of leagues away from the Va'Harot."

Gravely, he turned to S'baladin. "I believe that must be what happened to our men that day, to your father. The Y'cromahein men, recruited by the Gardener to open the streams with a spike, must have met with some delay or tragedy, routing our Br'thain to an unknown location." A deep frown wrinkled Sibrion's brow. "And somehow…though I have not quite worked this out, somehow that was planned by our enemy who lay in eager wait."

In the dim light of their buried campfire, every soul searched in the other's eyes for some glimmer of hope.

Sibrion shook off his frown and stooped down on his haunches, to peer at each young man, eyelevel. "With Ferusats in Rhünkai hands, it is risky to cross the Streams right now. For this reason, we cannot leave a spike continually in the ground while we are gone, lest they send a reign of terror down upon our people."

"But cousin, how do we enter the Streams without driving a spike into the ground?" asked S'baladin.

"But we will drive the stake into the ground, we must," Sibrion replied.

Met with looks of confusion, he gathered several sticks from a nearby dry desert bush into his right hand. "To ensure the safety of our people, and our successful return, we will draw from these sticks. Whoever gets the shortest stick agrees to stay behind as gatekeeper."

"One of us has to stay behind?" asked S'baladin.

"Yes indeed, Sy," answered Sibrion. "Someone must serve as gatekeeper, keeping watch over the spike in this stone outcropping. We will follow the Gardener's three hours of meditation. Once we leave through the Streams, the very second we disappear in an azure ring of light, whoever stays behind as gatekeeper must drive the spike into the stones on the third hour of the following morning and leave it in the stone outcroppings for the space of an hour, then remove it. The gatekeeper will repeat this on the sixth hour, and also on the ninth hour. Removing it after each hour with good hope will reduce the likelihood of any Rhünkai attempts to enter our world. In the Va'Giyyel, we shall all keep track of time, according to the Gardner's three hours of meditation. Our Ferusat shall not be struck unless it be one of those three hours. Stand and draw if you agree."

The boys all nodded their heads in accordance and stood.

Abán murmured solemnly, "May this ensure our successful return," to which Diero responded quickly, "And keep those Rhünkai brutes from entering our world!"

His fellows, too sobered by the drawing of the sticks, ignored his bravado. Comparing sticks, it fell upon S'baladin's friend Sabaca to assume the role of gatekeeper. His face showed disappointment, but this gave way quickly to pride as Sibrion clapped him soundly on the back and offered sincere thanks. To him Sabaca vowed, "I will not fail you, I swear it."

For the next hour, the fellows spoke excitedly about their adventure until they gradually drifted off to sleep around the campfire for a few brief hours of rest. Sibrion was first to wake. He scanned the horizon for the searchers they had seen the previous night. Satisfied that they were alone, he woke the rest of the boys. "Everybody up! Let us eat. Then on with our winter gear! A wild journey awaits us!"

A gnawing tension rose amongst them as each young man moved quietly from their morning fare to take up a coat, shiryon, leather helmet, and scarf. Each set aside parcels of food and fuel from their share for Sabaca. Each was deep in thought as they moved toward the middle of the stone outcroppings. The younger ones fought the temptation of turning back from their uncertain future. The older ones nervously considered the dangers ahead.

Now, I am about to enter a dark world.

Will we survive this journey?

Is there hope at the end for us?

Yet, a sense of adventure and daring blended with this nervousness.

"Listen here," said Sibrion, "Travelling through the Streams is serious business."

Vaez and Kelán tittered nervously but shrank back as Javatiel and Sibrion glared. The younger boys remained grim-faced, their eyes trained on Sibrion who continued sternly.

"If not done properly, the consequences are grave. Powerful currents lie far below us. The Streams will carry your life energy from one end to the other. You must bear no hate or rage when you travel the Streams. We must do as the Br'thain and take this moment to focus on positive thoughts before striking our Ferusat on the ground. Clear your minds of negative energy. Focus solely on the wisdom from the Infinite Garden."

So focused where they in their mediations, so eager for the journey that they failed to hear either the steps of a quadruped creature approaching them from one side, or the shadowy figure edging toward them.

Sibrion gave his final instructions to the gatekeeper. "Sabaca, once we leave, stay hidden deep inside those caves. The Br'thain will likely scour this whole country if they discover we have left." He pointed to the holes in the crumbling stone outcroppings. "Everything you need for survival we stored up inside those caves" Sibrion instructed Sabaca.

"I saw that," Sabaca smiled. "Thank you all for the dried meats, vegetables, fruits, and unleavened bread."

"There's plenty of candle wax, fuel, and wood for fire too. You'll be fine," added Diero from underneath his white fur and shiryon breastplate. Inaudibly, he muttered to himself, "You must fare well, else we will not."

"Very well boys, let us get going. We have a brother in arms to rescue!" ordered Sibrion.

Rays of soft light fanned outward to the east. The two strange entities on opposite ends of the stone outcroppings, shrank from the light, clinging to shadows, yet still they drew ever closer to the young men.

Sabaca stood a good distance away and drove his spike into the ground as the boys circled Sibrion. They held tight to him and one another as he raised his arms up high and drove the Ferusat into the stone surface.

Nothing happened.

Sibrion held the Ferusat into the stone a moment, then repeated the action.

"Nothing is happening!" Vaez shouted angrily.

Several of the boys put their ear to the surface.

"I hear nothing."

"Me either."

"Do you?"

"Still nothing," they whispered anxiously until Sibrion hushed them all.

Eventually, a low humming sound became audible. Suddenly, the sound of a ram's horn blasted the peaceful morning.

"What in blazes is that?" shouted the fellows.

"Hey there! What are you doing?" came a shout from the shadowy figure. With a ram's horn in one hand and a lit torch in the other, the warrior emerged from behind a tall bush as they huddled around Sibrion and his Ferusat.

"Dung upside down! Let us make haste!" cried Javatiel.

"Sibrion, hurry! Strike it now!" yelled Vaez.

The clan warrior hurried toward them shouting, "Stop there!" Opposite him, the quadruped creature loped toward the boys on silent paws. The band of seven clutched at each other's white furs as Sibrion drove the Ferusat into the ground. Still there was nothing.

"The Streams are not fully open, yet!" Sibrion yelled in frustration.

Never losing his grip on Javatiel's ankle, Vaez dropped his ear to the ground. "The rumbling grows louder!" he shouted. "Strike again!"

"Hold tight!" ordered Sibrion. The warrior, running now, blew his ram's horn several times as Sibrion's Ferusat struck the ground. A clang rang out against the stone. The warrior reached out to seize Sibrion, and Vaez yelped as something brushed against his arm.

A low growl rumbled from the quadruped. Its canine teeth snapped angrily as a furry figure leapt toward the assailant. The assailant drew back instinctively. Satisfied, Yashi leaned heavily upon Vaez' arms, licking at his face. The boys relaxed and grinned widely at each other. In a blinding flash of azure blue light, the group disappeared through the Streams.

Into the Va'Giyyel

Soft morning light filtered through a heavily wooded landscape obscured by mist. Here and there stretched grassy clearings where massive statues stood as mock guards. The stony sentinels were much eroded by the elements. Their feet were covered in undergrowth with moss and vines humbly clothing their proud bodies. Still, their gaze peered out above the pines as they had done for centuries.

Nearby, a stretch of farmland formed a neat grid of well-kept pastures. From one of the cottages dotting the landscape, an elderly farmer hobbled toward his barn, milk pail in hand. Cursing the dreary fog in rustic Hierundiel, he drew his hood of fur against the cold and dreary fog. Muttering to himself in a thick provincial drawl, he crouched to settle on a creaky wooden stool beside his bovine beast.

For many decades he had begun his day thusly, but today he frowned as an odd sound reached his aging ears. Suddenly, a blinding burst of azure light exploded in the barn. The poor man fell back as debris flew in every direction. Doused in cow's milk, the frightened old man cursed again. Dumbfounded, he stared as a curious youth stepped forward from the fading light. Adorned with armor of twigs and leather helmet, he bore a large burden on his back. The boy gawked back at him, then scanned his surroundings.

"Sorry for upsetting your barn, sir!" Jubal blurted as he dashed out the door. The poor farmer scowled after him in confusion, understanding neither the boy's Y'darit words, nor his appearance.

Jubal scanned the pasture nervously, cursing at the fog. Sibrion had said nothing of this possibility. We all travelled through the Streams together! As he ran across the farmland toward the woods, he scanned the countryside for his comrades. He gaped at the massive stone statues rising above the tree line. His brow furrowed as he gazed upward and struggled to orient himself. With the sun at his right, he moved in a northerly direction through fields of crops. After passing several hundred yards, the screams of women sent him cowering down into the mists between furrows of wheat.

Breathing heavily under his heavy pack of food supplies, Jubal inched closer as quietly as he could manage. Remaining low to the ground, he peered through the fog. A winding river could just be made out in the haze. Instantly, the mists shifted, and the shapes of several women burst forth, shouting in Hierundiel. Beyond them, laundry lay haphazardly scattered along the riverbank.

As they neared Jubal, he rose and made to calm them, but his Hierundiel was broken and rough. One of the women froze, pointed wildly in his direction and called to her friends, "Look! Another one!" They screamed and fled in various directions.

"Think it was the flash of light or just my face?" Abán quipped as he met with Jubal. With a sigh of relief, Jubal clapped him on the back in welcome before urging, "Come, let us find our fellows!"

"Perhaps we should hide. What if those women raise the local authorities? Or worse, the Rhünkai!" Jubal worried.

As if in answer, the fog shifted to reveal a large, fallen tree stretched invitingly across the width of the river. Wordlessly, they made for it. On the northern shore, they broke into flight through bushes, around trees, and over freezing brooks and creeks.

Before long they heard the calls of men ring out and froze. Both yelped with relief to realize that the voices were shouting their names.

"You are safe!" Jubal and Abán exclaimed in unison as they came upon their band.

"Yes!" Vaez cried out, "Even Yashi!"

The boys lavished the dog with caresses as he happily licked at their faces and hands.

But Sibrion frowned and observed, "Each of us were separated several hundred yards!"

"Who cares?" laughed Javatiel.

Sibrion ignored his rudeness and made for S'baladin. He grasped the boy's thin, wiry frame as it swayed back and forth. The stress and pressure of both the journey and the responsibility of the mission rippled across Sibrion's own neck, across his shoulders, and down his back.

"If you need time to rest, let us know," he told S'baladin.

The young lad gazed in wonder at cold vapors exhaling through their scarf-veiled face before responding. "I just want to find my brother and go home."

"Your mother will have my head if anything happens to you," Sibrion rebutted. "Have a care for my safety, would you?"

Before they could laugh, Sibrion fell violently to the ground under the force of a young man who pinned him. The stranger pummeled at his face. Instantly, the older boys ran to pull him away.

"Curse every one of you! Curse those infernal Streams! Why did you bring me here, you maggots!" cried the young man as the boys suppressed him.

"You!" cried Javatiel. "It was you at the stone outcropping!"

Vaez helped Sibrion to his feet as the young man raged. "We searched for you all night, you maggots! I tried to stop you, but you pulled me into the Streams!"

"If you had not laid a hand on us, just tended to your own business, then you would be back home," Kelán threw out.

The young watchman lunged at him, and the boys broke up a brawl once more. He wrenched his arms free and bellowed in anguish. "You do not understand! I was born here, but never did I wish to return!" In truth, the young warrior looked about to burst into tears.

When Sibrion urged him to explain, he complied. "I am not of the West, as you! I was among those rescued by the Br'thain. You think I cared to search for you damn maggots all night? No! But I was compelled to honor their commands out of respect for the great boon of my freedom!"

A deep remorse fell upon the boys. They muttered words of comfort and apology.

"Look here," said Sibrion. "We did not mean to drag you along, but we cannot yet return. We must first find T'balidor, S'baladin's brother, who went missing in the Caethain ambush. Then we will all return home together."

"If none of us die, then perhaps that is true," the young man uttered with a glare.

A silent foreboding fell upon everyone which Sibrion broke with introductions.

"I am Aejulan of Hierundia," the warrior responded begrudgingly.

"Perchance the universe brought you through the Streams, to guide us in your old country," said S'baladin.

"Do not trespass on my kindness," Aejulan said gloomily.

The hurt upon S'baladin's face conveyed the youth's genuine belief in such mystical powers. Noticing this, Aejulan sighed reluctantly and muttered an apology. "Keep silent as we cross the woods," he said, "Treacherous eyes are everywhere. Even in the sky."

Several hours of quiet trekking in the frigid cold brought them alongside a mountain cave. Heeding Aejulan's warning, they gestured noiselessly amongst themselves to pause and light torches. They entered cautiously, with weapons drawn against the appearance of some wild beast. Finding it to be safe, the younger boys sought tinder and firewood while the elder boys set up camp, deep inside the cave.

The cheerful fire they built warmed their weary frames. Jubal distributed fruits, dried meat and flat breads from his burdensome pack for all to share. From his own pack, Sibrion drew forth a map plotted out by the Gardener long ago. He beckoned to Aejulan to join him in surveying it.

"We are likely within the lower region of Hierundia, within these woods," the youth said.

"A week's journey from Va'Harot," muttered Sibrion.

Aejulan frowned in puzzlement, so he explained, "The Gardener teaches that Va'Harot was once a great ossuary. The Faeynül left behind deposits of bones, long before the arrival of the Y'cromahein. None in Y'cromeca know of it, for it its entrance is hidden."

"Then how do we find it?" he asked.

"Long ago, the Faeynül left colossal markers that indicate its location. Over the centuries, the growth of the forest has covered it. Now Va'Harot, supposedly, appears as a natural feature of the surrounding landscape."

Aejulan remained unimpressed, "If I am to be your guide, sleep is more important than legend," he said bluntly. "We only have a few more hours before the morning. Let us cast more wood into the fire and get our rest."

The boys settled comfortably by the campfire. Abán drew near with his lyre and to soothe their souls to sleep.

"The wind carries a sonnet from the kings of old.

The voices of our fathers call out to us.

Their words are a fire that burns in our hearts.

Into the Va'Giyyel, into the deep we go.

S'baladin's wracking cough rose above the tune and the roaring blaze. Sibrion quietly retrieved S'baladin's cough syrup from his pack and aided him in consuming a dose. The gangly youth smiled his thanks.

One by one, the boys began drifting into slumber. For S'baladin though, it was difficult to find any sleep. Though his cough had lessened, there was no balm for his mind or his heart. Already he missed his home. Worse yet, he bore a burden of guilt for increasing his mother's sense of loss with his departure. Yet, the danger of crossing into such a strange and terrible land excited him too.

"Hierundia," he wrote on a new scroll, "welcomes us in a cave, on a cold rainy night, fraught with peril and danger." But no sooner had he begun to write, then his body's fatigue quickly conquered his enthusiasm. He laid down his quill and rolled to one side.

The campfire's soft, warm glow, its pops and hisses, and Abán's tune transported S'baladin to Ferán. It roused warm memories of his father and brother. He fought against the tears of longing streaming down his face. An image of the Gardener rose in his mind's eye and a deep conflict rent his heart. On the one hand, he treasured the faithful teacher of his people, on the other questions circled emptily within him. Why did the Gardener not foresee the ambush? Why allow my papa to die in such a violent manner? And why leave us alone in such despair?

Sensing S'baladin's despair, the floppy-eared sheep dog rose up from Vaez' side and padded over to lay next to the lad. Through his tears, he caressed Yashi's shaggy fur until he eventually drifted into slumber.

The Presage at Realmhold Thaed-Rú

It had only been a matter of a month since the Haruspec took the highest seat of authority in the land, second only to Íraban Thaed-Rú. Though none in Kiérbangaal opposed him, the Haruspec anticipated doubt and curiosity to spread across Upper and Middle Y'cromeca upon hearing news of a strange new counselor. To bolster his rise, the Haruspec arranged for a grand parade in the streets of Kiérbangaal.

Children eagerly pulled their parents along to gaze at strange creatures harvested from the isle of Kaëyrbassad. His spectacular menagerie was composed of monstrous reptiles, colorful, plumed creatures, woolly, tusked quadrupeds, and beasts with armored plates covering sturdy frames. The people gawked in amazement as each of them meandered by, one after the other, as passive as could be. But the greatest wonder of all was the taming of the creation of the Cethin Arda, those symbols of untamed power of the skies, the Veyasaen birds. These frightful birds appeared toward the end of the vast parade with the Haruspec, as he rode upon a large carriage led by a team of twenty horses. The crowds cheered him on wildly, as others interspersed stood in awe and wonder at his sight.

The Haruspec's unprecedented dominion over these fowl mesmerized the spectators. They flew above the parade, landing on the ground and ascending once more at his command. His strange tongue vibrated the very air he breathed, taming the untamed and shocking all to admiration. A current of relief blew through the city as the people chattered eagerly.

"No more need we fear the Veyasaen talons!"

"Nor the dark creatures roaming in the woods!"

Just as he held sway over his wild menagerie, in the short span of a month's time, the Haruspec cast a subtle spell of charm over Upper and Middle Y'cromeca. Those who had yet to see him, heard of the spectacle of his domesticated menagerie, his tamed Veyasaen, from mercantile caravans and travelers. From the nobility to the peasant classes, word of his great power spread through the masses.

"They are children," he snarled to Grioppa in his chambers that afternoon.

According to Thaed-Rú protocol, royal guests were never allowed to confer in the privacy of their chambers out of concern of plots against the Thaed-Rú. Never had even a lowly house servant been allowed an unattended guest. But no one dared to question the Haruspec his private matters. Nor did any see the need to do so as the entire Thaed- Rú court was as deeply under the sway of the Mithengara as Grioppa and his retinue.

The ambassador chuckled now at his master's hatred. "Indeed! This land, and all its wealth, is ripe for the taking."

"Sit, eat," The Haruspec gestured to a feast. Grioppa hurried to comply as the giant turned to gaze out over Kiérbangaal. A sinister smile played about his shriveled lips as he watched men moving far below his lofty chambers. *Not children, insects really. Insects fully under my control.*

Even the Rhünkai armies had now shifted in their fealty from the Thaed-Rú to the chief steward of the Serpent in the Garden. A shift which Íraban and his court smiled upon benignly. Throughout the Eleven Dominions, the Rhünkai had received the Haruspec's altered Necropulpa plant. Enthusiastically, they ingested it and were rewarded with heightened strength and prowess. Without altering their appearances or personalities, it transformed them into powerful beasts. By the masses, these brawny soldiers offered their unswerving loyalty to the Haruspec.

The Haruspec labored heavily to turn from the window. He hobbled close to hover at the man's ear and hiss, "Very soon we shall see the fruits of my work come to pass, Ambassador Grioppa."

The ambassador looked up from his ravenous eating. His pale, gaunt features flared to life with a fiendish, beastly grin. "Oh! Master! I look forward to the day in which I too can rule as," he paused to wipe at dribbles and crumbs, then swallowed his half-masticated food and continued, "a token of my service to your benevolence."

The Haruspec nodded absently as he gazed at Grioppa. The man's visage filled the Haruspec with a deep satisfaction. His newest poisons left any who ate of his food consumed with the perpetual desire to devour more. Does not the body become more corpulent as a person consumes food lavishly? Yet, in contrast to the fruits he fed the army, this new concoction caused his victims to grow gaunter and paler, as their pathetic frames withered away.

"Soon," he muttered absently as he sank into a massive armchair. "Soon."

Thinking this a renewed promise, Grioppa grinned. But the Haruspec's thoughts were far from Grioppa's future. "So proud is young Íraban of his Cethin Arda," he scoffed. "Yet his manipulation of the Necropulpa plant is but a pithy attempt to wield its true power. Though his Scions engage in superhuman labor in the north, they are disfigured, their personalities altered, and they are limited to nocturnal efforts only."

Grioppa blinked ignorantly at him, "What of it, master?"

"Where has my sly fox gone, eh?" the Haruspec taunted him. "It is in his failures that I will cement my control of Hierundia. My Harmattan weed spies recently reported that as these Scions rest during the day, their bodies now emit a thick substance, forming a cocoon over their bodies. Just before nightfall, they burst from these pods. On the Isle of Kaëyrbassad, this was one of the final steps before I harnessed the true power of the Necropulpa."

"And before he discovers it on his own, you shall show him the way? Is that it, master?"

The Haruspec looked upon the man with condescension, but feigned approval by patting his shoulder absently. "Go. Arrange an audience with the Thaed-Rú court. I shall offer them a scroll of knowledge."

Days later, the Haruspec grandly presented this gift before the Bal-Rú's throne. Manipulating supernal agencies from Kaëyrbassad, the Haruspec's voice boomed across the court of thirty-two, past the crowds and into the air above the atrium for all to hear for leagues away. "In the Principate of the first Thaed-Rú lords of antiquity, innate powers brought down the Ballai from within. They manifested themselves to weak minds, strengthening them into a collective thought: to follow their ways to breach the walls from inside the provinces."

Íraban and the Thaed-Rú smiled in pride at the telling of their history, little knowing this time it was their minds that were weak, that it was the Haruspec's influence manifesting across their kingdom.

"I know of the failed attempt of the Thaed-Rú to breach the Ballai of the West," he added. "No Thaed-Rú, nor man, nor beast has ever penetrated the walls surrounding the savages of the West," he thundered. "Today we shall see the Thaed-Rú transcend those infernal walls from outside!"

The eyes of Íraban and the Thaed-Rú gleamed, drunk with power.

"Long have those vermin hidden behind their walls, secure and confident in their dusty dominion. They mock you, stealing your Scions away! But I tell you, darkness is coming to this land. And we shall take this darkness to the Ballai of the West. We will bring their fortresses down before their eyes. And we will plunder their world, as they have done ours!" he howled.

Bow grandly before the throne, he held out a scroll. "I offer you the fruits of the Serpent in the Garden, to manifest the strength the Cethin Arda."

Íraban swept down the stairs and seized it eagerly. His court gathered about him, peering over his shoulder, as he eagerly scanned the text. "But this..." he stuttered, "this is the missing link! My alchemists...they..." Wordlessly, he turned to stare at Teosifan who turned to the Haruspec.

"We thank you for this gift of knowledge," the elder Thaed-Rú said.

The solution, its effects instantaneous, relieved the Scions of their frightful appearances and altered personalities. Within the week, the Scions harnessed supernal strength both day and night in their efforts to build the Fortress City. The Haruspec's promise of darkness rang true as a new earnestness renewed recruiting efforts across the Dominions.

The lords of the Thaed-Rú world now believed his every utterance. Why would they not? Since his stormy descent upon the giant Veyasaen, they had endless validations of his promises and claims. Naturally, they now trusted his offering of fruits imbued with the dark power of the Serpent in the Garden. All the Rhünkai need do was consume them he promised, and any march on the Ballai of the West would successfully bring down its molten walls, from without. And so it was that across the realm, its people consumed his confident words as eagerly as the Rhünkai did his fruit.

· · · · ·

Over Realmhold Thaed-Rú, the Haruspec's shadow hovered. While his plot unfurled, Íraban and his court feasted daily. The young Bal Rú, prone already to drunkenness and pride, sank further into vice. Over savory treats, and sugary sweets, and flowing goblets of wine, his court laughed in fiendish delight at the growth of their wealth as the power of their Cethin Arda eclipsed the Y'cromahein world.

Of course, such a whirlwind of grand revelry could not exist forever. On a particularly dark night, with both the land and the moon shrouded in a cold mist, the Thaed-Rú court was graced by the rare presence of the Haruspec at their evening meal. Íraban stumbled from the head of the great table and offered his seat to his counselor with a sweeping bow which nearly sent him tumbling to the floor. Graciously, the giant accepted, a wide smile thinned his twisted lips as he beckoned for the royal cupbearer. "One more?" he asked the young Bal Rú.

Several feet away, a courtier slowly crumpled forward over the table. Occupied with toasting the Haruspec, Íraban did not notice as another slumped sideways, out of his chair to thud upon the floor, but a sinister grin spread over the massive giant's face. He rose from his seat at the head of the banquet table, ignoring Íraban's confusion. Followed by a lone minion in attendance, the dark figure hobbled past the wretched souls about the table as, one by one, they faded from consciousness.

The Haruspec sought one of these and gloated, "Teosifan! You served your Bal Rú well. Now shall you all transcend...forever...into the shadows of death."

The aging counselor of the Dominions, more skeletal than ever, turned his crystalline gaze upon the Haruspec. Lifting a thin finger, he pointed accusingly at the dark figure and cursed him, "There remains one...a youth...that may yet stop you, just you wait and see."

The Haruspec glowered down at Teosifan. He had discerned no threat against his plans in these lands, particularly none from a youth. Yet, the old counselor chortled out between his last breaths, "May others...succeed where we failed!...And may your soul...be damned!"

At this the dark figure chortled too. He kicked the lifeless corpse against the wall. Trudging heavily, he returned to the head of the table and stooped to peer at a slight frame. Its bony arm reached clutched weakly at the table, then fell.

The Haruspec sneered at the gaunt figure of the masked Bal Rú and bent to whisper in his ear. "Never shall you worry about those vermin from the West."

But Íraban was drunk with wine and poisoned by the very powers he had thought to harness. In his delirium, he mistook the Haruspec for his father. "Curse you, old man!" he cried. "See our feasting? See our success? We celebrate an accomplishment of which you never even dreamed!" He reached a spidery hand forward, but the dark figure before him easily evaded his grasp. Íraban's tongue grew thick and he struggled heavily to speak. "The Cethin Arda...it is revived!...It was I...It is you!...Curses..."

As the Bal Rú slipped further toward the shadows, the giant's massive, wrinkled hand removed the golden mask from his pale face. Ordering his minion in his arcane speech, he was handed another mask, which he placed on the Bal Rú's face. Carved of wood and painted black, it lay there heavily, grotesque in its exaggerated grimace of despair.

"Here is the last mask you will ever wear, young Íraban."

In the dimly lit chamber, the Haruspec raised his massive head upward, scratching and clawing his cheeks and his neck. With eyes closed he gritted his teeth. In his arcane speech, he cursed the sons of the Y'cromahein, the land of Y'cromeca, and the infinite Garden of Ages. In a sudden and violent jerk, he lowered his face down to the dark mask.

The withering Bal Rú slowly looked up at the Haruspec. As recognition dawned, he struggled to speak but could not. Disgust, then shock, then accusations of utter betrayal bloomed in his eyes.

"You thought to prove your father wrong, to master the dark force so many of your ancestors have failed to harness," the Haruspec wheezed. "It is I who have harnessed those forces, not you. Now you die a failure too." As if his word was a command, the last Bal Rú, Íraban, son of Theragad, breathed no more.

The Haruspec grunted in pain as he rose to his full height. His every breath was labored with the exhaustion of life. He muttered arcane words as he approached the man. A loud howl of pain bellowed from his girth as his countenance transformed. His clothing fell away to a shroud of shadowy robes of a strange and dark material. The visage of a genteel old man gave way to heinous features of stitched flesh. The beast's exposed tendons receded back to reveal a hideous, cracked grin exposing the sides of his eyeballs, his teeth and jaws.

He hobbled over to a man contorted in pain. As the terrifying giant paused to tower above him, Grioppa gazed up with effort. Though his body was paralyzed by the feast, his eyes popped wide at the gruesome visage of the Haruspec.

"Remember the words from your rancid kingdom of Paradmah, 'once a Gershuvyk, always a sly fox!' Thank you Grioppa...for your faithful service. You see my true countenance now, for I am not the chief steward of the Serpent in the Garden. I am the Serpent in the Garden!"

The ambassador, with horror in his eyes, realized for the first time the true evil of his lord and master just as he slipped into darkness.

The Haruspec surveyed the grisly scene of dead Thaed-Rú courtiers with satisfaction. "Pathetic!" he spat, then called out loudly, "Enter!"

Several of the Haruspec's minions entered the vast chamber hall. They reported to the Haruspec the successful executions of everyone who served in Realmhold Thaed-Rú, including Grioppa's diplomatic retinue, as ordered.

"Arrest each member of the Guild, their families, and their servants. Execute them all this very night," he commanded.

The following morning, from Íraban's own tower, his booming voice rang out across the capital. To the Thaed-Rú captains and their army in the courtyard below, he declared himself the highest authority over the land, explaining that the Bal Rú Íraban and the entire Thaed-Rú Court had died on their last feasting. So honeyed were his words that the seasoned warriors before him felt no alarm at all upon receiving this news. The Rhünkai too were unswervingly allegiant to his will as, by this time, most of them had digested his Necropulpa plant.

Out of the shadows of ages past, the ancient Haruspec arose to possess the land. Through cold mists foul beasts from another world roamed the countryside, as beholden to the Haruspec in their wildness as his menagerie had been in their passivity.

Now in his true form, the dark figure towered three times the size of a Thaed-Rú. From the parapets of Realmhold Thaed-Rú, he raised his ghastly eyes high above at the dark mass of Veyasaen careening lazily above, then down upon the vast army below. Its weaponry and armor were more advanced than any the Eleven Dominions had ever known. Satisfaction creased the twisted mass of scars and shriveled flesh that was his face. To them he howled, "I bring a maelstrom from across the seas. Sons of Y'crom, I have returned! I come to fulfill my vow of vengeance, sworn long ago."

As ordered, his captains dispatched legions into each province to wreak havoc against the governors of those territories, over their families, over their kinsmen, and over all who served under their governorships. Some he imprisoned indefinitely, some he tortured. Many he executed. As provincial leadership faltered, surviving vassals and noblemen went into hiding as the Rhünkai confiscated or burned their fiefs. The fall of Kiérbangaal and its environs opened wide the Province of Hierundia to the merciless advances of the Haruspec.

Hearing of the deadly feast in the capital, the Tribune Ansuz gathered the great army of Hierundia, the greatest army in Y'cromeca, and fortified his position at the southwestern corner of that province, near the entrance of the fallen Ballai which leads to Graëyhovan. He felt a little thrill at the sweeping loss of Thaed-Rú life, yet he refused to serve another master who sought to enslave him unto darkness.

Through the cold mist, he too rallied his troops. "We are the hope of Y'crom, the strong arm of the people, yet we are powerless against the Cethin Arda. Shall we remain to become the pawns of this monster, or perhaps to die at his behest?"

"No!" came the resounding reply from the ranks of men that stretched before him.

"We shall observe. We shall learn. We shall plan." The men before him remained silent and he paused, casting his eyes back and forth upon rank after rank of men. Clenching his fingers into a tight fist, he punched upward into the sky and shouted, "And when the time comes, we shall drive this beastly giant and all his twisted creatures from these lands!"

Through the great army before him swept enthusiastic shouts of allegiance accompanied by a wild clamor of gauntlets thumping against breastplates, spears and staffs beating the ground. The Tribune Ansuz grinned in satisfaction. He felt no remorse for the thousands of citizens left behind, defenseless to the onslaught of the Haruspec, such was the greatness of this war. He thought only *And when the last of the ashes have cooled, when this monster has eradicated the Thaed-Rú, with his own army lessened and my path made clear, I will rise to rule it all.*

With Ansuz's armies retreating to the southwest of Hierundia, the Tribunes of the northwest floundered in disunity. The Provinces of Tal-Ciddion, Rhühaven, Graëyhovan, and Molchaion fell rapidly. Rhünkai generals swept across the land, seizing the fortunes of the privileged and wealthy as their spoils. Turning to the east, the Haruspec sent out his minions to terrorize the

Provinces of Cahheramas and Cian. There, the Tribunes Wunden and Hagalaz were quick to surrender.

The loss of life and property at the hands of the Rhünkai crippled trade throughout Upper and Middle Y'cromeca. Masses of people, their world on the brink of collapse, suffered from lack of food and shelter. By the time the ambassadors of the southern Provinces arrived to treat with the Haruspec, it was not to threaten war but to pledge allegiance. In fact, in his presence, swayed by his dark powers, they pledged their armies eagerly to him. With the Provinces of Ir of the Fenrülk, Cerebantus, Bisantior, and Teras-Amin under his control, his conquest of Upper and Middle Y'cromeca was complete.

And all the time, the Lord High Counselor of the Dominions cared nothing for the misery of the people. It mattered little to the Haruspec if their economy fell, if women and children starved and suffered, or if men lost their sanity. Everything was falling into place for him. The devastation and collapse of the Y'cromahein world was a necessary impetus to draw out his ancient foe.

Mourning at Cerathmir

In the Province of Graëyhovan, dark clouds cast a heavy gloom over the crested ranges of the Eifandir Mountains. An evil foreboding hung upon the valley of Cerathmir. With great caution, the Gardener strode onto the miller's property and surveyed the destruction.

He picked his way around scattered debris, his eyes upon the muddy ruts of several wagons crisscrossing innumerable boot prints. Drawing closer to the house, his heart sank deeper as he recognized the charred remnants of kitchen utensils and broken toys. All else was reduced to smoking ash. The stone foundation itself was broken up and scattered. And the message was very clear. The Haruspec had the power to destroy a house, scatter and smash its intimate and private possessions and set it ablaze, as a warning to everyone who defied him.

The Gardener tightened his grip on his Tiller's Staff in anger. He roamed the property, searching for trails of blood or footprints, hoping for signs of the family's escape. Several yards away from the broken foundation of the home, he came upon a strange sight.

Cautiously, he made his way to a makeshift structure of debris. There, black ribbons fluttered eerily from a charred pole. The stake was driven into a pile of scorched stones and rubble. The Gardener fell to his knees, weeping as his eyes fell upon the center of this pile. Arbantio's dead body and the corpses of his servants and his family lay in disrespectful disarray.

Friendships are dear. Foremost amongst friends are those who selflessly align their will to those they love. A true and noble friend possesses enough courage to mend a broken and fallen world. No one in Y'cromeca understood this more deeply than the Gardener. Though he had sensed Arbantio's betrayal, it had long since been forgiven. "My friend! Oh, my noble friend! I am so sorry, my dear friend!" he bellowed.

His cry thundered so loudly across the valley of Cerathmir that it shook the land. Great avalanches of snow plummeted from the crests of the mountains as he rent his robes from the collar down.

A misty frost covered the land as the Gardener grieved. Finally, he moved to pull the dead, one by one. Alone, he made a proper burial for them, away from the miller's property beneath a great oak tree the flames had spared.

"Arbantio, M'zhalo, because your good men opened the Streams, thousands of young innocents are free! Now you too shall find rest for your soul. I shall miss our talks, but sleep now, my son. Enter the abode of the kings of old, wherein they gaze upon the renewal of spring."

After toiling at length to bury the bodies, the Gardener gathered what little he could and made a temporary dwelling beneath the tree. In his solitude that night, he repaired his soul through deep meditation. In the morn, he arose and ate. Determined and of a strong will, the Gardener began an arduous trek, making his way to Realmhold Thaed-Rú, in the province of Hierundia.

The Caravan

A gentle shake and Sibrion's call of, "Wake up, S'baladin!" roused the young lad.

Javatiel and Vaez hauled leather bags of water past from a nearby spring-fed source.

"Good morning, Sy!" they greeted him. He yawned a reply and rubbed at his eyes.

Jubal oversaw the roasting of the Gardener's special tea leaves over a campfire while the boys ate a simple breakfast of fruit. Everyone huddled about the flames for warmth, inhaling the fragrant earthiness of the leaves. Then Jubal proudly distributed the brew in small metal cups.

S'baladin, moving slowly, joined them for the tea. Because of his excessive coughing, Sibrion reached into S'baladin's pouch and gave him special leaves to chew upon. The boy did so absently, petting Yashi who remained at his side.

The youngest packed up their possessions while the older fellows went over the details of their next step. Insulated in thick animal skins, Sibrion inspected the early morning landscape from the mouth of the cave. Thoughtfully, he observed the drizzle.

"Boys, cover yourselves warmly. It is miserably cold out there." As they moved to ready themselves for departure, he added soberly, "Be cautious today, do not drop your guard."

The instant they doused their campfire, the frigid air bit against their scarf-wrapped cheeks. Melancholy dampened their spirits. They trekked warily all morning through a vast wilderness, crossing ice-cold brooks and creeks, ascending hills, and passing through valleys and ravines. Occasionally, they cringed and ducked as winged shadows of the Veyasaen above darkened their path and wilted their hearts. At other times, it was only screeching howls, clouds veiling their forms, which sent the boys shrinking for cover.

As the sun began to sink, they heard a distant roar. Momentarily, they froze in fear as the ground beneath them shook, the roar growing ever louder. "Damn it! Aejulan, what is this quaking of the ground?" shouted Diero.

Unimpressed, Aejulan urged them onward. "The Thaed-Rú alchemists are powerful. Ever since the Edict of the Scions of Íraban," he explained, "they have been experimenting with the power of the Cethin Arda. Before I was taken into Rhünkai servitude, I would often hear and feel such rumblings."

Uncertainty slowed their steps as they followed their guide. They longed for the desert heat of Ferán and the safety of the known. Sibrion nudged at the younger ones and spurned his peers onward. "Come, the quicker you move, the warmer you'll feel. Besides, we have a brother to search for!"

Abán was first to shake off his concern. He broke into a cheerful song of brave adventurers in a mystical land. Diero took S'baladin by the arm to stomp along behind him and the rest of the boys fell in line. Unaccustomed to the wretched cold, Abán, Jubal, Diero and S'baladin made a game of huffing and puffing, amused by the cold vapors they emitted.

"Hide!" Aejulan hissed, cutting short their game.

They ducked behind thick brush and peered out at a small detachment of Rhünkai in the distance, transporting runaway child slaves. They were fettered in chains and clad in thin garments. Their sodden frames were doubled over, in a vain effort to shelter themselves from the bitter cold. The boys gasped as one of the child slaves fell over from exhaustion, only to be punished by a Rhünkai whip.

They longed no more for the desert heat, but craved vengeance upon such evil. Their number too small, Aejulan waved them forward as the children marched away. Reluctantly, they turned away.

Aejulan spoke with Sibrion in hushed tones that night. In the morning, they ordered the boys to disguise themselves with the woven leaves, twigs and branches of their shiryon. Grateful for this camouflage, they merged into the undergrowth that day to peer out at a new threat. A herd of tall beasts the height of trees with long, thin spidery limbs lumbered along under lone riders. At the feet of these strange creatures, countless more trackers, moved warily through the woods, armed with archery weapons.

"Taenshuks" whispered Aejulan. "Each rider is a captain to the Ulkyrien trackers below."

From their hiding spot in the brush, in their shiryon attire, they peered, horrified at the Ulkyrien. Beneath dark, hooded coats, marbled eyes sunk deeply into dark sockets and yellowish canine teeth gave their scarred, ashen faces the look of death.

"Trackers? Those specters search for runaway slaves?" asked Sibrion.

Baring his shoulder to the cold, Aejulan revealed his slave's brand. "Aye," he said grimly, "for boys like me."

• • • • •

Travelling by night some days later, they traversed a deep crevasse. Leerily peering upward to a ledge twenty feet above, Yashi began to growl.

"Look at Yashi!" hissed Vaez as the gentle sheepdog's lips curled up around his teeth.

The bushes above their heads rustled. Then they became animated and moved, shouting at the boys, "Halt there!"

Yashi's growl turned into snarling barks. The boys reached for their weapons, but arrows whizzed down in warning. Vaez clutched at the dog's fur, hauling him back against the walls of the ravine.

From their limited shelter, S'baladin squinted upward. With some relief, he cried out. "They are not Ulkyrien! See, they wear thick furs, not hooded cloaks!"

Sibrion hushed him, "A second volley is coming! Seek what cover you can!"

The boys shrank further back against the walls of the ravine. But the men above paused to confer amongst themselves.

"What are they saying?" whispered Jubal fearfully.

Aejulan translated their Hierundiel as one man called down:

"How many more are with you? How many hidden in these woods?"

"It is only our group here!" answered Aejulan. "There are no others, save us."

"Stay there! Move one step and we will fire!" a man ordered. He turned and called for reinforcements.

Moments later, Abán warned, "Look ahead!"

Jubal and Diero shrank back as glowing orbs of gold floated eerily toward from within the dark reaches beyond. "It's just men with torches!" S'baladin whispered. The boys relaxed a little until they made out dozens of men with bows at the ready beside the torchbearers.

"Are they wearing our mark?" asked a man from the ledge. The men below moved amongst the boys, holding their torches up close to inspect their scarf-wrapped helmets of twigs and leaves.

"No! They are not with us!"

"What mark?" whispered Diero and received a warning punch from Javatiel who hissed, "Hush!"

To Sibrion's company a man ordered, "Remove your scarves."

"Why they are but lads!" cried one man.

"What is your business out here alone, like this?"

"Know you not that it is dangerous out here, especially at night?"

"We are merely passing through," said Aejulan.

"You speak well the language of trade and commerce, but you do not dress the part," said the men. "Where are you boys from?"

"We mean no harm," said Aejulan.

Sibrion concurred in fluent Hierundiel, "We are merely passing through!"

"Nonsense!" called a man from above and his fellows chuckled.

The man before them explained, "None of good intentions pass through these parts unless…" He trailed off and peered at the boys for a moment. "…unless they are on the run from Rhünkai trackers."

The boy's expressions, in particular the apprehensive aversion of Aejulan's eyes, betrayed them.

"Come!" the man chortled. "We know someone who would like to see you."

Fear engulfed Sibrion's company as the men disarmed the boys and confiscated. Puzzling over the Ferusat, they determined it was a weapon and confiscated it too. They herded the sullen little band and their sheep dog through the dark woods. A short walk led them to a massive, sprawling camp with numerous crackling campfires, hundreds of tents and two corrals full of horses. The boys gazed about them as they marched past a vast array of bundles stacked neatly beside the beasts of burden.

The sentries ushered them inside a large, warm tent. A bearded man with a thick, braided ponytail looked curiously upon them. Gathering animal furs about him, he rose from a comfortably curved wicker armchair and approached the boys. He scrutinized their strange aprons, leather helmets, and scarves but seemed most drawn to the peculiar breastplates of interwoven twigs protecting their chests.

"I can see that you are not from here," he said, his eyes suspicious. "We are a private guard, hired to protect and escort this great caravan for the merchant families of Valassentio, Vol-Thaladuin, Kol'maquin, Dur Beddasain and Dar Hamuil," he said. He gazed sternly for a moment at each of them. Seeing no recognition of these names in their eyes, he concluded abruptly, "We will keep you here until we decide what to do with you."

Throughout the night, the boys huddled together, captives in a guarded tent. As the elder boys ran through one plan of escape after the other, the younger boys spoke quietly amongst themselves.

They gasped as Diero muttered, "Where is the Gardener when you need him?"

"For shame!" said Abán, his loyalty unswerving.

But Jubal murmured his agreement and S'baladin too shrugged and said, "I thought he cared for the Br'thain of the West, I thought he loved my father."

Overhearing them, Sibrion rebuked the boys, "His absence does not mean the absence of that care! Hush and rest now, all of you!"

Despair fell heavily upon them. As they sank into an uneasy sleep, a fog slowly crawled across the nocturnal landscape beyond their camp. Its thick vapors moved along the forest floor in tendrils, choking the foliage and fauna. From a rocky ledge on high, a small detachment of caravan guards peered down uneasily.

"This fog moves with purpose," said one guard.

"Yes, like a large beast, stalking towards the camp," said another, frightfully.

The animals within the forest knew to run from it. Not because they feared the fog itself, but rather the furry creatures moving within. Despite their large frames, they moved as silent as owls in flight with maws stuffed full of jagged, tar-black teeth, hungry for flesh.

The fog made its way to the edge of the forest and halted. Between the camp and the tree line lay an open field, three times the length of a sower's barn. Had the sentries seen the fog in daylight, it would have resembled a pack of gigantic wolves with vaporous pointed ears obtruding from the fog. But these were not wolves.

The youngest of the three watchmen was first to hear their shrill call, rising from the edge of the clearing.

"Did you hear that?" said the young man.

Again, that strange shrill sounded, this time more distinct.

A knot welled in their throats. Hands trembling, they unsheathed their weapons. All three stood there, listening. The shrill sound varied in intensity, fading and rising rhythmically, like crashing waves. It was unmistakably familiar. It was the sound of a crying baby. A chill ran up the spines of all three men, as they stood with swords drawn, nervously scanning the fog.

They stood in silence again, listening to the wailing at the forest edge. The youngest one, sword trembling, stepped bravely forward. The wailing overwhelmed his senses until all else faded. Then, it ceased. Its absence sent him on edge. His hands and feet seemed frozen in place; every muscle of his body tensed at once. The only sound he sensed now was his own heartbeat, thrumming in his ear. It took every ounce of courage to speak in weak and trembling words. "Is-Is someone out there?"

No response. His own voice grounding him, he regained some composure and called out loudly, "Do you need help?" The forest was silent for what felt like an eternity. Slowly, he gathered his wits and edged toward the trees once more.

Then, something whispered back, "Do... yoU... neED heLLLp?" It sounded just as hesitant as he did, the words muffled and loose, but the cadence was wrong, unnatural. The phrase began repeating in horrifying imitation. His fellows called to him to return. He heard them not. A putrid odor invaded the young watchman's nostrils and a primal fear rose in his body. The young man fled, sprinting towards the warm glows of the campfires.

His scream of "Quick! Get the—" was cut short. Razor-sharp talons sank deep into the folds of his neck, dragging him back into the forest. His two fellows stood transfixed as the fog leapt forth, hiding the creature from view, hiding the others circling all about.

The young man's gargled screams merged with hundreds more as all about the camp, men shouted in confusion and pain. The commotion startled the young men of the West awake.

Sibrion and Javatiel sprang up instantly. From a compartment hollowed out in his heel, Sibrion drew a small dagger and crept toward the tent's flap.

"What is happening?" mumbled Vaez, still half asleep on his rut sack.

The other boys haphazardly sought their wits.

"Get up! On with your boots!" commanded Sibrion. "We are under attack!"

"Rhünkai?" Vaez asked in alarm.

"I do not know, but we need to leave, now. Javatiel, round them up!"

With that, Sibrion stormed out of the tent to investigate. The boys hurried to pack their things, but S'baladin followed after Sibrion. The cold night air struck his senses first, then the shouts of panic. Shouts of men, the commotion of their footsteps, the clanging of their weapons, the hoofbeats from horses, and the pungent smell of blood assaulted them. The camp was in complete disarray. Huddled by a nearby tent, a battle-worn and ragged man, rocked back and forth.

Sibrion approached him, "Who has attacked the caravan?"

The man continued to rock back and forth. He spoke in a whisper, fearful and sporadic.

"They are in the fog… in the fog…They…They cry like children. I thought they were children…" His rocking became more frantic. "Our weapons do nothing…nothing at all!"

Sibrion took a step back from the man, unnerved by his display of terror.

Two men from the caravan, carrying a stretcher, ran past the boys. S'baladin stared at the husk of a man they bore. The hot steam of blood met with the chilling night air as it oozed from massive chunks of missing flesh upon his torso. White marrow protruded from an arm where the teeth of some ferocious creature had left his flesh and tendons pulverized. All over his body were ribbons of dangling flesh.

S'baladin had seen this kind of damage before, when a pack of wolves devoured a wandering sheep. It brought him back to the Ballai for a moment.

"S'baladin!"

He snapped out of his fixation on the injuries to meet Sibrion's glare. "Get back inside, S'baladin! Right now!"

S'baladin could see the fear in Sibrion's eyes. They both knew it was not Rhünkai attacking the camp. It was something far worse.

"We must help the caravan, Sibrion!"

"Help? How can we help?" said Sibrion hopelessly. "You heard the man say our weapons, if we even had them, are powerless against whatever is out there! What can we do?" Sibrion urged S'baladin toward their tent.

S'baladin knew he was right, yet he refused to turn back. Something inside the young man pushed him aimlessly into the crowd of screams and beastly howls, despite his infirmity. Perhaps it was guilt, remembering how helpless he was to stop those wolves many years ago in Ferán. Perhaps it was logic, knowing that they too might perish if the men of the caravan did not survive. He did not know where to go, but something must be done.

Sibrion called after him, then followed reluctantly. "Surprisingly stubborn, for such a sickly lad," he muttered.

S'baladin ignored him as he wondered through the crowd of frightened people. He paused to gaze upward at the starry sky. As Sibrion caught up to him, he heard the lad whisper, "Yes, these creatures have supernal strength, but…"

S'baladin pivoted on his heel to face Sibrion, his face beaming. "The wisdom of the Gardener is a world of flickering starlight and infinite power from the universe. Let that be our focus against whatever is out there!"

Though S'baladin was trembling all over, there was a confidence about him that calmed Sibrion's nerves. The strength in his words and demeanor reminded Sibrion of Baltien. They moved cautiously through shouts of panic as the creatures' howls pierced the frigid air. Then, S'baladin stiffened as something struck him.

"That man, he said…" He whirled and dashed back towards their tent.

Sibrion dashed after the lad, panting, "Sy, what are you doing?"

As they slowed outside their tent, S'baladin wheezed. "I remembered something, something that can help us!"

The two burst into the tent and collided with their fellows who, packs upon their back, were making for the flap themselves. Diero fell to the ground. S'baladin's bag tumbled from his grasp, its contents all undone. The scrawny lad said nothing, as he knelt to scrabble through his belongings.

"Damn it, you jackass! I just packed that all up!" cried Diero.

The other boys gathered curiously about S'baladin's who, heaving and coughing, frantically emptied the bag.

Scrolls scattered to the ground, some rolling this way and that. Busily, S'baladin rummaged amongst them, then seized one and stood. Eagerly, he ran his fingers over its words.

Sibrion and the other boys exchanged confused glances as they hovered around S'baladin.

"What's going on out there?" Javatiel whispered to Sibrion.

"An attack of evil creatures from the forest, something unnatural."

"There, right here!" the scrawny lad interrupted. "I knew I had written it down."

S'baladin cast aside the scrolls and shoved a single parchment into Sibrion's hands.

"My father told me stories when I was small!" said S'baladin. That got a few chuckles out of the boys, but S'baladin's glare hushed them. "My father spoke of many monsters in the hinterlands beyond the Province of Hierundia where he and the Gardener once traveled."

Subdued, the boys listened more intently as he continued. "In northern Y'cromeca, they were stalked by something in the undergrowth, creatures who mimicked any sound they heard. A bird's call, a child's cry, even a man's voice."

"A survivor out there said he thought he heard children!" Sibrion commented to the fellows.

The boys tensed and S'baladin continued. "They were stalked for days. The creatures always kept their distance, their cries but distant echoes."

Sibrion, who had been scanning the parchment desperately, interrupted impatiently. "How do we kill them? What did the Gardener do?"

"They never killed one," S'baladin to responded.

The room seemed to sag in disappointment.

"They never came close enough. Probably because the Gardener was with him."

Abán's voice rose from the back, "Then what the hell do we do?"

"The Gardener told my father, if they ever did attack, all they would need to defend themselves was hyssop."

The boys all stared at S'baladin in disbelief.

"That is what he told me!" S'baladin protested. "Many times, both T'balidor and I heard the tale."

Sibrion sighed deeply, rubbing his temples, "Sy, what if it was just a bedtime story?" He motioned to the chaos outside their tent, "Do you trust a story to stop these things?"

"Listen to me!" S'baladin shouted. Tears of indignation formed in his eyes. "I know my father. And he—he never exaggerated! He told me those stories for a reason. And right now, we must heed them."

From the urgency in his eyes, Sibrion discerned that S'baladin believed with all his being what his father told him was the truth. He sighed deeply as the boys all turned to him, awaiting his decision.

"We shall trust Baltien, and the Gardener's wisdom, as we always have," he said gruffly. "Cursed luck that Sabaca drew the shortest stick!" he said. "Anyone know how to find hyssop?"

Outside the tent, men circled the campfires. Desperately they cast spears and fired arrows into the dark of night as the beast prowled the camp. Any man who edged too close was pulled into the darkness by those jagged teeth, all the while screaming for his life. Their steel did nothing to the creatures.

The men's morale was at a breaking point. Some froze, some ran as a ten-foot-tall creature with fur as white as the fog leapt forward. Its long jaw snapped against their swords and swatted them away with paws from which great claws flashed, slicing at their flesh. Wolf-like, it bore many arrows on its body. It paused and shivered. Audible popping sounds emanated from its pelvis. Then, it stood up on its hind legs in a bipedal stance.

It towered over the paralyzed men and was raising a paw to swipe when suddenly, frsssshhhh!, a well-aimed arrow pierced its rib cage. Unlike those of steel and stone, this one elicited a loud shriek of pain. It rattled the jaws of every man in the camp.

The moment of silence which followed was punctuated by Sibrion's cry of "ATTACK!"

Javatiel, Vaez, Kelán, and Aejulan charged past terrified guards. Their swords and archery weapons gleamed purple in the moonlight. Keeping low to the ground, they bobbed in and out of the howling creature's reach. The young Br'thain warriors took turns rotating swings at its exposed areas. Their small cuts proved effective against the creature. With each nick, the creature became more enraged, more dazed. Suddenly, it reopened its pelvis and returned to all fours.

Sensing its plan to retaliate, Sibrion took careful aim. Pulling back with all his might, he loosed one more speeding projectile. In a purple streak, it pierced the creature's eye to imbed deeply in the back of his skull. The great white creature let out one final roar as it came crashing to the ground in a sound akin to that of a great oak tree collapsing in the forest.

The men of the caravan stared in stunned amazement as the fellows whooped excitedly and clapped each other on the back. But this action enraged the rest of the pack. Standing bipedally, they moved closer to the firelight. Sibrion's face drained pale as he counted two dozen. As the young Br'thain warriors sobered and raised their weapons, something streaked past, beyond the guards and the four Br'thain.

It was S'baladin. Hobbling to the edge of the firelight, he faced the pack. His fellows stared after him in abject horror. Before they could run to save him, he lifted his hands high above his head. In them was a parchment scrawled with ancient words, the Gardener's words, passed to him from his father. In the pale firelight they almost seemed to glow upon the parchment.

An ancient tongue of power exploding from S'baladin's lips. They reverberated in the air and throughout the ground. These were ancient sounds that mortal men had not heard since before the Ballai were formed. They soared across the trees and into the mountains and hills themselves. These were words that had shaped the very lands of Y'cromeca, the words which forged the Streams of Feynhava, the hallowed utterances of Uraduin spoken over the lands by the Gardener eons ago.

All fell silent. The wolf-like creatures, the caravan guards, the young men of the West, and S'baladin himself. In the silence, the largest of the beasts stood upon his hind legs, stretching into the dark of night. It stood twice as tall as any of the men before him and they cowered backward. The Br'thain fumbled at their bows and readied their spears. But S'baladin raised his arm and called out, "Stay your weapons."

In the hollow eyes of the beast was fear, fear of the Gardener's power. As stealthily as the creatures had come, they shrank away into the night. The fog itself departed, and, gradually, the familiar sounds of a nocturnal forest returned. The air itself seemed lightened from a tremendous weight.

A curious crowd gathered all around the young lads. They beamed at them in gratitude and offered thanks and praise in Hierundiel. Sibrion gazed in wonder at S'baladin and hissed, "What strange power lies within one so sick? How came you upon such a scroll?"

Smiling shyly, S'baladin said, "It was the Gardener's Maleor gift."

Sibrion chuckled and shook his head. "Most of us receive weaponry or armor, but you? You receive words which trump them all!"

Just then, the caravan leader broke through the crowd with a barrage of questions.

"Who are you that speak like gods?" he demanded of S'baladin. "No man in Hierundia ever killed such creatures!" he spluttered. To Sibrion he asked, "Who are you that fight like ferrets? Where are you from?"

Sibrion shook his head at his fellows. None answered his questions. "We are a gift of fortune," he said vaguely. "In return for our defeat of these creatures, we ask you return our weapons and grant us our freedom."

"Very well," said the caravan leader. "You may leave at morning light. But know this, the people of our caravan will sing of this night for generations to come."

Sanctuary at Kol-Shebbala

Nine trackers searched cautiously about a fresh campsite. Wind Ghouls, hybrid canine creatures harvested from the Cethin Arda, sniffed the ground, growling with bared teeth as they moved from scent to scent. One of the trackers was on his knees like a predatory animal, his beastly nostrils sniffing the grounds of the campfire along with the Wind Ghouls.

A tall, lumbering Taenshuk plodded its way around the scene. From his mount a Taenshuk captain shouted down at his trackers below. "The runaways, were they here?"

The one who knelt looked upward and called out, "Yes!" He rose to report. "They camped here through the night."

"Aye. The charred ashes, their urine in the dirt, the rotting flesh of the fruits they consume. They cannot conceal their stench!" another tracker snarled.

Both trackers snorted beastly laughter out. Their fellows joined them with derisive howls.

"Cease your boasting, you fools!" the officer barked downward. "When were they last here? Which of you can answer that?"

A tracker shuffled forth. "The fire was extinguished hours ago."

Another tracker stomped out from the surrounding brush. "I have their scent. And multiple tracks lead that direction." He pointed a taloned finger as he spoke.

The officer on the Taenshuk silently studied the horizon, exhaling cold vapors. "Kol-Shebbala lies nine leagues to the northeast," he said. "It is uncharted. The terrain is composed of deep ravines and endless gorges. Take care guiding your mounts but move with haste."

The Ulkyrien trackers mounted their horses and moved through the forests at great speed. Hours later, they came upon the entrance of the scarred landscape of Kol-Shebbala. Thick woodlands all about the gashes in the ground made it even more difficult to traverse.

"A group of tracks lead into this gorge. We are close on their heels," hissed a vile beast man.

Just then, a haunting shrill screeched from a Veyasaen high above the tall pine trees. The monstrous fowl passed swiftly, disappearing into thick, dark clouds.

"Proceed with caution!" the captain ordered. "Many of our comrades have succumbed to their fates in these gorges."

"There are others watching us. I sense it," declared the lead tracker.

"Aye! But they hide well. I cannot detect their scent," spoke another.

Suddenly, the Veyasaen let for a series of ear-piercing shrills in short, single bursts. Ulkyrien trackers recognized this as the signal for runaways below.

"We have our boys!" hissed the captain.

The trackers moved stealthily to avoid detection, but morning passed into the noon day with no sign of runaways. Often, the trackers came upon their boot prints, but they did not find the boys. Each time, these tracks faded away upon their entry into the stone gorges. One of their many searches along the edges of ravines, led a duo of trackers to the base of five tall, wooden stilts.

Peering upward, they spotted five sagging corpses, dressed in tattered Rhünkai uniforms, lashed to the posts.

"A warning!" they called out to the others.

"None who inhabit these parts will aid us in our search," came the captain's reply. "Have none of you blaggards noticed? The Veyasaen no longer flies above."

"Strange!" and "And where have our Wind Ghouls gone?" another Ulkyrien muttered. Ironically, it was the very wind itself which unnerved them most as it howled fiercely throughout the canyon walls. A swirling vortex of pine needles and leaves, broken twigs and small branches rose up against them. Nevertheless, they forged through it, dogged in their search.

Eventually, the trackers came upon moist boot prints. Anticipation coursing high once more, they pursued the tracks until they diverged. Several prints went forward through a copse of tall brush, while the others took an alternate route above the ravine.

"You six with me on foot," called the captain. Turning toward the brush he ordered the others, "You three ride along the ravine."

It was the trackers on high land who spotted the forms of the boys, clad in layers of hooded furs, scarves and weapons, moving through the thick brush like bears. The path of the trackers descended into the dark ravine as frigid winds howled miserably through the gorge.

As they neared the boys, they strained to make out a conversation in Hierundiel. Instantly, they drew their weapons and dismounted. The low grunts of the Taenshuk moving through the tall pine trees announced the convergence of the trackers as the second group rejoined the first, flanking the runaway boys. Concealed by tall, thick brush, the three trackers spread silently, easing carefully past branches, across rocky terrain to surround the boys.

Suddenly, their conversation faded in the frigid wind.

Tired of their hunt and eager to capture their prey, the three Ulkyrien leapt from the wet brush into the clearing. But the only forms in sight were several massive boulders. Upon the wind, their heightened animal instincts heard a far-off shout. "Train your weapons on the Ulkyrien!"

"Those vermin are close! I sense it," whispered the lead tracker.

Sharp Ulkyrien eyes surveyed their surroundings. With a great grunt, the Taenshuk burst forth from the tall pine trees. To the Ulkyriens' shocked surprise, two youthful figures sat atop their beast. They looked at each other in confusion. What of their captain? What of the six on foot?

Infuriated, the trackers sent a volley of arrows toward the runaways from the West. The juvenile atop the Taenshuk steered the lumbering creature in their direction while his companion fired back. The three trackers sent along a second volley. One missile struck the grunting Taenshuk's torso, another his thigh. The giant animal froze, wobbled, then toppled to the ground.

Reloading their bows, the three trackers stepped cautiously over to the wounded creature, searching for the boys. They found them, clutching at wounds and crawling from beneath the shuddering beast. They fired multiple arrows into them both. In anger and triumph, as the youths choked rattling breaths past gurgles of blood, they let out a series of beastly grunts and howls.

"Where are the rest of them?" growled one as they ceased their cries.

"They are hiding still, somewhere in the trees...behind the boulders," roared another.

The third, with a frown, asked, "But what of our captain?"

"Look, they approach us now," said the first. Gesturing towards a rustling in the bushes. Confident from their kill, the trackers stood, defenseless, as several more of hooded youth sprang forth from behind the surrounding boulders to aim their bows at the trackers.

Skilled as they were, the Ulkyrien managed to notch arrows and release a volley, just as the boys released theirs. Each side sustained several injuries, and each side reloaded. Many of the arrows in this second volley found a home in the flesh of both boy and beast.

Each side retreated behind boulders and brush, pulling along the worst of the wounded. Those strong enough to fight, struggled to reload their crossbows, but their wounds made their efforts laborious at best.

Though his comrades were felled, riddled with arrows, the lead tracker remained on his feet. He too, was pierced through with sundry arrows, and the energy waned from his body.

"Wind Ghouls!" the Ulkyrien's voice rose to ride above the freezing winds. "Come! Now! At once!"

But the woods remained silent, with no promise of rescue from the hybrid canines.

"Where are the rest of us?" cried the Ulkyrien to his wounded comrades as he collapsed to the ground. "Have we been bested by a band of common lads!?" he growled in angry humiliation.

But his comrades, remained silent, the energy of life fleeting in their fiendish eyes.

A lad's trembling voice called from across the clearing.

"Why did you strike us? We are your kinsmen!"

Drawing his saber, he stood and hobbled painfully to the injured boys. Standing over them, he inspected their wounds. Through their arrow-pierced fur skins, their bodies bled profusely, turning the ground beneath them into muddied pools of burgundy.

"You are vermin from the West, as the counselor has called you. You stole into our borders," the Ulkyrien heaved painfully. His bodied swayed against a gust of wind as wheat would in a field.

"Why have you turned against your own?" cried another wounded soul.

"You think to escape the Ulkyrien with your lies?" heaved the beast-man. Following the Rhünkai policy of ending the life of any runaway sustaining serious injuries, the Ulkyrien plodded from boy to boy. With great effort, he rose his saber upward, over and over, stabbing it into each of their bodies.

Movement drew the tracker's practiced eye. Beyond a boulder, several yards away, one more crawled away from the bloody scene. This individual too was clad in hooded furs so thick it gave the impression of a bear treading on all fours. Resolutely, the Ulkyrien tread after him in pursuit.

Standing over the bleeding form, he lifted his blade back and brought it down upon the dying lad, but not before the youthful form rolled over on his back, produced a crossbow, and released an arrow. His arrow pierced the Ulkyrien's beastly neck and buried itself in his brain, killing him instantly. The boy too died as the blade plunged into his chest.

The frigid winds swept over the bloody scene, whipping through the tall grass and howling about the boulders, chilling the corpses. Moments after the final assault, a group of furry beings stepped warily out of the nearby foliage, approaching the bloody scene.

"I do not understand. These trackers, they were pursuing us, but chose to strike at one another?" Sibrion queried.

The boys surveyed the mutiny in wonder.

"Aye! They thought us runaways," said Aejulan. "But why turn upon their own?"

S'baladin's eyes peered through trembling branches. He took a few steps forward, squinting, then pointed a skinny finger and called out excitedly through chattering teeth, "Look! Over there!"

A company of dark forms rapidly approached. Fifty armed strangers circled about them. S'baladin sighed wearily as they pointed all manner of weapons at his little band who drew their own weapons upward in defense.

A youthful, female voice came from one of them. "We are not with the Ulkyrien, nor are we with the Rhünkai," she said in Hierundiel.

"And neither are we," cried Sibrion angrily.

"Who are you, then?" asked Aejulan.

The girl raised her crossbow, pointing it at him. "You are in no position to question us in our land! We will ask you the questions, and you will answer us!"

Outnumbered, the boys lowered their weapons. "You are the ones from the West," she said. "I have been waiting for you for quite some time."

The boys murmured their surprise at this.

Sibrion stepped forward to treat with her. "What do you mean? Who told you of us, and how came you to learn of our whereabouts?"

Another hooded figure, much her elder, spoke to the girl in Hierundiel. "The enemy now possesses Ferusats," she murmured. "Are you certain this is them?"

The young one turned her furry hood sideways to speak with her elder. "Yes. They bear, the mark. Look at their strange armor, its appearance foreign, of another world."

Her teeth clattered just as much as those of the boys, and she stamped her feet against the cold. The elder woman squinted at them all, then addressed them. "Follow us to our abode. It is warmer there…and safer."

The fifty-armed strangers lowered their weapons and marched alongside them through the brush. Finally, the group came to a towering wall of brush that curled and twisted upwards.

"As we pass through this wall, you must move your limbs slowly and press your bodies with care. Follow our example," the woman instructed.

The boys watched the ladies disappear into the wall of brush, along with the armed men around them. As they followed, the forests became eerily dense around the fellows as they passed through. Thick curls of twisted brush seemed oddly able to trap and repel the very wind.

"How grand, boys! It grows warmer, the wintry weather does not invade!" Vaez shouted excitedly. A soldier near him grunted sternly, reminding him to move slowly, lest he disturb the brush.

"It must be imbued with supernal powers!" Diero marveled.

The older woman leading the trek threw a little smile to the younger girl at that.

"Yes indeed!" exclaimed Aejulan. "The brush is solid, yet when our limbs pass slowly through it, it softens and bends, conforming to our bodies!"

"But look behind us, it is solid once more!" observed Javatiel.

The young girl, a wide grin upon her face stopped momentarily to address the boys.

"When strangers try to pass through here with brutish force, thrusting and swinging their blades about, the brush retains its solid state. It is impossible for them to trespass. In their frustration, they turn away," she said.

Impressed and curious, the boys raised eyebrows and murmured to each other. They emerged and blinked in surprise at the peaceful landscape before them. An open field stretched before them, populated by trees and plants of diverse kinds. Men moved about the fields and orchards while women worked busily within and without rustic hovels of straw, hay and wood.

"Once, they lived in the various Provinces, now left desolate by the Rhünkai," explained the girl, as she and the older lady pulled back their furred hoods. "Come now, boys. This way, please."

They followed the ladies past placid, grazing deer while rabbits and squirrels skipped and ran before them. Chickens too roamed freely near a pond where turtles lazily sunned and little fish swam and leapt.

"Though no man has ever been to the Garden of Ages, I can only wonder if it looks and feels as wonderful as this place," said Sibrion.

"Surely we are safe now," S'baladin whispered at his side. "They've left us our weapons and your Ferusat!"

"It certainly seems that way," Sibrion said, though he remained wary. He offered his arm to the boy who leaned heavily upon it as they walked.

They came to a cluster of giant stones in which there was a small opening. Beyond this was the wide entrance of a cave. A thick wall of leaves and branches cascaded beautifully down over its mouth. A small group of women stepped out from behind this foliage, holding back the living curtain to allow everyone to pass inside the mouth of the cave. "Herein is our abode," said one of them, as the band of travelers stepped over the threshold of the terrestrial dwelling.

Candlelight glowed warmly upon the smiling faces within. Women and children gathered around rustic tables and chairs for a meal. Curious, the children peered at the newcomers, giggling and waving. Several of the fellows smiled at them as they passed.

Kelán, Javatiel, Vaez and Aejulan gathered beneath provincial banners hanging on the walls, intrigued by their diverse colors and symbols. The eyes of S'baladin, Sibrion, and Abán fell hungrily upon the various ornaments, artifacts, and books strewn on the tables. It was the fire pits that drew Jubal and Diero, where one woman roasted tealeaves as others prepared a stew over a separate cauldron.

"You are welcome to stay the night and be refreshed with food before continuing your journey," said the older woman her voice echoing off the high ceiling of the cave.

"Thank you kindly. We certainly accept your hospitality," said S'baladin in Hierundiel. Sibrion squeezed his shoulder and they smiled together in relief. Shaking, S'baladin sat beside the fire, his body giving way to a series of coughs. Jubal hurried to him, drew a metal cup and a handful of tea leaves from his pack, and brewed a healing concoction for the boy.

The girl, quiet now, approached a fire. Messy blonde locks curled about her gaunt face. As S'baladin leaned toward her, intending to speak, she spun around startled, then smiled bashfully. Her smile quickly faded under the weight of worry in her eyes. He was drawn to those eyes. They were the deep azure of the evening sky but uniquely rimmed with the light sky blue of the brightest of Anterròs afternoons.

The girl gazed steadily at S'baladin as he coughed nervously into his scarf. Her eyes observed with feline intensity, her head swiveling slowly to follow Jubal as he offered his brew to the sickly boy. She turned to nod at a woman who informed her that their meal was ready to be served.

As a cat might, she jerked as S'baladin's voice beside her asked, "What is your name?"

"I am Ka-Lyn," she spoke softly, then nodded toward her elder, "She is V'leshkah."

"S'baladin," he said, tapping his chest. He pointed out each of the boys in his group, naming them one by one for her. She listened politely.

"Ka-Lyn, how was it that your company found us?" asked S'baladin.

She laughed gaily and said only, "You must be hungry! Come!"

The women treated the boys to a delicious stew of poultry and vegetables in simple, rustic steel bowls. They passed loaves of bread, butter and a jar of wild honey around the large table where they gathered.

S'baladin was pleased when Ka-Lyn sat beside. Quietly, she engaged him in conversation once more. "Our scouts followed your tracks from the time you entered Kol-Shebbala. We keep well aware of intruders. You may have seen what became of the Rhünkai who thought to find us." She peered up from her stew, saw him nod, and continued. "From our scouts, we believed you to be the young men from the West. So, I immediately set out to find you."

Hearing this from beyond them, Aejulan frowned and interjected. "But how did you know where we came from?" His tone drew the attention of the other boys and the table grew quiet.

"In my dreams, I have seen a group from your world enter ours."

Around a mouthful of his stew, Jubal chortled, "In your dreams!"

"You search for someone," she answered, unperturbed.

Around the table, eyebrows shot upwards. A few of the boys inhaled sharply.

"Just who are you?" asked Sibrion.

S'baladin spoke over Sibrion's question, "How is it that you have such dreams?"

Ka-Lyn paused from her eating. "This place of refuge, it was planted many years ago, when I was just a baby. It is incredibly special to me. And to V'leshkah, as well," she said. Turning to Sibrion, she said, "I am called Ka-Lyn."

Sibrion's eyes narrowed, and he pressed her for more. "That is not what I..." but S'baladin interrupted him "Who planted this refuge?" he asked, gazing intently into her feline eyes.

Gesturing about her, she explained. "This place was formed as a sanctuary for the weary, the oppressed, for those who are without a home, without a family, or name. It was formed by a powerful, kindly man out of his wisdom of the Streams of Feynhava."

S'baladin's face lit up with a smile. He was just about to shout, "The Gardener?" when Sibrion's foot connected solidly with his leg. He winced, realized in an instant the reason, and disguised his wince with a cough. Sibrion scowled a rapid warning to the others. They too remained silent.

A smile flashed across V'leshkah's face. "The Gardener is a very good man," she said.

"You are saying a Gardener grew your protective hedge? He must be powerful, indeed," S'baladin remarked casually, testing these women for deception.

Ka-Lyn laughed her tinkling laugh once more. "The hedge, the community, the people, all of this," she waved her arm in a wide arc again, "is his doing."

"He brings us good tidings of revelation every time he passes through these lands. He has also shared his feasts with us," said V'leshkah. "The Gardener's feasts signify rehearsals. They point to the future when all of Y'cromeca will return to the Garden of Ages. These are great times of rejoicing...even in a sad and broken world," she added.

The boys' countenances brightened, yet S'baladin shook his head slightly, still suspicious of Thaed-Rú duplicity.

"What is your story? What brought you to this place of refuge?" he pressed Ka-Lyn.

Her feline eyes turned to V'leshkah, who nodded slightly. "My parents...they gave me up when I was born. But V'leshkah, she knew them well, so she took me in and raised me. She has been like a mother to me ever since."

S'baladin sighed. The young woman seemed beyond deceit. He paused, then asked one final question, "Ka- Lyn, do you know what happened with the Ulkyrien trackers?"

Again, eyes of blue turned to V'leshkah, who gave another nod of approval.

"When we heard of your presence in Kol-Shebbala, I felt it deep within that you were the young men of the West, from my dreams. We hid above the ravine, behind the thick brush, following your company. That is when our scouts discovered Ulkyrien trackers following you, Wind Ghouls prowling all about you, and a Veyasaen on high," said Ka-Lyn.

She paused for a moment, cast her eyes downward, and fiddled with her cloak. When she spoke again, she seemed more guarded. "There is much that I cannot reveal to you, to protect Kol-Shebbala. In time, you will know all. But this I can tell you, it was I who caused the Ulkyrien to turn on one another. I exercise the power to enter one's mind. I can...suggest things. Things that are not...as though they are. I made the Ulkyrien to appear in your forms to one another. As one group saw the other, they each believed it to be you."

The boys sat silent and amazed, exchanging perplexed looks with one another.

"So, each of the Ulkyrien trackers fired arrows into each other, and thrust their swords into their own kinsmen, believing they were striking you," Ka-Lyn concluded.

"Through your powers of suggestion, you have indeed saved us from the Ulkyrien," said S'baladin. "I apologize that I was uncertain whether you were of our side or not." He nodded deeply toward her, bending his shoulders in deference. "We owe you our thanks."

She smiled kindly upon them as the others offered their thanks too.

"We are here on a special mission, to search for my brother T'balidor. He was left behind in our last attempt to liberate the child slaves," S'baladin offered one final test.

V'leshkah's eyes glimmered with genuine grief. "Yes. We know of your brave men and of the ambush under which they suffered great loss. The Thaed-Rú have led our land to ruin. It burdens us greatly here," she lamented.

"But they have received their just punishment. A wicked force has usurped their position. And now he sits on the throne at Realmhold Thaed-Rú." V'leshkah's kindly face grew dark. "But his time of reckoning is coming!"

S'baladin checked once more with Sibrion who nodded, turned to the ladies and spoke. "We are well acquainted in the West with the teachings of the Gardener. We have missed him greatly. He disappeared shortly after the great defeat of which you speak."

The women neither spoke nor reacted to this statement.

S'baladin attempted to fill the awkward silence. "We are in accord with you. The Gardener has spoken of his foe from ancient times. That great story, is divided into smaller narratives, as one person and his actions affect the next, and the next through the ages until now. So here we are here, sons of shepherds and farmers entering this story of the north."

"Aye," said Sibrion, "We have pledged to S'baladin to accompany him in rescuing his brother." He turned to Ka-Lyn, fishing for information, "...if he is still alive, that is."

"May your story come to a good conclusion," said V'leshkah. But Ka-Lyn, remained silent, offering no answers or advice.

The boys, Ka-Lyn and V'leshkah spoke of lighter things late into the night. The fellows shared stories of their home in Ferán, Rihován and Calasmorra. Ka-Lyn and V'leshkah were enthralled with the romance of the West. Though they loved the refuge of Kol-Shebbala, they were drawn to the stories of the desert. So, the boys told them of the Br'thain, the rite of passage called Maleor and the beauty of the desert mountains, caves, and valleys, of the Fieradeem and the Preceptans who were custodians of the Streams of Feynhava, and of the various B'naiynot, the houses. "And over all," S'baladin said proudly, "our desert world is governed by the goodness of the Gardener."

"This place reminds me of the Didderäsh in Rihován," commented Diero. "I never knew that, even here in the north, the Gardener offers similar shelters to those in need," he said.

"Yes, but this place can only hold so many people. It is not the great place of refuge like your Didderäsh," returned Ka-Lyn. The boys of Anterròs smiled proudly at that.

The last to remain awake talking, long past midnight, were Ka-Lyn and S'baladin. Accompanied by Yashi, they sat at the mouth of the cave, the living curtain at their backs.

"I sense you carry a heavy burden," Ka-Lyn said. "Is it your father?" S'baladin nodded his head.

"My condolences. The loss of a father brings such pain and sorrow," she said.

"It is more than that. The Gardener should have been there to prevent him from being killed in that ambush," spoke S'baladin in grim honesty. "After all, it was at his behest that my people put their lives at risk for strangers." A bitterness he could not banish crept into his voice. He cast his gaze downward.

Ka-Lyn peered soulfully into S'baladin's eyes, studying the conflicting emotions in his expression.

"We often disagreed, but my father was a good man – a great man, respected by many. Did you know that, at his funeral, people came from far and wide to pay their respects to him?"

His pain was a curiosity to Ka-Lyn, and her eyes studied him quietly.

Fervently hoping for answers from her visions, he gazed directly into her blue eyes and asked, "Why did the Gardener disappear through the Streams after the ambush? Why, when we needed him most, would he abandon us all?"

"Do you know who Arbantio M'zhalo is?" asked Ka-Lyn, to which S'baladin answered in the negative.

"After the ambush, the Gardener came to Kol-Shebbala to tell us about a miller in the Province of Graëyhovan. Years ago, his youngest sons were taken into Rhünkai service. It crushed Arbantio's heart into a million pieces. When the Gardener met Arbantio, he saw the miller's pain. Arbantio was key in the liberation of the child slaves. His servants opened the Streams during the Gardener's feasts. They are the fabric of bravery – nameless workers who travelled from Graëyhovan to Hierundia to open the Streams on the last day of every feast. Because of Arbantio's courage, thousands of children are now free. And this continued until the Harbinger came to possess Realmhold Thaed-Rú."

"The Harbinger?" interrupted S'baladin.

"That is what we call the new dark counselor of the Thaed-Ru. A counselor offers wisdom, the Harbinger offers only chaos, ushering evil along wherever he treads," Ka-Lyn paused to explain, then continued. "This Harbinger murdered Arbantio's family and all his servants and destroyed their home and mill as punishment for their intervention with the child slaves."

She sat quietly, allowing S'baladin to think on this.

"This is the reason the Br'thain were ambushed?" he asked, "There was no one to open the Streams?"

"Yes. Without their aid, they had no control over their destination and were steered by the Harbinger into an ambush. The Gardener realized immediately that the M'zhalo family was in danger, but he arrived too late. His heart is burdened, S'baladin," said Ka-Lyn. "And that is the great heart of the Gardener. Beloved by many beyond the West, he watches over all. He has spent much time with the Br'thain, training them, and teaching them his ways. He trusts them to do the right thing in a perilous time."

She laid a hand gently on his arm, "S'baladin, he did not abandon anyone. He left things in their natural course of action, because he trusts the sons of Alazar and Oliel."

S'baladin silently drank her words, a balm to all that had troubled him these many months.

"In due time, you and your family will find healing," she promised. "We must pass through the fires in order to be purified and strengthened."

"You speak truth, Ka-Lyn. Your words are a great comfort. I yet mourn my father, but no longer do I feel betrayed by our Gardener," he said.

She laid a hand kindly upon his and silence fell between them. For several long moments, they gazed upon each other's countenances.

"You leave in the morning and need your rest," Ka-Lyn said finally.

As they stood, she asked shyly, "Will we meet again?"

"It is said that when people who know the Gardener meet one another, their lives become forever intertwined," he said. "I wish you could join us. You would love the desert."

"I know I would," she smiled. "But I must remain here for these people. One day, I will visit Ferán," she promised.

"I hope so," he said.

They shared a warm embrace. Upon their two faces deep, abiding smiles shone with the stars, carrying the breath of the cosmos with it.

In the morning, after a hearty breakfast, the boys bid Kol-Shebbala farewell. As the boys stepped away from the numinous sanctuary, S'baladin cast one more look backward. Ka-Lyn's fragile, little smile stretched across the universe to him. It ignited the day with the brightness of the sun, and invaded his soul. But knowing they must not tarry, he followed the armed defenders of Kol-Shebbala who escorted the fellows through the supernal wall of brush, along the canyons of Kol-Shebbala unto to the pass that led to Va'Harot. S'ba-ladin, was grieved to face the unforgiving cold once more. Nevertheless, his love for his brother drove him onward, and, as they trudged through the cold, Ka- Lyn's smile warmed his heart.

Capture at Va'Harot

Several days later, the boys arrived at Va'Harot. The Gardener's wisdom and the advice of the defenders of Kol-Shebbala led the boys to a well-concealed entrance with ease. A pair of weathered Faeynül statues, their features faded to obscurity by the eons, flanked a rent in the canyon wall, overgrown by sticker patches.

The older boys chopped away at these with their swords as the younger ones kept watch. Eagerly, they descended the entrance that spiraled further down into utter darkness. The opening twisted and turned far below into a deep cavern. Carefully, they descended, torches aloft. Their lights revealed a monstrous heap of colossal bones scattered all about. Grim reminders of their mortality, the piles towered hundreds of feet above them. Warily, they passed beneath an archway of ribs.

Cupping their hands about their mouths, the boys called out, "T'balidor?"

When they heard no reply but echoes, Abán drew his ram's horn from his pack and its call sounded loudly through the cavern. From deep amongst the osseous heaps, they heard a faint cry.

"Did you hear that?" cried S'baladin eagerly.

"I heard it!" answered Aejulan.

Grinning, their hearts pounding with anticipation, the boys moved forward shouting, "T'balidor!"

"Over here!" the voice came, "This way!" growing ever louder.

Sibrion led the way, hopping over debris and picking his way around the massive bones. "We are coming!" he shouted.

Skirting a pile of bones, his eyes fell upon a campfire and he paused. Beside it, T'balidor resting on a mat of leaves and shreds of old, soiled cloth. Immediately, he leapt from it, then winced. He limped upon one leg, the other bound with two sturdy wooden sticks bound tightly with fibrous strips of woven plants.

"It is he! It is T'balidor!" shouted Sibrion. S'baladin, winded, struggled to catch up with the rest of the boys as they shouted in excitement and gathered round his brother in a powerful reunion of dear friends, of young hearts.

"It is you!" they exclaimed. T'balidor pushed the boys back, laughing, searching their faces and greeting them each by name in wonder. Finally, his eyes fell upon his ailing brother.

"S'baladin?" he pulled him into a happy embrace but asked. "What are you doing here? Surely mother did not consent to you partaking in such a perilous journey!"

His little brother shook his head in embarrassment. "She does not know."

"What happened to your leg?" asked Sibrion.

"After the ambush, I sought this refuge as instructed, but a pack of wolves chased me through the night. In my haste and with no torch, I slipped, falling twenty feet onto the stone foundations of Va'Harot. I limped all the way down to this damn cave!"

He laughed and brushed off their looks of concern. "Do not take pity on my sight! What has it been, three months?"

Sibrion nodded.

"I bound my leg and thus have managed to ascend and gather berries, hunt even," he said proudly, gesturing behind him. The remains of a deer lay near his fire pit. On a little shelf of rock beside his pallet lay a neat line of twenty or blades of various size and length, all hewn of bones from the surrounding piles. Beneath these was a stack of several spears tipped in shards of bone. It was obvious that T'balidor did not lack in the way of osseous weapons.

"Amazing how you managed to survive down here for all these months!" uttered S'baladin.

"Now that we found you, we must hurry back, that is if you can manage on that leg brace of yours. Perhaps you'd prefer to stay here?" chortled Sibrion. The boys all chuckled at this.

"I shall accompany you with pleasure!" T'balidor laughed. "For many weeks now, I have believed I was destined to contribute to these heaps of bones, my hope of any rescue long since faded."

In wonderous disbelief, he peered from face to face, then asked. "How came you past the Rhünkai? We were ambushed by strange, dark creatures under their control."

Before they could answer, T'balidor's face turned ashen. "The ambush!" he cried, then turned to his brother. "S'baladin...what of our father?" An invisible force gripped everyone's throats and stopped their hearts.

T'balidor searched his little brother's eyes and his own darkened as tears welled up in S'baladin's. "The ambush...it took his life," came the reply.

T'balidor closed his eyes against this news. He heaved a deep sigh. "Somehow, I felt that," he said. "In the chaos, I searched for him as best I could, but failed to locate him. He never would have left a battlefield. And, had he survived, I know he would have been among you, leading you."

S'baladin and T'balidor held each other in a heartfelt, brotherly embrace.

"I am so glad we found you," S'baladin said simply.

"Let us go! We must get back to the surface and open the streams!" said Sibrion.

Many hours later, the fellows scrambled up through a narrow exit, assisting T'balidor though his brace served him well for the most part.

"We must find a stone surface large enough to hold us all. There, we can stand together and drive the Ferusat into the ground," said Sibrion.

"There is a stone field beyond those boulders. I have seen it several times, whenever I came up to the surface. Follow me," said T'balidor.

They moved with great speed and anticipation. As they rounded a tall boulder, a horrible wave of nausea and shock stopped them dead in their tracks. Before them stood a vast army of Rhünkai soldiers. Their weapons clattered to the ground and they raised trembling hands in surrender. It was useless to fight such number of armed forces.

Several soldiers confiscated their weapons, while others bound their hands and feet in iron fetters. Wordlessly, the soldiers shoved the boys up a wooden ramp, into a steel wagon. The ramp clanged shut behind them. Aejulan curled into a little ball in one corner, shivering with fright at his horrible nightmare, relived again. Sibrion attended to Aejulan, murmuring words of comfort and comradery.

For the boys of the West, their capture was a new horror altogether. Javatiel and Diero rattled furiously at the locked ramp while the rest peered anxiously through thick bars at the countless soldiers, heavily armed beyond.

Many rode on horseback, while seven tumens of foot soldiers trekked on either side of the boys' wagon.

T'balidor glowered angrily, full to the brim with self-loathing. "Had you not come for me, you would all be free!"

"Bah!" said several of the boys, dismissing this and forgiving him for it simultaneously.

For weeks they huddled together, wondering if they were fated for execution or labor. When their muscles grew tight from disuse, they paced back and forth to stretch their limbs. Their only sustenance were the few crusts of stale bread and sips of water afforded them each day by the Rhünkai.

Finally, they arrived at a fortified camp populated by sentries all about steep ledges on high. The light of hundreds of fires glowed across the floor of an expansive canyon below with myriads of soldiers all about.

The boys were taken into a large tent, under heavy guard. They stiffened as gruff voices approached. Several men in high military regalia burst through. An overlord bearing the staff of a Tribune, flanked by six captains, three on each side, circled each of them, examining them closely. "I understand you boys speak Hierundiel," he spoke sternly. "It is what the leaders of your armies train you to speak, as you go about entering our Dominions to steal the Scions of Íraban."

Only silence met him. He and his captains observed their garments with the greatest of curiosity, just as the caravan leader had done. But, unlike he had in Kol-Shebbala, this time S'baladin needed none of Sibrion's warnings to inspire his guardedness.

The overlord prodded them. "So, you are the infamous savages from the West."

Sibrion noted a look of concern on the man's face and bit back a slight grin. *We are but youths, and yet they fear us!* He thought with glee.

"For too long, I have heard of the exploits of your ragtag bands of lowly shepherds, your farmers who dare to steal from the great armies of the Eleven Dominions!"

The boys' eyes narrowed with anger. Jubal whispered expletives under his breath. T'balidor, wanting to beat his condescending countenance to a bloody pulp with his fists, exchanged glances with Sibrion. Prudently, he shook his head, but bit at his lip in frustration.

The man's lips twisted into a smile. "For years, we thought of you as phantom raiders. None could stop you and none have known your identity. But the new ruler of the Thaed-Rú, in his omnipotence and great power, has revealed that you are nothing but desert whelps!"

He sneered at the boys as they held back their rage, then announced, "I am the Tribune Ansuz. I preside over one of the largest regions in Hierundia. From the first night you entered, my finest trackers have been following you," he said. Menacingly, he leaned forward to add, "Even as you passed into Kol-Shebbala and then descended to Va'Harot, always, they were near."

S'baladin cast his gaze downward as he felt the man's eyes piercing through the boys' souls.

Ansuz turned from them and ordered one of the captains to bring him the Ferusat. The boys shifted nervously as the Tribune studied the staff. After a moment, he set it aside and paced before them.

"Of greatest note to me in their reports was how efficiently you boys fought off those wild beasts at the trade caravan. Skilled guards were shred to ribbons, but you? You move like wild ferrets, strike them down, and send them into flight! One of my trackers was convinced that you lads were not even human," laughed the Tribune.

"In my sixty-four years of life, I have never seen such tactics," he said. Thoughtfully, he commented, "I find your skills laudable. Unfortunately, you lads have entered our lands in a very turbulent time," lamented the Tribune. He sank into an armchair of dark red wine upholstery, with the Thaed-Rú coat of arms in a golden disk above the head rest. Two of the captains moved to flank him, while the other four remained behind the boys.

"This regime of Bal Rú Íraban's creation, I abhor its practices. It lives on despite his death," fumed the Tribune, more to himself than the boys. "Their policies of experimenting on children are utterly reprehensible. But now their fate has been sealed with this new counselor." He snorted out a bitter laugh. "None who know me well would ever have imagined a day that I would prefer that upstart Íraban to this new ruler! He twists the Rhünkai to evil deeds more destructive than any Bal Rú in our history."

His sharp eyes met S'baladin's gaze as he added, "None are safe, and none are to be trusted."

S'baladin jolted at these last words. He had occupied his time during the Tribune's speech by studying his thin, gaunt features, specifically his eyes, searching his soul for any validation of truth, or falsehood. He remembered the words of the Gardener. The eyes of a person reveal their soul. The merits of life or the token of death, are revealed in one's countenance. But S'baladin struggled to discern the true intent of the Tribune.

Ansuz' gaze slid past the lad. Proudly, he bragged of his great army. "Despite the general unrest of the populace, the fealty of my army is beyond question. They are dutiful to the most inferior details. Even now they stand with me against this new counselor as legions of Rhünkai follow him, plundering the spoils of this takeover." With a heavy sigh he admitted, "Yet, even their fealty may not last under his sway." The Tribune fell into a moody silence.

To S'baladin, the thought of a greater evil than that of Íraban's use of child slavery was a heavy burden. His young mind searched for answers to this dilemma. Suddenly, his eyes gleamed and he stepped forward. In halting Hierundiel, the lad spoke, "Tribune, the power to bring about change, the power to challenge the Bal-Rú and his Rhünkai army, lies within your swelling ranks. What do you propose to do?"

His fellows' eyes grew round as saucers. Was this bravery? Had he another gift of the Gardener to wield? Or had his sickness worsened to depravity?

The Tribune Ansuz, in a blaze of anger, jumped from his chair and grabbed S'baladin's fur skins. The two captains pointed their spears at the frightened lad. Aejulan shrank back a step and sank his chin despondently to his chest. Two of the boys seized him by the arms, supporting him in his duress as the Tribune fumed at S'baladin.

"Here now, you sick little goat! You have only been in my land for a few damn weeks! You think you understand everything? I am a tribune of arms! I command tumens of soldiers! I do not treat with sick whelps who wipe their asses with sheep!"

T'balidor's anger flared once more. He itched to pummel the man to his death. He looked around the tent and glared defiantly at the sinister stares of the other four captains. But Ansuz shoved the poor sickly youth away and Diero hurried to support his stumbling, thin frame.

With a great huff, the Tribune straightened his regalia and regained his composure. All six captains paced cautiously around the nervous lads. "Those damn Rhünkai bastards! They never seem to let up on their bullying tactics on defenseless folks!" Aejulan hissed.

"You want to stem the tide of war?" bellowed Ansuz. "Fighting off the wild beasts of the Cethin Arda, like you did in that caravan, that is what I would need. Swell my ranks with men of those skills and we would have a chance against this plague of darkness upon our land. What we are up against are not mere soldiers, but beasts harvested with supernal knowledge from another world."

Despite the man's disrespect for these boys, S'baladin sensed the gravity of the impending threat of the counselor at Realmhold Thaed-Rú. Tribune Ansuz' division was the last defense keeping this murderous force from attempting to use the Streams to enter the Ballai of the West. Young as he was, S'baladin was not ignorant of the politics of Y'cromeca, nor of the darkness at its core. His visions and secret writings along with many well-read tomes of history came together now in S'baladin's mind. His body tensed with urgency, propelling him to speak further.

The Tribune Ansuz slumped into his chair and rubbed a thumb against his forehead. "They have my sons," he muttered. "My two youngest are among the Bal-Rú's Rhünkai, scions now. Would you have me order their deaths?"

S'baladin's eyes widened in understanding.

The Tribune chuckled darkly and nodded. "Aye, a clever pup, that Íraban. I refused him my tumens, so he took my sons, ushering them into his armed ranks to prevent any insurrection on my part. A clever pup indeed."

"Tribune Ansuz," S'baladin urged, "will you put the world at risk, your family and friends too, to protect your two sons?"

All in the tent gasped. Expecting the Tribune to lunge once more, the boys pulled S'baladin back Ansuz merely turned tired eyes upon the boy as his words hit home.

"Allow me to return home that I may call a meeting of our leaders of fighting clans. I will urge them to join themselves to this cause," said S'baladin.

"What pledge can I trust that you will honor an alliance and not abandon all hope for Y'cromeca?" The Tribune snorted, "Furthermore, what if your people refuse to help us?"

S'baladin looked down at the floor. He recalled the Gardener's departure, its sting of betrayal. All he had seen and heard in Kol-Shebbala assured him that the Gardener's wisdom yet persisted. S'baladin gazed upward at the Tribune earnestly and spoke again. "I say this – allow me to go back home and speak to my people. In the meantime..." he paused, a coughing fit seizing him momentarily before he could continue. When he did, his friends drew back in shock. "In the meantime, my friends, and my brother, will remain here, as surety."

"S'baladin? What is wrong with you?" murmured Sibrion. The rest of the boys, including T'balidor, stood in silent amazement. He turned to look at them, to pledge with his eyes that they should trust his plan.

"Very well. And should your leaders refuse aid, I will have no choice but to terminate your friends," threatened Ansuz.

A surge of anger rippled across S'baladin's sickly frame. He turned narrowing, rheumy eyes to Ansuz and struggled to hold his tongue. What an arrogant fool he is! His army is the key to the survival of people, he claims to oppose evil, yet is himself corrupted.

"Shall we appoint a time for their arrival? How can we know for certain your men shall agree?" Ansuz ruminated.

"If the Br'thain reach a decision before the next feast, we shall send a messenger through the Streams on the seventeenth day at the sixth hour of the morning," said S'baladin.

"Agree and I will depart on the third hour in the morning through the Streams. Our gatekeeper was instructed to drive the metal spike conductor into the stone surface in the third hour, the sixth hour, and the ninth hour for the space of an hour, to decrease the risk of the dark ones who have a Ferusat in their possession."

Behind him Sibrion hissed, "S'baladin!" but the lad ignored his protest.

"You must build a stone foundation in your camp," he instructed. "Stone is an excellent conductor for the underground Streams. Otherwise, travelers appear randomly in remote places, and we have no time to waste."

Ansuz stood in agreement. S'baladin could sense the man had no ill intent toward the Br'thain, simply the selfish desire to wield their power for his cause. The overlord stood and smiled wickedly. "The ninth hour is upon us. You shall depart at once."

S'baladin looked wildly toward his fellows. Mixed emotions ran across their faces. T'balidor and Sibrion stared intently at him, searching his expression for hope of some trickery, some power of the Gardener he intended to use.

"I am not abandoning you," S'baladin said firmly. One of Ansuz' captains seized the Ferusat, the other took him by the arm and ushered him out of the massive tent into the frigid cold, past campfires. According to his instructions about a stone surface, the Tribune and his captains led him several yards away to a stone surface, buried by nature and exposed by the weather elements.

S'baladin drove the Ferusat onto the stone surface to open the Streams. The shepherd lad held on to the Ferusat as he bent his ear to the stone surface and waited as the humming noise grew louder. He jumped up excitedly to cry out, "I can hear the Streams opening now!"

"Let me remind you that your friends will suffer a most horrible fate, should your leaders refuse to help us," Ansuz seethed viciously through his teeth.

This second threat against his fellows overwhelmed S'baladin with an impetuous anger. Forgetting his desire to look upon his homeland, he rallied all his strength to one arm and drove his Ferusat into the ground. Simultaneously, he flung the other outward. With all the strength his thin fingers could manage, he seized the Tribune's arm. The blinding flash of azure lights swallowed them both. One satisfied and the other shocked, they both sank down into the Streams.

A Tribune in the West

Far away from Hierundia, in the region of Rihován, the boots of twenty or so clan warriors rang out upon stone steps leading to the rocky outcropping where Sibrion and the boys had departed the week before. They prowled about, peering in and out of the many caverns formed by a crumbling old wall.

"Look here, somebody is camping here!" Sabaca heard one man call out.

"Dung upside down!" Sabaca he thought from where he knelt behind dry desert brush. His stomach tightened nervously as he watched the men gather around his cave dwelling.

He cast his eyes upward and cursed again. "The sixth hour is almost over! I must remove that spike!"

Fortunately for Sabaca, the metal spike was hidden underneath several large stones, some twenty paces beyond the clan warriors. As the men inspected his camp, he edged his way toward the spike.

Suddenly, Sabaca and the men alike jerked to attention as two azure lights erupted. The warriors pointed lances, drew swords, and notched arrows into crossbows, all while scanning the field for more eruptions.

A youth clad in shiryon stumbled forward from one burst while an older man, a rich cloak of fur hanging heavily over military regalia, appeared in the other. Too stunned to move, he swung only his head about in shock.

The boy's movement drew the man's attention. He lunged at the youth, tackling him to the stone surface, cursing him in Hierundiel as he choked him.

In an instant, the clan warriors descended on the man, striking with great fury. Their blows were smooth, cold and professional.

Released from Ansuz' grip, poor S'baladin rolled over. Gasping raggedly, he grabbed at his throat to massage it with a grimace. Beneath the fists of the Br'thain he despised, Ansuz fell to the ground, bloodied and unconscious.

The warriors forced Ansuz to kneel before them. Several younger warriors, friends of T'balidor, exclaimed,

"S'baladin!"

"We've searched across Ferán for you!"

"Who is this old man you bring into our midst, this man who thinks to harm you?"

S'baladin scowled at Ansuz, then gazed at him in bewilderment. Whitening tresses framed the Tribune's face, a face whose wrinkles deepened by the minute. The lad bit back a chuckle, Serves him right!

To the contingency of warriors he said, "This is the Tribune Ansuz. He commands one of the largest tumens in Hierundia."

The clan warriors grew slack jawed and saucer eyed. "Well, we now must deliver you before the Fieradeem, S'baladin. You are in a world of mule dung, my boy!" said the lead man.

"That is all well by me" retorted the coughing boy. "But first, they must hear what this man has to say."

Unmoving, Sabaca witnessed the entire spectacle from behind the desert brush. His attention was so drawn to the moment that he did not hear two more clan warriors approached from behind. Seizing him, they brought him to the others at the top of the stone outcroppings.

"We found this one," they reported. "In the brush."

"He has served as our gatekeeper," S'baladin explained, smiling wearily at his friend. "Sabaca has faithfully kept watch over the metal spike we used to travel through the Streams, inserting it and removing it three times a day to limit any risk to our people."

"Show us," grunted a warrior. Sabaca complied, uncovering the metal spike and removing it from the stone.

The clan warriors seized it and the Ferusat and marched S'baladin, the Tribune and Sabaca to the stone ruins of Duin Caeir. The two boys whispered together, sharing all that had transpired.

At the stone field, S'baladin and the Tribune were placed under heavy guard, while Sabaca was detained in a separate tent. Several Fieradeem arrived to meet with the former two.

"What are you looking at?" Ansuz growled as the lad scrutinized his appearance. "The Streams, they greatly aged you," S'baladin said quietly.

The Fieradeem explained that when he attacked S'baladin, he carried a great amount of negative energy through the Streams. In the short amount of time since his arrival, this had caused his physical body to be greatly affected, aging it many years.

Alarm showed for but a moment in Ansuz' eyes. Then he swatted at the air with his hand in dismissal and confronted the Fieradeem with gusto. Wincing, the Tribune rubbed at his injured ribs and heaved a weary sigh. "It was not my intent to cross the Streams. Though I issued threats against his fellows, I never laid a hand on him. Your shepherd boy grabbed me, as he struck that damn Ferusat into the stone." A wave of pain throbbed through his body, and he grunted as an attendant was ministering to his bloody wounds. "And I will gladly sacrifice a few years if it means the liberation of my province," he ended curtly.

"What was your intent in bringing this man here?" a Fieradin asked S'baladin.

The boy hesitated, unsure himself as to that answer. "I...I..."

Ansuz interrupted him. "I come from Hierundiel to treat with you," he said bluntly. "The Bal Rú Íraban is dead," he explained further, "but a dark and evil force has risen in his stead. I seek to form an alliance between your Br'thain and my vast army. So great is this new threat that it may well spill from our land even unto yours. Thus, my men have retained several of your young lads. I will gladly ensure their safe return, if you will only hear me out."

The Fieradeem about him exchanged looks of concern and interest but said nothing.

"I believe our united forces stand a chance at defeating the new counselor of the Thaed Rú," Ansuz urged. "My tumens form the single most numerous force that yet stands free of his influence." With a chuckle he offered a compliment, "My spies stumbled upon your lads as they brought down a creature of mystery, power and speed that none in my army have ever vanquished. I had always thought your methods more....rudimentary, but now...I am intrigued by the genius of your fighting methods. If the rest of your warriors possess the same strength and cunning as your boys did when they fought off that wolf creature..." he sighed and rubbed at his neck. "Well, we might just have a chance. United, we may succeed. Alone, we shall surely fail."

Still, the Fieradeem were silent. The elder gestured for guards to remove Ansuz until a later time. After his departure, the men spoke quietly amongst themselves.

S'baladin hovered on the edge of their group awkwardly. Pointedly, they turned their backs on him. Wearily, he limped to a stone bench to wait.

• • • • •

Puffs of dust rose from the desert boots of a young clan warrior as he hurried amongst the tents of Duin Caeir crying, "Lady Kalanit! Lady Kalanit!"

A woman in the dark attire of a widow appeared from of one of several tents along the path. After the boys left through the Streams, Kalanit had taken up residence with her family attendants near the stone ruins, along with the families of the other boys. Their mothers too came out of their tents to hear the messenger's news. Amongst several of them, hope was yet alive in their eager eyes. But the countenance of many of the women, including Kalanit, was darkened by the expectation of grievous news.

"The Fieradeem request your presence atop the ruins of Duin Caeir! S'baladin, he has returned! Please, allow me to lead you to the Fieradeem, and your son."

The other women rushed forward, asking after their sons and brothers. Kalanit was rooted to the spot, awash with relief. Her mouth, open in shock, suddenly spread into the most radiant of smiles. She clasped her hands together in joy, then composed herself with care as the other women gathered about her downcast, murmuring that it was only S'baladin who had returned.

"Come with me," she invited them. "Perhaps my son will have some news of them."

Together, the women moved through a scattering of dusty tents and curious souls toward the stone ruins, some four hundred yards away. Kalanit noted the sneers and scowls of many. *News of my son's return has reached their ears*, she thought, forcing a gracious smile to stay upon her lips. *The Gardener's disappearance betrayed them, now the travels of my son and his friends jeopardize their safety.*

Arriving at the base of the stone ruins, Kalanit and the women made their way up the hundred feet, or so, of wooden zig-zag stairs to the top of the massively sprawling stone ruins. As she tried to ignore the glares of people, Kalanit worked to ease away her anger toward the Gardener. Throughout the past few weeks, she had blamed him often for the sorrows of her family.

Yet the Gardener's Streams had brough her S'baladin home! Never should I have doubted! she reprimanded herself. It was, after all, the Gardener who had saved him from the verge of death. The frail little boy grew only weaker as he aged. The Gardener's early remedies from his Garden of Ages brought only minimal relief. Still, it was more aid than any offered by the many physicians of the West they consulted.

As the young clan warrior led Kalanit and her entourage through the crowds, she recalled the spring feast of S'baladin's seventh year. The Gardener had brought to their homestead the Fruit of Discernment. Once digested, it revealed the hidden mysteries in the boy's soul to him. He searched for what obstructions lay in S'baladin's life, what prevented him from receiving healing from the Garden of Ages.

Kalanit recalled her husband's steady presence at her side, their dearest family and friends all about, and the members of the Fieradeem present in her home that night. They gathered around S'baladin's bed, to watch over his withered frame.

To them, the Gardener relayed deeply hidden mysteries. "I see a soul afflicted by pain. Nevertheless, it is a soul with great wisdom. S'baladin will be a leader, compassionate for the weak. His heart longs to reap a harvest of justice in the world. So strong is his determination to serve that it brings affliction to his body. When all hope is gone, S'baladin will be a wonder to the world. He will sit in the Seat of Y'crom, and he will hold the Tiller's Staff. The people shall see a young soul harrowed by pain, but with the spirit to stand against the face of oppression. Many will follow him."

Silence had met this proclamation. In the silence, the boy's troubled mother had seized upon the hope in these words, believing all the Gardener promised. Now, as they moved through the crowds atop the stone ruins, their murmuring turned to shouts of accusation. Kalanit leaned heavily upon the woman closest her, fighting against the turmoil in her soul, struggling to trust the Gardener yet.

"Look! There is the widow of Baltien!"

"It is her son who reopened the Streams. He who put us all in danger!"

"Now he brings a Rhünkai warlord into our land!"

They moved past banners representing each of the B'naiynot, or houses, and multitudes of lesser coats of arms for the clans, waved dramatically in the evening breeze around a grand structure of large white tents. Kalanit was promptly escorted to a private tent of meeting where the House Varodduin - dominate in the vicinity of Duin Caeir - held S'baladin, feeding him well, and ensuring his safety.

Kalanit gathered her son up in a motherly embrace. He sank gladly against her for a moment, then pushed back and rushed to offer an apology. "I am sorry for the burden of worry I have caused you, mama. But the Fieradeem were wasting precious time deliberating. And...with papa gone, I could not bear the loss of my only brother too. I am sorry, mama."

She scolded him soundly. "You have your Maleor, then think yourself so fully a man that you may leave without a word to your mama!? To pursue your brother into the Va'Giyyel, fraught with danger and peril? All the West knows you are no warrior! Look at your bleary eyes! There is no color in your face." Tears ran down her cheeks as she threw out one last reprimand, "You could have died!"

S'baladin bit at his lip as they both remained quiet a moment, thinking of Baltien.

"And T'balidor!" his mother burst out into their silence, "What of your brother? Did you find him? Is he in good health? And what of the other boys? I heard that several of your friends went with you, S'baladin!"

S'baladin beamed. "T'balidor is safe! The rest of the boys are also in good health."

Kalanit wailed in relief. Now it was she who sank against her son's embrace. He patted her kindly but warned gravely. "Worry more for me, mama, as in the morrow, I must appear before the Fieradeem."

He will be a leader, echoed the words of the Gardener in Kalanit's mind. She laid a hand encouragingly on her son's bony shoulder. "You will do well, my son. I am sure of it."

• • • • •

A golden sun rose over a dusty world of cacti and desert brush, as Fieradeem, Preceptans and concerned citizens began to gather for the great meeting atop the stone ruins. They sat on straw mats under a sprawling tent with sheets of purple, gold and red rippling in the cool desert breeze. Stretching hundreds of feet in length, poles fifty feet high pushed upward along the tent's center, driving great peaks of colorful fabric skyward.

In the cacophony of voices within, Kalanit frowned. She took her seat at the front of the large crowd. She was unaccustomed to causing displeasure in others, yet her presence this morning was not well received. Fraught with concern for the fate of her son, she nervously smoothed her dusky widow's cloak.

Her eyes fell upon Sibrion's mother, the wife of one of Baltien's brothers. Kalanit stood to wave her over, grateful for a friend. "It appears that our boys are not popular with this crowd," she said in greeting as they sat.

"And yet, it is destiny itself which brought S'baladin back from the Va-'Giyyel," Kalanit replied, stubbornly clinging to her last shred of hope. "Why else would such a gangly child be returned to us whole by the Streams?" she contended.

"Yet he is received by a mob," her friend said sadly.

With nothing more to say, the women sat silently, hands clasped in their laps, amidst the buzz of anger. The crisp cool of morning gave way to the heat of the day as more and more people gathered. Finally, the meeting convened.

Seventy-five men stepped solemnly forward to blast their ram's horn. Hushed voices ran through the crowd as the Fieradeem took their seats before the people. Guards ushered S'baladin to a seat on the right of the Fieradeem while Ansuz, under heavy guard, was seated on their left.

A young Fieradin from the region of Calasmorra began the meeting. "We call this gathering to order. The Tribune Ansuz of Hierundia shall speak. We shall decide our next course of action." He yielded to Quispal an elder of Calasmorra.

The man stepped forward, puffing furiously on his pipe. "Tribune Ansuz, through unique circumstances, you have travelled through the Streams. You claim to head one of the largest Tumens in Hierundia and purport yourself to be the only Tribune willing to lead a charge against the Fortress City, with our forces as your auxiliary."

When the Tribune concurred with a nod, Quispal pressed him to describe the gravity of the new counselor's stronghold over the people of the north. In the space of an hour, the hearts of his audience sank. Ansuz spoke of a country beset with legions of Rhünkai, of a land where piles of their victims lay in various states of decay along highways beset by desperate thieves. He spoke at length of the destruction of life and property by strange creatures borne of the Cethin Arda and of the unnaturally wintry weather devastating the land.

Ansuz paused at the end of this report and his eyes narrowed. "I must add a curious detail. In exchange for provisions and shelter, many a starving man and boy from across Y'cromeca now fight in my legions. These soldiers often speak of the dreams and visions of their people." He held a hand up as murmurs swept the crowd. "I believe you are quite fond of superstition in this land, but I have not much stock in dreams, however..." he paused again.

Ansuz closed his eyes and cocked his head from side to side. He ran a hand through his newly whitened hair, hesitant to offer as evidence the stories of his people. "Whether hailing from coastal regions or deep into the south, so similar are these dreams that I must give them some credence. They see an ancient garden from long ago or of a husbandman cultivating vineyards and orchards of every kind. Some see colossal giants rising high above the towers of man."

The people of the desert sat spellbound, then they, and the Fieradeem gathered close in little groups and spoke together excitedly. A fresh hope flickered in S'baladin's eyes and a deep resolve welled within him.

"S'baladin," called the Fieradeem, "testify for us regarding your departure through the streams. Detail your journey from then until your return."

S'baladin rose from his seat to stand beside it. Leaning upon its back for strength, he spoke at length. He coughed violently and often, pausing many times to clear the bile in his throat. He finished his report but remained standing.

"I see today," he said, "the coats of arms representing multitudes of clans from every corner of the West. This convocation is the largest gathering I have ever seen. Inspired by your concern for our people, and heartened by these visions of our Gardener, I would share a parable with you."

It was a tale crafted before his father's death, before his heart had hardened against the Gardener, forged by S'baladin's love of history, his study of poetry and Gardener's wisdom. Quispal consented. From his memory, S'baladin recited in Y'darit.

A garden was planted in the West that grew rampant with wild berries and plenty of orchards and vineyards of every kind. All manner of creatures rested underneath the shades of its trees. From everywhere came fowl to rest on its branches. But in the north, wild beasts planted a dark garden with thorns and thistles that poisoned the minds of men.

These wild beasts spread their wrath across fields and forests, over mountains and valleys, leaving desolation behind in their path. They attacked the numinous garden in the West, devouring its orchards and vineyards. The people were fearful to labor on the garden a second time, lest wild beasts devour it once again.

So, the people lived, scattered and divided, too fearful to replant the garden. But, one day, the Gardener planted a small seed where this benevolent garden once grew. The fearful and divided peoples came to believe that this small seed would never grow though they waited many years. And so, believing the seed to have died in the deep winter snows, they lost heart.

Now, when the wild beasts of the north heard of the seed in the garden they had destroyed, they mocked the Gardener's efforts. But, far below the ground, its roots were spreading far across the land until one day, with the sound of thunder, its branches shot forth from the ground, springing high and wide into the sky.

The Gardener invited every tongue and tribe to gather under its shade, once more. The people came and sat under the leaves of this tree of fig and drank of its shade. The people saw that the miracle of life had finally sprung from the small seed.

This miracle united the people. As one across the land, all those who yearned for freedom, came together. They combined their strength, becoming as one a new Faeynül to fight against the dark garden of the north."

S'baladin paused to rub at his head which throbbed with pain. He had taken on a pale, ashen look, which gravely concerned his mother. The Fierra-deem urged him to sit, but he refused. The gathering stared at him, in awe of the strength of his passion. Respectfully, they pondered S'baladin's parable.

In the land of the West, along with a deep reverence for both the natural world and the realm of the mystical beyond, parables conveying wisdom and meaning were well divined by all. Yet, for the Tribune's sake, S'baladin interpreted it aloud.

"The Gardener promises to us all, this power will be restored again. This new Faeynül will burst forth from the deserts and glens to green fields and valleys. The colossal one will rise to drink from the Streams of Feynhava. With the blast of a thousand ram's horns, the new Faeynül will march on the Cethin Arda to tear out its very roots, casting it into the fire, destroying the wild beasts that planted it. The smoke of the Cethin Arda and the rotting flesh of the wild beasts shall ascend high into the sky, witnessed by all. All these things must happen, though all will think hope dead, beginning with a small seed."

A scattering of applause and cheers rose through the noisy murmurs sweeping through the tent. Quispal the elder, who had been translating S'baladin's speech to the Tribune, now explained, "The Faeynül giants once strode this land, many eons ago, forming and shaping its features. Whether you think them myth or not, the lad implies that a large gathering of people from our world and your lands will unite against this Harbinger, this dark counselor, in a force so great it would be like one of the colossal ones rising from the dead."

The Tribune gawked at the boy whose tale so closely matched the troubled dreams and visions of the north. It was to him that S'baladin now turned.

"We have crossed the threshold into these days. Many of us are fearful of what happened at the ambush. In the absence of the Gardener, we have slipped into disunity. When we first began our missions of liberation, we were strong, united."

An angry clamor came as many within the crowd, and several of the Fieradeem also, rose from their seats in protest. To these, S'baladin held up his hands in a plea for silence. When he did not receive it, he inhaled deeply, closed his eyes and spoke loudly enough for the Fieradeem to hear him. "I am the son of Baltien!" A few of them hushed and he cried out again, "I am the son of Baltien. These things I know!"

The Fieradeem grew silent and returned to their seats. Accordingly, the crowd began to settle, and S'baladin's voice rang out across the stone field. "I know these things because my father once told me. With each successive mission, many of our clans became more prideful and fractured. In Calasmorra, the clans of the Zadokai boasted of their great numbers during these raids..." He gasped deeply, then continued, "...In Rihován, the sons of Yotzrayim wagered against each other to take more numbers of the child slaves each time, only to boast that theirs were the most venturous of all the Br'thain. And in Ferán... the Balascayin...believed the child slaves were not worthy to be grafted into...the Tree...of Y'crom," S'baladin's speech dissolved into wracking coughs.

He squeezed his eyes shut against the embarrassment of his physical weakness before his people. The deep breaths he heaved sent a wave of nausea over him. He bent at the waist, clutching at his stomach. After several moments, and with heroic effort, he righted himself, but his vision blurred as he stood before the crowd. Swaying back and forth like the mast of a boat in a storm, he blinked unsteadily as spots danced brightly before him.

A hush fell upon the people. Into it Kalanit cried loudly, "Let him speak!"

"Hear the son of Baltien!" cried another of his kinsmen. Others added their support and cries of "Let him say his piece!" and "Listen!" rose from the crowds.

Heartened by these cries, S'baladin shook away the spots, then, blinking rapidly, continued. "Although we have carried out the Gardener's plan of liberating the child slaves, we are still divided in heart and intent. As clan has divided from clan, we have forgotten that we are united by the great deeds of the Gardener! It is because of the Gardener that we struck fear into the hearts of the Rhünkai, disrupted their progress. The Thaed-Rú, in all their power, were paralyzed by us! Shepherds and farmers."

Suddenly, the people gasped and rose from the seats once more. Ansuz scowled angrily as a woman rushed from the crowd toward S'baladin. A seasoned warrior, he noted fear in her eyes and leapt to his feet. His hand went to his belt as he followed their gaze and he grunted angrily at the absence of his sword. All about him, gasps of horror erupted. Then, his eyes fell upon S'baladin beside him. The boy was heaving up blood. Ansuz sighed and sank back into his seat with a frown.

Preceptans offered him sips of water and a cloth to wipe the blood as Kalanit hovered near. She longed to pull him into an embrace, to help him to his seat. But her boy, now truly a young man, shook his head at her, smiled bravely, and hobbled to his seat. He sat there, well composed, catching his breath in shallow gasps in the respectful quiet of the tent.

Ansuz, unmoved, tapped an impatient rhythm with his foot against the stone. *Will they join me or not? I can hardly destroy the Cethin Arda with this sickly boy as my only support in the West!*

Once more, S'baladin spoke. "There is a deeper purpose as to why the Gardener has called us to this liberation of souls in the Va'Giyyel. Have you forgotten? These souls are descended from the Branches of Y'crom! They are our brethren. They are deserving of our aid. Their Ballai, breached long ago by the Thaed-Rú beasts, fell as ours remained. But were our fates to be reversed, would not we be deserving of their aid?"

The people murmured at this wisdom, then hurried to hush each other as S'baladin raised a trembling hand for silence. "Removed as they are from the Gardener's wisdom, they know nothing of the Garden of Ages, nor of the Streams of Feynhava. As the Gardener has told us, 'It is gone from the memory of men, in that country.' Yet, you hesitate to unite with the Tribune? Do not forget our shared heritage! Are we not all descended, so long ago, from that First Patriot?"

S'baladin slumped in his seat. With his chin supported by his hand, his elbow on his knee, he looked out over his people. They gazed at him with a collective respect. As their eyes met his, many smiled encouragingly. Kalanit's heart trembled as she watched this. Even as the pain of her son fractured her heart, her pride in his words wrought healing within. Casting misty eyes downward, she whispered, "Look upon our son, Baltien!"

The Tribune's fidgeting ceased. A triumphant smile played at the corners of his lips, threatening to burst into a grin as the people of the West conversed. The Fieradeem looked upon the son of Baltien in awe of the depth of his wisdom, yet they were torn. Never had the warriors of the West deferred to the wisdom of youth, nor had they been led by the ill. Yet, S'baladin's passion deeply affected them.

At length, the Fieradeem conferred, then moved to reconvene with the Tribune in private. A new spirit, a stirring of hope, swept through the people's minds and hearts and flowed from their tongues as they streamed forth from the tent.

Northern Dreams and Visions

After much deliberation, the Fieradeem agreed to an alliance with Ansuz. They set a period of three months for the conscription of an army in the West. On the last day of the last week of the third month, a small gathering populated the stone field of Duin Caeir.

The Fieradeem had accepted S'baladin's idea of keeping the Streams opened for the space of an hour on the third hour, the sixth hour and the ninth hour, but limited this to the last day of each week. This allowed for the messages to pass between the Fieradeem and Ansuz, whom the Fieradeem had hesitantly supplied with a metal spike and single Ferusat for his armed camp in Hierundia.

Despite his self-serving nature, Ansuz was a man of his word, and a shrewd one at that. He knew well the risks of using the Streams with a spike in the hands of the Haruspec. Aside from the return of S'baladin's fellows, he had refrained from using it till now. Thus it had been a surprise to all when, one week prior, a messenger of the Tribune requested the presence of the fellows in Hierundia.

Graeyba, now a full-fledged Preceptan, on the cusp of leadership over a company of the Br'thain, was overcome with a deep longing to accompany the fellows. The Fieradeem granted his request under two conditions. His son must remain to finish his training, and, should he return the boys all safely home before the Gardener's Feast in the spring, he would be granted a leadership position amongst the Fieradeem.

D'thalien embraced him now as he prepared to leave. "Look for Aidan amongst the men, papa," he urged.

"Of course," said Graeyba and offered comfort to his son. "Remember the Gardener's words. 'The time will come. Did I not promise you that, once separated, you would be brought together again? The time will come.'" Yet he kept from D'thalien that it was only in the deep mediation he had learned in the West that these words had come to him, helping him conquer his desire to break from the group and search Y'cromeca far and wide for Aidan.

Beside them, Kalanit wagged a finger at her youngest. "The only reason I'm allowing this foolishness," she grumbled, "is because I trust T'balidor to look after your safe return." To her eldest she said sternly, "Do not let him out of your sight!"

The young men chuckled at this and protested. Reminding her that they were no longer boys, they embraced her warmly, then turned to join their fellows, Graeyba, and a small contingency of Br'thain.

Eagerly, Sabaca beckoned to them, "You may already know what it is like, but I have waited long enough to see the north!" he urged.

In good spirits, the little band struck their Ferusats and were welcomed by the Streams. They burst out of its current upon a new stone field roughly five hundred square yards, several hundred yards outside the perimeter of Ansuz' camp. Under strong guard, this was the place where the Br'thain of the West would appear from the Streams. Several of these guards led them to Ansuz' great tent.

Within, the boys were surprised to recognize a stranger who nodded familiarly to them. The man, clad in thick furs, was the leader of the caravan they had saved from the wolf creatures.

Ansuz greeted them, then handed S'baladin a scroll. He scanned the Hierundiel scrawled upon it, then smiled. "These are my words," he said. "The very words I spoke at the ruins of Duin Caeir. What of it?"

Ansuz turned to the caravan leader. "Tell them more of this scroll," he said.

"After your departure, we found several scrolls in the tent where you were held," explained the caravan leader. He stepped forward, bent his head respectfully toward S'baladin and spoke. "A scholar translated the Y'darit to Hierundiel. For centuries, all Y'cromeca thought of the people of the West as wild beasts, with no measure of thought or civilization. But now we see that a son of shepherds carries the passion of the wind in his words, with fire in his quill and ink."

T'balidor nudged him proudly. S'baladin's cheeks flushed, but a deep satisfaction warmed his chill frame. It was good to have his brother alongside him on this journey.

The caravan leader explained earnestly, "We were amazed by the words of this letter for they pointed to the dreams and visions we have had of late. Now this ancient foretelling has entered our world, it consumes our minds. The hope that it inspires collides against a time of great convulsion and upheaval."

"My own dreams of the garden in this parable compelled me to share the tidings of this scroll with all I know. I bid the people of my caravan to write as many copies of this scroll as possible. Altogether, one hundred and fifty- seven horsemen rode across the land, heralds of your shepherd's words."

The older boys gasped. But Jubal and Sabaca jostled S'baladin in pride while Sibrion murmured, "So many?" in disbelief. Graeyba smiled, his heart full of how proud Baltien would have been to hear this man's words.

The caravan leader grew animated, his face alight with pride. "They carried his tidings to the trade routes and marketplaces within weeks, with great haste. And now," he grinned, "we are seeing the fruits of their expeditions. These scrolls have been read and passed on to peoples everywhere, throughout all of Y'cromeca."

"This is partly why I have summoned you," the Tribune interjected. "For many years, my people have existed in a deep despair, fearful of their safety, battling starvation, mistrusting all they meet. But, because of S'baladin's parable, hope is spreading." He beckoned them to follow him outside the tent, "Come, there is something you must witness."

His soldiers led them beyond the camp to an expansive highway. Travelers passing through the breach of the Ballai paused, drawn to the strange sight of the young men from the West. Many, noting S'baladin's sickly frame, murmured amongst themselves in wonder and admiration.

"Is that the poet?"

"That must be the shepherd of the West!"

At his side, Ansuz murmured to S'baladin, "Throughout Hierundia and beyond, you are well known, my boy. I believe their hope will be enough to rally them in the weeks to come, to give them strength. If indeed it does, and if my sons are returned to me safely, I will owe you a great debt."

S'baladin said nothing. He remained leery of Ansuz and his intentions. He trained his gaze instead upon the rag-tag line of travelers on the road, and a great compassion for them spread across his countenance.

· · · · ·

The next morning, a large horde of people stormed the camp. Ansuz lancers and swordsmen quickly formed a perimeter and held them at bay. Graeyba and the boys, under heavy armed guard, watched them from a safe distance. Listening to their accusations and outrage.

"A story of gardens and giants alone will not liberate us!"

"Aye, give us not words but food!"

"You breach our world and steal away to safety at your will!"

"You ferry our children away to foreign lands!"

A young, unarmed peasant stepped forward and turned to call out to the crowd. "The dark counselor holds the great Scepter of H'dhar. Now, a shepherd boy holds scrolls with promising words. Which are we to trust?" He threw a fist into the air, "I say we trust neither! I say we appoint a ruler of our own!"

The crowd roared in support. S'baladin was overcome with a great sadness. I knew Ansuz was not to be trusted. It is unrest beyond his settling that caused his summons.

Graeyba, meanwhile, fought a kindling anger. In a flash he mounted a horse and cantered toward the mob. From behind the lancers and swordsmen Graeyba called out, "Sons of Y'cromeca, hear me speak!"

Curious, they quieted. "There is truth in what you say. Hope alone will win no wars," he declared. "But you must realize that it is this new power's rise at Realmhold Thaed-Rú which is your enemy, not us."

"Who in damnation are you?" shouted a man.

The young man hushed him but offered a rebuttal. "For all we know, you desert thorns and thistles plan to invade our lands! We trust no foreigners with our fates!"

"I am no foreigner!" came the swift reply. "You wonder who I am? I am Graeyba Khalevad, of Graëyhovan," he called out loudly. "In the Forests of Merungild, I raised my family. There I fought against the Edict of the Scions, evading the evil of the Thaed-Rú arm, but even so, my sons were taken, forced into servitude. You think that you were better off under their rule? You wish your sons to wither away in labor at the Fortress City? I tell you Íraban and his Edict were no friend to the people of Y'cromeca. Just as this new counselor plagues you all, so too did he! But my youngest son was rescued by the brave men of the West." In a great passionate, his voice rose into a war cry. "You are right in calling them thorns and thistles of the desert. For many more of them are coming. And they will pierce through this new counselor and rip apart the flesh of the Thaed-Rú!"

The Tribune and the caravan leader, side by side, stepped forward, their boots crunching twigs and leaves. The Tribune raised his Scepter of H'dhar high above his head as a signal to an officer who stood higher up on the steep mountain, higher than them all. Immediately a Minghan of Rhünkai descended the steep mountain. From the opposite mountain, another column descended into the other side of the valley. The thunderous sound of galloping horses filled the valley, surrounding the roiling mob.

The Tribune leapt onto a white steed and galloped toward the mob. He pulled his horse to an abrupt stop. It reared and wheeled about as he berated the crowd, "You have said your share! And you have heard the words of Khalevad. Much is taking shape in our world." Scowling at their ignorance he shouted, "Have you not heard, this new counselor murdered the entire Thaed-Rú court? His forces fill your lands with destruction and death! Yet still, you think yourselves safe? Shake off your stupor! The dark sway of his influence holds you all in bondage! Free yourselves of it, I say!"

As the people murmured and shouted amongst themselves, he spoke in hushed tones to his steed, and the animal stilled. "My great Tumens stand with these people from the West. I tell you now: they are your only hope," he declared. "We must storm the Fortress City! We must overthrow the dark counselor!"

With a scowl, the Tribune commanded the people, "Choose now your side. Remain with us, under our protection, or depart."

• • • • •

That day, many left the mob to join the Tribune's mighty entourage, the rest returned to their own misery. By nightfall, the newcomers to the camp formed a large gathering around S'baladin's tent. Torches and lanterns too numerous to count glowed as warmly as their hearts. The armed guards policing them rapidly realized they need not fear this crowd. They neither mocked nor accused the poet, instead their shouts were borne of curiosity and wonder.

"Where is the steward of the scrolls?"

"How is it a foreigner shares in our visions of gardens and vineyards?"

"What is their meaning?"

Graeyba and the Tribune pushed through them and entered the tent. To S'baladin, the Tribune said, "This crowd is too large to turn away. They have journeyed far in search of a sign amidst chaos."

S'baladin remained seated as his companions stood. His health had worsened further with travel. To the point that the boys had spent most of the day in the tent to keep him company as he rested. They had spoken much of Ansuz' summons. Few of them believed the tale of the scrolls to be the true reason behind the request.

"S'baladin," Graeyba urged gently, "this is the moment of opportunity. Seize it, son of Baltien. Speak to the people, refresh them with your words."

Seeing his friend's hesitation, Sabaca, the botanist now turned medical attendant, reached into his large leather pouch. "S'baladin, last year at the Gardener's Feast, he gave me this root. He said it would serve you in a time of great need. I sense that time is now."

The boys gathered around to marvel at the root, a twisted mass of thick fibers.

But T'balidor, ignoring them, whispered in S'baladin's ear. "Little brother, your sickness worsens, you need not do this. Do you hear me? Graeyba can speak to them again, or Ansuz."

S'baladin shook his head, but even that was done heavily. "It must be me," he said. "I cannot allow this weed of sickness to stand in the way of a vast garden."

To Sabaca he said, "I am not sure exactly how this root will serve me, but I trust the wisdom of the Garden of Ages. I will lend my voice to this gathering."

Ansuz and Graeyba spoke their approval of his courage. Sabaca reached in his pouch once more and brought forth a powder of deep umber from the Garden of Ages. This he mixed with a bit of the Tribune's wine to amplify S'baladin's voice. The lad drank it down and offered up his arms to Javatiel and Sibrion who, smiling encouragingly, helped him to his feet and escorted him outside.

As the frosty night air met his throat, it sent him reeling into a fit of coughs. In the light of hundreds upon hundreds of torches and lanterns, the people looked upon him with sympathy. The boys hoisted S'baladin's sickly frame atop a very tall boulder. It sat atop a little hill overlooking the massive gathering that spread down a slope and across the wide valley.

Young Sabaca found a depression in the ground beside the boulder. He scrabbled at the frigid soil, planted the root and covered it with dirt. Softly, he whispered over it. "Breathe the ancient words of Faeynhava over S'baladin. Confirm his words with signs and wonders."

The Tribune and the caravan leader snorted at this, dismissing it as rustic superstition. Graeyba, however, remembered the Gardener's grand display at S'baladin's Maleor and echoed Sabaca's words, "Confirm his words with signs and wonders."

From their belts, T'balidor and Sibrion seized their ram's horns. Flanking S'baladin's boulder, they sounded a blast that shook the valley. Never the people heard such a sound. The cacophony of their eager cries fell instantly to silence.

S'baladin's frail form shivered as he nervously surveyed the people. But his voice was loud and strong when he spoke. It shook the ground and all were frightened by this, including the Rhünkai.

In Hierundiel, he spoke, "I am S'baladin, son of Baltien, from the house of Eirun-Vala, of the Branch of Alazar, of Anterròs in the land of Ferán. And these are my friends who have accompanied me from the Ballai that still stands."

The powerful vibrations of his voice gave life to Sabaca's root and it rose instantly. A vibrant, green stalk sprang fifty feet into the cold night air. All present, including the Tribune and the caravan leader, were astonished. Murmurs ran through the crowd at this strange, mysterious sight. The most familiar supernal occurrences to these people were the predatory elements produced by the Cethin Arda. None had ever witnessed supernal beauty. It fortified their hope. As the brave words of the sickly lad fell upon them, amongst the pure hearts gathered there, all doubts and fears faded, only trust and love remained.

"You seek explanation for shared dreams and visions of a gardener planting vineyards and orchards," his voice thundered. Cold vapors curled into the air before him. His knees trembled as he succumbed to another fit of coughing. But the people waited quietly, respectfully, so he continued bravely, "I will share with you now the meaning of the scrolls that pass through your lands.

The Gardener, whom many consider a myth, is the greatest ally of our people in the West. He is the Steward of the Isles of Feynhava. A distant island, it is home to a garden of infinite power, transcendent throughout all of the ages of time. Its glory is great beyond the fragile clay of mere men. Eight immortal guardians bind its borders, keeping it safe for all times from perilous danger. They are known as the Aëlruk," said S'baladin.

"In your world of progress, the truths of the past have slipped from your grasp. The story I now tell you, once known, has been lost in the winds of time; lost through manipulation and deceit. In the West, from a young age, we are all taught the Gardener's wisdom. During his appointed feasts each year, he instructs the children himself, and throughout the year, teachers further his learning." His voice booming across the valley, he told of the Sheddukem theft of the seeds from the Garden of Ages, the corruption of them into the Cethin Arda, and of the First Patriot, Y'crom who, working in alliance with the Gardener ousted the Sheddukem and destroyed that first dark garden. He told of the rise of a dark entity, from a far-off island, of the terror it brought to their land, of how the Ballai brought about the end of the Sheddukem and drove away this entity.

"This dark one swore to annihilate the Y'cromahein," he said, his face grim. Age after age, the Ballai kept him at bay, until the age of the Thaed-Rú, until they were breached, opening our world once more to this dark entity, the dark counselor as you know him. All you here are but innocent victims of these evils."

The people stood in awe, never had they known the source of the Ballai. Never had they known its breach was to their detriment. A murmur ran through the crowd while S'baladin paused to cough painfully and spit bile. The boys, sitting below, stood to attend him. But he waved them away, and his thundering voice shook the valley again.

"The dark counselor has seized your Eleven Dominions, from forth Realmhold Thaed-Rú, he has ushered in a terrible pestilence across your lands. My people, the Br'thain warriors of the West, pledge themselves in an alliance to the Tribune Ansuz in the battle against this harbinger of darkness. He brings with him a power that supersedes nature. His strength is greater than that of armies and weapons forged by man. Therefore, no army can conquer him. Only the Steward of Feynhava can bring him to justice."

"What!?" muttered the Tribune to the caravan leader. But before the man could respond, S'baladin's gaze fell upon them. His eyes narrowed as he noted their frowns. Yet, he merely raised his hand toward Ansuz and offered his laud. "Alone, the great Tumens of the Tribune Ansuz remain unbent to the will of the harbinger at Realmhold Thaed-Rú." To the people he called, "I urge you all to join the Tribune and the warriors of my people, to destroy the Cethin Arda and the numerous Rhünkai that are holding its position."

A man in the crowd with the thick braided hair of a warrior down his back spoke up. "Why does the West wish to join us? What interest do you have in our world? Was it not your men who entered our domains to steal our sons for your slaves?"

Some hushed him while in others, doubt resurfaced.

"Silence! Listen to the boy speak!" The Tribune bellowed, but his voice was lost in the cacophony of murmurs.

It was S'baladin's voice, thundering once more, which quelled the crowd. "Your sons live. They are well!" As the crowd hushed, he explained, "They were rescued by my people from their enslavement to the Thaed-Rú, from their heinous experiments of the Cethin Arda! There was no safety for them here, but they are safe within the Ballai of the West. My people humbly and lovingly tend to them, feeding them and teaching them our ancient wisdom and truth!" he thundered.

The braided warrior sighed. He glanced at the towering plant beside the boulder. More humbly, wearily even, he asked as a child might, "But why?"

"Because we are all descended from that First Patriot, Y'crom, from his seven sons Aeduthir, Aelgad, Dürthaliun, Visanthiel, Faëlgrey, Alazar and Oliel, the seven branches of Y'crom."

S'baladin's eyes became moist as he surveyed the crowds. "A sonnet in the West heralds this very truth," he said. Abán reached for his lyre and accompanied S'baladin as he sang the ancient words.

> *"We saw the Gardener plant a garden in the desert.*
> *Its borders were the Quinassa and the mountains of Ferán.*
> *Its roots stay nurtured in the Streams of Feynhava,*
> *so long as the faithful follow his ways.*
> *A day will come when he will plant anew*
> *in this garden of the West.*
> *For on that day, he will graft many branches.*

*And together as one shall we grow,
with our roots nurtured in the Streams of Feynhava."*

The people stood, mesmerized. Many of their upturned faces seemed to glow with a newfound sense of understanding. Yet, those with callous hearts were harder to read, and understandably so. The people were accustomed to harsh rule by the Thaed-Rú, to the treachery of the Rhünkai armies. Many, like S'baladin himself, remained unsure as to the Tribune Ansuz' true loyalties and few had ever heard of the Gardener of which this boy now spoke.

"I shall soon return to my people," declared S'baladin. As many in the crowd expressed dismay, he waved away their fears and spoke confidence into them. "Fear not, I return to ready the Br'thain. The Gardener's Feast of the Spring approaches. It is a great gathering in the West, a celebration of his wisdom and the life it brings. And this year, it will serve to rally my people for war. When next you see the people of the West, it will be with a host of great warriors bent on destroying the Cethin Arda and its ruler."

The people cheered and celebrated amongst themselves as S'baladin slumped down into the arms of his friends. T'balidor and Sibrion strode into the crowd, clearing a pathway through them with muscular arms. Graeyba and Ansuz flanked the sickly lad protectively, ushering him back to his tent. There, he collapsed upon his bed and fell into a restless sleep.

• • • • •

It was now the last day of the week. The third hour of the morn was approaching as Graeyba and the boys slipped out with their spike and Ferusat. Conferring long into the night, watching over S'baladin's rest, the older boys and Graeyba had agreed the crowd was best avoided upon their departure, lest any try to accompany them.

"Wait!" the Tribune's voice rang out behind them. Cloak swirling, he hurried after them. "There is one sight left for you to see. From there you can depart, unencumbered by the masses that will soon approach to bid you farewell. It is but a short ride through the forest."

Javatiel snorted to Diero, "And are we to trust such a request?" who muttered darkly, "I think not!"

The older boys hushed the two juveniles. Sibrion and Graeyba studied Ansuz' face at length, then turned to confer with S'baladin who urged them to consent to the request.

Protected by a mighty escort of Ansuz' soldiers, they rode on horseback for an hour through deep forest. T'balidor gripped his brother, mounted before him, protectively. Wary of every sound, every rustle of movement the band of boys scanned dark shadows for threats.

Arriving at the Baliencora Marshes, a deep sea of melancholy engulfed the hearts of the boys as their eyes fell upon a dismal sight. Graeyba let out a low whistle as he gazed upon a cluster of dead trees, sodden and black in the midst of the marsh, a little ways back from the road. The morning light failed to penetrate the thick canopy of trees above them, nor could it pierce the eerie fog that hung about the marsh. In the half-light and through the mists, they barely made out the shapes that chilled them. Dead, rotting naked bodies hung from the dead, dark branches.

Clumped beneath the cluster of trees was a tiny isle of mud. The heads of thirty-two dead bodies buried there protruding from tufts of marsh grass. Their flesh mostly decayed, the whiteness of their exposed skulls offered the only bit of light in this dark place. Strange thorny vines slithered in and out of their orifices like serpents.

Silently, Graeyba and the boys exchanged wild looks. Had the Tribune, served by their words to the people, brought them here to such a fate? Steel scraped as the older boys withdrew their swords. The younger ones followed suit, notching their bows.

But Ansuz readily assuaged their fears. "The ones hanging on the branches, their corpses bear governors' medallions around their necks. Others have the markings of nobles, and lesser lords," he said.

From one of these skulls, a wooden mask hung askew. Its twisted expression depicted a grotesque sadness. Ansuz drew their attention to it, saying, "When we removed that mask, we recognized it as the face of the Lord Íraban Thaed-Rú.

"The counselor at Realmhold Thaed-Rú sent this message in the form of a mock garden." Deeply offended, S'baladin's voice was small. Cold vapors rose from his lips to join the mist and he shivered beneath his heavy furs. "This counselor's counterfeit blasphemes the numinous garden."

"When you return to your Fieradeem, tell them everything you have witnessed in my lands," said Ansuz sternly. "Tell them of these trees of dead bodies in Baliencora. Tell them of the people rallying to your cry. Tell them that our victory depends on a band of shepherds and farmers who follow the ways of your Gardener."

There was no arrogance or threat in the Tribune's words, yet Sibrion's eyebrows furrowed critically, "So this is why you summoned us, to view your discovery here, in these marshes?" he asked.

"Among other things," Ansuz said shrewdly. "There is a clearing near here," he said. "My men will lead you to it."

Graeyba and the boys mounted their horses. T'balidor offered S'baladin his hand, but the lad turned to speak quietly to Ansuz.

In the air between them hung words unspoken. *It is not the Tribune Ansuz that will save the Y'cromahein. An army alone will not win this war.*

S'baladin winced as T'balidor lifted him into his saddle. "What did you say to him, brother?" he asked as they followed the soldiers to the clearing. But S'baladin merely shook his head. His body convulsed in a fit of wracking coughs, and he leaned heavily back against his brother as they rode.

· · · · ·

The words of Graeyba, Ansuz, and S'baladin spread. In the months following the departure of the men of the West, hordes of displaced peoples offered their fealty to Ansuz. From far and wide, across the provinces, came thousands of refugees to form scattered settlements about the camp.

Upon their arrival, one such group sent four emissaries before the Tribune Ansuz, seeking his audience. They wore tribal tunics of earthen tones with strangely embroidered designs, and boots were of a strange dark leather. In their rustic, provincial custom, they knelt before him.

"We are sons of the Anil-Gevra, of Ir of the Fenrülk," said the one with slate grey eyes. "I am called Teima by my people." He gestured to his companions and named them as Naddú, Isayar, and Tzeytvara.

The Tribune's eyes flickered. Judging by their accent and nomenclature, he discerned at once that these four men were from the southern provinces. "Is your master the steward of Iemil?" he asked.

"Yes, great Tribune," said Naddú.

"The bonds of friendship between he and I go back before you young men were even born. I have found that nobles and aristocrats are never to be trusted. Yet, Master Sulla alone among them was always a fair and honorable man. Rise, tell me, how is my old friend Sulla?" asked the Tribune.

The young men stood, a quiet dignity in their bearing.

"I am afraid that we are bearers of bad tidings," lamented Isayar.

Long hair the color of honey, pulled tightly back and held in place by leather cords, swung forward to cover the tribal tattoos upon their faces as the four men bent their heads in grief.

Ansuz turned from them sharply to gaze at the crisp white fabric of his tent. His body weakened from his trip West in the Streams, a deep sense of Ansuz' own mortality came over him. Shaking his head both against such fears and the loss of his old friend, he turned back with a query.

"Before, his death, I well remember Master Sulla pledged the Anil-Gevra to me, were I to join them in fighting Íraban. Tell me, with that young puppy gone and the dark counselor to replace him, what has become of the Anil-Gevra?"

"Great Tribune, this is our reason for appearing before you this day," said the last of the four, Tzeytvara. "Our loyalty is rooted in the estates of Iemil. After the death of Master Sulla, the Rhünkai seized his properties, displacing us. In our anger, we swore never to serve the Thaed-Rú nor their infernal garden. Over the last year, we have gathered our numbers, training constantly for war. We four are the leaders of the great divisions of Anil-Gevra. With the scroll of S'baladin inspiring hope across the Provinces, our ranks swell daily now. Even as we speak, the vast companies of Anil-Gevra march this way from Ir of the Fenrülk."

Bowing his head to the Tribune, he declared, "We wish to join your men in storming the gates of the Fortress City."

The Tribune's generals gasped and murmured excitedly. For the first time, Ansuz' hopes formed into a solid belief. "Together with the men of the West, a strong alliance we shall be!" he cried. Feeling a new surge of life through his tired body, he exclaimed, "Together, let us drive the darkness from Y'cromeca!"

The Great War

Gatherings

For several weeks, the dusty town of Anterròs bustled with activity as the Br'thain gathered their weapons, their shiryon, which is to say their body armor, and other such inventory of war, to prepare for storming the gates of the Fortress City, in anticipation of Ein-riyon, the month of the Gardner's seven-day Feast in the spring.

Several days before the eve of the last day of the feast, a great concourse of people gathered at the ruins of Duin Caeir, celebrating with music, dancing, and food. S'baladin's entire family, even his most distant relatives, were there along with Kalanit's attendants. Among the honorable guests to the Feasts of Duin Caeir were Graeyba, newly named a Fieradin, and his son D'thalien, now a Br'thain. Both had rapidly earned the respect of their peers in their respective positions.

Against the backdrop of music and celebration, S'baladin slipped away one night, as he often did, to enjoy the peaceful bliss of momentary solitude. Savoring a roasted, buttered corncob, S'baladin's torch and a full moon led him away from the sweet noise of music, chatter and laughter, and into natural surroundings of cacti, sagebrush and shrub. Clad in his brown Dolscareb, with his pouch over his shoulder, he wandered a hundred or so yards.

Gradually, his walk ascended to a rocky ledge, some fifty feet high, overlooking the nocturnal desert floor. With his practiced shepherd's eye, S'baladin noticed a dark, round coil underneath a shrub, several feet away. S'baladin remembering how his father taught him to stealthily sit on the ground close to a coiled snake, without fear of its strike, did so now.

Time passed and the moon became so bright it turned the sky a shade of azure similar to the color of a Ferusat's burst. S'baladin roused and turned his gaze to the stone ruins of Duin Caeir. They rose, as pale as the moon, out of the desert floor. Hundreds of campfires blazed atop the ruins where celebrants had made camp. He shivered in the cool night air but did not seek their warmth.

Occasionally, a faint wave of musical strains, or laughter, made their way across the valley floor to S'baladin's position. Pride and love bloomed in his heart for the good people of the West. His time in the North had drawn to an end. As satisfying as it had been to return to his mother, to his hometown with T'balidor, triumphant, greater trials yet remained. These trials he well knew, held no place for a young man so plagued by illness. The time of the Br'thain had come. The time of the great uprising drew nigh. A great melancholy fell upon him as he thought of his father and felt sorely the loss of his involvement, and leadership, in their plot.

A trail of torches made their way to S'baladin's perch. As his friends scaled the rocky ledge, he shook off his reverie and called out a warning, "Be careful of that snake coiled there!"

Unperturbed, they skirted the shrub and called out cheerful greetings.

"Sabaca saw you head this way from the feast. What treasonous plots you were hatching, Sy?" quipped Jubal.

Diero, Jubal, Abán, and Sabaca sat in a circle with S'baladin while Kelán, Vaez, and Javatiel gathered wood for a campfire. Yashi bounded from one to another, licking joyfully at their hands and faces.

In the fire's warm glow, the boys chattered of music and poetry of the Gardener's Feast, of the power in the ancient tongue of Uraduin and the beauty in the poetry of Y'darit, the offshoot of Uraduin. Javatiel, although he was older than S'baladin, turned to him for confirmation. "Sy, did not the Gardener say that one day the peoples of Upper and Middle Y'cromeca would learn to speak Y'darit?" he asked.

"Yes, that is true. The Gardener has said before that many will come from the north to take their place at his feasts. From here, they will learn of his ancient tongue, even unto Uraduin," answered S'baladin.

Suddenly, Jubal let out a whoop. "T'balidor, Sibrion, welcome!"

Sabaca peered into the darkness, then called out, "Look, they have brought along Aejulan and D'thalien! Welcome, friends!"

These last two, children of Upper Y'cromeca, had become fast friends during their Br'thain training, deeply bonded by their trials and losses. The boys shuffled to make room for the newcomers in their circle.

A broad smile flashed across S'baladin's countenance, "My brother, my cousin, my friends, it does my heart good to see the Br'thain attending us."

"You know something, Sy," began Sibrion. "I have truly come to appreciate each of you young men. You are all as brothers to me now."

The boys smiled proudly, some putting their hands to their hearts to accept the pledge and some nodding their quiet acceptance.

"As the Br'thain of the West formed their ranks and moved into the Va-'Giyyel to liberate souls, so too, we formed our own enterprise to liberate T'balidor, although sometimes I wish we had left him in the Va'Giyyel!" Sibrion grabbed T'balidor's head in a tight grip and ruffled his hair.

"Brother, indeed!" T'balidor joked to Sibrion as he squirmed loose. "After how I see them treat their siblings, after how I have treated mine," he threw a grin to S'baladin, "I have never wanted an older brother, but I suppose I have one now."

Raucous laughter rang out from all save Aejulan and D'thalien. The two shared a look of deep understanding.

Noticing this, S'baladin frowned, his own grin fading. He moved to sit beside the pair. "What troubles the two of you?" he asked quietly.

A lump in his throat, Aejulan nudged at D'thalien to reply.

"You may have heard that at the same time I was taken into slavery, my brother was taken into servitude amongst the Rhünkai." S'baladin nodded. "Aejulan also has a brother," said D'thalien. "Like mine, he too was taken."

Beyond them, Vaez frowned and leaned toward the little group. "Aejulan!" he exclaimed. "I had no idea you had a brother. What happened to him?"

Aejulan's stare into the fire intensified, his eyes grew wide and blank. "He did not survive the caravans of caged wagons. Sickened by the foul conditions in which they kept us, he died in the cold. The Rhünkai did not care whether he could even work to serve them. They cared not to remedy his illness. When I was liberated, I thought at first that evil creatures were whisking me off to another world. I was both terrified, and relieved. I thought to myself 'Maybe these creatures will end my misery. They will devour me and the pain of separation from my family.'"

The young men murmured sympathetically at this, yet few of them knew such despair. "The day that the Rhünkai came for me and my brother," he continued, "My mother cried and cried, but my father remained distant in his sadness. Then, to stave off his own tears I think, he grabbed me, shook me and slapped my face, telling me not to cry, that I would have to grow up and be a man. Well, the Necropulpa plant cured my grief awhile, unnatural though it was. But now, here, hearing you speak of brotherhood, I often wonder how my parents have fared under the burdensome weight of their emotions. Likely, they still believe us both to be alive."

The tears he had fought to hold back streamed down Aejulan's cheeks. Each of the boys pretended ignorance of them, and Sibrion spoke loudly. "It is for them, and others such as them, that we intend to fight!"

A chorus of shouts greeted his declaration.

As they settled, Aejulan murmured to T'balidor and Sibrion, "You joke of fraternal insults, I would give anything to be the brunt of my brother's teasing once more. To throw one last punch at each other as our parents scolded us for fighting..."

"As I wish for the same," said D'thalien at this side. He bent his head forward, yet even his thick crop of blonde curls could not hide his own tearfulness.

Respectfully, the boys averted their eyes, quietly honoring their grief. Gradually, Aejulan's eyes refocused and a look of hope framed his countenance. "Now that I have drunk from the Streams of Feynhava," he said, "and after reading Sibrion's parable of redemption for the lands of the north, I have hope now, whether or not I see my family again. I did not journey with you recently as I could not bear to return, but I am ready now, I will join you in this war."

The boys whooped excitedly and smiled encouragingly. Yet, D'thalien remained silent. Aejulan's mention of the Necropulpa had set a plague of memories upon his mind. Face after face of the slave boys of the Fortress City floated through his mind's eye. Some were covered in lesions and boils, some were balding, all were bent to the will of the Rhünkai taskmasters, their bodies corrupted by the Necropulpa.

"Want to know a secret?" D'thalien interjected suddenly. "While I was slaving for the Thaed-Rú, the Necropulpa did nothing to me."

Aejulan looked at him in amazement. "Just now you spoke of it, which caused me to remember," said D'thalien. "It is true! My face was not altered, nor was I reduced to a mindless tool of labor."

Sibrion drew near, intrigued. "You alone among them?"

When D'thalien nodded, Sibrion turned to Aejulan. "Tell me, did you ever see any others with such immunity?"

"Never," said Aejulan.

"Why you?" asked Sibrion, his brow furrowed.

"I knew not then," he said. "But now, after studying the wisdom of the Gardener, I believe it was a boon from the Gardener himself. We crossed paths with him in the forests of Merungild, as we sought to evade Rhünkai pursuit. We drank of tealeaves he had freshly brewed. Surely it was these which protected me while I was enslaved by the Rhünkai. I spoke of this to my father, and he agreed, telling me of tealeaves the Gardener gifted him, tealeaves which healed the foul poison of the dark garden."

The boys gasped in awe and murmured amongst themselves.

"I had only ever heard of the fruits of the Garden reversing the dark effects of the Necropulpa," Sabaca said in wonder.

"He intervenes so often for the good of all!" smiled Abán.

"Aye! In ways great and small!" nodded S'baladin.

"Very soon I hope such fruits and tealeaves relieve the unnatural state of all the sons of Y'cromeca who yet toil in the darkness of the Cethin Arda," Aejulan swore.

"May it be so," many of his fellows agreed.

As the young men broke into lesser conversations, T'balidor moved to sit beside D'thalien and scrutinized the curls framing his face. The youth looked curiously at the Br'thain warrior. When T'balidor spoke, his words were abrupt, his expression stormy. "I think I saw your brother, the day my father died."

D'thalien's initial joy at glad tidings faded to darkness as T'balidor added, "He fought amongst our enemies."

"The Necropulpa," D'thalien said bitterly, "Aidan did not drink of the Gardener's tea that day in the ruins."

Understanding dawned on T'balidor's face and he softened his composure toward the youth.

"His name is Aidan?" T'balidor asked, "With curls just like yours? And skill in archery?"

D'thalien nodded. "He is alive? He looked well?"

Remembering his leadership against the Br'thain that day, T'balidor nodded somberly, "Yes."

"The Gardener promised we would be reunited if ever we were separated. I trust it will be so. And when that day comes, I trust he will be liberated from the dark sway of the Cethin Arda."

"May it be so," T'balidor murmured.

Their brooding silence was broken by a cry of "I am anxious!" from Vaez who leapt suddenly to his feet and strode about in an air of excitement. "Soon we will storm the gates of the Fortress City alongside the Tribune's great tumens, beside the legendary warriors of the Anil-Gevra! Just think of it! We are about to change the history of our lands!"

Javatiel, chuckled at his friend's enthusiasm, but spoke more somberly. "Perhaps we will see a new and better world for the lands of the north. The Gardener's dream is to see the sons and daughters restored to their fathers and mothers. They are freed now of the Thaed-Rú, may true freedom dawn soon, may the Rhünkai and their evil counselor's shadow be no more."

The boys yelled and whistled as a fervor ran throughout their circle. Even the boys of the north were drawn out of their melancholy and into the ardor of the Br'thain.

Kelán spoke up. "Together we shall stand for rightful justice in this crooked world!"

Sibrion rose to stand beside him. "Indeed! A great battle is upon us."

S'baladin alone remained seated as the boys all leapt to their feet to join them. T'balidor was quick to dismiss the shame upon his face, "Brother, this war we are to wage is all of your doing, else innocents will continue to die, powerless against great evil."

"Aye!" cried Sibrion. "You shall not travel with us this time, yet our unlikely brotherhood, is bound together in its stand for rightful justice, as Kelán has said. On your feet, S'baladin, for it is your words which have lit a fire in the hearts of the people! Abán, play for us! Let us celebrate!"

In the light of crackling embers that floated into the darkness, Vaez and Javatiel lifted S'baladin on their shoulders. The boys danced heartily around the campfire.

In Y'darit, Abán's voice rose into the night in an ancient tribal melody.

"The Streams of Feynhava move through the ground.
The strength of the Faeynül rises through our feet.
Of all the trails in life, there is one that matters most.

*Our people and our lands are all we have.
And we will fight and live to sing this song."*

• • • • •

Far from the Feasts of Ferán, on the last day of the Gardener's Feast of the Spring, a bitter frost gipped the southwestern district of Hierundia. Sheltered all about by deep forests, the soldiers of the Tribune Ansuz' camp worked continuously to expand a massive clearing for the ever-expanding camp. In the third hour of the morning, about this field, a gathering of the Tribune's officers move through the chill darkness. Protected to the front and back by numerous soldiers, they lined the stone field beyond the tent city.

Precisely as the Fieradeem had pledged, the Br'thain of the West appeared through the Streams of Feynhava in an array of hundreds upon hundreds bursting azure domes of lights. The faces of Ansuz men glowed as clan warriors ascended through the stone surface. In place of the beastly fur skins of the Aerrukán, they were clad now in shiryon, their strange armor of woven twigs.

The Tribune strode forth to greet them, then led his guests to his great tent. His soldiers, meanwhile, welcomed the clan warriors out of the bitter cold and into their own tents for rest, refreshment, and entertainment.

Though the winds howled without, within it was little noticed. The hours whirled by as several Fieradeem, leaders of the Br'thain, worked with Ansuz' officers, poring over maps and rejecting, arguing, opposing, and negotiating various strategies for the attack on the Fortress City.

Finally, the men arrived at a conclusion. A twofold plan of attack in which a company of Ansuz' men and several of the Br'thain would climb the mountain and secretly enter the Fortress City to hammer a Ferusat. The second attack would involve an army of the Br'thain entering the Fortress City through the Streams to destroy the Rhünkai guard. Afterwards, they would liberate the last of the child slaves. Only then would they, finally, destroy the Cethin Arda via the wisdom of the Garden of Ages.

The Tribune Ansuz remarked, "If all goes according to plan, expect a counterattack from the rest of the tumens surrounding the mountain base. Then we shall finish them off!"

The Fieradeem nodded their consent and a nervous tension fell quietly upon them all. The familiar shadow of fear was visited upon everyone. Seasoned warriors imagined the battle that was to come. The dreadful taste of rusted metal filled their mouths, and the foul stench of death filled their nostrils.

"How many separate camps do your men harbor at this moment?" asked a Fieradin.

"Ten within the Forests of Ixzaril, two weeks from here on foot. They lie many leagues to the northwest of the Fortress City and are well concealed within a series of deep, narrow ravines. No man passing through that country can detect their large numbers," answered Ansuz. "A great host of messengers throughout those ravines ensure constant communications between the camps, day and all night. We rely on that communication to keep our unity intact," added the Tribune.

Dusk fell and, as they worked out logistics for joining the camps of Ixzaril with Ansuz' main force, servants busied themselves lighting candles and oil lamps. Graeyba, the newest Fieradin amongst them, stepped forward as the meeting neared conclusion.

"You speak of weeks of preparation," he said. "I feel I am little needed here."

Several of the Fieradeem spoke reassuringly, but he held up a hand, "I seek permission to journey into the hinterlands south of Graëyhovan."

The eldest of the Fieradeem scrutinized him. "To seek your missing son?"

Graeyba frowned. "Would that I could," he replied honestly, "but the Gardener assures me we will still yet meet. Now," he gestured to the map table, "is not that time. I seek to leave in hopes of mustering the strength of a hidden ally in those parts."

A chorus of "Ah!" and "Oh?" greeted his statement.

But Graeyba, saying no more, merely looked to Ansuz for consent. With little deliberation and much hope, the council granted his request.

A Summoning

It had been weeks since Graeyba had felt the warmth of the West in his bones. Covered in thick fur skins, he tread doggedly through a snowy ravine. Thick clouds obscured the sun, shedding silent snow across a forbidding landscape. His eyes scanned the snow before him for footprints. But his thoughts were in the Didderäsh.

In the mountain caves, at that first feast following his reunion with D'thalien, Graeyba had relayed to the Gardener his experience with the hairy giants of these lands. From his pouch, the Gardener had offered him a little packet of strange berries.

Graeyba recalled the Gardener's instructions. "If ever you should find yourself in the wild country of those hairy giants again, these tart berries, chewed until dissipated, will protect you. It is strange they acted with such hospitality. For I have come across their beastly race numerous times. Their chirps and whistles can turn deadly if provoked. Many have vanished without a trace in their lands."

The sour taste of those berries now in his mouth, Graeyba strode fearlessly throughout the snowy landscape. Finally, he came upon a trail of large footprints in the snow and followed them up and out of the ravine. Each was nearly two feet in length and the stride between them six feet long. From several hundred yards away came an unfamiliar sound. Looking warily about him, it struck Graeyba that the sound was the thunk of a large branch striking a tree.

"It is them!" thought Graeyba excitedly. He followed their prints further as more tree knocking echoed from a different direction. This sound was closer than the first. Excitedly, he continued his course, then froze as a large rock hurtled past him, landing just to the side of his path. He searched the dark forests. Nothing could be seen, only felt.

Respectful of the warning, Graeyba stilled. As he stood, a lone man amongst the vast whiteness, he felt the power of the woods. Somewhere in the darkness was heard the indistinct chatter of chirps, barks and whistles. Memories of that shadowy cave beyond the waterfall overwhelmed him. From all about him came the sounds, as the creatures communicated with one another. Sentries perhaps, he feared they warned a gatekeeper of sorts that an intruder was present in their domain.

Silence fell. Graeyba tensed. Several yards in front of him, a dark, monstrous silhouette appeared amongst the trees. It stood twenty feet tall, framed by tall pines on either side. From forehead to chin, it bore a deep scar that Graeyba well remembered. Its monstrous form swayed from side to side as it took several steps forward, crunching through wild brush. Graeyba held his position.

Suddenly, a collective roar filled the woods. The terrible sound of snapped branches and smashed trees shattered the hush of falling snow. High above, grunts and roars came down the ravine toward him, but the berries he had digested protected him from their sound waves. Strange, indecipherable voices came from inside the tree line all around him. He remained immune to their efforts and the sounds turned to blood-curling shrieks of frustration.

The scarred creature in front of him roared a final warning, but Graeyba stood his ground. "I seek your help," he said. An ear-piercing shriek rose to a howl that shook everything within the ravine for leagues away. Nevertheless, Graeyba stood firm.

"Hear me speak!" ordered Graeyba. He lowered his furry hood and stepped forward. Immediately, upon seeing Graeyba's eyepatch, the hairy creature bellowed in anguish.

"You remember me," observed Graeyba calmly. "You cared for me, nurtured me back to life." The many growls and shrieks surrounding Graeyba gradually died down to echo the anguished groans of their leader.

"I understand your pain in the treachery of this world," sympathized Graeyba. "I know that long ago, the dark once stole into this country and robbed your ancestors of their souls. A dark and hulking giant altered the course of your existence. Once men, you roam the country now as wanderers, cursed by the dark one. You haunt the forest and valleys. In your wandering of late, you must have seen the dark one's return, the terror he has wrought once more upon the world of man. I know your heart. This treachery grieves you. Now is your chance to strike back," challenged Graeyba.

Silence hung about them for many moments.

Loudly, Graeyba called out to the gathering of Ghost Kings lurking in the forests, "Join me! Help me strike back at the dark one and his army!"

He reached into his pouch and dropped a single seed to the ground. Instantly, a peculiar, red-petaled plant sprang to a height of two feet. "Keep these separate," the Gardener had said as he handed him a handful of tiny seeds. "Do not ingest them. They bear a great power. It was harvested from a plant that sprouted instantly beside a dear fellow I once found near death. In those wintry hinterlands, I planted a seed such as this. The creatures ate of it, and it revealed to them a deep, universal purpose to care for those whom death pursues."

The creatures gathered about the plant curiously, then began to eat of it as the Gardener had said. Graeyba watched the plant regenerate, bursting forth new growth just as the tea plant had beneath the vines of thorns. He was deeply moved to think of the Gardener's care for him, a simple man of Graëyhovan. Years before he had come into existence, even then had the Gardener had laid his plans for a time such as this, saving his life by bending the will of the creatures that they might care for him and fight for man.

"If your clans agree to help the struggling seed of man, if you wish to rally with us in a great battle against the dark one, follow these red plants north. They will lead your people to the men of treachery," said Graeyba. With that, he parted from the creatures' domain.

Raid Upon the Fortress City

Knowing full well that his return to Y'cromeca would incur the wrath of the Gardener, the Haruspec amassed his greatest defense to protect the Cethin Arda. Summoning Rhünkai tumens from every province, he formed one massive force about the Fortress City. Himself he remained at Realmhold Thaed-Rú where daily from the parapets he used supernal powers to gaze far and wide across his new Domains.

One morning, just weeks after Graeyba's trek to the hinterlands, the Haruspec's senses prickled at the threat of an impending conflict. Yet, there was no unease in his posture as he strode to the window of his chambers. Around the city stretched league upon league of black tents in perfect rows, just as they did around the base of his Fortress City. The Haruspec's ruse was in place to draw out the Gardener. He welcomed an attack.

He cast his eyes upwards from the armies of men to cry out triumphantly in his arcane tongue. Across his Dominions, hordes of his supernal defenses stirred, responding to his call. Dark clouds of Veyasaen swarmed above his army's camps, Wind Ghouls and wolf creatures howled in packs about their vast perimeters.

Despite the Haruspec divination, in the vast camp around the base of the Fortress City, military business went about as usual. Taenshuks and horses each lumbered heavily across their immense corrals, toward their morning fare. Rhünkai soldiers bustled about their morning duties while officers assembled the captains of their vast divisions to issue instructions for the day.

Among these, General Muredka stood inside his massive tent surrounded by fifty captains. He concluded a string of commands with an assurance, "Each of your tumens has their place around the base of this mountain. Remain vigilant, and none will breach strong defenses!"

From forth the ranks of men, Captain Khalevad called, "And the Fortress City? Suppose insurgents found a way to enter with those mystical canes of theirs?"

"I see your point, young Khalevad." Muredka approached the youthful officer. While his words had been respectful, his countenance bore cold scrutiny. Face-to-face with Aidan Khalevad, the favorite amongst his men he said, "Consider this," he sneered, "should a ragtag band of shepherds and farmers appear atop our summit and somehow conquer the Fortress City's army, they'd face our armies below, and the creatures prowling all about."

All about them, officers chuckled at the very thought of such an effort succeeding.

Muredka guffawed and crowed, "Believe me, after the counselor's ambush at Caethain, those shepherds will think twice about attempting another attack, but they are certainly welcome to try!" Laughing he called out loudly, "We could use a little sport, eh gentlemen?" and was met with rowdy agreement.

The meeting over, the men departed. Aidan returned to his tent, kicking at the slush of snow and muttering curses against the arrogance of his fellow officers. Tilting his head far back, he stared up into the misty morning at the mountain summit of Fortress City. Stark was its black silhouette against a dark gray, cloudy sky where thunder and lightning never seemed to cease.

Huffing at the flares of lightning above, he spun about and made for his tent. He barked commands at his lieutenants. As they hurried off to do his bidding, he barged into his tent and sank into a chair. There, inner turmoil gnawed at him. It was not the fear of battle, as Muredka pointed out, no force could threaten theirs, but a disgust for the army which he served. Once, he had felt a loyalty to the Rhünkai order. But with the new counselor suspending every aspect of Y'cromeca's economy, the Rhünkai had fallen into a foul routine of raping and pillaging. The Rhünkai ate of his fruits and grew strong as all about them weakness begat weakness. Aidan considered himself a soldier, but aside from the daily routine of camp life, he had done little soldiering of late.

He was not alone in these sentiments. There was great division amongst the ranks. Morale had sunk since the counselor took over. Insubordination was everywhere. He stood, unbuttoned his coat and tossed it on the chair. Flopping on his mattress with a snort, he scowled. *It is a marvel the tumens still hold together.*

A round of several rumblings from the mountain shook the land for leagues in every direction. Though used to these sensations, his senses prickled oddly. He sprang from his tent to scan the camp and the Fortress above but found nothing out of the ordinary. Biting at his lower lip, he returned to his tent where he paced nervously, deep in his thoughts for the better part of the morning.

Many leagues away, at the Tribune Ansuz' camp, his little brother D'thalien appeared through the stone foundation with his Ferusat. Clad in shiryon armor of the West, he followed the route of busy military traffic, unnoticed. As his father had taught him, he clung to the brush beside the road to the Fortress City, never straying too far away from the trail. And no one ever spotted him, nor detected him, in their busyness.

• • • • •

The following morning, for hundreds upon hundreds of leagues, a deep fog enveloped the frigid landscape. Near the mountain base, horrified cries rang out from Rhünkai moving frantically about the great camp.

"Over here!"

"Another?"

"There's more here too!"

The blood of seasoned patrols ran cold as they discovered corpse after corpse in a wild disarray of limbs. Half-naked, frozen bodies hung eerily, dangling down on high from the trees. Some were decapitated, some dismembered. They were all surrounded by countless sets of giant footprints, ranging from eighteen to twenty-five inches in length.

"What manner of persons could do this?" wondered a young Rhünkai soldier.

But his fellow merely shook his head as he gawked at a collection of bodies wedged tightly between large branches sixty feet or so above. "To carry a body alone is a feat, but to hoist them to such lofty heights...?"

"'Tis the work of the savage beasts of the Cethin Arda," declared an officer as he rode by. "Back to the base, now, all of you!"

As they hurried to their tents, the young soldier contradicted his officer. "The beasts of the dark garden act in rampant violence, there is a pattern here, an intelligence."

"Aye," came the other's reply, "As if the beasts are storing their prey to feast upon later!"

As news of this horrid encounter reached the ears of every man, back at the mountain base, the Rhünkai eagerly sought those to blame. Many blamed the mysterious powers of the Br'thain, the shepherd warriors. Others thought perhaps the men of Tribune Ansuz had done the grisly deed. Officers proposed marching tumens against Ansuz' camp to the southwest.

Nevertheless, firm orders came swiftly from the Haruspec's aides. No tumens were to leave the base of the Fortress City. Having no idea of his deeper intent, that he was biding his time, the Rhünkai armies assumed he feared more of these attacks.

Later in the day, the severed bodies of the slain Rhünkai were brought into the great camp for medical inspection to determine the cause of death. Fear overcame many as it was discovered no weapons, only brute force, had been used. The great tumens of men had long been confident in the strength of their numbers and the proud rule of their armed dynasty. Now, many souls were deeply troubled.

The frigid evening ushered in the greatest storm they had yet seen. Its radius extended from the Fortress City far into the distance. In the flares of lightning, the men engaged in tense conversations about their campfires.

Despite the storm, Aidan Khalevad left his tent to engage in nightly patrol of the camp's inner perimeter. Though none had assigned him this duty, he regularly roamed the base of the mountain, gazing up its steep stone walls. He knew not why. Some impulse called him, urged him toward the great walls of the Fortress City.

In his patrol tonight, the ominous portent of the attack on the camp clouded Aidan's sharp mind. He felt compelled to escape, to run far away from everything, from the Rhünkai service and the never-ending game of watch and wait that was guarding the Fortress City. The dark abyss of loneliness that gripped his soul swelled ever larger. His role as captain, and the admiration of his men had long been a balm for his pain and sorrow. Yet, no camaraderie from any among the Rhünkai had ever conquered it.

These lone patrols of his were a self-imposed punishment for the pride he took in his work for the Rhünkai. He had long since pushed away all memory of his family, yet there remained a subconscious shred of decency. He knew not these were echoes of his upbringing.

From the same depths of his soul came a lingering connection between he and the Fortress City. Something that, in its obscurity, inspired him to search for meaning, though he found none. Tonight, was no exception. With the sound of whips upon the backs of child slaves ringing down from high atop the mountain crest of the Fortress City, he found no respite from the turmoil within.

• • • • •

Though Captain Khalevad's patrol was a solitary one that night, the Haruspec's aides meanwhile, were engaged in their own routine patrol. Atop the Taenshuk beasts, they patrolled the perimeter of the mountain base camp, searching for anything amiss, for giant creatures with ill intent. The Veyasaen also patrolled though their howls were muffled by the thick clouds and drowned in booming thunder. About the camp, the night watch stood on high alert. Fearful of both storm and beast, their watch was fraught with tension.

To the north of the Fortress City, sentries were in the nearby glens of Vartenca. Through dense fog, they patrolled, heads swiveling to squint at every rustling in the misty woods. Their alarm grew as a horrible, wretched stench hung in the air. They paused, and the rustling paused. They moved, and it moved. Ever growing in intensity, the scent was unfamiliar, its potency nauseating.

"Who goes there?" called the sentries. The only reply was the pounding of their own hearts against their metal breastplates.

Suddenly a guttural howl rang forth. It lingered several seconds before crescendoing into a high-pitched scream that spilled into the surrounding hill country. As the gut-wrenching sound wave passed through the patrols, they fell as one. Squirming, their hands clasped bloodied ears as they succumbed to a strange, dishonorable death.

In the western hill country of Vindakyr, mounted patrols paused as heavy footsteps thundered through the dark forests. Their horses neighed nervously, rearing back, even as their riders whipped them forward. Then, the crunching of large branches and debris gave way to a deafening silence which engulfed the nocturnal woods. Into this burst a chorus of chirps, whistles, and grunts.

"We are heavily-armed!" said the mounted patrols, nervously. "Show yourselves!" The strange sounds ceased for a moment, but then thunderous fate of their sentries of Vartenca fell upon the Vindakyr patrol.

To the east of the Fortress City, along the remote edges of the marshes of Faeynoga, another detachment of eleven patrols hesitated, as a ghostly mist crawled toward them over marshy waters. An eerie silence fell over the dark landscape. Into the flares of lightning, shrouded forms leapt toward them. Splashing through the marsh, their feet pounded and sucked against the muck. As the mist closed in on the eleven, it concealed them from each other, concealing too their foes.

"Hold your place! Identify yourselves at once!" shouted the patrols. They drew their weapons, but the sounds drew ever closer. To their right, a group of heavy bodies splashed. As they brandished weapons at their unseen foes, a soldier yelled, "They have flanked us!"

To their left another group of creatures waded heavily through the marsh. In the darkness, bones cracked, flesh was shredded, and horrible cries of pain filled the marshes of Faeynoga.

In the southern ravines of Ganuyar, three flanks of patrols navigated a deep ravine.

"Arm yourselves men," commanded the company leader. "Something seems…off."

The men agreed. Swords and crossbows in their hands, they inched forward in the pitch-black. A rock clanged loudly against the back armor of one of the patrols in the last flank. The soldiers froze and turned as the sound echoed through the walls of the ravine.

"Who threw that?" the soldier said with a scowl.

"This is no time for jest," bellowed the company leader. "Are you boys or men? Now forward, all of you!"

Suddenly, a twig flew through the darkness and hit the helmet of another soldier. "Something just hit me too!" winced the soldier.

Their superior's rebuke faded on his lips as a foul stench filled their nostrils. The hair on their arms and necks stood in fear as dread came upon all amongst the three flanks.

The leader's eyes gleamed intensely beneath his helmet visor. Nervously, he fixated on the darkness before them, cold vapors exhaling from his nostrils.

"Ignite a signal flare and hand it to me!" ordered the leader. Flare in hand, he took several brave steps forward but could see only the dancing shadows of wild brush and trees. The putrid stench intensified as he stared into the dark void before them. He flung the stick flare high into the air.

The soldiers watched anxiously as its light arced into the darkness. As it thudded to the ground, the silhouettes of a dozen monstrous, hairy forms appeared some thirty feet away in front of the company. Man and beast stared at each other in the dim light. Then, the fire sputtered against the stone and went out. In the darkness, the company leader and his sixty men ran fearfully for their lives. Along with a chorus of beastly howls raging in the darkness, their horrible screams of pain echoed off the ravines of Ganuyar.

With morning fast approaching, came one final assault. Inside the outer perimeter of the great camp, a massive array of black tents was situated on the steep slopes of a hill. As the thousands of men of many tumens soundly slept, a grove of trees upon the slope began to move.

A young sentry squinted upward in confusion. A cluster of dead tree trunks appeared where he was sure none had been before. Four to five feet wide, they appeared darker than the surrounding landscape. A brilliant flash of lightning crackled against the slopes. This time, he was sure of it, the dead tree trunks appeared further down the slope, closer to the camp. Paralyzed with fear, the sentry could neither shout for alarm, nor move. Persistently, the forms inched nearer until the sentry could no longer deny his suspicions. Surely these must be the beasts that tore apart our men!

His voice failed him as more lightning showed them bending on their haunches, their massive girths preparing to bound forward. "To arms!" he squawked. Clearing his throat and unsheathing his weapon he shouted bravely, "To arms!"

Yet his cry came too late. All about him were the shouts and screams of pain, the sounds of struggle, of cracking limbs pulled from their sockets. Ten to twenty Rhünkai died under the hands of one beast, their weapons doing little damage. Beastly growls of rage shattered the darkness. Corpses and scattered human limbs were flung into the heights of oak trees. Some snagged and dangled, others fell to monstrous, wooly paws which flung them upwards yet again until the trees received them.

When the sun crawled above the horizon, its soft light fell on the sobering sight of mutilated bodies scattered through the outer perimeter of the great camp. Giant footprints, now familiar, crisscrossed scenes of destruction. In the latter part of the morning, each of the tumens reported their death tolls. It was found that one fourth of all their soldiers had been slain.

Confusion and tension seized the heart of every man. In a fury, the Haru-spec's aides issued new orders. Eager to track the beasts, to find some means by which to end them, Aidan glowered as the masters of his tumen ordered a retreat of sorts.

Initially, the frequent rockfalls of the mountain had caused the Generals to set up camp some distance from the base of the mountain. Now, reluctantly, Captain Khalevad ordered his men to join the army in moving their tents closer to the base of the mountain as the camp shrank away from the forests.

The Tip of the Sword

The next several days saw a flurry of activity throughout the great camp. By night, soldiers fell in and out of uneasy sleep, tense and fearful of another beastly attack and unnerved by new sounds issuing from the forest. It was the snarls and shrieks of creatures snorting and sniffing at giant footprints which they heard, creatures under the sway of the dark counselor, creatures hunting for the wooly beasts.

In the vast, chaotic traffic of soldiers, equipment and weaponry, twelve Rhünkai soldiers made their way by day up the mountain. They moved not on the well-worn path to the stone archway at the summit, but unseen, along their own trail.

"There is the summit, boys. Remain alert at all times," announced Graeyba. The youthful warriors' sighs of relief exhaled in cold vapors.

Fifty feet above this ledge, Graeyba discerned a pair of tall stone archways in partial ruins shrouded in thick fog. Beyond them led a walkway, ascending to the Fortress City. Spectral in appearance, twenty or so Rhünkai moved in and out of the fog ahead.

Huddling his little band together, he laid out his instructions.

"This is it, boys. Remember this, darkness shackles multitudes of people in Y'cromeca. A vast number of freedom fighters imbued with the will for slaughter lie ready to storm those gates. We are the tip of the sword, gentlemen. And you young men, you are about to cross over a new threshold, to surrender the boy, in exchange for the man. There is no turning back," said Graeyba.

Hunkered down behind dark bushes, the friends exchanged awkward stares and gulped cold breaths in fear. Graeyba turned to try and fix his eyes on the stone ruins leading up to the walkway. His gaze shifted to the colossal trees above the old archway, flares of lightning aiding his sight.

"T'balidor, Javatiel, climb those trees, high enough to get into firing position upon the guards inside those stone archways," he ordered. "Sibrion, Vaez and Aejulan, initiate the first blow. Climb further up the mountain. Close in on the stone ruins. You must get a clear shot from high ground. Pick the most vulnerable targets on that platform. As soon as the first daggers find their targets, the rest of you fire your arrows into the rest of the group. Understood?"

The boys nodded grimly.

"The men are nervous too. Most likely, some will make for that stone walkway, flee toward the Fortress City. Kelán, discharge lances in them at once, prevent them from sounding the alarm. Should you miss those targets, our mission will be compromised."

Graeyba cast his eyes from face to face. "Any questions?" he asked.

When met with silence, he offered them a grave smile, then waved them forward. The young men moved stealthily, undetected.

As Sibrion, Vaez and Aejulan positioned themselves above the stone field, two sentries stepped over to the edge of the stone platform to relieve themselves. In the flare of lightning two vicious daggers gleamed toward them with furious strength, piercing their hands to their private regions. The two guards elicited a painful yell that startled the others guards to their feet.

They scrambled for their weapons. Several fled up the walkway to alert the Fortress City, as Graeyba had predicted, but a flurry of lances violently and quickly felled their bodies. The remainder of the guards on the stone platform met their end under volleys fired by T'balidor and Javatiel.

Graeyba and the young men cautiously stepped out of the fog and onto the stone platform, to survey the slain.

"Great job, boys!" smiled Graeyba, then corrected himself, "Great job, men! The Br'thain taught you well."

He was met with smiles of pride. T'balidor stepped forward eagerly, "Hurry, we must drive these Ferusats into the ground up there," he said.

Gesturing to his attire, Graeyba said, "The Tribune Ansuz said this uniform belonged to one of his top captains. I doubt we will have any trouble slipping inside the Fortress City."

"Let us proceed in haste, before our presence is discovered," Sibrion urged.

Graeyba and Aejulan led the band up the stone walkway. Despite the gravity of their mission, the boys peered curiously into the lightning at the eerie sight below them. They cringed at the sight of several slain soldiers impaled in the twisted mass of gigantic vines of thorns and thistles of the Cethin Arda below.

"Solid hits on those targets, men," Graeyba praised them as they ascended. "You remind me of my oldest son. He never missed a target."

The walkway ran alongside the towering fortress wall. A natural archway of giant vines grew over the steps and scaled the walls. At some length, they passed through it and slowed their pace. This was the very area that Graeyba had entered through, almost a year ago, in search of his sons.

A pair of wooden doors three times a man's height towered over a group of guards huddled around a campfire. One strummed a stringed instrument to sad Hiérundiel lyrics while the others conversed. They bragged of their threats to the weak and oppressed, the poor and the wealthy. They laughed insidiously as they swapped tales of forcing possessions confiscated from innocents forced to flee their homes.

As Graeyba's team approached they were met with a swaggering guard. Arrogantly, he demanded, "What is your station, and your purpose here?"

At precisely this moment, his bragging comrades broke into raucous laughter. Echoes bounded off the crags which clad the gates. None of his comrades noticed him stagger, then fall lifelessly to the ground as one of Aejulan arrows found his throat. The laughter of the guards was silenced by a vicious volley of arrows. Survivors scrabbled for their weapons, but Vaez and Kelán rushed to thrust their daggers into their sides.

"Two groups now brought down!" Graeyba said approvingly. "Now, two hundred yards inside those gates is the town square. It is very large and may be busy, but it is the only area with enough stone to guarantee safety. Their Ferusats are in the ground, let us drive ours down and open the Streams! Hurry!"

The twelve men of the West ran through the cobbled streets, over debris. Statues of the Bal Rús loomed in various states of completion. *They will never be finished, now!* Aejulan thought triumphantly.

They crossed one intersection after the other, undetected. Then, a hideous visage stopped them dead in their tracks. Their blood ran cold as, out of a spectral fog, dozens of beings ambled eerily through the street. Patches of hair clung to heads whose features were gaunt. Deeply sunken eye sockets housed ghostly eyes. The bones of their rib cages were oddly exposed, their ashen skin beneath it. A disturbing number of stiches marked the loose grey skin about their bodies. Aimlessly, they drifted through the dark streets.

"Let them be," muttered Graeyba.

"Curse those wretched alchemists and their experiments!" hissed Aejulan.

The rest of the group stood paralyzed. They had, indeed, crossed over a threshold, exchanging the boy for a man. For in this moment, they were faced with the hypnotic power of evil.

"We can do nothing for them. Heed the warnings of the Gardener who has said many times 'Do not swallow the seeds of the harbinger, for he was a manipulator of men from generations past. Drink from the Streams of Faeynhava'," said Graeyba. "T'balidor! Sibrion! Time is running out, move!" he urged.

The strength in his voice stirred them. Slowly, they turned from the frightful monstrosities and made for the main square where Graeyba issued rapid orders. "T'balidor, take to the stone column to the east of the square! Drive your Ferusat in front of it. Sibrion, take to those trees to the west. I will attend those massive stones to the north. The rest of you, stand guard while we drive these Ferusats. Kill any Rhünkai who approach," ordered Graeyba.

Just then, a distant shout of "Close the gates!" came to them upon a chill breeze. It was followed by urgent calls of "The city is breached!"

They hurried to their posts as a clamoring rose, far away at first, then closer. His fingers frigid about his Ferusat, T'balidor whispered a song. It was a sonnet, oftentimes sung around campfires in the West.

"Into the Va'Giyyel we go. With the favor of our papas..."

Between the booms of thunder, a low rumble began.

"...To rekindle a light. Snuffed out so long ago. To restore that which was broken."

From the south, an arban of Rhünkai archers approached at a run, their captain shouting "There they are! Take aim and fire!"

They loosed a barrage of arrows at Graeyba's company. But their positions behind the stone columns, behind the trees and massive stones offered them protection as they worked away at the stakes.

T'balidor smiled as small currents of electricity ignited from the stone foundation.

"Extol the Gardener. He trains my hands for war. From the Garden of Ages. Comes my wisdom for battle—"

In a brilliant flash, a thousand azure blue lights of clan warriors filled the square. The Br'thain were met with a volley of arrows, but their shiryon deflected them. Straightaway, small detachments of fifty warriors sprinted to defend Graeyba, T'balidor and Sibrion, to prevent any disruption to the Ferusats which might close the Streams.

But the Rhünkai were paralyzed by the domes of light. The sight of thousands of Br'thain melted their discipline with fear. Their many dreams and visions and the recent attacks of giants in the night caused their hands to tremble. To the great surprise of the men of the West, the Rhünkai turned and ran. Many Br'thain pursued them, slaughtering them throughout the streets of the Fortress City.

In a flurry of movement, the rest of the clan warriors moved into fifty formations. Stealthily, with great speed and agility, they spread rapidly into the avenues of the Fortress City. The fiery words of young S'baladin's parable propelled them forward. In a way, they too were crossing a threshold. The ambush of their countrymen had left them fearful and disheartened. On this day however, their courage rekindled to imbue their souls with the will to slaughter an ancient evil.

At the northern wall of the city, Rhünkai patrols numbering seven hundred and fifty were huddled around their campfires in the cold rain, unaware of an enemy presence. The Fortress City being the most prestigious of posts, these were the most evil and corrupt of all the soldiers in Y'cromeca, the most deserving of death. As the guards had done, they swapped in mocking laughter, stories of dark deeds against children, of rape, and of pillage.

Suddenly, these brutish fiends prickled. A mysterious sound, blast loudly through the rain. It was the ram's horn of the West, heralding the first clash between the Br'thain and the Rhünkai patrols at the northern wall of the city. The soldiers gawked for but a moment at a large contingency of foreign warriors inside their fortress walls before surging to their feet.

In a flurry of chaos and cursing, they rushed to arm themselves. Rhünkai officers' shouted for reinforcements. Meanwhile, the clan warriors descended. With all their regimented, professional training, the Rhünkai were no match against the shepherds and farmers. Several soldiers fell at the hands of each clan warrior.

They were organized into ancient clans according to their districts and family patriarchs in each territory. Beyond the element of surprise, this was their true strength against the Rhünkai soldiery. In frigid conditions that were alien to them, against a great evil, they fought side by side with fathers, brothers, and cousins. This brought them great strength and comfort as they sought vengeance for those slain by such as these. As they butchered the patrols, the Br'thain shouted,

"Remember the ambush!"

"You murdered my father!"

"You killed my brother!"

The clans of the house of Eirun-Vala shouted "Remember Baltien!" and "Long live the Garden of Ages!" as they struggled against the Rhünkai.

As fearsome as the storm that raged about them, the Br'thain, though smaller in numbers, descended with fury upon the vast numbers of patrols. The northern wall fell to them quickly, then they swept through all the rest.

Few among the Br'thain fell, but many sustained injuries. These were offered immediate relief from rapidly administered herbs from the Garden of Ages, then transported safely back through the Streams. As Rhünkai resistance waned, small detachments of the Br'thain liberated children from their forced labor. To them they offered fruits from the Gardener, to heal the effects of the Necropulpa plant.

In the attack, many of the Thaed-Rú scientists, alchemists and administrators evacuated the city straightway. For they knew well the evil experiments wrought upon countless innocent souls placed them well beyond the hand of mercy. With them, the few Rhünkai who managed to survive, fled down the mountain to warn the others.

The Br'thain shouted cries of triumph. The booms of thunder and flashes of lightning now seemed a celebration, the heavy rains a purifying force. In the sixth hour in the morning, their ram's horns sounded victory over the Fortress City. The clan warriors made one final sweep through the city. They searched amongst the piles of slain Rhünkai for Br'thain comrades wounded or dead and gathered the remaining child slaves.

Meanwhile Graeyba, T'balidor and Sibrion left the Ferusats at the main square to the guardianship of the others. As planned, they bid farewell to their fellows and made their way to the heart of the Cethin Arda. Upon entering through a tall stone archway, the trio held torches aloft to light their way and ensure the quality of air. Each wore a cloth mask about their neck in case the flames guttered in polluted air.

Cautiously, they stepped into a dark ravine and shivered as the temperature dropped dramatically. The wretched bodies of slain Rhünkai and Thaed-Rú stretched before them, bordered by thorns and thistles. It seemed the branches of the arching trees above were hideous creatures stretching down their threatening claws as they passed below. They gasped in horror as their torchlight fell upon a failed harvest of the Cethin Arda. Throughout the floor of the ravine, human heads in various stages of decomposition protruded from the ground. Vines wove in and out of their orifices, like serpents. Countless human bodies intermingled with the carcasses of strange creatures.

"What...?" Graeyba began, then trailed off, speechless.

"They grafted man and beast into the garden," Sibrion said grimly. "Who knows what harvests such an effort reaped."

"Come," said Graeyba to Sibrion, pulling him away from the gruesome sight.

T'balidor, bile rising in his throat, turned away and pushed onward, saying gruffly, "This place... I hate it!"

"Indeed, it is completely opposite of the Garden of Ages," agreed Sibrion. "The Infinite Garden uses the sun's warmth to harvest life. Yet this counterfeit garden uses cold darkness to breed death and destruction."

They made their way along carefully, until they spied a sinister, dark form. It was hunched over a tall stone several yards away, its massive wings outstretched. Its visage alone caused their hearts to race. Then the tension left their bodies and T'balidor let out a low chuckled. "It is just a statue!"

"And thankful I am for that!" Sibrion said in relief. Gesturing to a carving upon the stone pedestal, he asked, "Graeyba, can you decipher the meaning of these letters?"

"It is ancient Hiérundiel," explained Graeyba, "first spoken by the primordial Thaed-Rú." He held his torch closer and read, "'Herein is the Cethin Arda, the dark garden of promise for all Y'cromeca. Its knowledge is too deep to fathom; therefore, it is dark. Its power is too great to harness; therefore, we labor to subdue it.'"

"Come boys. Let us undo these cursed words!" said Graeyba.

As the trio passed the winged statue, their torches began to sputter. Cautiously, they pulled their masks up to cover their mouths and noses, then set their torches carefully at the base of the statue to retrieve upon their exit. Beyond the statue, lay a large, oblong pool over one hundred feet wide and three times that in length. A pale light emanated from the cold mist on its surface. Beneath this eerie glow, patches of ice floated atop a dark void of deep water. Menacing trees extended their branches into this pool. The trio was appalled to see human corpses hung from these branches in a grotesque manner. Their torsos hovered above the water, while their limbs were hidden beneath. Smaller vines slithered from their bodies into the icy water, or perhaps the opposite was true.

Graeyba reached inside his fur coat and withdrew a packet of cloth from which he removed an exceptionally large seed. He cradled it in his palms and the trio peered down in awe. Thin, wiry vines wove a tangled covering all over the root of the greenish, brown seed.

Wearily, Graeyba cast his eyes about the evil surrounding him. Drawing several deep breaths through his mask, he relayed their mission. "I recall the Gardener once said, before he disappeared from the West, that all seeds are planted to bring forth life. Yet the seeds of the Cethin Arda bring death. The dark one came long ago to plant the Cethin Arda. He brought about the dark roots of the Thaed-Rú. And now their thorns and thistles have spread to cover the land of Y'cromeca. But now this evil shall end!"

"Yes!" cheered Sibrion.

"Let it end!" said T'balidor solemnly.

"Those who oppress the innocent, harm the widows, abuse the fatherless, and torture those without a voice for justice, they shall reap the harvest of wrath from this seed!" declared Graeyba. He released a frustrated huff of warm breath. It passed as cold vapors through his mask to curl upward over the pool.

Then Sibrion spoke. "Years ago, in his wisdom, the Gardener uttered words over this seed. His words of life and order of purpose I repeat:

Root of Kal-Hezek, in the Isle of Feynhava, spread the plague of pestilence across the Cethin Arda. When you are planted at the bottom of the dark pool, mingle your roots with the icy waters and spread a plague throughout the mountain. Destroy everything upon its crest. Then shall the sound of the ram's horns blast throughout the forests of Ixzaril, the glens of Vartenca, the marshes of Faeynoga, the hills of Vindakyr, and the ravines of Ganuyir.'"

Breathlessly, the trio leaned forward as Graeyba dropped the seed into the water with a little plop. The sound resounded against the walls of the ravine and, instantly, the ground beneath them trembled. It sank, and great ripples spread forth from it to spill over the edges of the pool.

"Evacuate! Run!" shouted Graeyba. They snatched up their torches and ran. Through the eerie fog, over and around corpses, beneath the threatening trees, past twisted vines, thorns, thistles they fled. It was with great relief that they exited the Cethin Arda, yet they did not slow their pace until they arrived at the main square.

"Hurry!" Vaez shouted as they buckled over at the waist, wrenching off their masks and gasping for breath. "I have held the Streams open for you!" Vaez called. "We are the last ones to evacuate this mountain!"

They lurched forward to cling to his Ferusat as he drove it into the ground. Immediately, they disappeared in an azure ring of electrical currents, into the stone foundation.

Battle for Y'cromeca

Throughout the great camp, word spread of these savage shepherd warriors, of the massacre they afflicted when they stormed the gates of the Fortress City. With the beastly attacks decimating a quarter of their combined armies just days prior, this second wave cast fear and dread upon every soul in the great camp.

With desertion rampant, untold numbers braving the dangers of the forest over unknown threats to come, a cloud of doubts fell upon the remaining Rhünkai force. With no confirmation as to whether the shepherd warriors had verily occupied the city, the Rhünkai consulted with the Haruspec's aides. It was decided that they would lead a reconquest up the mountain. Their intent was to utterly destroy the Br'thain whom they assumed had occupied the mountaintop city.

As night fell, large numbers of Rhünkai soldiers followed the Haruspec's aides. Veyasaeyn flew overhead, screeching and howling through an icy storm. Another plague upon the minds of the Rhünkai, the same massive storm had clung to the area for days, with little sign of sun by day. Surrounding the entire mountain, they climbed doggedly for hours in darkness. To all who watched from the camp below, they seemed as ants, carrying sustenance to an anthill.

Meanwhile atop the mountain, a green plague had indeed sprung from the stagnant waters of the pool in the Cethin Arda. Tendrils of green spread everywhere, germinating everything within the dark garden and covering it with an algae-like substance. It moved now beyond the Cethin Arda, into the streets, covering half-finished buildings, obscuring the unfinished statues.

In the pre-dawn, the Haruspec's minions reached the summit to enter the gates of a deserted, silent city. Boots rang out against cobblestones, echoing emptily as soldiers moved about the square, then poured through empty streets and into the Cethin Arda. Yet, whether disguised by the heavy fog or cloaked in some supernal protection, no one seemed aware of the green plague.

It was found that no shepherd warriors remained, and the Rhünkai quickly moved to secure their foothold on the mountain, once more. By the noon hour, thousands upon thousands reoccupied the deserted Fortress City. This time, they were determined to set up a massive force of guards for an indomitable hold on the city. Only then did they begin the process of collecting the bodies of their slain comrades.

Meanwhile, the sound of a giant shook the land. It was an echo of the ancient Faeynül, the colossal ones that lived long ago, in the age of Ulmeca-Dül. Today, this colossal sound of the Faeynül trod not out of the past but out of the Forests of Ixzaril. It was the great war cry of the ancient mountain clans of the Mon-Herra, the Fin-Faiza, the Ir- Aranon, the Breytha-Ul, the Ler-Bahnya, the Er-Orba Feron, the Bok-Faiza and the Tir-Volkai. It rang out from the fifty thousand who heard the call of S'baladin's letter in the fields of Molchaion, from the twelve-thousand insurgents in the Upper Vales of Miórgelân of Graëyhovan, from Ansuz' twenty-two thousand in Hiérundia, from thousands upon thousands more banded together from the snow-covered mountains of Tal-Ciddion, from thousands of armed militia groups near Laëthoban and Hánuthir, from the four great divisions of the Anil-Gevra of Ir of the Fenrülk, and from the lands in the West from the brave and noble men of B'naiyth Varodduin, B'naiyth Eirun-Vala, B'naiyth V'oar, B'naiyth Ur'uhuk, B'naiyth Inaruhuin, B'naiyth Vizzarayn, B'naiyth B'rukkain, and B'naiyth Valantorat.

This colossal horde, fighting on the side of goodness, roared forth against the Rhünkai. Through dreary fog, they marched, through the forests of pine trees and wild brush, up rocky crags, across the rivers, row upon row, rank upon rank, column upon column, their numbers covered the valleys and crested the hills surrounding the high mountain of the Fortress City.

On this cold day, they were united as one from across the land. All those who yearned for freedom, weary of the oppression of the dark garden of the north combined their strength to become as one of the Faeynül. And the words of S'baladin and the wisdom of the Gardener rang true.

The new Faeynül will burst forth from the deserts and glens to green fields and valleys. The colossal one will rise forth to drink from the Streams of Feynhava. With the blast of a thousand ram's horns, the new Faeynül will march on the Cethin Arda to tear out its very roots, casting it into the fire. The new Faeynül will destroy the wild beasts that planted it. The smoke of the Cethin Arda and the rotting flesh of the wild beasts shall ascend high into the sky, witnessed by all.

• • • • •

While vast forces gathered around the Fortress City, far away in the provincial capital of Kiérbangaal, a lone, hooded man moved through early morning shadows. Countless pillars of smoke rose high into the clouded skies where a single Veyasaen wheeled about aimlessly. It was the smoke of desolation. It rose from giant heaps of the dead in neighborhoods razed by fire.

A few miserable souls lamented their dead. Fur clad children wandered about in search of food and shelter. Some sought warmth in the fires consuming their dead. Tears of lament ran down the Gardener's cheeks at their sorry state. Beggars warily approached him, seeking food. He reached into his pouch and drew out seeds from a special compartment. He tossed the seeds into the air, and uttered "The choicest of fruits, pomegranates, henna with nard plants! The people of this city shall be partakers of these fruits."

Instantly, countless plants rose through the cobblestones wherever seeds had fallen, producing fruits of various kinds. All eyes turned from the death and destruction around them to new life springing forth.

"When the land is restored and the power of the Haruspec is broken," proclaimed the Gardener, "this street shall be known as the Way of the Fruits of Life, and the provinces shall eat of its fruits."

Children and women came to pluck their share, squealing and murmuring in delight, thus giving thanks to the Gardener. He continued through the city's ruinous state, routing the foul beasts that haunted the dark, deserted streets with sound blows from his Tiller's Staff.

Late in the morning, he sought rest amidst the city's debris for a spell. He ate of numinous fruits, to regain his strength and fortify his power against his ancient foe. Before he rose, he scooped a small depression into the ground at his feet. From his pouch he planted, all together, a cluster of seeds so tiny they were nearly microscopic.

"Follow my steps deep underground," he whispered, "until I summon you. Though my call will be still and small, as you are now, you will be a great auxiliary unto me." Then he gathered his belongings and rose.

An hour later, he arrived at the heavily wooded, rocky outcroppings of a sprawling butte on the outskirts of the city. Spread across the top of this butte was Realmhold Thaed-Rú. The sides of the slopes were completely covered by heaps of corpses far greater than those in the city. Vultures and Veyasaen alike feasted upon them. The Gardener used his scarf to cover his nose against the putrid odor of rotting flesh. Carefully he picked his way through swarms of flies, over thousands of rotting corpses. "This is certainly the deed of the dark one! Only he delights in murder on such a scale!" he muttered. Gazing out at endless mounds of death, he shook his head, pained. "It is just as Teosifan predicted many years ago."

At Íraban's coronation, when last the Gardner had visited Realmhold Thaed-Rú, Teosifan had threatened any who defied the Edict of the Scions:

Your province shall be laid waste. It will become a haunt of ghostly specters and fowl beasts. That province will become a graveyard for the rotting corpses of men!

"Though he little expected it I am sure," scoffed the Gardener, "the words of Teosifan have turned upon his own kind."

Much later, he trudged up a steep slope toward the Hall of Towers. Strange, dark pods lay scattered everywhere amongst thorny weeds. They twirled around towering pillars, through archways, and over walls where they bit into the tattered black and red banners of the Thaed-Rú.

The Gardener found it very strange that no opposition barred his way as he entered the great council hall. He peered upward through the open-air atrium, in search of Veyasaen, and smiled. The sky above him was absent of the beastly fowl. The Thaed-Rú stronghold was eerily silent, deserted. The only soldiers left to meet him were corpses in countless number scattered about the stone structures. Some of these bodies appeared frozen in time - caught in a struggle to escape - with frightful grimaces on their faces. They seemed an omen, a self-revealing description of a dark and murderous entity.

The mists before him dissipated slightly to reveal a colossal heap of human skulls and bones. The base of this osseous matter rose seventy feet tall and spanned a space twice that in length. Flies swarmed about it. The fog slowly swirled away to reveal a dark, monstrous form atop this heap. It was crouched and gripped a staff.

"Are you come to contest my ownership of these lands?" spoke the monstrous figure. "The Thaed-Rú have signed all over to me."

"I know these lands," interjected the Gardener, cold vapors exhaling from his lips. "I was here long before you drifted to this world. I planted my garden in the West before the wretched Sheddukem appeared. I know the energy running far below the ground."

The figure above him howled in rage. "You are nothing! I am the rightful owner of Terra Y'cromeca."

The Gardener denied him fiercely. "Though you lay claim to it, nevertheless, I am the true husbandman of this soil. You forget the oldest truth that governs husbandry: though the land may yield forth thorns and thistles, the wise sower will plant a harvest of goodness. The same shall remove the cursed weeds, in order that his roots may spread throughout the land." The Gardener's voice echoed through Realmhold Thaed-Rú. It pierced the fog which dissipated with increasingly rapidity.

The dark form rose, the shredded tendrils of his black robe billowing like serpents. With every step of his descent, bones crunched and crumbled beneath his massive weight. The Gardener stepped backward as the dark form finally reached to the ground amidst an avalanche of bones.

The two stood still before each other. The dark one breathed heavily, exerted while the other stared calmly into his countenance. Slowly, the Gardener reached into his pouch. Then, in one smooth motion, he knelt and sprinkled a handful of seeds in a wide arc on the stone floor, all the while gripped his Tiller's Staff tightly, never taking his eyes from his foe.

"It has been many ages," spoke the Haruspec, undaunted.

"Indeed, it has," responded the Gardener.

As the Gardener hauled himself to his feet with his Tiller's Staff, the long wooden staff of the Haruspec became limp. It bowed toward the ground and the Haruspec swung it into the heap of osseous matter behind him. From the wooden staff burgeoned multiple vines to coil around the bones and skulls. With great speed, the Haruspec swung forward, releasing a terrible volley of osseous matter at the Gardener.

The words of Uraduin which the Gardener had whispered as the little arc of falling seeds now caused strange branches to shoot forth from the stone floor. They interlocked in a defensive formation ten feet tall. In a blinding flash, the volley of osseous matter crashed against them. Osseous matter erupted violently in an ear-shattering explosion. A cloud of tiny shards of bone and dust fell to the ground before the Gardener's interlocked branches.

"You possess great speed and cunning, Steward of Feynhava!" chortled the Haruspec. He clutched his staff once more. The fog thickened now. It swallowed the massive form of the Haruspec. Guarding his hideous face with his staff, he moved around the Gardener's shield of branches, searching it for weakness. Finally, he came upon an opening of the arc of branches. Within was crouched a shadowy mass shrouded in mists. The Haruspec swung his wooden staff heavily upon it. Shattered leaves and twigs burst into a powdery cloud which, once cleared, revealed only an empty space within the shelter. With a growl of frustration the Haruspec spun around, beating angrily at the fog with his staff, searching wildly for the Gardener.

• • • • •

As the age-old foes were locked in battle, the Rhünkai at the northwest perimeter of the base camp trumpeted an alarm as a massive army of insurgents approached. While Rhünkai masters shouted orders to form defensive columns, alarms sounded from sentries to the northeast as a great armed force approached there also.

Among those in the northwestern army, Graeyba and Sibrion led an advance guard of seven hundred Br'thain. The two blasted upon their ram's horns and then it was that a great chorus of seven hundred horns pealed forth from those of their men. The great sound thundered loudly across the valley floor to collide against the mountain. The sound spread through crags, leaped over great ravines, and summitted the mountain peak to echo through the Fortress City.

The green plague constricted in response and the mountain convulsed with a tremor that shook the land for leagues in every direction. The mountain summit erupted. Boulders launched into the air as massive missiles and splintered shards of rock rained down upon the sides of the mountain. Mammoth trees violently snapped and ripped apart, reduced to splinters and shards of wood. Myriads of squawking birds fled their nests, dipping and swooping in the chaos. Even the Veyasaen screeched in terror and wheeled away, only to swoop furiously down over the terrestrial destruction of their domain.

Then there erupted the dreaded sound of a maelstrom thundering across the valley floor. A monstrous tower of green-tinged dust consumed the tents of the Rhünkai tumens. They, along with the Haruspec's aides, fell to their miserable doom, asphyxiated by the cloud of green, impaled by branches, and crushed by boulders. Instantly, hundreds of thousands of Rhünkai soldiers fell, as did their catapults and other mechanisms of war.

A vast cry of victory came from the surrounding forces of insurgents and Br'thain. But another sound surpassed it, a strange sound erupting from the nearby woods. It was the monstrous howls of anguish of the forest beasts. The insurgents stared at the woods around them. Many exchanged quizzical glances. As howls, shrieks, and growls filled the cold air, they drew their weapons and fell into defensive formations.

From high above the clouded chaos, flocks of Veyasaen swooped down through the haze, attacking and devouring the soldiers loyal to the Haruspec. These war birds were the very symbols emblazoned on each shield and banner. Yet now, they turned on these Rhünkai.

There was scant notice that the Veyasaen had concentrated their attack solely on the dark order of Rhünkai. Nor did the insurgents notice a young girl standing high atop a fallen boulder, sheltered by thick foliage and protected by several armed individuals. V'leshkah, and a troop of bodyguards clustered protectively around Ka-Lyn whose bright blue eyes were transfixed upon the war birds. Her eyes, her thoughts and her words directed the Veyasaen to exclusively attack the dark souls of the Haruspec's men.

"Destroy the Rhünkai! Descend upon those whose hearts are knit by murder and bloodshed," she cried. Leave the others alone! came her thoughts.

This attack of beastly fowl caused great confusion for the Haruspec's men. Long had they trusted in the dark counselor's control over the fowl. In their confusion, Rhünkai soldiers wandered in a daze, past a great number of their dead comrades who now lay buried under mountainous heaps of rock and debris. A few among the survivors scaled the mountainous rubble, search for comrades under the debris. Most however turned toward the advancing armies of insurgents, while many deserted, fleeing the Veyasaen, fleeing the great army.

Hundreds of yards away from the chaos and dust-covered destruction, Sibrion ordered the seven hundred to blow the ram's horn once more. This time, it was the battle cry unto war. Great hordes of insurgents shouted as they drew closer and closer to the confused Rhünkai. Standard bearers carrying banners of every tongue and tribe marched. Their mouths and noses covered by scarves, they struggled through the heavy clouds of dust. Small particles of debris, appearing as snowflakes, floated amidst shouts and struggles.

A great battle ensued. The Rhünkai clashed with warriors and insurgents. Officers and chieftains shouted orders into the haze.

Across the valley, the Tribune Ansuz and his generals sat upon their horses on a high ledge, surveying the war. Attendants, lesser officers and couriers stood around them, while a great host of soldiers guarded their lofty position.

"General Nitha, move the first and second phalanxes into the field!" Ansuz ordered his general.

Nitha's horse galloped him away to dispatch his men into action. They marched into the dusty cloud of conflict, shields up, swords drawn, spears down. They fought bravely against the Haruspec's soldiers, but many reappeared, driven back by desperate men.

"General Beizara!" the Tribune ordered his next officer. "Order the third column to repel them back!" Beizara's third column, a massive force of foot soldiers, lancers, bowmen, and equestrian fighters, marched into the fray of battle, amidst insurgents and Br'thain. As the strength of their numbers overwhelmed the weary Rhünkai, a flock of Veyasaen swooped again, carrying off more men. Some of these giant birds tussled with each other over their victims, ripping them apart like a rag doll, high above the field of battle.

The Tribune Ansuz watched as multiple groups of young men from the Br'thain slipped into the colossal cloud of dust which yet rose high into the sky over the fallen mountain. They bobbed along - close to the ground - like ferrets, then sprang suddenly upon Rhünkai soldiers who, blinded and dazed by the dust, were quickly slain. It was a curious sight for the Tribune Ansuz to see. He chuckled and shook his head. *Many a strange sight I have seen today. It is as I always knew, alone my men were nothing against the evil in this land.*

He watched as the Rhünkai lines broke under the onslaught of Br'thain. The one consisted of armor, weapons, shields and heavy equipment, large numbers, and organization, in contrast with smaller numbers, which were quicker and faster, with lightweight daggers and shorter swords fashioned by the smithies of the desert. Dipped in the mysterious waters of the Quinassa River, their metals held a strength beyond any in the Eleven Dominions. It was said that long ago, the Gardener stood by the headwaters, pouring vibrant mixtures into the Quinassa. The Tribune Ansuz stood dumbfounded as the blades of the shepherd warriors splintered shields, dented armor, and shattered steel. The deathblows of their swords were swift and sudden. Still, many Rhünkai archers yet fired arrows into the hordes of clashing warriors.

Amongst them was the consummate archer, Aidan Khalevad. Man after man fell beneath his merciless arrows. Rallying his archers to him, they merged with numerous mounted Rhünkai. From horseback, their volleys joined with long rapiers and sabers to thin the crowds, striking down, or wounding, insurgents by the hundreds.

• • • • •

While the battle ensued over the ruins of the decimated Rhünkai camp, the Haruspec howls echoed against the great stone walls of the Hall of Towers. He called out loudly as he sought his foe. His long, skeletal finger traced the scar upon his face. "This mark you left has echoed through time! Now, in retribution, I have left a mark upon your people and this land!"

The Haruspec froze in his hobbling pursuit as the Gardener's voice came from within the fog. "Why carry this infernal rage across time?"

"Long ago, pitiful souls journeyed to the Isle of Feynhava. They searched for immortality, knowledge, strength and power. Yet you denied them!" Out of the thickness of the fog, three large wolf-like creatures came alongside the Haruspec. He hushed them and together they prowled while he continued berating the Gardener, "You offered only healing for their ailments. You feared them! Fearing they might seize your power, you limited their harvest."

He stroked the fur of the creatures and spoke over them in his cursed tongue. They emitted a strange sound, like joints popping and stood upright on their two hind legs. Their bodies rose into the fog as bones amidst more bony bursts until each stood ten to twelve feet tall. Their muscular bodies were covered in patchy hair and hideous battle scars. One of the creatures was missing a limb.

The Gardener cautiously approached the Haruspec and his hairy brood. Everywhere the Gardener trod, hundreds of thin, wiry vines moved out of the ground to protect him. When he stepped to the side, the vines moved through the cracks of the stone foundation with him.

"You twist the truth!" replied the Gardener staidly.

"Do I?" said the Haruspec.

To his bellows of mocking laughter, the Gardener responded. "You know well I only guarded them from tragic paths, from inclinations to destroy the course of peoples and lands. The Fruits of Discernment, you know also, revealed their true intentions in seeking the Infinite Garden."

The Haruspec snorted. "Only I saw the potential of unleashing more fruits to benefit souls, to transcend the clay of mere men. To make a stronger creation, the life essence of men must mingle with creatures. That is how I harvested these," said the Haruspec, and he pointed his staff at the three wolf creatures.

Momentarily, the thin, wiry vines that protected the Gardener lowered into the stone foundation as he peered at the heinous wolf creatures. Instantly they lunged. Razor-sharp talons clawed through his raiment as they leapt upon him, tearing bloody gashes across his back and on his arms.

As the Haruspec's laughter howled out into the chamber, the Gardener retaliated. He swung his Tiller's Staff in a violent arc which sent froth a blinding flash of supernal power. His vicious blow struck each of the hairy giants simultaneously with great force. They fell to the ground, shaking their heads and growling in pain and the Haruspec fell silent.

But the dark creatures were battle seasoned and the Gardner's attack served only to incense their fury. Howls echoed across the chamber and they rose to their feet, once more surrounding the Gardener. In a flash, they leapt forward as one, and a fiendish roar of delight echoed over their attack. But the wiry vines, thin as they were, shot up through cracks in the stone foundation to protect the Gardener. Millions of them wound about the creatures, thus catching them in midair. Their growls filled the vast chamber of the council hall as they struggled to free themselves, slicing viciously at the tangle of vines. But the more they fought, the more vines grew.

The supernal vines now wrapped themselves around the creatures' necks. Futile against the ever-tightening vines, they continued clawing away. Base instincts overcame the wolf creatures. All desire to appease their master faded as they struggled to breathe. Kicking, scratching, and pawing at the air, slowly, one by one, the creatures died.

• • • • •

In the dust and debris of the fallen Fortress City, what little daylight pierced the hazy cloud began to wane as the sun descended. The spirits of the men sank too. Their bodies were sore from exhaustion, their limbs ached from constant struggle. In the massive field where once a thousand rows of crisp black tents had proudly stood, men sloshed through rivers of blood, past piled corpses. The wretched stench of battle filled their nostrils, and all about them the horrified screams and vile cursing of the wounded filled the air.

Still, the Haruspec's troops persisted, defending naught but what lives were left amongst the rubble. The cloud of dust was slowly dissipating. Through it, tall, lumbering Taenshuks appeared, carrying officers, followed by more of the Haruspec's troops. Their powerful, muscular limbs trod over Ansuz' men, crushing them instantly.

From behind the Taenshuks, archers yet loosed arrows upon the insurgents. Many of these found a fleshy home. The brave men of the ancient mountain clans of the Mon-Herra, the Fin-Faiza, the Ir-Aranon, the Breytha-Ul, the Ler-Bahnya, the Er-Orba Feron, the Bok-Faiza and the Tir-Volkai rallied to strike down row up row of the Haruspec's men with lances and swords. Heavy battle-axes bit into the Taenshucks legs and they came groaning down upon their sides. In the mountain clan tongue of Vayezdar, chieftains ordered their brigands to finish them off, then marched them onward, toward the main body of Rhünkai gathered about the greats of the heaps of dust and rubble.

The great divisions of the Anil-Gevra merged with them in a charge against the Haruspec's men who held high ground. The Generals Isayar, Teima, Naddú and Tzeytvara led their men furiously into battle. Their standard bearers carried banners bearing the name of Iemil, the war cry of those who had worked for the noble master, Lord Sulla of Ir of the Fenrülk.

"Iemil!" they shouted as they thrust their lances and wielded clubs against the Rhünkai. In their anger and wrath, they struck down many an expertly trained Rhünkai who had held their position, guarding what remained of the mountain debris.

Shouting "For Baltien!" the Br'thain from B'naiyth Eirun-Vala joined the fray. Graeyba, T'balidor, and Sibrion each led groups of these into the calamitous and dusty milieu. Vaez, Javatiel, Kelán, Aejulan fought valiantly against the Rhünkai order alongside a host of other shepherd clan warriors. Their shiryon breastplates, fashioned by wooden twigs from the Garden of Ages, held a supernal protection against their foes. No Rhünkai weapon used against them could prevail.

Breathing laboriously from battle fatigue and exhaustion, Graeyba's eye-patched countenance constantly swept the battle scene not just for danger, but for any sign of his son, Aidan. Covered in soot and smeared with blood, he crouched low, to thwart the swing of blades. Graeyba spun his body each time he bobbed upward, to deliver his entire weight along with each blow or thrust. In the gathering twilight, blood splattered in the air above him, mingling with floating particles of dust and ash.

Suddenly, a hundred roars of anguish rolled across the forests. Familiar only to the Rhünkai, the soldiers froze in horror, then scattered in rapid retreat into the nearby forests. Confused, the freedom fighters paused momentarily, awaiting orders. Sibrion, frowning, ordered his seven hundred to sound the ram's horn for retreat.

Dusk had deepened and though they peered about them, none could see the sound's source. The Tribune Ansuz' men, the Anil-Gevra, and the Br'thain of the West retreated, carrying their wounded away to medical tents. The rest of the insurgents followed suit while the Haruspec's men tried to rally their surviving forces to what remained of their base camp.

Another primal scream filled the evening darkness. Then, with no further warning, they appeared out of the dark forests, the nocturnal giants that had decimated one fourth of the Rhünkai just days before. Their dark, monstrous forms sped through the tall brush, to leap from behind trees, over the rolling hills of rubble and debris. Their howls filled the cold evening, sapping the warmth from the blood of the men.

A series of clicks and chirps travelled back and forth around the perimeter of the decimated camp. Inside the perimeter, the Haruspec's men huddled together, swords trembling in the dark as the thundering sound of footsteps hurtled towards them. Thick, muscular legs, carried the Ghost Kings through the evening darkness with furious velocity. The Haruspec's sway over these men waned as base fear welled within. As the hairy giants descended upon them, they dropped their weapons and ran to a man.

In a fury, the creatures pursued the Rhünkai, seizing them and ripping them apart. More were hurled against trees or dashed and tossed violently upon boulders. A chill breeze carried the screams and shouts of men into the evening darkness and across the valley floor.

Far away, safely withdrawn from the perimeter, even the most seasoned warriors amongst the freedom fighters cringed at the frightful sounds of beastly battle. As the night stretched on, eventually the base camp fell silent. None among the great, triumphant army, dared to venture close for fear of creatures lying in wait.

• • • • •

At Realmhold Thaed-Rú, as frigid night drew nigh, the Haruspec hoisted up his withered weeds, the Harmattan. Crushing their leaves, he tossed them into the air. They formed a massive whirlwind which released a cacophony of disturbing sounds and voices. They spoke of the Sheddukem plots and downfall, the Thaed-Rú's plans, the age of men, and the rise and fall of the Ballai. The Haruspec's own voice echoed across time as did the howls of his victims.

As the great turmoil of recent times spun out from the dark whirlwind, the weight of it sent the Gardener to his knees. His yell of outrage shook the very foundation of Realmhold Thaed-Rú. The Haruspec hobbled toward the Gardener, mocking him in derisive laughter.

"Look what the history of Y'cromeca has yielded," he said, a fiendish grin on his twisted lips. "My gift of seeds to the Sheddukem spawned the Thaed-Rú, you destroyed my Sheddukem but the Thaed-Rú breached your precious Ballai, making way for my return."

With deliberate steps, he approached the kneeling form. "My little mythical gardener," he said, "the Thaed-Rú are my creation! They are the real husbandmen of this land! They trampled the weeds of Y'crom, beating them into submission until they crushed their spirits, ruling over your pathetic people…"

The Gardener swung his hooded head up at this to interrupt angrily, "…But you destroyed this creation of yours as I would never do to mine!"

"I now possess the land," the Haruspec said, with a shrug. "The Thaed-Rú served their purpose, and now," he sneered, "my knowledge of the dark nature will prevail over your pathetic army. They shall be mine!"

"Never!" the Gardener railed against the Haruspec. "I mourn all the innocent, even the Thaed-Rú, who have died because of your vain attempts to conquer! You rebel because I withheld the wisdom of the Garden of Ages from the people? Yet you slay your own Thaed-Rú?"

He rose heavily to his feet, burdened by the evil of his foe, but his voice was strong, his mind sharp. "Your dark nature, as you say, shall never prevail over the noble men who rose this day against your forces!" He rubbed wearily at his forehead. 'You never knew the proper mixture of seeds. This ignorance is why you bore your infernal rage throughout time, against me, against my benevolent garden."

The sadness of a father clouded the Gardener's countenance. "You will never master your own corrupt heart, thus will your gardens always be perverse, twisted and dark. In the end your creation serves no one, not even you."

Raising his staff, the Steward of Feynhava declared, "The wisdom of the Streams of Feynhava protects and nurtures the hearts of men. Your selfish aims, your desire to evolve all things to serve your dark and twisted intelligence, ends now!"

Hatred rampant on his features, the Haruspec crashed his wooden staff with both hands against a tall, spiked weed near him. The weed shattered into fractured splinters and thorns that shot across the dark fog. Already weakened from the wolf attack, the Gardener was barely able to draw more seeds from his pouch in time. They filled the air like dust and powder. Millions of splinters and thorns were deflected by an invisible field surrounding the Gardener. But some of the thorny shards cut into his face.

"You know nothing of my creation, or my experiments!" growled the Haruspec, exhaling cold vapors. "I harvested plants that have opened portals, grown shrubs that enable me to speak with voices from the dead, and I have travelled through dimensions." Cold pride and hatred fumed from his ghastly countenance. "You make fruit for the sustenance of many people, while I have conquered dark nature itself, to use it at my will for illimitable dominion! My knowledge and power transcends the Garden of Ages!"

The Gardener jabbed his index finger at the face of the dark one and shouted reprimands. "You are a sire of vain dreams! You are the greatest of fools! The fullness of your dark knowledge has run its course. For out of the seed of the Thaed-Rú, there is one remnant whose bloodline remains pure from any dark inclination. Indeed, I have grafted her into the Tree of Y'crom, she is watered by the Streams of Feynhava."

In the fog, the glow of a bright smile formed upon the Gardener's face. "I have raised this young girl from birth. She now stands ready to inherit the throne of the Thaed-Rú, which is her rightful place. She shall rule a new world, and usher in a new era of prosperity and healing. She will banish the old ways of oppression from the dark seed you harvested!" declared the Gardener.

The Haruspec turned his ghastly head in disbelief. A frown crossed his beastly countenance. Never had he heard of any such girl, sired by the Thaed-Rú, from his Harmattan weed spies.

"You have rid the world of the wretched Thaed-Rú and usurped their rule over the people. But in doing so, you have prepared the way for this young girl to take her rightful place!" the Gardener chortled.

Outraged, the Haruspec bellowed dark words in his cursed tongue. Instantly, sinister dark weeds upon the walls and floor of the hall writhed with life. Those on the wall became animated, turning into spiky creatures crawling downward to the floor. Giant figures covered with thorns surrounded the Gardener. Meanwhile, from along the floor, spiked vines slithered with the look and sound of serpents.

One dark creature crawled toward the Gardener on eight legs, like a giant, thorned spider. Another black creature dragged itself on the floor, with only two limbs, and a long-spiked tail like a scorpion. The vines wound about one leg and made for the other. The Gardener fought valiantly against these with his staff and seeds. One by one, he drove them away as they attacked. Still, he sustained several stings from the poisonous thorns they bore. The pain of these was greater than any man could endure or survive. He fell to one knee, still swinging his Tiller's Staff. Then his other leg bent too, yet on he battled.

After several minutes, a smile spread across the face of the Haruspec, for the Gardener was motionless, his head lowered in silence. The dark form hobbled toward his fallen foe. In his foul tongue, he spoke blasphemies against him and against the one true Infinite Garden. The evil waves of sound emanating from his cursed lips popped into millions of sparks as they met the Gardener's huddled form.

Aghast, the Haruspec's steps slowed. As the Steward of Feynhava lifted his head to speak, he cringed and stepped backward.

"For centuries, your Thaed-Rú seed have spread their cursed weeds across the land. This infamy will be erased, in time." He gestured to the vines and weeds about him, "See? Your darkest entities attack me, poison me..." thumping his chest, he proclaimed, "...yet, I am still here!"

His foe struggled to hear him as he whispered. "Now my justice is rooted in the smallest seed." The land began to tremble, tremors rippled across the landscape. Massive vines, lithe and green, broke forth through the stone foundation of Realmhold Thaed-Rú. They rose from the ground to overturn slabs of stone, slither up the walls and swirl around the great stone pillars of the council hall. They tightened their grip around the Haruspec's creations, crushing the life out of each dark entity.

Meanwhile, smaller vines raced across the stone floor, over cracks, under upturned slabs. Before the Haruspec could sense their presence, they swirled violently and painfully around his legs. He growled in anguish as tiny thorns upon the vines sought purchase in his flesh, sending piercing pain through his muscles. More vines swirled around his arms. In the grip of misery, the Haruspec lost focus on his surroundings. He lost contact with his otherworldly creatures and entities. and what remained of them crumbled to dust. His tongue failed him. Indeed, his very faculties became paralyzed.

The Gardener struck his staff against the floor and leaned heavily upon it. In a loud voice he called out, "The curse of the Thaed-Rú has turned on itself, striking down the Thaed-Rú court, their families, their leaders, and this very mountain with the wrath of the Cethin Arda! All that remains of their rule shall be laid waste, save one young girl." declared the Gardener. "Cursed is the ground on which Realmhold Thaed-Rú sits! May thorns and thistles devour your harvest of darkness!"

The landscape shook once more. Where his staff met stone, the foundation of the hall split in half. The Gardener retreated some distance from the fissure. As he witnessed larger vines rise to wrap themselves around the anguished Haruspec, he digested a special leaf from his pouch which brought healing to his wounds. Meanwhile, swirling tendrils of verdant vine twisted tightly around the Haruspec's massive girth. Then, in a great groan, the split in the foundation yawned wide. Violently the vines dragged the Haruspec into a deep chasm far below.

Now the Steward of Feynhava moved with great haste to abandon the remains of Realmhold Thaed-Rú. The vines that slithered throughout Realmhold Thaed-Rú tightened their grip on the stone columns, pillars and walls of every corner. The Gardener did not look back, for the sprawling buildings and structures behind him crumbled with a violent tremor that shook the nocturnal landscape, followed by a colossal cloud of dust and debris.

The mountaintop, the centuries old seat of Realmhold Thaed-Rú, was now reduced to a heap of stone rubble populated only by giant vines of thorns and thistles and the corpses of men. Without a backward glance, the Steward of Feynhava used his knowledge of the Streams to ferry himself back to the brave men yet fighting amongst the ruins of the Fortress City.

• • • • •

In the aftermath of battle, the surviving insurgent forces made camp in a field near the ruins of the Cethin Arda. Sentinels and guards established a perimeter for a night watch against the beastly remnants of the garden. A guard was also set about the hundreds of prisoners they had taken, lest they escape. Meanwhile, soldiers loaded wagon after wagon with the slain, moving them to the perimeter.

A deep frost drove the noble warriors of the West to the hundreds of campfires which spread across the valley floor. Even the Tribune's men and the Anil-Gevra, accustomed to frigid weather as they were, drew close to the fires tonight.

The morrow ushered in a thick white fog and the Gardener with it. From the Streams of Feynhava, he appeared in an explosion of azure light the glow of which spread throughout the fog and reduced it to mist. Immediately, he expelled the dreadful beasts from the ruins of the garden. Yet the Br'thain met him with silence.

Where has this benevolent figure been?

Why did he not aid us as great numbers of our men fell?

They knew not the greater battle he had waged, arcing over the politics of tribes, tongues and lands.

The Gardener strode regally toward the Fieradeem. Beside them stood the Tribune Ansuz and the four great generals of the Anil-Gevra. Men of every creed and rank gathered around them, straining to hear their words.

"The words of S'baladin have been fulfilled," came the solemn voice of the Gardener. They echoed across the cold evening air.

"In my absence, you have proven yourselves as rightful stewards of the Streams of Feynhava. The struggle to band together and fight for justice laid within each soul here," he added.

Hopeful smiles appeared on many of their faces at this. Quispal the elder made his way through the crowd until he stood before the Gardener. "My lord, we have brought down the Fortress City, even as we have destroyed the Rhünkai Order. But the counselor to the Thaed-Rú still remains at Realmhold Thaed-Rú."

At this, the Gardener's powerful voice resonated across the valley of debris and rubble.

"I come to you from Realmhold Thaed-Rú. I saw the counselor fall to the justice of the Streams of Feynhava. Large vines of thorns burst upward from the ground. Breaking the stone foundation, they wrapped themselves around the counselor and bore him far below."

The people gasped in awe of these tidings.

"Moments later, a colossal rent in the ground was opened by the Streams of Feynhava. Into, I saw the last of Realmhold Thaed-Rú crumble before me. Every stone of that massive fortress fell deep into the ground, atop the counselor."

A shout of joy and victory came at this. It resonated warmly across the gathering of weary warriors.

Previously, Ansuz had imagined a silly little man who gabbled incessantly of plants and flowers. But now, amidst shouts of praise, as the warriors patted each other's backs, some hugging one another, Ansuz knelt before this grand figure clad in robes from another world. The Gardener smiled upon him knowingly as Ansuz recognized the hooded cloak as that of Sulla's messenger years prior. All doubts of S'baladin's parable, or suspicions as to the verity of the dreams and visions of his people vanished. The Tribune, and his generals after him, knelt before this powerful ally who transcended governments and kingdoms, armies and nations. A chorus of murmurs rose all about them as each of the various divisions and clans fell to their knees as well in one great, rippling wave.

During the military business which followed, the Tribune Ansuz deferred to the Gardener. It was he who decided which of the allied insurgents to appoint as stewards of the fallen mountain and its ruins. It was brought to their attention that the clans of the Ir-Aranon once laid claim to the mountain, when their ancient chieftain, King Elar was lord of the land in the age of the Thaed-Rú warlord, Ceinad the shapeshifter.

The Gardener suggested, and it was agreed, that the ancient and noble birthright be restored unto the Ir- Aranon. "This is a fulfilling quest," said the Gardener, "that here, where once the Cethin Arda lay, where once the Thaed-Rú swayed mankind to evil ways, the descendants of the Ir-Aranon now shall restore to their people that which was stolen so long ago."

Sibrion offered thoughtfully, "In Uraduin, there is a saying, t'cayn uloma, it means to restore this broken world from the infestuous weeds of the dark one. This restoration is meant to occur one soul at a time, one day at a time."

"An apt name for such a place," the Gardener said solemnly. And the generals of the Anil-Gevra, and the Tribune Ansuz and his generals solemnly echoed these words.

For several weeks, Ansuz' men continued to arrest injured soldiers of the Haruspec. Ansuz' men and the alliance of noble warriors scattered amidst the mountainous ruins, searching for fallen comrades and arresting enemy survivors. Ansuz and the generals, even those of the Anil-Gevra, were shocked when the Gardener suggested they offer the enemy hospitality – a policy unheard of in the Rhünkai armies.

Graeyba, who had naturally fallen into a role as intermediary between the insurgents and the Br'thain, explained the Gardener's wisdom. "Joined first by the fallen Ballai, joined now in our survival of the darkness that has long reigned over these lands, should we not join in our recovery from a great conflict, now over?"

So it was that on the outskirts of the fallen camp, Ansuz' men expanded their medical units. In tents for Ansuz' men, and tents for the enemy, healing came to all in need.

• • • • •

High up in the mountainous debris, young D'thalien Khalevad made his way in stealth, hidden behind boulders. He was guided by his father's teaching that altitude had its advantages. If one hid as far up a mountain as possible, they could survey the entire landscape, searching out an opponent far below. Whenever he felt watchful eyes upon him, D'thalien stilled for several minutes. Then, slowly, he moved to observe from behind the rocks until he deemed it safe to scramble to the next boulder.

But young D'thalien's was not evasive. He was on the hunt. Ruled by an extraordinary hope, he had never given up on finding his brother. It seemed a simple truth to him that if life was good enough to bring him back to his father, then surely, he would find his brother again.

Both boys, sons of a keen hunter, were skilled in surviving the cold and unforgiving landscape of Hiérundia. High up in the mountainous ruins of a fallen camp, D'thalien found spaces in between the broken and cracked boulders, large enough to crawl through. In such places, from gathered debris fires warmed him through the nights. By day he watched. He heard the voices of Ansuz' men, and sometimes the Rhünkai, near his hidden space, yet no one ever detected him, nor the smoke from his fire.

As evening drew nigh, the clanking of armor drew him from his hidden space to spy on the men far below. His eyes surveyed the scene with caution and care. Clad in the fur skins, scarf and helmet of the West, and armed with a bow and arrow, D'thalien appeared far older than a youth.

Was this the end of the battle? Which side was the victor? he wondered to himself.

The sound of the beasts feasting on the flesh of the dead had surrounded him in the weeks following the battle, before the Gardener had appeared to drive them away. He had seen the hooded man in the distance, waving his Tiller's Staff in wide arcs. Separated by piles of rubble he had remained at his post, ever vigilant, ever trusting that soon his eyes would fall upon the sight of his brother. These days, he leaned heavily on the Gardener's words, 'All good works will find their way to your heart. Your brother will be restored unto your father.'

Young D'thalien followed the clattering sound far below the ruins. A contingency of warriors urged a group of captives forward. He squinted at the faces of their prisoners, then sighed and turned back to light his evening fire.

Then D'thalien gasped as an arrow whistled down and sought purchase in the flesh of one of the noble men. Dragging his body to shelter, the little group sought cover behind ruins and boulders. Half a dozen arrows struck them as they fled.

D'thalien scanned his surroundings fruitlessly for the location of the sniper. Below, men shouted orders and several volleys of arrows zinged across the general area where D'thalien hid. He squirmed on his belly to another pile of rubble several yards away. From there, less than a hundred yards below, his sharp eyes spied a dark form amongst a clutter of wood debris. Between a pair of cracked boulders, the sniper sat.

The man wore a hooded cloak of fur and was barely distinguishable from his surroundings. Is he Rhünkai or of the dark order? D'thalien wondered.

The sniper readied for another volley. Quickly, D'thalien notched an arrow and aimed at the sniper's back. Then he froze. A skilled bowman, by chance it might be Aidan down below. Besides, he reasoned that, if he missed, the sniper might turn on him and kill him. These thoughts stayed the young lad's hand.

The men ceased their return fire. All was quiet for a time. Then, slowly, one of the nobles began to crawl in a wide arc toward the sniper. Though invisible to the sniper, his efforts must have been audible, for the hooded man seized a long wooden staff at his feet. As the man sprang over a large, cracked boulder, he rose it high, just in time to block a deadly blow. With it, the sniper pushed his opponent's staff away, then swiveled in a complete circle, and plowed his staff hard against his opponent's head. Whirling in the opposite direction and lowering his body as he spun, he struck against the back of his opponent's knees with vicious speed and force. The man flew over backwards from the second blow, smashing the back of his head on a rock. The sniper rose finished him with a lethal head blow, then sank back down amongst the boulders.

D'thalien watched in dismay as two men bravely followed their ill-fated companion, one wielded a sword, the other bore a crossbow. Expertly, the sniper blocked their attacks with swings of his staff, and nimble dodges. With lightning speed and powerful deadly blows, these two fell also.

Every move the sniper made seemed familiar, so similar were they to the teachings of his father. D'thalien grew more and more convinced that this man was Aidan. Here is where the student imitates the teacher.

As he fought hand-to-hand against the pair, another man positioned himself between two great boulders. Through these, he rapidly fired three arrows and they struck the sniper from behind. All of D'thalien's honed instincts vanished. Forgetting all the caution Graeyba had taught him, he leapt into action. Grabbing his staff, he skipped over timber and bounded over rocks and ruin in a nimble descent toward the stricken sniper.

"Aidan!" he cried. "Brother!" Moving as smoothly across the terrain as a ferret, he dodged a volley of arrows, one of them grazing his jaw. Unphased, the excitement in him running high, he did not feel its burning sting. But when D'thalien came to where the sniper lay, he could not locate him. As he looked around, confused, a hard blow struck his back, thus knocking him forward on a boulder.

Another blow came toward him, but he rolled away in good time and the bo staff thudded against a boulder. D'thalien's training came flooding back, and he raised his staff to block his assailant's blows.

"Aidan! It is I, your brother! It is me! D'thalien!" he shouted through his scarf and helmet.

But the sniper continued to swing his staff. As the two opponents swung, twirled and skipped around each other, arrows narrowly missed them.

Beneath the sniper's hood helm, he caught glimpses of the man's eyes, of curly blond locks framing his face. His heart leapt. "Stop! Aidan!" he shouted. "What is wrong with you? I am D'thalien!"

But his opponent said nothing. He only continued to assail him with vicious thrusts from his staff, striking down upon him with cruel force. But D'thalien, Br'thain training aided him in parrying every blow.

"Aidan! Father and I...we were rescued...by the men of the West!" he called out between dodges. "We live there now!" As if caught by this curious statement, the vicious sniper paused, tilting his head back to peer from beneath his hooded helmet. A great wave of love came over D'thalien as he looked full upon his brother's face for the first time in years. Nonetheless, Aidan composed himself and returned to his assault.

"Aidan! I bear you no ill will! I love you brother!" He paused to catch his breath, blocking blow after blow. "Papa searched many months for you! His love for you has never failed!" he choked out. Tears welled now in his eyes.

The sniper's strikes began to lose their energy. D'thalien's words sapped his fervor. Aidan began to heave and gasped with each blow, yet still he struck relentlessly.

"My family is dead!" he cried. With great fury, little D'thalien's strength surged forth at these words. His training with the Br'thain and all that their father had taught him crystalized within. He turned his wrath on his brother's staff. Now it was Aidan who strove to fight and block every lethal blow from D'thalien's staff.

"Release the hatred from your heart, brother! Trust not the lies of the Rhünkai. I release you from your loyalty to them! Remember how you hated them? Remember our mother?"

In a series of powerful strikes from his staff, D'thalien momentarily lost control just as Aidan froze, recognition dawning in his eyes. D'thalien landed a powerful blow to his hooded helmet, thereby knocking it off his brother's head. Aidan's strength failed him. Stumbling drunkenly for several steps, his knees buckled and he collapsed backward to the ground.

D'thalien took up his brother's staff and splintered it to pieces upon a rock. With utter disregard for the arrows still assailing them, D'thalien bent over his brother's weakened form. Grabbing him by his fur skins he shouted, "Cut my flesh into a million pieces if you will, but every one of those pieces will yet love you! You are my brother, Aidan! I forgive you, absolving you of all you have done. I love you!"

Tearfully, the young man searched his brother's body for injuries. Two broken arrows were lodged in Aidan's back, while the third arrow was lodged above his right shoulder. But it was not the pain of these that overwhelmed the young captain. It was the great and guilty wound of his failure to reject the Rhünkai, to search for his family as they had searched for him. In a moment undefined by time, the two brothers held each other. Their faces were veiled in tears. Neither uttered a word. There was no need to.

Moments later, the noble warriors surrounded the two brothers to arrest them. By lucky happenstance, Vaez and Javatiel happened to be amongst them. "Wait!" Vaez cried. Javatiel stayed them with a hand. "We can vouch for this one!" they cried in unison, pointing to D'thalien.

"Take us to the medical tents!" D'thalien ordered, "My brother needs attending to!"

His friends gasped. Seeing that the wounded captain was unable to walk, they exchanged concerned glances, then called for a gurney.

• • • • •

As he had for many nights, Graeyba busied himself in the medical tents. Dozens of young lads worked beside him, volunteering aid to the skilled men and women attending the injured. They heated water over cauldrons and ferried medical supplies from one tent to another. As a vicious frost spread across the night, they brought covers and blankets. Then they moved to feed both friend and foe alike, for the Gardener's fruits were ripe to heal their hearts and minds. Such was the nobility of Graeyba Khalevad, leader, warrior, hunter to pause from his virile role and serve the wounded.

"Where is Graeyba?"

"Have you seen Graeyba?"

"Oh! There he is!"

Graeyba turned as he heard familiar voices to see Vaez and Javatiel hurrying toward him, anticipation gleaming on their faces.

"Graeyba! Hurry with us to the stewards' tent! Come!" they urged.

Moments later, they entered a large, sprawling tent. Men and women scurried about with blankets, heated water pans, medicine and food. Graeyba followed the boys around the wounded in beds, dodging busy volunteers.

Around a bed nearby, his eyes fell upon a gathering of familiar faces. Aejulan's face was shining with joy as he stepped aside, to make way for Graeyba at the head of the bed. There, Graeyba's quick, gainful steps slowed to a crawl. Slack jawed, he saw Aidan in bed, an attendant binding his wounds. Kneeling beside him, was his little D'thalien. Time slowed as the father knelt beside his sons.

"Aidan...It is you!" said the father. His hand fell softly upon Aidan's uninjured shoulder.

"Papa...I am so sorry for everything that has happened between us!" his son burst out.

But his father merely leaned over the bed to gently hug his son with one arm and pulled D'thalien into the embrace with the other. "My sons! You are both safe! I knew I would find you again!"

"Your son?" Aidan said, and his eyes flared impishly. "This cannot be little D'thalien. He fights like a demon! My little brother never bested me!"

D'thalien grinned proudly. But Graeyba's face had dissolved into rivers of tears. He choked and coughed a bit, navigating his grief, then spoke. "I have trekked across the land in search of you! At times, I almost gave up hope. Once, I almost took my life, for the loss of heart I felt in not finding you!"

This revelation sent a shadow of concern across D'thalien's face. Moved by compassion, he placed a hand upon his father's shoulder.

Graeyba smiled tearfully at him, "Darkness and shadows have claimed my heart! But now life has given me the greatest reward of holding my sons again!"

The fellows around them, stood awkwardly, patting one another's shoulders as emotions overcame them all. From those in the Br'thain, to Sabaca their gatekeeper, to the youngsters once viewed as juveniles, all had become men of honor and strength. In the brief time that they had known Graeyba, they had seen him only as a powerful leader, a fearless warrior in the field, but now they saw his father's heart.

Standing behind them, in the mix of medical attendants was the Gardener. Tears of joy streamed down his face as he watched this long-anticipated reunion. Slowly, he moved to stand opposite Graeyba beside Aidan's bed and the gathering fell silent.

"Son, do you remember this man?" asked Graeyba. Aidan looked upward, then nodded. "From the ruins, yes! I remember the tune he played."

"I wish it was the taste of his tea you remembered, brother," D'thalien said, his face forlorn, "How different your path might have been."

"Put all that behind you now," the Gardener said kindly. Offering Aidan a ripe pomegranate, he said, "Eat of this fruit and be healed of the dark influence over your heart."

Aidan ate, painstakingly. Turning to his father, he asked, "Who is he, papa?"

"A man of great destiny," Graeyba said proudly. "This is the Gardener. He is the chief steward of an infinite garden beyond our world. He rallied the men of the West and schooled them in supernal ways to liberate the child slaves. He is the impetus behind the great battle which brought down that vile Cethin Arda."

Aidan sat up in his bed, and stared at the Gardener, eyes falling on the queer tassels hanging from his peculiar robes. All of the energy and power of the stars seemed to emanate from the man, as if he had travelled through thousands of years to arrive at his bedside. Aidan was truly humbled.

"You have been through much sorrow, young Aidan," said the Gardener. "Your eyes have seen a great injustice from the Rhünkai. And your hands have shed much blood. Now is the hour to rid yourself of the great force of anger that was once bound up inside," said the Gardener. He laid a hand, radiant with healing energy, on Aidan's head. "Release it, my son! And I will restore unto you all the years that the locusts have eaten!"

Aidan's proud shoulders slumped and tears flowed freely as he sank back to his bed. The fellows and attendant alike stood in quiet awe of this powerful moment.

A New Seed is Planted

Without a sovereign, a temporary congress governed the war-torn land. Two years of reconstruction passed, and each successive meeting of the congress grew increasingly intense. Fraught with the conflicting interests of man, the voices of many were set against the Gardener's ways. Nevertheless, the Gardener stepped forth to convene today's meeting of sixty-three men.

They gathered inside a massive stone hall in the city of Kiérbangaal. Twenty long oak tables of various lengths, temporarily appropriated from across the city for this purpose, lay end to end in two columns of ten. The Gardener began by repeating a prior suggestion to appoint local patriarchs as judges over each of the Provinces, then he sat down amongst them.

An elder patrician from Cian, a region of great discontent with the Gardener's ways, stood to respond. "You mean well in your counsel, nevertheless, we still need a sovereign ruler to lead us into a stronger future!"

"Take care," the Gardener warned grimly from his seat. "The sons of Y'crom eagerly elected the first Bal- Rú." More kindly, he explained, "Local leadership is often more successful than a single sovereign, and it has served you well these twain years."

Grumbles arose from the representatives as they shifted in their seats. It was the Tribune Ansuz who stood and raised his hand to silence this cacophony. Though his virgin trip through the Streams had grayed his hair and set deep wrinkled in his skin, he yet remained a man of great inner strength, well respected during the many years of restoration.

The men subsided at his behest, and the Gardener rose to pace the aisle between the tables. The men craned their necks to gaze in awe as strange plants bloomed where he trod. Though many had their doubts as to his leadership, though some still doubted his origins and intentions, none could deny the goodness of his great powers.

"Men of Y'cromeca, long have you sought a sovereign amongst your most respected generals, chieftains, and noble warriors. Most of you have found unity only in your rejection of any sovereign carrying Thaed-Rú blood, and I would be inclined to agree with you."

"Here, here!" shouted many of the men.

But the Gardener held up his hand and added a condition, "If such a person were to threaten Y'cromeca's safety and your way of life. But…what of one of mixed blood, Thaed-Rú and man, one who was raised far from the reach of Thaed-Rú hands? I beg leave of this congress to share the story of such an individual."

For years, rumors of a special candidate for sovereign, groomed by the Gardener himself, had swirled. Begrudgingly, spurned by their curiosity, the congress conceded the floor to the Gardener. Dissenters on the counsel muttered amongst themselves,

"I knew he had someone in mind!"

"Of course! But a Thaed-Rú!"

"We cannot allow it!"

The Gardener held a hand up for silence, then conceded, "As many have whispered, there is a young lady whom I have groomed from birth."

"A female!?" many of the men murmured. This time it was the Fieradin Graeyba who shushed them.

"Twenty-three years ago," the Gardener continued, "In the forest of Graëyhovan, I crossed paths with a woman, cold, tired, and hungry. She held a baby to her bosom as a mother would. I offered her the warmth of my campfire and a share of my evening meal. She was fearful that soldiers were pursuing them. To me she confessed her life had been spent in the service of the Thaed-Rú, as a mid-wife. Many of us know of the infamy of the Thaed-Rú, but few knew then and less know now how they rid themselves of female offspring, in order to breed strong rulers." Anger choked the Gardener's voice as he said, "When a Thaed-Rú concubine gave birth to a girl, it was the mid-wife's responsibility to end the baby. Burdened by the guilt and shame of bending to their will, after several such dark deeds, this mid-wife vowed to never again kill a life she had delivered. So it was that she absconded with the last child born to Teosifan, second in power only to the Bal Rú Íraban, whom he served," said the Gardener.

He watched as representatives broke out into dozens of conversations. It was uncomfortable news for them in many ways.

After several moments, the Tribune Ansuz once more shouted for silence, this time striding forward to speak. "The wisdom from the Streams of Feynhava has proven to help rebuild our world!" his voice boomed over the men. "I vouch for the Steward of Feynhava when I say that he carries no intention to usurp our world, as the Bal Rú's did, as the dark counselor did. Now, hear him speak!"

The chaos of the congress subsided, and the Gardener continued. "I assured this mid-wife that I had no connection to the Thaed-Rú, nor would I turn her in. When she confessed to me the parentage of the baby, I gave the infant some morsels to eat from the Fruits of Discernment. I saw the true intent of her heart, that there were none of the dark weeds of her father, nor of the Thaed-Rú before him, save one. She has the power to harness the Veyasaen. It was she who caused them to attack the Rhünkai during the fall of the Fortress City, she who swayed them from attacking those with noble hearts. No Thaed-Rú, not even Íraban, whose power swayed mothers and fathers to offer their sons to him as slaves, has ever been endowed with such powers."

"Hoping such a child would one day serve to overthrow the evil of her race, I took her and her guardian into my care. For them, I created a garden sanctuary where she was raised in safety, protected from the outside world. Every year, in my journey to the West, I stayed with them, planting seeds there from the Garden of Ages and educating the child in the wisdom of the Streams of Feynhava." With a proud smile he added, "During the oppressive years of the Scions of Íraban, refugees were permitted entrance to this sanctuary. They gravitated towards this girl. Over time she became their respected leader."

"Where is this place of refuge?" A dissenting patrician from Cahheramas called out.

"For her safety, it remains a secret," answered the Gardener. "Not even the Tribune Ansuz knows of its whereabouts. In time, all will be revealed."

But the patrician from Cahheramas scowled and asked, "If it is a secret, then how did others know to find it?"

"As I came across those displaced from the ravages of the Thaed-Rú, I led them there," the Gardener patiently explained.

"The dark counselor's dominion surely necessitated such a place of refuge," the patrician conceded. His fellows shouted in opposition but stilled as he smiled darkly and continued. "Those dark times are now behind us. How are we to rebuild a new world forged on trust, if the wisdom of Feynhava denies us that trust?"

A wave of agreement passed through the majority of the men at this. Yet some, fascinated by the tale, urged them to consider the Gardener's pick for sovereign, to trust the efforts of his many years of care.

The Gardener watched them, his countenance grave. Finally, he interrupted. "Listen to the dissent amongst you!" his rebuke boomed forth, silencing their many voices. "There remains a hesitancy amongst you to trust in the wisdom of Feynhava. Some of you wish nothing to do with it, while others have learned to trust it."

Long had the Tribune Ansuz endured the petty politics of restoration. In the Gardener's proposal of a candidate, he found great hope. Springing to his feet, he shouted, "Men of Y'cromeca, hear me speak." The Gardener yielded, the dissenters hushed, and he spoke, "A leader of soldiers, I am no statesman. Though some have approached me as a candidate, I am not fit to rule. Who amongst us is?" His bushy white brows furrowed in a fierce scowl as he strode between the tables, gazing from one dissenter to another. "Who amongst us did not fall under the sway of the Thaed-Rú at some point before the war?"

Many cast their eyes down, while others avoided his steely gaze.

"Now, in the aftermath of a dark and terrible reign, we desire to rebuild our defenses, to serve and protect our people justly. We have all lost. Lost our livelihoods and lives of those we love." His eyes darkened at the memory of his two young sons, counted among the many Rhünkai slain, and of his dear friend, Sulla, driven to an early death before the fighting ever began. Sighing wearily, he continued, "The years drag on. Some amongst you seek to return to the old ways, to risk the good of the people for your own profit." He let his eyes linger on the representatives from Cian and Cahheramas, who had recently, foolishly, voiced their support of indentured servitude to stimulate the economy. To their credit, they shrank guilty under his gaze.

"I too was skeptical of the wisdom from the West! But this is not the time to be mistrusting of good and noble souls," shouted Ansuz. "As thousands will bear witness, the Steward of Feynhava overthrew the dark power, orchestrated the liberation of our child slaves, and spearheaded the restoration of Y'cromeca in the name of love and charity. Ansuz glowered at the congress but did not sit. His eyes flickered, then narrowed.

The Gardener smiled.

"Many of you served under me in the war," Ansuz declared, his voiced strained. "Thus, you know me well. But I have never told a single one of you what I will tell you now."

"A day of secrets, eh?" a voice cried out.

Ansuz smiled shrewdly, nodded, and continued. "You think me borne of men, and that is true. My ancestry is rich with the blood of Y'cromahein." He turned to Generals Teima, Naddú, Isayar, and Tzeytvara of the Anil- Gevra. "Did you never wonder why old Master Sulla would entrust leadership of the Anil-Gevra to me? The blood of the Anil-Gevra runs in my veins too, several generations removed." He observed the congress fall to quiet conversations once more. "But there is also one dark branch in the history of my family, further back than that of the Anil-Gevra. As a child, I was told of a Thaed-Rú ancestor, a powerful master of the dark arts, who fell deeply in love with a beautiful woman, many times my great-grandmother. The blood ran shallow within my family for centuries, and the tale would likely have faded to oblivion, had not the blood taken root in my veins, had not I chosen to share this tale with you today." His voice rang out over the murmuring crowd, silencing them. "Gentlemen of this congress! How is it you imagined I resisted the sway of Íraban? How is it I among the Sovereign Tribunes bent not to his will? How else could I have rallied my army and secreted them away, also resisting the power of the dark counselor…were it not for powerful Thaed-Rú blood coursing through my veins?"

He raised a fist into the air, proffering his wrist to them, where a large vein, bulged, pulsing. "You balk at the thought of a leader with Thaed-Rú blood," he chuckled, "yet you have had one all along! And have I not served you well? Have I not been just?"

The Gardener bent his head in a low nod as the Tribune strode past and took his seat amongst an eruption of dialogue. They both remained silent, observing the men, listening to their conversations. Gradually, the men were pacified as one patrician from Hierundia rose to speak. To the Gardener he said simply, "We would hear more of this young lady," and sat.

A warm smile beaming on his face, the Gardener continued his tale, "Like a husbandman who pulls the weeds before he plants a vineyard, so too did I with this young girl from the time of her youth. On the day of Íraban's coronation, I took this young girl to see her father, to show how he had bent to Íraban's will and counsel her against the policies and practices of the Thaed-Rú. We travelled throughout Y'cromeca. As she grew, so too did the misery and ruin worked upon the land by the Thaed-Rú and their Cethin Arda. The day she came of age, I revealed to her my purpose. My friends," the Gardener smiled fondly, "immediately, she expressed a fearfulness to rule, fear of the dark, heathen blood of the Thaed-Rú flowing in her veins."

"And unto her I said, as I say unto you, 'Should the people seek a flawless leader, one who has never seen war nor famine nor pestilence, they are foolish. Such a person is not fit to put their hand to the plow. They can neither sow, nor reap a harvest for the people. What Y'cromeca needs is a strong leader with wisdom and fortitude, one who has seen the oppression of the people. Such a leader understands the misery of their struggles. The first Thaed-Rú was grown and nurtured in a dark garden. As a result, the Thaed-Rú inflicted oppression and misery on the people.' Unto her I said, 'you, my daughter, are nurtured by the Infinite Garden. You are the good seed that will infect these lands with compassion, justice and mercy. You come at such time as this to lead with goodness.'"

The sixty-three men of the temporary congress sat silent, weighing the words of the Gardener, pairing it with the confession of the Tribune.

Quietly, the Gardener urged them, "If we do not take care of the garden, more weeds will spring up and choke the good seeds we have planted. We must seek unity by setting aside our stubbornness. Let us vote and see where we now stand."

It was recorded on this day that fifty-seven men cast their vote behind the daughter of Teosifan. The few who abstained were the lowest amongst these men, governed by fear, lacking in trust, and torn by their own selfish desires to rule.

• • • • •

Months later, from chilly Tal-Ciddion in the far northwest to sunny Bisantior in the southeast, citizens flocked to Kiérbangaal. From booths throughout the streets and tents in the surrounding countryside, vendors hawked their wares.

"Scarves of finest wool!"

"Fruits of the Gardener's own seeds!"

It was Entiyoh, the month of the Gardener's autumn feast, which was now celebrated by all in Y'cromeca. This year, the festivities extended from a single day to an entire week, to include a coronation.

Where once the Veyasaen hunted, the skies were empty now but for a few wisps of cloud, for Ka-Lyn's innate powers had subdued them. Men, women, and children thronged to a great public square. The wonderful aroma of scented primrose, plumeria, nicotania, viburnum, tuberose and lily of the valley hung lazily in the air and towering trees lent their shade.

Ansuz' handsome soldiers stood before colossal stone archways and pylons overgrown with verdant vines. Elders from every province stood in attendance, as did the wealthy and powerful. Their banners waved gloriously in the air.

Also present were the Br'thain of the West and the Fieradeem and Preceptans from every corner of Ferán, Rihován and Calasmorra. They stood beneath their own rippling banners and standards, representing the various Houses from each of the territories in the Ballai that still stands.

Between two great pylons depicting the Gardener's Tree of Y'crom stood the Gardener himself, clad in shimmering robes of azure. Upon an altar of stone beside him gleamed a silver crown of delicate filigree crafted in the shape of vines. About him stood the greatest leaders and most celebrated warriors of Y'cromeca. Amongst these were the Tribune Ansuz, Graeyba and his sons, Baltien's sons, and Sibrion's band of fellows.

The great cacophony of jubilant voices fell silent as the boots of seven hundred men marched forward. Placing their ram's horns to their lips, they blasted forth the once foreign, now familiar, sound. A young lady in white raiment appeared before the Gardener's entourage, escorted by a private guard and her attendants. Although she possessed no regal bearing, nevertheless, the people were drawn to her humble demeanor. Her inner beauty and her feline eyes radiated like the sun, for in these days, the sun now shone as never before.

The Gardener's voice thundered across the great plaza. "Today, I give you the name of your new steward. For many years, her identity was kept hidden for her safety. Yet on this solemn day, she comes before you at the behest of your Provincial leaders. I pledge on her behalf that her heart is good. She desires only to serve and lead these lands with justice, compassion and mercy. To you all shall she bring healing from the grievous pain inflicted by her predecessors."

For months following the congress' election, gossip and debate had been upon the lips of all as to their leader's identity. But the good people of Y'cromeca had far more reason to trust than doubt the Gardener's wisdom. Through his feasts and from the helpers and builders of the West, they knew of his good deeds and wisdom. For this reason, men, women and children, young and old, came to know him and drink from the Streams of Feynhava. Where their leaders had struggled, they accepted this new sovereign with ease.

The Gardener smiled. "I give you a symbol of new beginnings for all of Y'cromeca! By the wisdom of the Streams of Feynhava, I give you Ka-Lyn of Kol-Shebbala, the Veyan Fehru, the Ruler over the Veyasaen!"

To a chorus of resounding cheers, Ka-Lyn approached and knelt before the Gardener as he crowned her golden locks in a gentle flourish.

Ka-Lyn rose to thunderous approval. After the cacophony had subsided, she spoke to the masses.

"I am honored by your trust and grateful for your support of my stewardship of our great land. Many of you have journeyed far, from across the Eleven Provinces and the three regions in the West. Never in our history has there been such a gathering. As a husbandman nurtures and cultivates the garden, even as it requires the warmth of the sun for its growth and sustenance, so I shall lead our new world with compassionate rule, with humble wisdom and righteous justice."

Ka'Lyn's composure faltered, and her voice strained as she spoke openly to her people, "As a daughter of Thaed-Rú blood, I bear the burden of their injustice. I grieve for the reign of terror committed by my ancestors. And for this...I ask of your forgiveness."

The people stood aghast at such unprecedented humility.

"As your new sovereign, I ask we work together to shake off the burdens of anger, hurt, shame and guilt that divide us. The wisdom of the Streams of Feynhava says that a soul that is always at war with others is never at peace within itself. Together, let us cultivate a garden of gratitude."

Tears of hope filled the eyes of many, and the city shook with the cheers and shouts of a land united.

To conclude the ceremony, the Gardener raised his right hand over the people and spoke in Uraduin. *"I SEE THE TREE OF Y'CROM. ITS*

BRANCHES ARE THE SONS OF THE Y'CROMAHEIN. THEY ARE MY GARDEN PLANTED IN THE WEST. I SEE THEIR ROOTS REACHING BACK TO HALLOWED ANTIQUITY, TO THE PLACE WHERE TIME BEGAN."

Not since the ancient days of Y'crom did such numinous power shake the land as these hallowed words. For years to come the people would tell of how fruit bearing trees and flowering plants sprang forth across each of the Eleven Provinces that day. It was then that people accepted once and for all that it had in fact been the Gardener, in ancient days, who formed the Ballai to protect the people from a great foe desirous of wiping their seed from the land.

• • • • •

The evening sun cast golden hues on Kalanit's face as she moved through her garden of various desert plants and flowers. She eyed the long wooden tables before her and directed attendants to set an array of roasted meats, sauteed onions and various vegetables and unleavened bread upon them. From a little bower of flowering vines nearby, the pleasant sounds of musicians of Anterròs rose in rustic tunes to accompany Y'darit lyrics. Smaller children laughed and chased one another amidst chatty parents and relatives. Kalanit was determined to make the tenth anniversary of S'baladin's Maleor a memorable occasion.

As with every year before, his younger cousins and closest friends were in attendance. "Thank you all for coming, Aejulan," S'baladin said in welcome as he gathered with the fellows from his first journey North.

"Oh, I can never turn down a feast of desert cuisine!" said Aejulan. The men about him chuckled, but their smiles faded as S'baladin turned aside to cough at length.

Their dispositions brightened as Graeyba, Aidan and D'thalien joined their group. The Khalevad men were met with hugs and hearty recognition. S'baladin shoved aside his bodily pain and greeted them with gusto. T'balidor steered him toward their table, inviting the men to join them.

"Tzevi," S'baladin called fondly to one of old Yashi's pups. The furry mutt loped over to happily lap at table scraps. As his friends exchanged stories from their journey in the Va'Giyyel, S'baladin absently petted the pup as he considered the weaving of the tapestry of life. His heart was warmed as he joyfully took inventory of the smiling faces glowing all about in the flickering candlelight upon the tables and the torches posted all about.

It is amazing how life has changed so much in the last two years, for all I love, all who helped me in my darkest hours, he thought. He smiled as T'balidor, relieved his wife of their infant son that she might eat. *My brother now a proud papa, and I...an uncle!* he mused.

Sibrion, too sat beside his wife, their one-year old son upon his lap.

Meanwhile, the bachelors, Vaez, Javatiel and Kelán rose to lead a group of young ladies in a dance. A warm feeling came over S'baladin as he watched the young men laughing with their chatty young ladies.

As Jubal and Sabaca made to join them, the botanist said wistfully, "Would that you and she could join us, S'baladin!" With a smile he waved them on, but within he too yearned for that to be so.

How I wish you were here by my side, Ka-Lyn, he thought *We would sit under these stars and discuss the mysteries of the universe, of life, and of our journey together. I wish to see your smile, your eyes that make me weak at the knees.*

He started as a man sank heavily into the chair beside him. "Sy, I bring good news to your feast!" said Graeyba. "Aidan here has pledged himself to a young lady from Kir-Geyzot! A dark-haired girl with brown eyes," he added with a chuckle. "Can you imagine such a beauty with this blonde mess?"

S'baladin's face beamed with joy, as he glanced at Aidan who stood behind his father. "The children they will make!" D'thalien chortled as he set down cups of wine before them. Aidan Khalevad, the greatest of the Br'thain archers, blushed wildly and downed a cup of wine without a word.

S'baladin smiled kindly and spoke wisely, "Where once we met with great struggle, it seems that love now seeks us all."

Graeyba and D'thalien responded "Well said!" and "To love!" as he toasted Aidan's match.

• • • • •

Many days later, S'baladin reflected on the moment from the steep, craggy slopes of the Yedara Mountains. *And I?* he thought as he gazed upon a flock of grazing sheep. *What lies ahead for me?* He stooped down from his seated position on a rock to caress Tzevi. Another series of violent coughs disrupted the young lad. He clutched at his mouth with one hand and rubbed against his temple with the other, to stem the misery of a headache.

Straightening, he fingered the branches of the Tree of Y'crom pendant hanging from a simple leather chord about his neck. Ka-Lyn, knowing how fond he was of the Gardener's symbol, had presented him with the necklace on the day of her coronation. "I honor you with this gift, a token of respect for the great work you have done. Together we have banished darkness from these lands," she had said shyly.

Though dusk was deepening, S'baladin lingered. To the winds about him, he murmured how much he loved her, how much he wanted to be with her, and how he could not stop thinking upon her. He remembered how those strange blue feline-eyes lit up each time they met.

S'baladin's thoughts were interrupted by Tzevi's light-hearted growl. His flock bleated and shuffled nervously below. He had thought himself alone at the summit, but the crunch of gravel sounded from behind. Stunned, he turned to see a tall, hooded form approach him.

"My lord? Is it really you?" S'baladin's called out. He struggled to his feet to meet the Gardener. His Tiller's Staff in one hand, he used the other to push back his hood to reveal a hearty smile that lit up the darkening landscape.

"What brings you here?"

"I came to visit with a good friend."

"Here in Anterròs?"

"Here on this summit," the Gardener chuckled.

The young fellow felt a wave of goodness at this honor. Never had he spoke at length in a private audience with the Gardener. To his shame, in the cool evening air, a coughing fit overcame him. Gently, the Gardener helped him to a seat upon a large flat stone then moved to build and light a fire from the shepherd's woodpile nearby. Over this, the Gardener roasted tea leaves in a pan he took from his pack. S'baladin thanked him humbly as they sat side by side on folded legs.

"Tell me, young son of Baltien, how are things with the lady Ka-Lyn?"

S'baladin spoke openly, as he would have to his own father. "She is always in my thoughts. I see her beautiful smile in the clouds. The wind carries her laughter. After her coronation, we spent much time together. In between her duties as a new ruler, we talked of many things. Of the future together..." he trailed off. With a bashful grin he added, "...of our love."

The Gardener smiled widely at this but noticed how S'baladin's eyes drift into melancholy as the boy stared into the crackling fire. Silently, the Gardener inspected the tea leaves roasting over the fire. He uttered soft words in Uraduin. So soft that S'baladin could not discern them.

"What deep longings are lodged within?" he asked S'baladin, who held his head from the tortuous pain of his headache.

Taking a deep breath, the sickly young man gathered his thoughts. He gazed into the glowing embers and spoke. "It has been two years since the fall of the Fortress City. And yet I still hear my brother, and my cousin Sibrion, and the others talk of battle. I marvel at how they all played host to a critical and important role that has now altered our world. They did not merely take part in a battle for spoils. They wrote anew the pages of history."

"Many will speak of you in those annals," the Gardener comforted him. "They will write of the young bard whose immortal words awakened the mighty Faeynül to…"

But S'baladin held up a hand. "It is not such recognition, nor their tales of honor that I envy," he explained. "I envy the strength of their bodies."

"Ah," the Gardener murmured. Inspecting the tea leaves once more, he leaned in closer to S'baladin. His smiling eyes conveyed a strong intent, as he whispered indecipherable words in Uraduin. Then he spoke to the suffering shepherd.

"I bring tidings from the Streams of Feynhava. My dear young man, your parable, dispersed across the Va'Giyyel, awoke a giant. Across the far-flung regions of Y'cromeca and from the desert world of the Ballai that still stands, your words empowered a great gathering of peoples to come together, united as one."

The young shepherd momentarily turned away to expel his terrible coughs. The Gardener patted his shoulder in sympathy, then moved his right hand over the vapors from the tea leaves and gazed heavily upon them. "I know that you wanted to help in their struggle. To take up a sword, a lance, an archer's weapon, any weapon, into battle."

"Indeed, I did," spoke S'baladin as he studied his numinous guest, puzzled as to his intent.

"And yet, your letter served a far greater purpose than you realize, son of Baltien."

With a terrible pain running through his body, S'baladin struggled to concentrate on the Gardener's words.

"I told you that I brought tidings," he said. As the leaves began to simmer, the Gardener reached into his pouch. In the firelight, a small bowl fashioned of a blue ore glowed in his hands. Upon its gold plating within, the ancient script of Uraduin was etched in black. Holding the bowl at S'baladin's stomach, the Gardener swept an index finger in a circular motion around the edge of the bowl. S'baladin chuckled nervously as a high-pitched vibration rose into the air.

"My lord...these vibrations...they are ringing through my body," he said in wonder.

With a satisfied grin, the Gardner poured the tea into the blue bowl, uttered more words in Uraduin, and handed his concoction to S'baladin.

"My young friend, drink of this tea, and relax your soul," he ordered.

Without question or protest, the suffering young shepherd drank of its contents voraciously. A warm sensation spread from his stomach to intermingle with the vibrations in his lungs, his limbs, his chest. Breathing deeply, S'baladin carefully handed the bowl to the Gardener and sank into the warm sensations. His throat and nostrils tingled. Then, he closed his eyes as warm vibrations spread into his head, pushing gently against his skull.

When he opened his eyes, the Gardener was standing over him. A hearty laughter erupted from the mighty Steward of Feynhava. "Rise up my son, and quickly! For you are healed! Never again shall this sickness plague you. By the merit and token of the Streams of Feynhava, are you made whole, son of Baltien."

S'baladin, in perfect trust, leapt to his feet and strode rapidly about the campfire. He spun about with a little laugh, then felt at his throat in wonder. "My cough, it is gone! The headache too, and my body feels so alive!" Tears ran down S'baladin's cheeks as he turned to the Gardener and expressed his gratitude.

"The time has come to display the edges of the universe to a child of the stars" said the Gardener. "Every soul born into this world is given something to work for, and your soul chose to struggle with your sickness for a reason. You might wonder soon why this healing was not offered before. Many years ago, I stood by your bedside as you laid near death. I read the Fruits of Discernment before your family, and I saw in the Streams of Feynhava that this time of healing would come this very day and not before. The deep purpose of the legend of your soul was not complete till now."

"And what was the purpose of the legend of my soul?" S'baladin asked, humbled, for he longed to understand the marvel of this act of healing.

"Everything has a reason, though often time must pass before we can discern those reasons. Without your afflictions barring you from training with the Br'thain, you would have grown to be a strong and brave warrior the same as your brother and your father. Yet, you would have certainly died with your father in battle. T'balidor too would have died, lost in Va'Harot."

The shepherd pondered this.

"S'baladin," the Gardener continued, "without your words to muster the call to unity, the call to battle, without the hope you offered unto man, the Va'Giyyel would have plunged into a deeper abyss under the dark counselor. So empowered, the Ballai of the West would soon have crumbled, and every man, woman and child here murdered."

S'baladin sat down on a nearby rock to digest this alternative. Despite such chilling thoughts, the warm vibrations continued to strengthen S'baladin's body as his mind ingested the revelation from the Streams of Feynhava.

"For thousands of years, the swords of the Thaed-Rú Dominions oppressed the people. In the space of a few months, your quill and ink brought down their order," the Gardener said. Proudly he clapped S'baladin upon his back.

The shepherd smiled widely as his new, sturdy frame received the gesture with nary a single cough. His heart leapt as he thought of Ka-Lyn, of the joy she would take in his healing, of the new possibilities such a gift held for their future. The Gardener's eyes met his and smiled at the hope he saw in them. The two locked in a deep gaze that moved across the universe.

Then the healed shepherd spoke. "It all makes sense," he agreed. "I realize now, and accept, the purpose of the legend of my soul, my lord. One thing I must ask of you. Many years ago, my father spoke of a foretoken from you. You once said that when the Haruspec finally died…the Ballai that surrounds the Eleven Provinces will crumble to the ground of their own accord, including the Ballai in the West. In accordance with the wisdom of the Streams of Feynhava, you told my father there would be no need of them."

From their campfire high up in the Yedara mountains, the glowing walls of the Ballai could be seen far way. S'baladin gestured to them, saying, "Yet, the Ballai in the West still stands."

The Gardener rose and stepped away from the campfire to gaze at the molten walls.

"You carry an excellent memory, son of Baltien. What your father said is true."

The Gardener pivoted slowly. His sharp eyes pierced into those of the shepherd. "The Ballai still stand…because the Haruspec is not yet dead."